Rochester Public Library
Rochester, New Hampshire

DISCARDED

ALSO BY BRAD GEAGLEY

Year of the Hyenas

A Novel of Murder in Ancient Iraq

DAY OF THE FALSE KING

BRAD GEAGLEY

Simon & Schuster

New York   London

Toronto   Sydney

SIMON & SCHUSTER,
Rockefeller Center
1230 Avenue of the Americas
New York, NY 10020

This book is a work of fiction. Names, characters,
places, and incidents are products of the
author's imagination or are used fictitiously. Any
resemblance to actual events or locales or persons,
living or dead, is entirely coincidental.

Copyright © 2006 by Brad Geagley
All rights reserved, including the right of reproduction
in whole or in part in any form.

SIMON & SCHUSTER and colophon are registered trademarks
of Simon & Schuster, Inc.

For information about special discounts for bulk purchases,
please contact Simon & Schuster Special Sales at
1-800-456-6798 or business@simonandschuster.com

Book design by Ellen R. Sasahara

Manufactured in the United States of America

1 3 5 7 9 10 8 6 4 2

Library of Congress Cataloging-in-Publication Data
Geagley, Brad, date.
Day of the false king : a novel of murder
in ancient Iraq / Brad Geagley.
p.   cm.
1. Government investigators—Egypt—Fiction. 2. Iraq—
History—To 634—Fiction. 3. Babylon (Extinct city)—Fiction.
4. Egyptians—Iraq—Fiction. I. Title.
PS3607.E35D395 2006
813'.6—dc22   2005052756
ISBN-13: 978-0-7432-5081-8
ISBN-10: 0-7432-5081-8

For
Randall R. Henderson

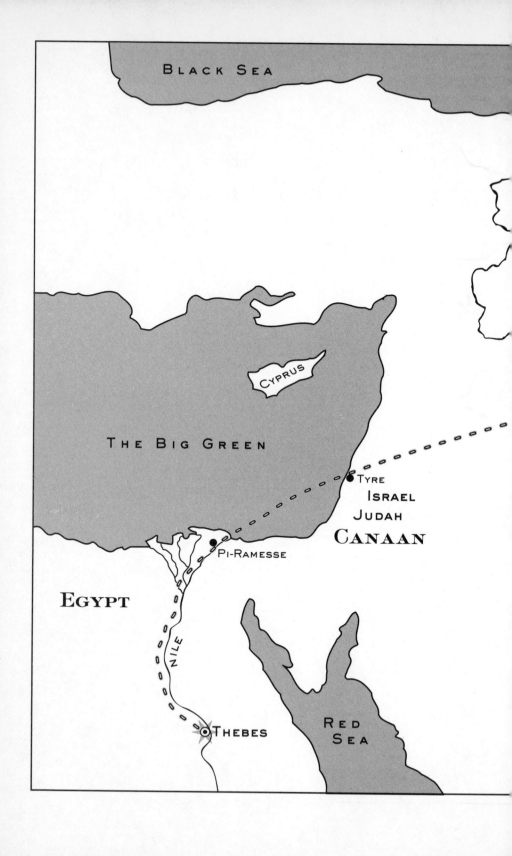

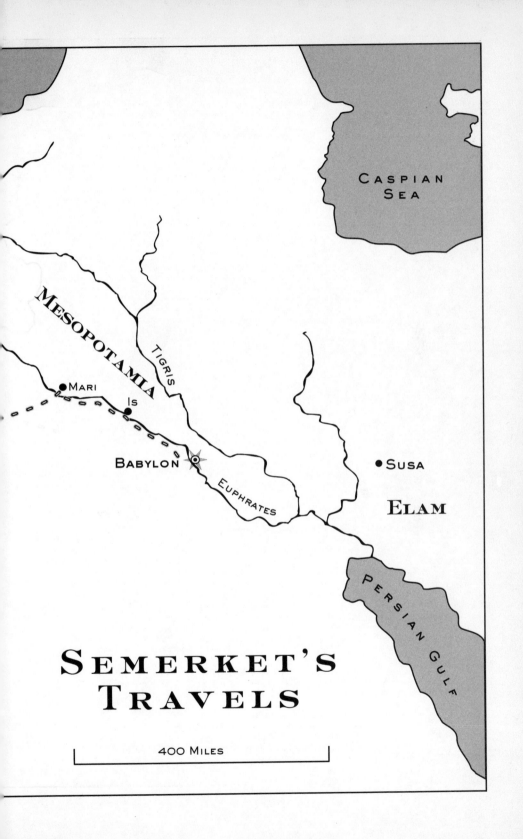

CASPIAN
SEA

MESOPOTAMIA

TIGRIS

MARI

IS

BABYLON

EUPHRATES

SUSA

ELAM

PERSIAN GULF

SEMERKET'S
TRAVELS

400 MILES

INTRODUCTION

DAY OF THE FALSE KING continues the story of Semerket, Egypt's clerk of Investigations and Secrets. The time is approximately 1150 BCE, and the conspirators who plotted the overthrow of Pharaoh Ramses III have been tried and executed. But the old pharaoh has succumbed to the wounds inflicted by his Theban wife, Queen Tiya; it is his first-born son who now rules Egypt as his chosen successor, Ramses IV.

Day of the False King takes place mainly in the city of Babylon (ancient Iraq). Geographically placed at the center of the Old World, where East literally meets West, Babylon was the crossroads for conquering armies and adventuresome merchants, and the prize of dynasts. From cruel tyrants to far-seeing visionaries, an ever-changing set of rulers have claimed Babylon's throne as their own. But they were not god-kings as in Egypt; in fact, there was no term for "king" in any of the Babylonian languages. Instead, they were called simply "strong man" or "big man." Then as now only martial strength determined who ruled. Strangely, or perhaps inevitably, the rights of the individual were first codified and set down as laws here.

Around the time that *Day of the False King* occurs, the Middle East is undergoing—just as it is today—a tortuous, protracted transformation. The old regimes have vanished, setting the stage for the aggressive emergence of the new nations of Phoenicia, Israel, and the Philistines; it is the fourth of these new peoples, the Assyrians, who will achieve dominance in the years ahead.

Babylonia in particular has suffered a series of cataclysms. The old Kassite Dynasty, themselves invaders from the north, has been toppled. The nation of Elam (soon to be known as Persia) has launched a massive war to conquer Babylonia from the southeast. Native tribes in the country also see this moment as their own chance to evict the foreigners and re-establish a dynasty of their own.

Into this roiling alchemy Semerket's adored ex-wife, Naia, is thrust. She and Rami, the tomb-maker's son, have been banished to Babylon as indentured servants—punishment for their accidental roles in the Harem Conspiracy against Ramses III.

As in the first novel, most of the events in *Day of the False King* actually happened, and many of the characters actually existed. The Elamite invader King Kutir and the native-born Marduk truly vied for the throne of Babylonia. There really was a festival called Day of the False King, where the entire world turned upside down for a day, when slaves ruled as masters—when the most foolish man in Babylon was chosen to become king.

Brad Geagley

Alas my city! Alas my house!
Bitter are the wails of Ur
She has been ravaged
Her people scattered.

—The Lament for Ur,
  Traditional Sumerian poem

BOOK ONE

MESSAGE FROM
BABYLON

WAKING WITH A SHARP CRY, HE FELT HIS heart thump madly before he realized that he was on his pallet in his brother's house. Once again, he had dreamed of his wife, Naia, slaughtered before the eyes of his wandering night's spirit. He sat up in the dark, rubbing his forehead. Every time he had the dream, his old wound stung.

Throwing his mantle over his shoulders, he slipped from the courtyard gate. He had taken to walking the Theban streets late at night when he could not sleep, which was most nights now. Turning from the Avenue Khnum, where the bonfires of Amun's Great Temple blazed, he slipped into a dank and twisting alley behind a riverfront warehouse. Picking his way through the rot and refuse, he came at last to a tavern. The sign hanging above its door depicted a hippopotamus besieged by hunters.

It was very late and many of the patrons were snoring over their cups. The Wounded Hippo was a venerable dockside haunt, centuries old, and its brick walls were crumbling to pieces. Unfortunately, the current owner's apparent devotion to the antique did not extend to the vintage he served.

He trod silently to his usual corner and signaled the tavern's owner. "Wine," he said. "Red."

At the hearth, the innkeeper poured some wine into a terracotta bowl and gave it to his serving wench. "See that man over there?" he asked, keeping his gruff voice low. The woman was recently hired, and unfamiliar with the tastes of the tavern's regular patrons.

She turned her head discreetly, whispering in the same guarded tone, "A gentleman!" Her posture perceptibly straightened so that her breasts might be displayed to better advantage beneath her tight linen sheath. "What's he doing *here,* I wonder?"

The innkeeper ignored the unintentional slur to his establishment. "Every night he comes in and wants the same thing."

"Well, that's hardly strange—not much to choose from, is there?" The wench laughed, which she often did these days, proud of her new teeth made of elephant ivory and wired into her mouth with copper bands. "I mean, it's either white or red, now, isn't it?"

"That's not the point." The man's voice fell to a whisper. "He never drinks it."

The woman caught herself in midchortle. The idea of a man coming into a tavern and not drinking struck her as odd, somehow, almost obscene. "You're joking," she said.

"May my Day of Pain come tomorrow if I am," the innkeeper said. "Just stares at the bowl all night, and never once brings it to his lips."

The woman peered suspiciously at the man. "He's not a ghost, is he? They say ghosts can't eat or drink, but still they pine for it terrible." She shivered. "I won't serve ghosts."

"He's alive all right—though Egypt would've been better off if he wasn't. A 'follower of Set,' he is. He's the one accused all them at the conspiracy trials last year."

"That's *Semerket?*"

The innkeeper nodded. They stared.

Semerket's aggravated voice abruptly cut through the room. "Must I wait for the grapes to be harvested?"

The innkeeper looked down at the bowl still clutched in the wench's hands. "Better take it to him. Don't want my name on any list of his."

The wench swept her mass of braids away from her face and crossed the room to where Semerket sat, her generous hips swaying as she walked. She placed the bowl at his side.

"Your wine, my lord."

At her unfamiliar voice, his head snapped up. She was struck by the sudden tense collision of emotions on his slim face. His eyes, glittering dangerously in the firelight, were the blackest she had ever seen. He was not handsome, but far from ugly. She dropped her eyes before his powerful stare, and the woman was surprised to feel something unexpectedly warm flush through her loins.

"You're new," Semerket said, handing her a copper snippet. It was not a question.

The wench bobbed her head, and the wax beads woven into the ends of her braids clicked together softly.

Semerket looked away, his black eyes going opaque. Still the woman lingered a bit, collecting the empty bowls strewn around the rug. He did not appear to notice her.

"My lord?" she whispered at last.

He looked up, surprised to find her still there. "What?"

"I don't mean to pry, but—but my master over there says—well, he tells me that every night you order wine, but that you…"

"But that I never drink it." Annoyance flickered behind the obsidian depths as Semerket glanced in the direction of the innkeeper. "I wasn't aware he found me so fascinating."

Though his voice was cold, the woman persisted. "I thought you was a poor spirit, maybe, some sort of ghost, now, didn't I? But up close, I see you're a fine, strong man. Very alive, indeed. So why do you not drink?" She smiled at him encouragingly.

"My wife doesn't want me to," he said dully. "And I promised her… something…"

"Well, if you don't mind me saying it, what you need is a more forgiving woman."

He grabbed her wrist, and her words ended in a tiny yelp. She gasped at the strength in his grip as he pulled her down so that her eyes were level with his. In the firelight his face was haggard and drawn, his expression tormented.

"I need the wine because I know if I can't deal with my life any longer, one little sip and the gods grant me a merciful release. Do you understand now? It's a way out."

She nodded, her eyes wide, the ivory nervously glinting. "Yes, my lord. Yes. It does a body good to get out now and then. I understand. Truly."

The odd lights in Semerket's eyes suddenly extinguished, and he let go of the woman's arm. She comprehended nothing.

Rubbing her wrist, she retreated again to the hearth, never to come near him again that night. Semerket hardly noticed. He gazed instead into the shadows, as if looking for something. It was very close now, he knew, the thing that sought him. He felt like some helpless rabbit, spellbound by the cobra's approach.

For a year, he had sensed it coming. Lately the feeling had become worse. Rarely did he sleep through an entire evening without seeing his banished wife, Naia, slain by a spear's thrust. The dreams were a warning, he believed, some intuitive communication he had received from her. Perhaps she was in some kind of danger in Babylon; perhaps she needed him. It might be that she was—

He clenched his eyes tightly, rubbing at his brow, refusing to consider that obscene possibility.

At long last, through the doorway, he saw that the night was turning from black to gray. He rose, another evening gone. Outside, shrill birdsong poured from the reeds and grasses at the Nile's edge, and from the Temple of Thoth came the distant barks of the sacred baboons heralding Ra's approaching solar barque. He stood at the river's edge and closed his eyes, inhaling deeply.

The air was clear on the river. The Nile had only recently receded, leaving its yearly gift of silt upon the land. The odor of rich black earth rose in his nostrils. Tassels of sprouting emmer wheat and flax fringed the distant fields with a delicate green. It would be a good harvest this year, he thought, if the gods did not afflict the crops with locusts or snails.

The food vendors soon appeared from the dark alleys to set up their stalls on the concourse. When the smells of frying onions and spiced fish began to scent the boulevard, he turned and walked back to his brother's house. Nenry was the mayor of Eastern Thebes and occupied an estate near the Temple of Ma'at. Semerket's fretful mind was a void, for once, and he was unprepared for the sight that met him at his brother's gate.

A cohort of Shardana guards waited in the alley. They were Pharaoh's elite northern guard, composed of Egypt's former enemies, the Sea Peoples. An empty sedan chair waited with them. It was no modest equipage, for eight liveried attendants wearing Pharaoh's colors carried it.

Semerket saw that Nenry and his wife, Keeya, stood at the gate. From their anxious expressions, he sensed that the news was not good. Keeya clutched Huni to her chest, the child Naia had left behind in Egypt for Semerket to raise. Even the infant's dark eyes were full of fright.

"Here is my brother at last," Nenry said, his face wreathed in nervous tics.

The Shardana chief turned as Semerket approached. "Lord Semerket?" he asked.

Semerket nodded mutely.

"Pharaoh requests your presence at Djamet Temple."

Semerket swallowed, trying to find his tongue. "May I . . . may I know why?"

"There is a message for you, I'm told—from Babylon. Pharaoh wants you to come immediately."

He would have fallen if the guards had not leapt to catch him. As they eased him into the carrying chair, he cast a stricken glance at Nenry and Keeya. He felt Nenry's hand squeeze his shoulder as the chair was lifted high by the bearers.

As she held Huni for him to kiss, Keeya whispered into his ear, "The gods go with you, Semerket."

It was too late for gods, he knew; the thing he feared had come. Resolutely, he turned his face to Djamet Temple.

SEMERKET STOOD at the grated window in Pharaoh's private chambers, straining to make out the blurred and water-stained words written on a piece of brittle palm bark. The first ones he managed to pick out were ominous:

. . . attacked by Isins.

He had no idea what or who Isins were—or even who had written the letter. The next few glyphs, smudged beyond recognition, offered no help. He could make out only those that spelled these words:

. . . the house of Menef to . . . Prince of Elam . . . Naia . . .

His breath caught when he saw the name he cherished actually written down. The only glyph he could further distinguish, and that with difficulty, was the most chilling of all—*slain.*

Then, at last, the signature, smudged and barely legible. *Rami.*

He raised his head. Surrounded by his scribes and servants, the fourth Ramses sat on a thronelike chair at the end of the room. Beside him was another man, a foreigner. Though it was late winter and the temperature was climbing every day, Egypt's king had wrapped himself in a heavy, embroidered cape of red wool. Charcoal braziers were placed everywhere about the room to warm it.

"Does Your Majesty know the contents of this letter?" Semerket asked.

Pharaoh nodded, and gestured to the foreigner, who also sat in a chair. "My cousin Elibar, here, brought it to me last night. We read it together—or as much of it as we could."

Semerket, surprised, looked closer at the other man, and noticed that Pharaoh and the foreigner indeed shared a physical likeness he had not appreciated at first—the same slim, prominent nose; the pale eyes and skin. Indeed, though the stranger's long hair and beard had turned to gray, their hue had once been the same russet that characterized all the Ramessid family. He must be related to the king's Canaanite mother, Semerket thought.

Ramses drew a breath to speak again, but instead began to cough. A faint sheen of sweat erupted on his forehead and he pressed a kerchief to his lips. Semerket noted the instant concern that flared in Elibar's eyes. With a wordless gesture, the hovering chamberlain directed a servant to remove the soiled kerchief and bring another. Though the room's light was dim, Semerket thought he saw a faint tinge of pink froth staining the cloth before the slave hastily folded it. Elibar himself filled a goblet with wine and held it to Pharaoh's lips.

When he had finished drinking, Ramses sat back on his gilded chair, weakly mopping his brow with a fresh kerchief. "Now," Pharaoh's voice was stronger, "you will no doubt want to ask my cousin about that letter you hold."

Without pleasantries, Semerket nodded and began to speak. "How did you come by this letter, lord? And when?"

Elibar answered slowly, taking time to consider his words. "A caravan entered Canaan from Babylon a fortnight ago. This Rami of yours had given the letter to the caravan's master to bring to Egypt, or to pass to another merchant who would."

Though Elibar spoke an excellent Egyptian, his voice was so deep and oddly inflected that Semerket had to watch the man's lips to determine the words he actually spoke.

"In my own land people know that I'm Pharaoh's cousin—not always to my advantage, I might add—so the letter was brought to me. I recognized your name at once, for my aunt, Pharaoh's mother, had written to me about how you rescued my cousin from the conspirators. I hurried here, knowing of his majesty's regard for you."

Semerket could not conceal his disappointment. "Then you weren't the one to actually see the boy?"

Elibar shook his head.

"Is he still alive? Did the man indicate—?"

"He only said that he was very sick—that he suffered from some kind of head injury."

"Did he mention where Rami might be found?"

"Well, there I can be of more help to you. He told me he met the boy on the outskirts of Babylon, at an oasis near a ruined estate. The man used a stick to draw an outline of Etemenanki in the dust, making a circle around it—"

Semerket canted his head, not sure that he had heard correctly, "Etemenanki, my lord?"

Elibar paused in his narrative. "The devil Bel-Marduk's abode, yes—the ziggurat at Babylon's center. The man took a stick and—"

The word caught Semerket by surprise, and before he could stop himself, he asked, *"Devil?"*

Bel-Marduk was the Babylonians' name for the god that Egyptians called Amun-Ra. Never before had Semerket heard the father of the universe referred to as a devil, and he felt almost superstitiously affronted by Elibar's casual blasphemy. Quickly he made the holy sign in the air.

Pharaoh spoke from his seat. "Elibar worships a nameless god of the desert, one so jealous it considers all other gods to be demons or devils or frauds. Pay no attention to my cousin, for his religion is simply another family sickness I must endure."

Elibar smiled indulgently; it was obvious that theirs was an argument both cousins had waged amiably for many years. The Canaanite continued to speak.

"As I say, the man drew the outline of the ziggurat in the sand. Then he made a circle around it—this I took to be the walls of the city. Two wavy lines on either side of it were, of course, the Tigris and Euphrates. Then he took the stick and pointed to the upper left of Etemenanki, outside the circle but between the rivers. I assume he meant that your Rami could be found to the northwest of Babylon, on the river plain."

"Did the caravan master tell you if . . . if there was a woman with him?"

"He said there were many women—many men, too—but unfortunately they had all been massacred by bandits."

Semerket abruptly felt light-headed, as if his legs had somehow disconnected from his body. Black crowded the edges of his vision.

"Get him a chair!" Pharaoh ordered, and the servants scrambled to obey.

"No," said Semerket. Sternly he forced himself to breathe regularly, to stand erect. After an imperceptible moment, he turned again to Elibar. "And these Isins," he managed to ask, "who or what are they?"

It was not Elibar but Pharaoh who answered. "A native tribe in Babylonia. Egypt has very cordial relations with them, for my father felt they had a fair chance of becoming the next rulers. Of course, that was before the Elamites invaded."

Semerket nodded. "And Menef—who is that? It's an Egyptian name, isn't it?"

Pharaoh nodded. "He is our ambassador, appointed by my father before he died." He looked at Semerket with an odd expression. "I've already sent a special dispatch to him, directing that he help you find your friends when you arrive."

It was a moment before Ramses' words penetrated Semerket's clouded and anxious mind. He raised his head, surprised.

Ramses nodded, confirming his previous words. "I have named you my special envoy to their new Elamite king, and have also prepared documents of manumission for your friends. Your wife and the boy may return to Egypt whenever they wish."

To Semerket's surprise, he saw that guilt laced Ramses' expression—a quality rarely found in a Pharaoh.

"I should have freed them after my father died." Ramses sighed. "It was the only reward you ever asked. But with the trials . . . my father's burial . . . I thought the matter would keep. I was mistaken. My only hope is that they're still alive to enjoy their freedom."

Sensing Semerket's discomfiture, Ramses continued to speak. "When Elibar returns to Canaan, you shall go north with him under his protection. It's only a short journey to Babylon from where his family resides."

"May I ask—" Semerket had to swallow before he could speak further. "May I ask when Lord Elibar will be leaving?"

"The day after tomorrow," Elibar answered, "at dawn. A royal galley will take us to Pi-Ramesse, and from there we sail on the Big Green to Tyre, on one of my own ships."

There was nothing more to say. Stretching forth his arms at knee level, Semerket began to back out of the room. There were a thousand preparations to make before he could depart. But Pharaoh held up his hand, preventing him from going. "Semerket and I must now speak privately," he announced curtly.

Without asking the nature of this private business, Elibar raised his fingers to his lips and made the gesture of kissing the earth. "A hundred years," he said, uttering the traditional blessing to Pharaoh as he backed from the room.

As the rest of the servants melted into the shadows, Ramses wrenched himself from his chair. "Follow me," he told Semerket.

Ramses seized an oil lamp to light the windowless and winding halls of Djamet. Soon they came to a far door, which the guards pulled open. Within the room, an immense model of a new city was set upon trestles. The length and breadth of it took almost the entire chamber.

"Look at it, Semerket." Pharaoh gazed lovingly on the model. "The new capital of Egypt. My engineers tell me it will be the greatest project since the pyramids—the legacy of Ramses the Fourth."

Semerket knelt to inspect the model. Miniature temples, causeways, palaces, workshops—all were laid out in meticulous detail. He could even see the rounded ovens in the temple bakeries. Pharaoh's architects had thought of everything, down to the new capital's last alleyway and square.

"It will take generations to complete," Semerket said, mentally calculating the city's phenomenal size.

Ramses looked at him so piercingly that Semerket felt the color rising in his face. Pharaoh suddenly went to the door and peered into the hallway in both directions. He dismissed the guards that waited outside, telling them to post themselves further away. Satisfied that no one loitered in the corridor, he motioned for Semerket to come closer.

Pharaoh brought his lips close to Semerket's ear, lowering his voice to barely a whisper. "My physicians tell me that I will live a hundred years or more," he said, "but that only means they're not sure how long I will live at all. The priests have cast my horoscope, but it's so vague it might mean anything. I've sacrificed to every god and goddess in the land—I've given them new garments of rare silk, and gifts of gold and ivory to their priests. Yet still the gods do not help me." Again he looked around, as if searching for spies. "And this is the other reason why you must go to Babylon, Semerket, a secret reason. There is something you must do for me, for Egypt, when you arrive there." Once more, Pharaoh looked about the room, squinting into the shadows.

Semerket stared at Ramses, waiting.

"In Babylon, you will go to their new king Kutir. You will offer my greetings, and extend Egypt's official recognition of his rule. You will tell him I stand ready to assist him with arms and gold to strengthen his dominion over the country."

Semerket allowed his black eyes to glitter. "And the price for Egypt's support?"

Pharaoh's gaze took on a dreamy look. "Babylon's god Bel-Marduk must make a state visit to Egypt. When he arrives, I will take the idol's golden hand in mine and gaze into his eyes, for it's said that doing so will drive out my every demon and pain."

Suddenly Ramses began to cough again, and his glance filled with incipient terror. "Time, Semerket," he pleaded when he could catch his breath. "Bring the idol back to me, that I can see this new city rise in the Delta, greater than any other. Death is in me, Semerket. I can feel it gnawing at my vitals like a rat at the grain."

Semerket's eyes grew wide.

Pharaoh's hands gripped his shoulder. "My son is only six years old. If I die, the priests of Amun will appoint regents to rule for him. And who will they be?"

Semerket considered quickly. Tutors? The child's mother? These had been the traditional choices in the past. But such persons, however close to the prince, would not be enough protection in these uncertain times. The priests would certainly favor the appointment of stronger, abler men from the royal family—

"Tiya's sons," Semerket said instantly.

Pharaoh nodded grimly. "Exactly. My half-brothers, sons of that murderess who killed my father. How long will my own son last, then, do you think? Such a small matter to arrange some 'wasting disease' for him. Like father, like son, they will say, dead of the same ailment." Ramses' fingers dug so hard into Semerket's flesh that his nails left crescents. "And after my son, who next will they turn their eyes upon?"

Semerket knew the answer to that question, too—they would seek the one who had exposed the conspiracy hatched by their mother and brother, the one who had brought their own side of the royal family into so much disgrace.

"Me," Semerket breathed.

"You—to begin with! And after you're dead, none of your family will be safe. Do you understand why I chose you for this task? You have as much to lose as I."

Semerket swallowed. He saw clearly that it was not only Pharaoh who needed the years the idol could bring; he needed them himself—at least enough time for Pharaoh's son to become a man. Though he had little faith in the curative powers of foreign idols, he had no choice but to believe with his king in the magic of Bel-Marduk's statue; it seemed their only chance.

"Yes," Semerket said firmly. "I'll bring this god back to you."

WHEN HE HAD ARRIVED earlier at Djamet, the temple had not yet fully wakened. But as Semerket came through the door that connected the palace with the temple proper, he saw that the halls and sanctuaries now teemed with priests, singers, nobles, and guards. He cursed silently, knowing what was ahead. As he passed through the hall of soaring columns, he heard them whisper his name nervously as he passed, sounding to him like the flutter of quail wings. "Semerket . . . Semerket!" They probably imagined that he and Pharaoh conferred about plans to hunt down any remaining conspirators, many of whom still roamed these very halls.

Semerket felt his heart sinking, for in the group of people clustered at the doorway was Prince Mayatum. The youngest son of Queen Tiya, half-brother to Pharaoh, Mayatum would be one of the regents for Pharaoh's son should the unthinkable occur. Though Mayatum wore a priest's vestments, being the prelate who governed the city of On, he exuded the oleaginous superiority common to all of Tiya's brood.

Semerket tried to hurry past the prince and out to the Great Pylons beyond, keeping to the walls. Whatever they had to say to one another could not be pleasant, for Semerket had presided over the execution of his older brother, Prince Pentwere. In fact, Semerket had been the one who had conveyed the white silken rope to the prince, with which he had then hanged himself. As for the princes' witch of a mother, Queen Tiya, whose plotting had been responsible for the entire tragedy, she had disappeared from the royal palace, spirited away under cover to some unknown destination. Some said that she had become the victim of Ramses III's final act of vengeance. Whatever had happened to her, her scheming had proved treacherous for everyone, and Semerket had no wish to confront the prince and re-open the wounds. But Mayatum, alerted by a servant, turned just as Semerket was passing and hailed him.

"Why, isn't it Semerket?" he called out warmly. "How fares the great hero of Egypt, the man who saved my father... almost?"

Though the words the prince used were flattering, Semerket still sensed an insult in them. He kept his head lowered, staring at the black basalt tiles.

"I am well, Highness," he said.

"I take it you've been meeting with my brother?"

"Yes, Highness."

"And how is his health today?" The prince's loud words seemed somehow too caring, too concerned. "Is his cough any better? Not spitting up more blood, is he?"

Semerket kept his voice low, answering obliquely. "Pharaoh's health will improve, no doubt, upon seeing your highness again."

Mayatum flicked his whisk of horsehair at an imaginary fly. "I've been out of the country, you know, meeting with our allies in the East. Very secret, you know. Very hush-hush. In fact, I'm on my way to make my report to Pharaoh now."

Semerket felt his tongue withering in his head. What did the prince expect him to say? Semerket was nothing to him, beneath his notice. "I'm... I'm sure the king will be anxious to hear what you have to say," he muttered.

"Oh, ho!" Mayatum smiled. "So you're dismissing me, are you? You were always so direct, Semerket, so honest. Some said to a fault, but never I."

The prince dismissed Semerket with a wave of his flywhisk, turning his back on him with seeming indifference.

Semerket left the temple quickly, almost running to where the fer-rymen congregated at the docks. Ever since the trials, he had dreaded meeting any of Tiya's remaining sons. It could have gone worse, he supposed. Perhaps the prince had concluded that it would be best to leave old hostilities behind and endure the shrifts a new reign had imposed on them both.

As Semerket crossed the Nile again to Eastern Thebes, he stood at the prow of his boat. The sky above the city was afloat with streamers that soared from a thousand crystal-topped spires. From Amun's Great Temple, the distant voices of the temple chorus pricked his ears with familiar psalm.

Every part of him was electric with anticipation. Yes, the news he had received from Babylon was devastating, and the secret of Pharaoh's declining health was worse. But the thing he had dreaded for so long had appeared to him at last. He knew the worst, its shape and size, and its power over him was gone. Now he could do something about it.

He knew in his heart that Naia was not dead; he was absolutely convinced that she waited for him just beyond the eastern horizon. Nothing could prevent him from bringing his wife and Rami back to Egypt. Semerket felt the warm winds on his face blowing from the east, and in them was the scent of Babylon.

THE CREW TOOK UP the ship's anchor stone at the first reddening blush of sunrise. Shakily, Semerket thrust his head over the thatched gunwales. His stomach clenched. The only thing he could see in any direction was the vast heaving ocean that the sailors called the Big Green. No land. No birds. Only the endless swells.

Semerket pulled himself to his feet, swaying unsteadily with the motion of the ship. He was in time to see the sailors unlash the single huge sail, painted in bright red and yellow squares. As it billowed outward with a sudden, lethal snap, the ship lurched forward so quickly that Semerket, already off-balance, fell backward onto the deck.

"At least the ship's moving again," he thought sourly.

On the previous day, the crew had not been allowed to ply their oars, for it was the Sabbath of Elibar's strange and only god. Even food was forbidden them. Not that Semerket could eat. For almost the entire three days of the voyage, he had been so sick he thought he was going to die. Strangely, he seemed to be the only one aboard affected by the malady. If he survived, he vowed to himself, he would never again sail abroad on this salt sea, no matter how much time it might save him.

The ship began its relentless pitching and tossing as it skimmed across the white-topped waves, assisted by the ten pairs of rowers. Semerket felt his guts twist again into painful knots. The captain must have seen his beleaguered expression, for he came aft and bent down to speak reassuringly to him.

"Now, now, sir," the captain said, "no need for that face. Coastal waters soon and we'll be moored in Tyre by nightfall."

Semerket nodded, unable to speak, and attempted once more to stand. This time he was successful. He looked in the direction of the ship's prow and saw that Elibar and his four sons had already gathered around the bronze cooking brazier.

Elibar saw him standing, and cheerfully hailed him from the fore-deck. "Can you manage something to eat today, Semerket?" he asked in Egyptian. "We've slaughtered a sheep to break the fast."

Semerket shook his head weakly. In response, he heard the low snickers of Elibar's sons, who had joined them in Egypt's northern capital of Pi-Ramesse where they had been visiting their aunt Ese, Pharaoh's mother. Though the youngest of them was still beardless, they were all strong, competent men, tall in stature and hard in appearance. Their eyes were the bright and piercing bronze of hawks, and their skin darkened from weeks spent herding their father's immense flocks of sheep. They had been quick to tell Semerket that though their ancestors had settled in Canaan, they considered them-selves members of the Habiru tribe—or tribes (Semerket gathered there were more than one). Their country was a new one called Israel, or perhaps it was Judea; they conversed so rapidly in their strangely accented Egyptian that Semerket was unsure. Whatever its name, it seemed to be a nation where there were no kings, but rather judges, ruling by the consent of their fierce desert god.

Seeing him awake, the young men gathered around Semerket to question and pester him. "Is it true you're going to Babylon to bring back the devil's idol for Cousin Ramses?" asked the youngest.

"I'm going there to find my wife," Semerket said, choking back his stomach. He was shocked to learn that the lad knew of his quest for the idol of Bel-Marduk. Ramses must have confided the secret to Elibar.

"Egyptian women are harlots." This from the eldest.

"My wife is no harlot," Semerket said firmly, an edge to his voice.

"Yet our father tells us she is not really your wife at all," said the tallest son. "He says she divorced you to marry another man, a traitor who raised his hand against our dead Uncle Ramses. Is that true?"

Semerket's stomach churned dangerously. "She wanted a child," he managed to gasp. "I couldn't give her one. She didn't know he was a traitor when she married him."

"Is that why you Egyptians allow your women the freedom to bed whomever they choose? Must they search everywhere, then, for men who can give them sons?"

"That isn't why we allow freedom to women—"

"Look what happened to Uncle Ramses—killed by his own wives. How shameful is that? In our land, you would never hear of such disgrace. Women should keep to their homes, raising their children and spinning the good wool."

Semerket truly did not feel up to such debate, but attempted to answer the lad reasonably. "Men and women in Egypt take their example from the marriage of Isis and Osiris," he explained. "Osiris could not be King of the Dead without the help of his wife."

At this, Elibar's sons burst into contemptuous laughter. "But they are false gods," said the third oldest. "They don't exist! How can you even mention them to us?"

This comment provoked the young men to lapse into their native tongue, all shouting together and gesticulating violently, turning their backs on Semerket. He took the opportunity to slip away unnoticed and join Elibar at the ship's prow.

The ship rolled suddenly, and Semerket was surprised to find he suffered no accompanying urge to vomit. In fact, the mutton stew in the swaying cooking pot smelled almost tempting. Perhaps he had at last obtained his—what did the captain call them?—his "sea legs."

In the prow, beneath an awning, Pharaoh's cousin Elibar was praying, with his shawl drawn around his head. Semerket waited for the man's muttering and keening to cease before he spoke.

"Your sons are very passionate," Semerket said when Elibar opened his eyes.

Elibar canted his head to regard the four young men. "It's a good thing for men to be passionate about their beliefs," he said with his usual deliberateness. "Sometimes, only a deeper conviction gives us an advantage over our enemies. Sometimes, it's all we have."

"I would have thought it was your god who gave you the advantage."

Elibar shrugged, indicating that the sentiment was understood.

"They certainly despise Egyptians, though," Semerket said, looking back at the youths.

"Perhaps you didn't know that the Habirus were once enslaved by the Egyptians," explained Elibar, "or so our tradition tells us. But we prayed to our god, and he sent a hero to rescue us; his name was Moses."

Semerket, who had never heard this story before, shook his head doubtfully. "But Moses is an Egyptian name, or at least half of one."

"Moses was a Habiru who was drawn from the Nile and raised as a prince in Pharaoh's Golden House. So, yes, you can say that he was an Egyptian—or at least half of one."

"Why have I never heard of your 'hero'?"

"Perhaps because he lived over three hundred years ago."

"Elibar," said Semerket with a trace of condescension, "in Egypt, that's like saying 'yesterday.'"

Elibar regarded him skeptically, smiling to himself, but saying nothing.

"Do you believe the story?" Semerket asked.

At that moment, a school of fish suddenly swarmed near the surface, breaking the water in a flurry of froth and furious spume. Their silver flanks sparkled in the rays of the rising sun. A few sailors took a moment to cast lines into the sea in the hope of snagging a meal.

Elibar answered Semerket in a low voice, so that his words would not carry on the winds to his sons. "I will tell you what my cousin Ramses believes, if you're of a mind to listen, for he claims to have read the suppressed scrolls."

Semerket shifted uncomfortably. All too often knowledge of the truth brought with it its own kind of penalty. Nevertheless, he nodded, indicating that Elibar should speak.

Elibar leaned in close. "Ramses says the Habirus first invaded Egypt alongside the Hyksos. One of them, Youssef, even rose to become high vizier under the Hyksos king. He was given the task of exterminating the native Egyptians in the Delta, and drove their survivors south into Thebes. Ramses insists the Habiru legend is actually wrong side up— that it was the Egyptians who were oppressed by the invaders."

Semerket shrugged. Every Egyptian knew of the Hyksos. Their invasion was the national scar on the nation's conscience, and their expulsion Egypt's greatest victory.

"When the native southern kings at last prevailed," Elibar continued, "they enslaved those Habirus who had stayed behind and slew their every male child."

"The usual punishment dealt to Egypt's invaders," said Semerket reasonably. "It's told about the Libyans, the Shardanas, Danites, the Sea Peoples—any of the tribes who invaded Egypt."

"But only the Habirus produced a Deliverer."

"Ah, yes," said Semerket ironically, "the Slave King raised in a palace."

Elibar regarded him patiently. "Will you hear more?"

"Go on."

"Ramses believes Moses was one of his own ancestors, a Prince *Thut*-moses, a nephew of Queen Hatshepsut. My cousin says that Prince Thut-moses made common cause with the Habirus, planning to use them as warriors in his attempt to take the throne. But the coup failed. Only the intervention of Hatshepsut allowed him to escape Egypt, together with a handful of Habirus. It was then that he began to worship a single god of the desert, where he wandered like a crazed wizard for many years."

Semerket was silent for a moment. "Why do you tell me these things?" he asked.

"To illustrate, perhaps, that all life is merely a point of view—that nothing is what it seems."

"You tell that to me, clerk of Investigations and Secrets?" Semerket laughed shortly.

"I mean it as a warning, Semerket, to guide you perhaps to where you are going. You must remember that Mesopotamia is a different world from Egypt altogether. It's disordered and chaotic. Often you cannot see what is right in front of you; often you will see what is not there."

There was a sudden yelp of glee from one of the sailors. He had snagged a large fat fish, enough to feed them all that night. Others ran to help him scoop it from the sea.

Elibar pointed. "That's how it will be for you, Semerket—like that fish there, ripped from the only world it ever knew into one it never imagined. Not even the air you breathe will be the same."

"I'm not so complete a fool as you may think," muttered Semerket. "I've been to Babylonia before, you know, though not as far as the capital; I can even read their language, though slowly."

"Perhaps that will be enough," Elibar said doubtfully.

They watched the big fish struggle on the deck, gasping and snapping futilely at its captors. Finally, the laughing sailors fell on it, clubbing it to death with their oars.

A tiny droplet of fear crept into Semerket's soul. He would have liked to ruminate over Elibar's words, to twist them around in his mind and dredge them of their hidden meaning—but suddenly, from the lookout's nest above the sail, came the shout:

"Land!"

They had sighted the coast of Asia. Semerket uttered a quick prayer of thanks; at least now, if the ship foundered there would be a chance of making it to shore.

By noon, the ship had joined the long line of others that were crowding into Tyre's newly built harbor. As the sailors prepared to moor the ship, Semerket returned to where he had stored his travel sack. Within it was the glittering badge of office that Pharaoh had given him, designating him Egypt's special envoy. It was a thing of heavy and magisterial beauty, a falcon whose outstretched wings covered most of his chest. Semerket had not yet donned it; the first lands through which he would travel had once been colonies of Egypt and their inhabitants still harbored bitter resentments toward their one-time masters. Sometimes they killed the occasional Egyptian wayfarer to settle old scores. "Evil has an Egyptian mother," was the saying in these Asian lands.

Also within the leather pouch, beside the letters that manumitted Rami and Naia, were five clay tablets that Pharaoh had given him. Inscribed with the strange, wedge-shaped characters of Babylonia, they entitled him to draw monies from temple counting houses throughout Mesopotamia. Each of the five tablets bore Semerket's thumbprint, for the Babylonians believed that the swirls and loops etched into every person's thumb were unique. The temple priests believed they could tell if the bearer was truly the person to whom the monies were entitled. Semerket found this to be an absurd notion, but if all it took was his thumbprint to freely access Pharaoh's bullion, who was he to dispute the custom?

In the pouch with the clay tablets were the only other items he had brought along with him. The first was the brittle piece of palm bark from Rami. The second was another letter, Naia's only message to him from Babylon, inscribed on a piece of papyrus she had filched from the ambassador's waste pits. Perhaps for the hundredth time, Semerket unfolded the brittle paper to read:

> My Love,
>   I have arrived in Babylon, and the Egyptian ambassador has placed me in his house as a maid. I am well and Rami is with me. We are content here, though everyone talks of the coming war with Elam. A merchant who leads a caravan to Thebes promises he will deliver this letter to you. Kisses to you and Huni, a thousand times. You are not to worry.
>   Naia.

Semerket's heart began to beat with excitement when he heard the splash of the anchor stone. He realized that only a couple of hundred leagues separated him from his beloved.

"I'm here, Naia," he whispered. "Do you feel it? Look up, and you will see me."

•   •   •

SHAUL, THE ELDEST SON of Elibar, together with a few of his father's more burly shepherds, escorted Semerket to the Babylonian border. Though the land differed in no way from the rolling hills in which they had been traveling for at least a week, Semerket knew the land to be Babylonian by the tall, slim boundary stone that marked it. He stepped from Shaul's four-wheeled chariot to the ground. Dutifully, he knelt and kissed the earth, thanking the gods for his safe arrival.

The boundary stone stood flat and gray at the junction of two roads, carved with the names and images of the Babylonian gods, invoking their curses should anyone violate the hospitality of the people living behind it. Fierce gryphons with slashing claws stood sentry on either side of the stone, promising swift punishment to those who disregarded its warnings.

Semerket watched as Shaul and his companions turned their chariots, returning to the west. He waited until they disappeared over the rise; then, fighting an almost panicky feeling of abandonment, he began to walk down the road that led south.

It took him the entire afternoon to reach the next city. In all that time, he saw no one on the road. To his relief, just as the sun began to fall behind the western hills, he caught site of the ancient walls of Mari. A haze of black smoke hovered above the city, thicker than the usual smut of cooking fires. As he came nearer, he saw that the walls bore witness to siege engines recently used against them. Holes gaped in their brown brick flanks, and scars of soot and smoke zigzagged crazily across their ramparts.

In all the other cities of Mesopotamia through which he had passed with Shaul and his companions, the noise of human traffic and habitation had risen loudly to greet them. At Mari, he heard only the occasional screeches of the carrion vultures wheeling in high circles above. As he came nearer the walls, he saw bodies heaped haphazardly in the fields on either side of the road. The temperature had risen precipitously as he ventured further south, and the bloating corpses seemed to melt together like fat left in the sun. His nostrils curled at the sinister smell of rotting meat, overlaid as it was with the pervasively acrid scent of human waste.

From behind the damaged city wall, he unexpectedly heard male voices yelling in excitement. A gang of Elamite soldiers suddenly burst through the ruined city gate, kicking a leather ball, passing it to one another between their feet.

The squad of soldiers stopped abruptly when they saw Semerket standing in the road. The ball came bounding over to where Semerket stood, and he set off to catch it for them. When he bent down, however, he saw that the leather wrapping covered a perfectly distinct human head. Semerket recoiled, allowing the head to roll into the field of corpses, losing it in the long shadows.

"Who are you?" one of the men asked in poor Babylonian.

Semerket spoke haltingly. "I'm Semerket, from Egypt. I've come to meet with your king Kutir and bring him Pharaoh's blessing." Now that he had left the former colonies of Egypt, he felt it safe to call himself by his own name.

When the lieutenant had translated his words, the Elamites smiled cordially and nodded. "Welcome to the kingdom of Babylon, Egyptian, or what's left of it," the soldier said in his queerly accented Babylonian.

Semerket's gaze wandered to the ruins behind the gate. "What happened to this town, Lieutenant?" he asked.

"Its people gave—how do you say it? Hiding? Protection... ?"

"Shelter?"

"Yes! Just so! They gave shelter to Isin traitors. Our brigade was sent here to..." The lieutenant paused to once again search for the correct word. "...to *demand* that they turn the Isins over to us, or be destroyed."

Semerket looked about. The citizens of Mari evidently had not yielded to the Elamites' request.

"Is everyone dead, then?"

"Eh." The lieutenant shrugged philosophically. "Most fled to swamps. Very disappointing. Mari is poor city. No gold for soldiers, you know. No loot."

Stepping over fallen bricks and charred lumber, Semerket turned to the lieutenant. "I don't suppose there's an inn where I could take rooms? I've walked most of the day, and would be glad of a bed."

"Priests of Bel-Marduk keep a hostel for travelers—but they, too, flee to marshes."

"What about food?"

The lieutenant shook his head, but then his eyes brightened with joy. "You eat with us! With officers! We share our rations with you and you tell us stories from Egypt. Come . . . come."

Just as the last rays of the sun deserted them, they reached the Elamite headquarters. From a half-burned-out building at the far end of the walkway, he heard a cacophony of voices spilling into the courtyard, all speaking a gregarious Elamite.

"This way," said the lieutenant, pointing. "We take our meals in the cooking shed, yonder."

As Semerket entered the ruined shed, the soldiers gathered there turned to stare at him—twelve of them, Semerket counted. Old instincts in him made him note all the doors and exits. When he was sure of their location, he turned his attention again to the men. They sat on the floor on a carpet, in the center of which was a large steaming kettle.

The lieutenant spoke rapidly to them in his own tongue. Semerket could not follow most of it, but thought he recognized *per-ah,* the Elamite word for "Pharaoh." *Ramses* came out "Rah-may-seeyu"— at least, that is what Semerket assumed the word meant.

The commander was a short, thick plug of a man with sinewy arms lavishly scarred from battle. Without rising, he hailed Semerket from the carpet.

"Egyptian!" he called in his gravelly voice, speaking a more unintelligible Babylonian than even the lieutenant. "Here! Come!" He indicated a seat of honor beside him.

Semerket walked carefully around the perimeter of men and took his place beside the commander. A slave lingering near the hearths, a man of Semerket's age, staggered forward, gripping a ewer and a basin. Chains, Semerket noticed, bound the man's legs together.

The slave placed the basin on Semerket's lap. In perfect Egyptian he said, "I am going to wash your hands now, sir."

Semerket's head shot up. His expression must have been one of shock, for instantly the Elamite officers roared out in protest, jumping to their feet and reaching for their swords. They lunged at the slave as if they would hack him to pieces on the spot.

"No!" said Semerket quickly. "No, I was just surprised to hear him speak Egyptian. He only wanted to wash my hands!"

As if debating whether Semerket spoke the truth, the commander hesitated, then gave a shake of his head. The officers sat back down on the rug, but kept their hands on the hilts of their swords and menace in their expressions.

"Slave is nothing," said the commander. "Only Dark Head we capture in battle. We kill later." He drew his finger across his throat, and laughed.

The slave hurriedly dried Semerket's hands with a towel. With his back to the Elamites, he whispered so that only Semerket could hear, again in Egyptian. "Help me, lord," he said. "I'm a dead man if you don't prevent it."

Semerket's expression did not change. The soldier next to him passed him the basket of bread. Semerket took a piece and dipped it into the pot of tasty stew. The meat was surprisingly flavorful, though he was unfamiliar with the animal from which it came. He only hoped it was not the flesh of some Dark Head slave.

"So, Egyptian!" the commander said between mouthfuls. "You are ambassador and friend of Great Rah-may-seeyu. You are rich."

"I'm his servant, not his friend." Semerket scooped some more stew into his bread. All the soldiers' eyes were hard upon him.

"Is long way to Babylon," the commander said, smiling. "Many Isin traitors hide behind rocks. I send men with you tomorrow. Protection for you. In Babylon you must go to my friend, General Kidin. Head of all Elamite forces. Much help to you!"

"Kidin," Semerket murmured, noting the name.

The commander then said something to his soldiers, smirking. His men laughed with him, and turned to regard Semerket with enigmatic expressions. The slave went around the circle of soldiers, wiping their hands on a cloth. When he reached Semerket he whispered, "Beware, sir. He tells his men that you are not destined to reach Babylon."

Semerket felt a rush of paralyzing fear surge through his body.

These barbarians planned to murder him for the gold they imagined he carried, no doubt to make up for their lack of swag in Mari! He cast about feverishly in his mind for a plan. He did not know the country-side, or even the layout of the city. Semerket's eyes instinctively found those of the Dark Head slave at the far end of the shed; when their eyes met, there was understanding between them.

Semerket thrust his legs forward, stretching luxuriantly. Solemnly he thanked the soldiers for sharing their food with him. Then he yawned, feigning great fatigue, saying that he would find accommoda-tions at the ziggurat of Bel-Marduk, even though it might be deserted. Would the escort promised by the commander be ready to leave at an early hour?

The Elamites nodded vigorously. Yes, they were quite sure they could be ready by then. Semerket noticed the surreptitious glances the men exchanged.

Semerket rose to his feet, inclining his head in thanks. As he started to the doorway, he turned, as though seized by an incidental after-thought. "You know," he said, "I was thinking that I'll need an inter-preter. My Babylonian, as you can tell, is very poor. Will you sell me this slave of yours?" He pointed to the fettered man at the hearth. "I'll give you three—no, five—gold pieces for him. Egyptian gold." By this, he meant the gold was worth more to them than the debased pieces found in Babylon since their invasion. He fished out the five glinting rings from his belt and saw the sudden hunger in the soldiers' eyes. "Do this, and I'll be sure to praise you to your king Kutir."

The commander spoke again in Elamite to his men, who readily enough agreed to part with the slave. The slave was no further use to them, and, in any case, they were eager to rejoin the bulk of their army in retreat—

"I mean 'in retrenchment,'" the commander said quickly.

Semerket nodded graciously.

They brought the slave forward and struck the chains from his ankles. Semerket made cheerful farewells to the Elamite soldiers, promising to see them again at first light. The two men left the kitchens rapidly and went into the dark of Mari's streets.

When they were out of earshot, Semerket murmured to the slave in

Egyptian, "Do you know the city? Can you get us out of here now without being seen?"

The slave nodded. "The walls to the east have been destroyed. We'll slip out there, and continue on to the river. They won't think to look for us if we go in that direction. When they find us missing, they'll go down the southern route first."

It was a good plan, and Semerket willingly agreed to it. "What are you called?" he asked.

"Marduk."

"Like the god?"

The slave nodded.

Semerket considered the name a lucky omen.

MANY HOURS LATER, just as the sky became light, Semerket and Marduk reached a small town of reed-dwellers, perched on a wide estuary of the Euphrates. The villagers greeted Marduk lustily, and he hurried forward to speak with them in a dialect with which Semerket was unfamiliar. After much animated conversation, Marduk returned to where Semerket waited.

"Give me a gold piece," he said peremptorily.

"Why?" asked Semerket, surprised.

"I've bought us a boat so we can take the river down into Babylon. It's safer than the roads, and faster."

Semerket dutifully handed over the gold piece, again admitting to himself that Marduk's plan was a good one.

"It was a fortunate day when we met," Semerket said aloud. "When I think what might have happened to us if you hadn't been able to speak Elamite..." He shuddered.

Marduk's brow lifted in surprise. "What are you talking about? I don't speak Elamite," he said.

Semerket looked at him without comprehension. "But, in the kitchen last night—how could you know that the soldiers meant to kill me today?"

"I never said that."

"You did!"

"No, lord. I told you that the commander said you were not destined to reach Babylon. However, upon reflection, he may have said something entirely different."

Semerket could only sputter, but Marduk held up his hand in an imperious gesture, silencing his protests.

"I said nothing other than what I had to," the slave said easily. "The rest you told yourself. But let us forget this misunderstanding and bless the Golden One whose name I bear, for now I have a new master and all is well."

Semerket glared at Marduk with narrowed eyes. "I could have had an armed escort all the way into Babylon."

"But now you have me. Moreover, I'm certainly far cleverer than they are. You won't regret it, lord. You'll see. I'll keep you safer than any Elamite."

As Marduk moved off to confer once again with the villagers, Semerket told himself that here indeed was a trickster race. Never again would he trust anyone in the land of Babylon—particularly those slaves who made such fools of their masters.

BOOK TWO

THE GATE
OF GOD

MARDUK, IN REALITY, HAD NOT PURCHASED A boat; he had merely hired one. Semerket learned of the deception the next morning when Marduk introduced him to a merchant at the river's edge. The man, a wineseller, had agreed to escort them all the way to Babylon, Marduk told him.

"And here is our transport," he announced with a flourish, indicating a vessel floating a few cubits away in the stagnant marsh water.

Semerket's eyes widened.

The thing—it could hardly be called a boat—was made of skins stretched over branches. Perfectly round, possessing no stern or bow, it resembled nothing so much as a gigantic floating disc. Straw covered its insides, on top of which the merchant had piled hundreds of clay wine jars. Its other occupant was a donkey, delicately nibbling the straw.

"You don't mean that this *thing* is what I paid good gold to sail in?" said Semerket.

Marduk fixed him with a flat eye. "What's wrong with it?"

"There's an ass in it, for one thing!"

"My lord," Marduk said, taking him aside and whispering, "when you're in a foreign country, it's very rude to mock the local customs."

"You're saying my refusal to sail with an ass is rude?" Semerket's voice was loud in the morning air.

"I'm saying, my lord," said Marduk, "that on the Euphrates the traffic goes only from north to south—*with* the current. When this man and his son reach Babylon, they'll dismantle the boat and sell its hides. How do you suppose they'll return to their village if they've no donkey?"

Semerket breathed deeply before he answered. "I don't mock the custom," he said carefully. "I'm only saying that I think we should purchase our own boat—one that doesn't include any livestock."

Marduk brushed away Semerket's words. "Absurd," he said emphatically. "I don't know anything about navigating a river. Do you?"

Semerket took another deep breath. "No," he admitted.

Sighing dismally, Semerket carefully climbed into the craft and seated himself in what appeared to be the only space available—next to the donkey. The beast appeared to find him a sympathetic pilgrim, for its lips drew back to form a smile of almost certain joy and it began to butt its head aggressively against Semerket's thigh.

Semerket recoiled, but the ass continued to nudge and nip at him until finally he was forced to scratch the beast between its ears. Contentedly exhaling a fetid gust of fermenting hay from deep inside its gut, it rolled against him, hooves thrust in the air so that Semerket might tend all his parts equally.

"Groom to an ass," Semerket muttered dolorously to himself.

Onshore, a crowd some two or three deep had gathered around Marduk. They all called loud blessings on him as he headed to the round boat. Some of the mothers held their children up for his kiss.

What is *this* all about, thought Semerket.

The merchant and his son hurriedly spread rugs to make a soft cushion for Marduk when he came aboard. Semerket, miffed, attempted to claim the seat for himself; he was the master, after all, and it had been his gold that had purchased their accommodations. But nothing could budge the affectionate donkey, and Semerket remained helplessly pinned beneath it.

It was only then that he raised his head to look out upon the river, and saw that the odd boat had already reached the center of the marsh without his being aware that they had cast away. He was surprised at how steady the vessel was; he had to admit that she took the water well.

As the wine merchant and his son rowed, one pushing and the other pulling, they navigated easily through the reed-filled estuary toward the main channel of the Euphrates. The sun was hot in the glades, lulling Semerket into a kind of torpor. Having had no sleep the night before, he soon nodded his head.

He jumped awake, swearing in fright, however, when the donkey began to bray. The beast struggled to rise; almost too late, Semerket realized the animal meant to defecate. He scrambled out of the way just in time to avoid the shower of dung—much to the glee of the Babylonians. But when Semerket attempted to push the animal's rump over the side, wanting to prevent the donkey from fouling the boat any further, their laughter turned into protests.

"No, no, my lord," said Marduk amiably from his seat of honor. "The dung is to be collected and dried in the sun. That way, in a few days we'll have fuel for a fire when we go ashore. Even scrub wood is too precious to burn in Babylonia."

His fellow sailors decided that since the ass had developed such a touching bond with Semerket, it would be his task during their travels to collect and form its dung into bricks. In patient kindness, the merchant's son showed Semerket how to do it.

LATER, WHEN HIS MOOD had improved sufficiently, Semerket began a polite inquisition of his new slave.

"I'm curious," he said to Marduk. "How did you come to speak Egyptian so well?"

Marduk considered a moment before he answered. "I lived there for a time," he said carefully. "In my youth."

"From your accent I gather you lived in Lower Egypt?"

"In Pi-Ramesse, yes."

"Ah! Who was your master? Would I know him?"

"I doubt it."

"He must have been a kind man, to see that you were so well educated."

Marduk turned away from Semerket to gaze across the river, his glance inscrutable.

"Is your master still alive?" Semerket continued the inquiry.

"No."

"Did you escape from him?"

Marduk shook his head, still looking away toward the lavender hills on the eastern horizon. "When my master heard that the Kassite king couldn't last on Babylon's throne much longer—and that Elam planned to invade—he freed me. My country needed me more than he did, he said."

"But then the Elamites took you prisoner."

"Yes."

"So you were again a slave."

Marduk turned and looked at him fully. For the first time Semerket noted the man's well-formed features. Marduk's intelligent brown eyes, contrasting pleasantly with the paleness of his skin, were set far apart and deep, below a smooth high brow. His nose was strong but not beaked, and his lips beneath his mustaches were full. Like most Babylonians, he wore his dark hair long, and though it was now scraggly from neglect, Semerket saw the straightness of his back and the determined set of his shoulders.

This Dark Head, as the native Babylonians were called, was no man's slave, and never had been. The fact that Marduk had naturally taken charge of their expedition and ordered Semerket about so highhandedly was testimony to a long habit of command. Why, then, Semerket pondered, should Marduk pretend he *was* a slave? Some pertinent facts, he sensed, remained unspoken.

"I don't believe you are a slave," said Semerket finally, "or ever were."

Marduk was wry. "Yet you nevertheless paid five gold pieces for me."

Semerket shook his head sadly. "I'd have done better to throw them to the river god as an offering, for no doubt you've already planned when and where you'll escape."

Despite himself, Marduk laughed aloud. He did not confirm or deny Semerket's accusation.

"I would ask a favor of you in return, however," Semerket pressed. "Will you stay with me after we reach Babylon? For just a few days, anyway. I need someone who knows the city well. I'm looking for a person—two, in fact. One of them is my wife."

Marduk stopped gazing at the distant hills and turned his incredulous face to Semerket. "Why is she in Babylon, then, of all places?"

Perhaps it was the fact that Marduk was a foreigner, Semerket later thought, or that he seemed a sympathetic listener, but Semerket divulged everything to him. He described Naia's banishment, and the reasons behind it. Marduk interrupted him only once—when Semerket told him of the strange message from Rami and how the word *slain* had appeared near the phrase *attacked by Isins.*

"Isins?" asked Marduk sharply. "Are you sure that's what the message said?"

"Why? Do you know who they are?"

Marduk shrugged his shoulders, glancing again toward the shoreline. "They're a tribe who ruled as kings before the Kassites invaded from the north. Now their fight is with the Elamites. They're hardly murderers, Semerket—in fact, we native Babylonians regard them as patriots."

Semerket snorted derisively. "May the gods preserve me from patriots, for their crimes are always so noble."

They spent the rest of the afternoon's voyage in silence. Semerket gazed out at the vast brown plains that edged the river, an endless sea of furrowed ruts of earth, crosshatched by canals and dotted with waterwheels. The fields rose imperceptibly to become hills, which in turn changed abruptly into tall cliffs and canyons through which the Euphrates snaked. Here the current was markedly fiercer, but the little round boat proved just as steady as she had in the barely stirring marsh waters. River otters gamboled among the reeds, and once Semerket saw a cheetah warily lapping at the water's edge. At their approach, it turned and slunk back into a ravine. Soon enough the canyons gave way again to marshes clotted with reeds. Small at first, the reeds were soon as tall as trees, overhanging the river so that the Euphrates seemed a tunnel of green, filtered light.

"Like the heavenly fields of Iaru," Semerket murmured.

From time to time, Semerket glimpsed black, viscous pools of some bubbling ooze forming at the river's edge. Once, a black stain crept all the way to the boat itself, glimmering with a dirty iridescence. Semerket pointed at it, asking Marduk what it was.

"Bitumen," answered Marduk. "The bane of Babylonia's farmers. It leaches up from the ground, like some pestilence from hell, spoiling the crops and poisoning the earth."

"Bitumen? I've seen statues and furniture carved from it. I thought it was a kind of stone."

"When it dries, yes, it's amazingly hard. You see it now in its natural state, thick and greasy. The only good thing about it is that it can burn for hours."

Semerket plunged his finger in the passing water. It came back filmed in gooey black, smelling vaguely of sulfur. It was difficult to imagine this wet, sticky stuff aflame.

"Is it a good source for lighting, then, or heat?"

Marduk shrugged. "It throws off such a stinking cloud of soot we only use it when there's no dried dung. If you ask me, that stuff is something the earth goddess has vomited up and wants buried again. But I know that the ladies of the gagu have taken out a license to exploit what they can find."

"The 'gagu'?"

"A convent of women whose religion is trade. As we get nearer to Babylon, you'll probably see some of their caravans. You'll know it's them because all their drivers and guards are females."

"And women have found a use for this bitumen?"

Marduk only shrugged again and fell silent.

The river began to bend lazily to the east. Coming around a promontory, Semerket saw the distant walls of a city. Like Mari's, they bore the scars of recent warfare, but he noted that they had not been breached. As in all Babylonian cities he had encountered, Semerket saw the gilded tip of a distant ziggurat thrusting up above the other buildings. As they drew nearer, the sounds of vital city life began to reach them. They soon came to a long, flat beach nestled against the city walls, where a superfluity of merchants was already encamped.

"Where are we?" Semerket asked.

"In the place where we will stay the night," Marduk answered. "In the city of Is."

Semerket raised his head. "*Is?* As in '*Isin'?*"

Marduk nodded. "Their ancestral home," he said.

THOUGH THE ELAMITES had laid siege to the city of Is the previous year, its defenders had repulsed them. This made Is a magnet for any rebel or dissident who hated the Elamites, and the city had in effect become the unofficial capital of the Babylonian resistance. Gangs of mercenaries and ragtag refugees continually streamed into it from the east and south. Any one of them might be an Elamite agent or Babylonian turncoat; consequently, Marduk told Semerket, trust was not in plentiful supply in Is.

Shortly after they set up their camp on the riverbank and lit their dung fires, Semerket announced that he wanted to go inside the gates. "I mean to find an Isin mercenary," he told Marduk. "Someone who knows of any recent attacks against . . ."

He stopped. Attacks against whom? The only thing he really knew was that Naia and Rami had been employed in the Egyptian ambassador's household. Surely if the ambassador had been assaulted, someone would have mentioned it to him before now. However, it was all he had from which to begin.

"Anyway," he said, "I'm going into the city."

Marduk instantly protested. "If you go blundering in there, asking questions about the resistance, you'll last all of ten minutes before someone plunges a knife between your shoulder blades."

Semerket thrust out his chin obdurately, saying nothing.

Marduk said that he would go inside the city himself. "It may be I know someone in there. Perhaps I'll find someone you can speak with—someone who might know of any Isin raids." He rose to his feet, brushing off his tunic. "Just don't go in there by yourself. It'll be your death if you do."

Though Semerket cared little for arranged meetings, always suspecting that much else had been arranged as well, he knew that Marduk was giving him good advice and—this time—he would take it. Semerket settled back against the city wall. His eyes smarted from the low-hanging cloud of fetid, brown smoke emitted from all the surrounding dung fires. He found it difficult to breathe and took himself to the river's edge where the air was clearer. As the night passed, however, swarms of ferocious mosquitoes rose from the stagnant water to pester and bedevil him. Semerket kept up such a racket of slaps and curses that the wine merchant's son took pity on him and brought him an evil-looking black balm, gesturing that he should apply it to himself. Semerket sniffed at it and the harsh scent of bitumen assaulted his nostrils. Apparently there was a good use for the stuff, after all, for after he had slathered it on his face and limbs, the mosquitoes were not quite so determined to leach him dry.

But he became suddenly aware that water scorpions and long-limbed spiders of disgusting hairiness were glaring at him from the river's edge. The scorpions clicked their foreclaws, advancing toward him stealthily. The insects in Babylonia were immense, he discovered—the largest he had ever seen. He looked around suddenly to find that a legion of spiders and beetles, mantids and other crawling things encircled him. He jumped to his feet with a small cry. At his movement, the insects skittered back a few paces, only to begin inching aggressively again in his direction as soon as he was still.

Fighting down feelings of immense disquiet, he took himself back to the dung fires where the other merchants slept; the insects did not follow him to where the flames flickered. Nevertheless, he was uneasily aware of their flat, opaque eyes, staring at him from the grasses. As the night passed, Semerket made sure to move and flail his arms about from time to time, if only to convince the creatures that he was still awake. ·

The moon was settling low over the horizon when Marduk reappeared. He tapped Semerket on the shoulder and nodded with his head in the direction of the gates. Semerket got to his feet and followed him silently into Is.

Just off the main square, Marduk opened the door onto a small tavern. Its vaulted ceiling was black with the soot from centuries of unvented cooking fires, its ancient murals obscured by grease. Marduk led him to the rear of the tavern, where two men waited, their faces veiled by the black scarves that distinguished them as Isin rebels. Semerket sat on the bench opposite them, while Marduk took his place against a far wall.

Semerket voiced his thanks for meeting him and signaled the tavern owner to bring some beer. Served in a large bowl, syrupy and unfiltered, it had a scum of fermenting husks floating on its foamy surface. The tavern-master brought them long flexible reeds so they could suck out the clearer liquid at the bowl's bottom.

"I'm Semerket," he said after they drank.

"We know who you are," said the taller man curtly.

"May I know your own names?" Semerket asked after a moment.

"Why? So you can tell the Elamite usurper who we are?" asked the taller man with a sneer.

"I'm sorry. I only meant—"

The shorter man interrupted tersely. "Just what do you want?"

"I'm looking for a woman and a young man, both Egyptians. I heard that Isins attacked them—that the boy was injured. I don't know the woman's condition. Can you tell me if you've made any raids recently?"

"Not so often as the Elamites would have you believe," answered the taller man carefully.

"Not as many times as we'd like," insisted his comrade.

Semerket rapidly calculated in his head. "This one would have happened some ten or twelve weeks ago."

"Where?"

"To the northwest of Babylon."

The men looked at one another. "No," they said simultaneously.

"How can you be sure?"

"Because the Elamites retreated there, to protect the capital. It's too dangerous to make raids with so many of them around—not worth the risk."

Semerket's voice was suddenly harsh. "Have you ever killed women in your raids?"

"Maybe," said the taller man.

"*Elamite* women," the other clarified.

"What about an Egyptian one?" Semerket asked.

"Are we supposed to sort one from another, then, nice and tidy?" the taller man asked with a short laugh.

"Besides, we have no quarrel with Egypt—that is, until we met you."

Semerket blinked. "Why? What have *I* done?"

Hot words bubbled to the men's lips. "We hear you bring Pharaoh's greetings to Kutir. You'll talk of treaties—"

"And 'friendship between nations'—"

"Pharaoh will send him gold—"

Semerket impatiently interrupted their litany of grudges. "The alliance between Babylon and Egypt has existed for centuries. Only good comes from it, whoever rules."

"Your pharaoh shouldn't negotiate with an invading criminal," said the taller warrior, slamming his fist down on the table.

"Who should he negotiate with?"

This question seemed to disconcert the two men, and they shot uneasy glances at one another. "With the Heir of Isin," said the shorter one. "The real king here in Babylon."

"All right," replied Semerket in a reasonable tone. "Take me to him. Show me his capital, that I can bow before his throne. Parade his armies before me, that I can measure his might with my own eyes."

The men would have spoken harsh words, but from the corner of his eye, Semerket saw Marduk slightly shake his head. The men swallowed their unuttered sentiments with difficulty.

"There'll come a time," whispered the shorter man between clenched teeth, "when you will do exactly that."

"In the meantime," replied Semerket, "it's Kutir who's the latest strong man in Babylon. That's your word for king, isn't it—'strong man'? But we Egyptians are a practical people. When this Heir of Isin sits on the Gryphon Throne, I can guarantee that Pharaoh will negotiate with him. Until that time, however . . ."

Realizing that this would be all the information he could get from them, Semerket rose to his feet, and waited at the door while Marduk spoke to the two men alone. The men shot dark glances in his direction. Semerket could hear the reassuring timbre of Marduk's voice as he sought to calm them. Semerket went outside into the street to wait for his "slave." When Marduk emerged into the dark a few moments later, they did not speak as they made their way back to the riverbank.

THOUGH THEY WERE STILL a good fifteen leagues away from Babylon, the river soon became dense with little round ships all converging on the capital at once. When Semerket exclaimed at their number, Marduk remarked that the Euphrates seemed desolate to his eyes.

"Trade hasn't recovered since the invasion," he told Semerket. "Merchants are still suspicious of the Elamites, and most have stayed home in their villages this year."

Semerket was skeptical, for hundreds of the round leather boats encircled them, laden with their disparate cargoes. A heap of furs lay piled in one boat, while another carried the skinned and fly-covered corpses of recently slaughtered sheep. Some bore sweet-smelling spices, or cut flowers, or mounds of seeds. Babylon and its surrounding cities were home to over a million persons, and their provisioning was a massive logistical effort.

"No wonder the Elamites covet this land," Semerket said, "if this is so 'desolate' a year for trade."

At that moment, another of the river ships pulled alongside their own. The craft held ten or twelve huge clay jars, with dark stains of honey running down their sides. The honey's spicy tang floated to him, vaguely reminiscent of wildflowers. So strong was the scent that it bordered on the pungent, and Semerket imagined that he could taste the honey's sweetness in the very air. From the corner of his eye, he saw Marduk and the wine merchant bow their heads and make a holy sign. Then he noted the strange priestly robes that the boat's pilots wore.

"Is that the costume of your beekeepers?" asked Semerket.

"What did you say?" asked Marduk with a short, disbelieving laugh.

"There, on that boat that just passed?"

"They're embalmers, Semerket," Marduk explained. "Each of those jars contains someone who's died—probably on their way to be placed into their family crypts."

Semerket had heard that honey preserved flesh almost as well as Egypt's natron, but had never imagined the bizarre burial customs that accompanied the notion. A sudden chill ran up his spine, and he shuddered. Despite his resolve never to allow himself to imagine such things—for by thinking them he might give the thoughts existence— he could not stop the sudden onrush of images that blazed in the recesses of his mind...

Would he find Naia's body, or Rami's, in such a jar? He could imagine how it felt to reach into the jar's dark ooze, how the honey's cool stickiness would close around his fingers, clinging to his arm as he searched for a clump of slimed hair... how he would seize it in his fingers, pulling the body into the light... seeing the honey running down her forehead—

Semerket cried out, wincing.

The others in the boat gazed at him with concern, but he did not see them, too horrified by his vision. Fiercely he commanded himself to put the images from his mind. Naia was *alive*. If she were dead, he would have *sensed* it. He would not, *not* find her in one of those terrible jars. Pain abruptly radiated from his forehead. His viscera churned and bile rose in the back of his throat. Marduk held him as he vomited weakly into the Euphrates.

A touch of river fever, Marduk said soothingly, a common affliction for foreigners visiting Babylon. Semerket accepted a dose of stomach-cleansing elixir that the wine merchant produced from his pack. But Semerket knew that it was not his fever but the horrifying vision looming so suddenly before his eyes that had caused him to retch. He prayed silently to all the Egyptian gods, hoping that he had not glimpsed the future.

• • •

THE FOLLOWING AFTERNOON the ramparts of Babylon came into sight. For hours, they had seen a cloud of smoke growing on the horizon, so thick that it blanketed the city from their view. At first Semerket thought the smoke was from war, that Babylon was in ruins, and he raised a fearful finger, pointing. But Marduk assured him that what he saw were only the emissions of a hundred thousand hearths and altars.

"Babylon will never be destroyed," Marduk muttered resentfully. "She survives as she always has."

Semerket looked at him, surprised to hear the sudden acidity in Marduk's usually calm voice. But Marduk did not notice his glance, and continued speaking in the same low, sour tone.

"Babylon the withered strumpet, opening her skirts to every swaggering invader. This time the Elamites think they've conquered her. But they'll only end up as soft and vitiated as the Kassites. You wish to know the real reason Babylon's walls are intact, Semerket? She gives herself freely to anybody with an army. She alone will prevail in the end."

"You sound like a spurned lover," Semerket said.

"Do I?"

"What is it, Marduk? Are you bitter because you have no armies of your own? Tell me what I don't know."

Marduk's voice was withering. "Some moonlit night in front of the campfire, perhaps," he said.

The smoke and haze thinned as they drew closer to Babylon, and Semerket discovered that the Euphrates actually flowed through the center of the city. On the right side of the river, as tall as a pyramid, the ziggurat called Etemenanki dominated the flat landscape from all perspectives. Seeing Semerket's expression of awe, Marduk regained some of his good humor and explained that the name Etemenanki actually meant "the cornerstone of heaven." The tower was not in reality a temple, he said, but an observatory dedicated to all the sixty thousand gods in the Babylonian pantheon.

"I thought the ziggurat belonged to Bel-Marduk," Semerket said.

"The Lord's temple is actually on the other side of the river. See there—the building covered in gilded tiles? That's where he's worshipped. But it's true the Golden One sleeps every night in a room at the very top of Etemenanki."

Semerket craned his head to squint at the distant level to which Marduk pointed. The highest tier, painted a shimmering azure, seemed impossibly far away, melting without effort into the sky above. It was no wonder that the Lord of the Universe chose to sleep there, for it seemed the exact place where earth became heaven.

"It's where he couples every night with a different virgin," Marduk added casually.

Semerket tore his eyes away from the ziggurat to look at Marduk in shock. In Egypt, the invisible gods were colossal figures, many cubits tall—the reason why the Egyptians, in fact, constructed their temples on so grand a scale.

"And the maidens survive such an ordeal?" Semerket was incredulous.

Marduk regarded him quizzically. "Of course. They're considered very lucky women for a man to marry. But, then, they're very beautiful, too, as you can imagine; only the best are chosen for the Golden One."

"Has any of them . . . um . . . ever described their night with the god?"

It was Marduk's turn to be shocked. "Not only would that be sacrilegious, Semerket, but tasteless as well. I'm surprised at you. What human words could ever describe such an experience?"

"What words, indeed?" murmured Semerket ironically. The maidens' collective silence was certainly a very convenient tradition. With a start, he suddenly wondered if Bel-Marduk would demand the comfort of virgins during his trip back to Egypt. He certainly hoped not, for he had no wish to become a procurer, even for a god. And if the Lord of All did indeed desire such companions, where was he supposed to find them on the dusty roads of Mesopotamia? He sighed, resolving to deal with the problem when it arose.

By now, river traffic surrounded them utterly, and forward motion on the Euphrates came to a halt. Semerket became irritated to find himself confined in an unmoving boat in mid-river. Standing up, he gazed far ahead to see what the holdup was, only to observe yet another wonder—a solid stone bridge that spanned the entire breadth of the Euphrates. He gaped at the continuous stream of vehicles and pedestrians that traversed it from one side of the river to the other. It was quite the most amazing feat of engineering he had ever seen, for the bridge was almost an entire furlong in length. In its center an immense gangplank of wood spanned the two stone piers that made up its bulk, and he saw that it was through this relatively small gap that all the river traffic was being funneled; hence the delay.

In the enforced idleness of the backwash, Semerket raised his besotted eyes to the public buildings that lined the river. A note of pride crept into Marduk's voice as he saw Semerket gazing at the immense city walls. "Are they not impressive, Semerket? Why, they're so wide," he boasted, "that four chariots can ride atop them—abreast!"

Semerket was about to churlishly remark that surely with such thick walls Babylon need not have surrendered to the Elamites so hastily. He still hoped to goad Marduk into revealing the reason for his bitterness. But distant tinkling bells stopped his words before he had a chance to speak them, and he turned in the direction of their sound.

A train of donkeys was leaving the city, going to the north. The asses bore baskets across their backs filled with chunks of what looked like glistening black rock. Semerket saw that the drivers were women—undoubtedly the members of the mysterious gagu Marduk had mentioned earlier. Though the women were clad from head to toe in shroudlike woolen cloaks, allowing only a glimpse of their eyes, there was no mistaking them for men. Even the train's guards were females, though they were sensibly clad in practical leather armor.

"Do these gagu women make a success of their livelihood?" he asked.

"They've lent their wealth to every king and prince in Asia for centuries. If the women were to go bankrupt tomorrow, the entire region would collapse—they're that powerful."

"And it's this trade in bitumen that's brought them their wealth?"

"Hardly. Bitumen is just one of their interests. No, they've become wealthy because they're scientists, Semerket—masters of astrology."

Marduk told him that the gagu's predictions were so astonishingly accurate that kings and satraps from around the world consulted with them. No one was more adept at divination than the women of the gagu, Marduk swore, and their every business decision, every loan, investment, and purchase was first subjected by them to the prism of heaven, the true reason for their success.

As Marduk spoke, Semerket abruptly sat up straighter in the boat. Something familiar had caught his eye. What had it been? He again scanned the long line of donkeys and the women who drove them.

There . . . !

A woman walked beside a big two-wheeled cart piled with chunks of dried bitumen. Shrouded like the others, there was nevertheless something oddly familiar about her—the way she walked, how she held her head, the curve of her hidden leg beneath the shroud. Taller than the rest, certainly less compact (for he was beginning to notice a certain stockiness common to Babylonians of both sexes), the woman possessed a distinctly Egyptian stance.

Semerket stared after her. His mouth dried up. His heart beat a fierce rhythm. His lips suddenly parted, for he was going to shout—to scream—"Naia!"

His throat ached from the effort it cost him to choke back her name. He turned away, fiercely telling himself that the last thing he needed to be doing was imagining Naia in every likely woman that passed. If he continued to do so, he realized, he ran the risk of failing to recognize her when she was truly there.

"What are you looking at so intently?" asked Marduk.

"At . . . at the baskets on the donkeys. They're full of bitumen, aren't they? It must be heavy stuff."

"On the contrary, it's very lightweight. That's why it's so perfect for the gagu to handle—a woman can easily manage a load of it."

Semerket looked sharply at Marduk. Had he not noticed the way the bags sagged over the donkeys' backs—how the hardy little beasts seemed almost to stagger under their weight?

"Yet . . ." Semerket fell silent. So the gagu indulged in a little smuggling. What merchant guild did not? It was none of his business what those women were up to, and such speculation would only cloud his mind with irrelevant detail. Perhaps he had only imagined it, anyway. In his mind, he heard again the deep voice of Elibar, warning him of the perils of Mesopotamia. He would see things that were not there, and become blind to things that were . . .

It was late afternoon when their little round ship finally squeezed past the bridge and found a place to moor on a distant riverbank. Only the donkey seemed sad to see him go, reaching out its head to forlornly nuzzle his hand. The wine merchant and his son raised loud cries of lamentation to see Marduk depart, however, bowing before him abjectly and kissing his hands, fervently asking for his blessing. Marduk at last extricated himself from their embraces, and led Semerket forward into the city.

Babylon possessed eight gates, each named after one of the city's chief gods. In fact, Marduk said, the name Babylon itself actually meant "The Gate of God." Semerket and Marduk entered through the Ishtar Gate, the grandest of them all. It was one of the few mud-brick structures glazed in expensive enameled tiles, and its deep blue color was sacred to the goddess. Trying to look less a bumpkin at his first festival, Semerket obediently stepped into the customs line and forbade himself to gawk.

"You must do the talking for both of us," he whispered to Marduk. "Don't give them my name—I don't want anyone to know I'm Pharaoh's envoy. Tell them I'm a merchant seeking spices, or some such thing, and that I can't speak Babylonian. I need to explore the city on my own before any officials know I'm here."

He had decided not to announce his arrival to Babylon's new king until he had completed his own mission. Only then would he begin negotiations to bring Bel-Marduk's idol back to Egypt. In the meantime, he meant to work far away from the attention of great ones, for he had begun to suspect, given the Elamites' weakened position, that if the native Babylonians knew he was close to Kutir more doors would close to him than open.

Marduk did not answer him, but merely averted his head, and began to follow a few steps behind, cringing and gawking like a simpleton. Semerket smiled to himself, marveling at Marduk's endless mutability. He was a true shape-shifter, able to blend into any crowd, enact any role.

However, when they came to the Elamite immigration clerks and tax gatherers, Marduk remained silent, still affecting his empty gaze. He hung his head and seemed confused and intimidated by the Elamites' sharp questions.

"What's the matter with you?" Semerket said in Egyptian. "Answer them."

But Marduk only peeped dully at the men from behind Semerket. Drool began to string from his mouth. The customs clerk turned his head away in disgust and addressed all his questions to Semerket, refusing even to look at Marduk.

In the end, Semerket had to declare himself to the authorities, for they had searched his pack and found the tablets bearing his name. They then exclaimed and bowed low before him, showing him a list of expected foreign dignitaries, with his own name placed among the most prominent. Instantly, a palace clerk appeared to usher Semerket and Marduk away from the others and into a private room located within the gate itself.

"You are most welcome, Great Lord," gushed the clerk in precise Babylonian. "We will send a courier to inform the palace that you have at last arrived."

Semerket was appalled. "But I don't want that!" he blurted out before thinking.

The Elamite clerk stared at him, taken aback. "But . . . but what will I say to the king when he asks why you don't present your credentials?"

Semerket hastily improvised, with no help from Marduk. "You may inform the king, of course, of my arrival. But tell him . . . tell him that before I present myself at court, I must first purify myself through prayer, to thank the Egyptian gods for my safe arrival."

Semerket knew that the Mesopotamians regarded Egyptians as religion-mad, and hoped the Elamites would accept his excuse, suspicious as it was. The clerk looked doubtful and began to shake his head.

"Or perhaps I should return to Egypt?" Semerket asked darkly.

"Oh no, sir!" The clerk held up his hands in a supplicating manner. "King Kutir would be extremely disappointed—angry, in fact—if you were to depart from Babylon now. His troops would find you, in any case, for he is anxious to hear Pharaoh's greeting from your own lips."

Semerket considered quickly. Either Kutir must possess a formidable network of spies, or Pharaoh's instructions to Ambassador Menef had been extremely thorough. Either way, he had to find a way to gain some time.

"Before I kneel before his throne," he continued to insist, "I must first kneel to my gods."

The clerk's voice was weak. "When do you think you will be content to present yourself at the palace?"

Semerket answered obliquely. "I will give sufficient warning before I come. Meanwhile, my slave and I will look for accommodations in the Egyptian Quarter." Semerket shouldered his pack decisively.

"But rooms are waiting for you at Bel-Marduk's temple hostel, Great Lord! It will be my pleasure to escort you there myself."

"The rooms won't be necessary."

The clerk's face succumbed to his anxiety at last, crumpling into a mask of abject fear. He confessed that a lingering death in the Insect Chamber would be his fate if Semerket vanished within the city. He begged Semerket to see reason, and spare him so terrible an end.

Cursing his luck, furious at Marduk for his silence, Semerket reluctantly agreed to follow the hapless clerk to the hostel. There, Semerket knew, the priests would spy on him, reporting his every movement back to the palace—exactly what he had hoped to avoid.

The clerk mopped his brow, relieved. "And if you wish, the priests can surely furnish you with a proper valet."

"I already have a servant." Semerket tersely indicated Marduk, who reached out to grab, entranced, at a passing fly.

"Forgive me, Great Lord . . . but . . . but is he quite right in the head?"

"He's new," Semerket said, lips thinned with suppressed anger, "recently purchased. I haven't broken him in yet."

The clerk nodded. "We have a saying in Elam, Great Lord —one must turn a slave inside out before they become a proper servant."

"A sage piece of advice," said Semerket ominously, narrowing his eyes at Marduk. "And one that I will certainly try."

From the Ishtar Gate the trio walked down Processional Way, a wide boulevard paved in stone on which the city's massive celebrations took place. Semerket attempted to speak to Marduk in whispered Egyptian, demanding to know what possessed him, but Marduk continued to affect an idiot's shuffle and refused to speak. Semerket grew increasingly frustrated; all his plans for seeking Naia and Rami from the shadows were in ruins, thanks to this stubborn man. He deliberately turned his back on Marduk then, listening as the Elamite clerk pointed out the city's wonders with a pride born of recent acquisition.

"And its walls are so wide," the man concluded with a flourish, "that four chariots can ride atop them! Abreast!"

Semerket murmured appreciatively.

The hostel was a massive six-story affair situated along the Processional Way. Semerket's rooms were on the fifth story, as sumptuous as any he had seen in Pharaoh's palace. Skins covered the tiled floors, and a wide doorway led out onto a terrace overlooking the city. Gazing down from its ledge, seeing the people congregating so far below, Semerket suddenly felt a wave of profound dizziness overtake him. Never having been so high up before, he was astonished that his reaction could be so immediate, and so acute. Semerket retreated hastily into his rooms, to stand as far away from the terrace as possible. At that moment, he heard a cry from the Elamite clerk, who had discovered the final and most amazing of the suite's luxuries—pipes that conducted hot and cold water into his indoor privy. Diverted, Semerket crossed the room to pull at the silver taps, first with timidity and then with delight, allowing the water to spew forth into bronze basins.

"Come see this, Marduk," Semerket called, forgetting his irritation. "Tell us how it's done!"

But no answer came. Semerket grew angry again, tired of Marduk's pretense at simple-mindedness. He turned, a scowl on his face—but Marduk was not there.

A quick examination of the rooms told the rest of the story. Marduk had slipped away while Semerket and the clerk marveled at the gushing water. Even the priestly servants who waited in the hallways had not seen Marduk leave.

Semerket smiled ruefully to himself. He should have expected it; Marduk had never promised he would stay.

For the first time since Mari, Semerket was alone. As he gazed out to the darkening city, careful to avoid the edge of the terrace, he saw Babylon's myriad cooking fires begin to light up the sky. It was only then that he truly appreciated the city's immensity, for it gleamed in front of him like a blanket of rubies without ever seeming to end.

Sweet Osiris, he thought, how was he ever to locate Naia and Rami in such a place?

DAWN FOUND SEMERKET on his way to Babylon's Egyptian Quarter. A man was following him, he noticed, a rather disreputable-looking fellow with a sparse beard and ponderous belly. Semerket turned to stare at him, and the man halted, overcome by a sudden urge to study the contents of a nearby vegetable stand. Semerket almost laughed aloud. Did his pursuer really think he was being subtle—that Semerket did not know him for a spy?

Semerket decided to confront his pursuer, striding pointedly toward him. "Since we seem to be headed the same way, stranger," Semerket said, bringing his face close to the man's, "perhaps you can tell me: am I on the right path to the Egyptian Quarter?"

His spy at first pretended that he did not understand Semerket's accented Babylonian, and glanced about. To Semerket's repeated inquiries, the man simply turned on heel and fled. In his haste to get away from Semerket, however, he made the mistake of peering to the rooftops.

Semerket looked up, knowing what he would find. Another agent stared down at him from behind a balustrade. The man, thinner but no less disreputable-looking than the first, quickly slipped from sight.

Semerket hurried down a side street, shaking his head at the spies' clumsy tactics. He headed east, where the hostel's priest had told him he could find the Egyptian Quarter. Once there, he planned to mingle with his fellow citizens, to ascertain whether any of them had heard of Naia or Rami, or of any recent attacks made on Egyptians by Isins. He would also attempt to find where Ambassador Menef's residence was located, for he knew from Naia's letter that she and Rami had last been living there.

As he wove through the swarming Babylonians, who had risen early to open their innumerable shops, he heard his spy leaping noisily from rooftop to rooftop above him. The streets were so narrow this was not a difficult chore. Yet even this small bit of athleticism seemed too much for his hapless pursuer. From below, Semerket heard an aborted scream and a crash. He looked up to find the man clinging frantically to a parapet. Semerket debated whether he should rescue the man, but the spy's fat friend quickly appeared to drag him back onto the roof. Several broken mud bricks rained down on the narrow street with a tremendous crash. Semerket leapt easily aside, but some of the bricks struck an old crone selling blooms. She lay senseless in the alleyway, sprays of mountain lupines strewn about her in a pathetic circle.

"Look," Semerket called up, "if you want to know where I'm going, it's to Amun's temple in the Egyptian Quarter." His spies made no answer, but cowered behind the roof's ledge, pretending to be invisible.

"Morons," Semerket muttered darkly. If these spies were the best Elam could produce, he thought, their occupation of Babylonia was doomed to be a short one.

Semerket discovered that the streets of Babylon seemed to radiate from successive squares like spokes on a chariot wheel, never leading to where he expected. It was not very long before he had passed the Egyptian Quarter altogether, finding himself in an area of town where merchants sold mud bricks, pots, ewers, and molded terracotta statues. He stopped to ask directions from a seller of religious figurines.

"The what?"

"The Egyptian Quarter. The Bel-Marduk priests told me it's somewhere east of the river."

"I'd believe them if I was you."

"That's not the point. I've lost my way."

"East of the river, you say?"

"Yes."

Shaking his head, the man turned to shout at the potter across the courtyard.

"The Egyptian Quarter? Ever hear of it?"

"The what?"

Semerket felt his gut clench. He detested being lost. As the two men argued, it was clear that they knew very little about their own city. At any other time, he would have asked directions from one of the omnipresent Elamite foot soldiers who patrolled the streets in small units. But he had no wish to approach them, and went out of his way to avoid the Elamites. This was not easy, as most of Elam's army seemed to be stationed in the capital city—an intimidating, menacing presence on almost every street corner.

It was noon when Semerket realized that the signs and notices painted on the brick walls had changed from cuneiform to glyph. He had at last arrived in the Egyptian Quarter. To his dismay, however, the upper floors of his own hostel loomed over the rooftops not a furlong away; Semerket had come almost full circle from where he started.

He cursed aloud, using an epithet he rarely spoke.

Though the quarter's featureless mud-brick facades resembled every other place he had seen that morning, eventually his eye found some rudimentary Egyptian embellishments. A single lotus column supported a sagging roof, while a fallen statue of some ancient pharaoh lay forgotten in its courtyard, covered in bird droppings. At best, the quarter was only a tired and dusty refuge for Egypt's unwanted outcasts.

These outcasts congregated in the square, loitering in doorways and stables. None seemed to be actually doing anything, and they stared back at him with vacant, surly expressions. Semerket bent to ask a woman sitting in the shade of a spindly palm where he might find the local temple. Listlessly, she pointed to an alley.

"End of the street," she slurred, idly waving away the flies that foraged on her grease-stained robes.

His two spies waited for him behind the temple's walls, ducking out of sight when he approached. He was pleased to see them, for then they could honestly report to King Kutir that Semerket had done what he said he would do: he had gone to pray to his gods. The two men would never guess that he intended to go directly to the rear of the temple and over its wall to continue his investigations alone.

Once inside the temple compound, however, Semerket was temporarily flummoxed. There was no hall of columns, no sacred lake, no altars—in fact, the place did not seem like any Egyptian temple he had ever seen. Tentatively, he went inside the unkempt courtyard, where a couple of parched fig trees were its only ornamentation.

Crossing into the darkened sanctuary, he met a miserable collection of chapels and shrines, though not a single statue of the gods occupied them. The murals, too, seemed poorly painted. A faint though pleasant smell of stale incense clung to the room, but it was clear that no rituals had taken place in there for some time. He looked vainly about for any priest or acolyte.

Shrugging his shoulders, he plunged forward into the temple, toward what he assumed was its rear. He had gone no more than a few paces when he heard footsteps coming down one of the gloomy hallways.

"My lord!" A thin craggy voice bleated in Egyptian to him from the dark.

A gnarled priest of incalculable years was advancing slowly toward him, all the while attempting to straighten his threadbare wig. Behind him padded an elderly woman, her lips quivering in alarm.

"You must not go that way, my lord," the priest said. "Only a consecrated priest may enter."

"I'm a priest of the second grade," Semerket said, not precisely lying. All who learned how to write the 770 sacred writing symbols of Egypt in a House of Life, as Semerket had, were designated second-grade priests at their graduation. It was just that Semerket had never truly graduated.

"Nevertheless, you are a stranger here and you have not been purified..." The aged priest's voice trailed into muffled uncertainty. "You *are* a stranger, aren't you? We've never met?"

"No."

The old priest seemed relieved that his mind still functioned, and stood up straighter. "Then I must ask you to leave the way you came."

Semerket thought quickly. "But I wanted to offer up a prayer of thanks to Amun, for seeing me safely to Babylon."

The old priest glanced at him sharply. "A prayer—? You will make an offering?"

This was more than Semerket meant to do, but he shrugged. "Yes, all right. Why not?"

"You'll purchase onions and bread for the altar?" The priest was smiling with surprised delight. He turned to the priestess behind him. "Mother, today is a fortunate one for us!"

To Semerket's distress, he saw that tears flowed down the old woman's cheeks. Impulsively she reached forward to take his hand and kiss it.

"It can't be so strange," Semerket said, a trifle embarrassed, "for wayfarers to offer thanks to the gods?"

"Around here it is," the old woman said forthrightly. "Most of the Egyptians in this neighborhood didn't come to Babylon willingly. They have very little to be thankful for, and blame the gods for their misfortunes. Hardly anyone makes offerings nowadays."

Semerket knew that Egyptian priests and priestesses lived mainly from the sacrifices of bread, vegetables, oil, and other foodstuffs given to the gods. Seeing the old couple's eyes shining from their sunken faces, Semerket grew concerned.

"When was the last time you ate?"

"It's of no importance. We serve the gods in joy."

"*When?*" Semerket's voice was perhaps harsher than he intended.

The woman spoke quickly. "Two days ago."

"Hasn't Ambassador Menef sent you provisions, or workers to help you? Isn't it his duty to maintain this temple?"

The thin, little woman narrowed her eyes. "He has his own private chapel, on his estate, with his own priests. He doesn't come to our services anymore. He said——"

"Mother."

The old woman fell silent, staring at the floor in shame. Semerket noticed how her tunic, though meticulously cleaned, had been patched and repatched so many times that there was more Babylonian wool to it than good Egyptian linen. Semerket bent to regard the woman's tired eyes.

"Tell me."

With a fearful look at her husband, she whispered, "He said that my husband and I have done too little to lure the people here—that's what he said, 'lure'—as if this place were a circus and——"

"Mother!"

But the old woman's words continued to pour out in ever more aggrieved invective. "We've even had to sell the gods' statues from their niches in order to keep the temple up. We traded the last one a month ago, and then only for what its bronze was worth. What's next for us? My husband forbids me to beg—he says it demeans our calling—though sometimes the pains in my stomach are so sharp, that I—that I—" The rest of her words were swallowed in a sudden, silent convulsion of weeping.

The old priest stepped between Semerket and his wife. "I'm sure the ambassador has many reasons for why he hasn't sent us sustenance," he said firmly. "The war with Elam, I know, has caused much suffering. We're not the only ones who go hungry in Babylon, you know."

Turning suddenly, Semerket retraced his steps through the gloomy temple and out to the gates. The old couple hobbled after him in alarm, believing that he was leaving them for good.

"You two!" Semerket shouted to the spies when he reached the gate.

They peeked from behind the wall where they hid. "Do you mean us?"

"I need you to get some things. Go into the marketplace around the corner. Bread, onions, honey, oil. A goose, if you can find one." He turned to the wide-eyed priestly couple. "Do you think the gods would like some beer?"

The elderly priest seemed too dazed to speak, but his wife chimed in hopefully, "Oh, yes, please! The August Ones haven't had beer in so long."

The spies frowned. "Who the hell are you to order us around!?" the thin one railed.

"Semerket, envoy of the fourth Pharaoh Ramses, come to parley with your king Kutir—as you well know, since you've seen fit to follow me around all morning."

"That's a lie—!"

"We never—!"

The obsidian flash that glinted then in Semerket's eye made them abruptly cease their protests. "Do I really have to tell the king what inept spies he sets upon me?"

The men grew alarmed. The fatter one swallowed and asked in a humbler voice, "What is it you want, again, sir? Though we don't admit to your accusation, mind you, we'd be glad to help."

Semerket named the items, and gave them a gold piece. He told them that another would be theirs if they would be quick. With many grumbles, the Elamites went into the nearby marketplace.

"And some incense," he called after them. "A big ball of it!"

"I'm afraid you won't see them again, young man," said the priest. "We've never been able to trust the locals."

"They'll be back," averred Semerket, staring after them.

Despite his impatience to begin his search for Naia and Rami, Semerket assisted the aged couple in preparing the altar for the receiving of sacrifice. They scraped away the lichen growing on the stone and threw away the dead blooms from its vases. At one time, the old priest told him, when Egypt's eastern empire flourished, the Babylonian temple of Amun had been much larger. He pointed beyond the wall, telling him that the real temple had once stood next door but that it had been lost in a bad business deal with some crooked Babylonian scoundrel, who had razed it to put up a warehouse. Only this collection of odd rooms was left of the original temple, which had once been only its storage area.

"It's no wonder the gods have turned their backs on us," said the old priest mournfully. "My wife and I, I'm afraid, have been very poor stewards of their glory." He sighed as he bent to sweep up the dust. "Though I doubt anyone ever loved them more."

Defying the old priest's gloomy predictions, the two spies returned with the provisions, and Semerket assisted them in bringing the goods inside the temple. They heaped the groceries on the altar and set wildflowers in the vases. Despite the rumbles coming from their stomachs, the old couple insisted that they celebrate all the obsequies and ceremonies before they themselves partook of the food.

They lit the incense, and genuflected before the altar, insisting that Semerket perform the rituals with them. Verbosely, the old ones thanked the good gods for the safe arrival of their guest, praying earnestly for his welfare, and begging the August Ones to protect him in all his endeavors.

Semerket had always disliked ritual and ceremony. He preferred instead to commune with the gods in his own way, silent and solitary. For all of this, his first day in Babylon found him intoning the litanies and psalms he had learned as a child. And after the priest and priestess concluded their prayers, Semerket—who liked to think of himself as a hard-bitten man of little sentiment—meekly asked the old couple to add a prayer or two for the safety of his wife and young friend, whom he had come to Babylon to find.

"NAIA WAS DEVOTED to the gods. I know she must have made an offering here. It's what she would have done when she arrived in Babylon. Why can't you remember her?"

Senmut the priest and Semerket sat together in the soft light of evening, their backs against the warm granite altar. Senmut's wife, Wia, had cleared the remains of their dinner away, and had taken the leftovers to the spies who still waited outside the temple gates.

"Ah, yes," the priest smiled. "How could I fail to recognize such a paragon from your description?" He paused, and then recited, "'There is no one like her, she is more beautiful than any other, a star-goddess rising, with hair of lapis and sweet lips for speaking...'"

"You remember your poetry well enough."

"I was young when I learned the song. You'll discover when you're my age it's easier to recall a poem from your youth than what it was you did yesterday."

"I'm sure if you tried—"

"Semerket," Senmut admonished, "you describe a goddess, but I must recall a woman. And the world is filled with so many."

Semerket tried to hide his disappointment from the priest, making his voice deliberately light. "Then if the most beautiful woman in Babylon *does* come here, with skin the color of smoke and eyes like the Nile at flood, will you send me word?"

"Of course. But perhaps there is some other way I can help you." The priest scratched his brow, struggling to remember. "Mother?" He called over to Wia, who had returned to the courtyard. "Mother, what is the name of that singer?"

"Nidaba," said Wia distinctly, instantly knowing who her husband meant.

"Who?" asked Semerket.

"Nidaba. A singer of ballads and poems. You must go to her house. It's where everyone in Babylon meets to find what they need."

Semerket was intrigued. "For instance... ?"

Wia, who seemed the more practical member of the family, looked at him slyly and tapped her nose. "The kind of things you don't find in the regular souks or bazaars, if you know what I mean."

"Black market?"

Wia nodded. "Yes, that, of course. But mostly one goes there for information. If anyone in the city has seen your wife and friend, you'll find them at Nidaba's."

"Where is her house?"

"We've never been there, Semerket," said Senmut. "It's not an ... *edifying* ... place for a priest to be seen in. But I believe it's in the old section of town."

"How did you find out about it?"

"When we had to sell the statues of the gods, we made inquiries. Someone from Nidaba's house came to collect them. Apparently she knew someone who has a passion for Egyptian objects."

Dusk had fallen over the city. Semerket rose to leave, for the Elamites had imposed a nighttime curfew, allowing only those with a pass onto the streets. Semerket hurriedly made his farewells to the old priest and priestess; the gods alone knew how long it would take him to find his hostel. As Wia stood on tiptoe to embrace him, he slipped a few pieces of gold into her tattered sash.

"You will come back, Semerket?"

"Of course. It does me good to speak Egyptian again. I hadn't realized how much my throat ached, speaking only Babylonian as I've done."

"We will ask after this lady of yours," Senmut promised earnestly. "And the boy, as well."

That night, Semerket discovered that someone had rifled through his belongings while he had been out. The seals on Pharaoh's letters freeing Naia and Rami were broken. Though his intruder had tried to mend them, Semerket saw the hairline fracture that faintly scarred the wax intaglio. With rising panic, he clawed through his pack, searching for the clay tablets. They were there—a relief, since he must soon go to the temple countinghouse for more of Pharaoh's gold. The fact that the tablets were still in his pack proved that whoever had searched it was more interested in information than gold.

He chastised himself for having left his belongings behind during his day's roaming, for now the Elamites knew that he was searching for two Egyptian nationals, and who they were. He had not declared such an intention to the customs clerk at the Ishtar Gate, and the Elamites would wonder what importance Pharaoh or Semerket attached to the recovery of these individuals. He had no wish to become embroiled in any international gamesmanship, and knew that time was fast running out for him. A few days were all he had left before Kutir would surely demand to see him. He must work quickly, he decided, and without any spies reporting his every move back to the palace.

AFTER HE LEFT the hostel the following morning, Semerket moved in a slow, circuitous manner, certain that his two fumbling spies would be following him. Just as he thought, he soon heard the wheezing and panting of the larger one coming down the road.

"Good morning," he said, stepping into their path.

Even though they had been amiable enough the day before, the men became instantly wary. They glanced nervously around the crowded streets, suspicious of the nobles and bureaucrats converging on the various government buildings and temples in the area. They beckoned him into a dark doorway. There, they indignantly told him that it was their job to keep him in sight, and not the other way round.

"Please, sir," whispered the heavier one, "it won't do for you to keep surprising us this way. What if someone important should see us together? What would they think?"

"We'd lose our job, that's what," added the other man, his voice as taut as a lute string. "It's hard enough since the invasion to get honest work. Just go on walking, sir, like you was doing. We won't bother you if you don't bother us. Live and let live, that's what we say."

"How'd you like to work for me?"

Both men were speechless for a moment. Then the thin one exploded in protests, regardless of who saw them, saying that a dungeon—or worse—awaited them if they changed allegiances. Semerket gathered from the man's repeated entreaties to the sixty thousand gods of Babylon that the Elamites were not liberal-minded in such matters.

"Let me rephrase it," Semerket said. "What if I pay you *not* to follow me? In that way you can collect two salaries at once."

Again, the thin man began to bewail his fate, but his compatriot's face took on a shrewd expression beneath its folds of fat. "Let us hear this gentleman out," he said, "for even though he's an Egyptian, there may be some sense in what he says."

Semerket quickly sketched his proposal: for the next week they could earn a gold piece per day if they were to let him go about his business alone. It amounted to almost a whole year's salary, he said, since he would be paying them in Egyptian gold. Moreover, at the end of the week, Semerket promised, he would dutifully present himself to King Kutir, and no one would be the wiser.

"But what do we tell the Elamite captain who pays us?" asked the fat one. "He wants a report detailing your movements at the end of every day."

"You'll follow me to the Egyptian temple in the morning," Semerket blithely assured the two spies. "And every evening I'll come out the same way. You can report that I've been praying all day, and as far you can tell, it's true. Everyone thinks Egyptians are god-crazy, anyway; it'll be easy for you to convince your captain."

The larger of the two spies contemplatively stroked his scanty beard. Even at rest, the breath going in and out of his lungs sounded like a punctured bellows. "I confess it's more appealing to me than following you around the city all day, going in circles as you do. I'm a large man, as you can see, more accustomed to the comfortable benches of the occasional wineshop. The thought of collecting two salaries at once is very tempting—very tempting."

"We'll be caught," the other man whispered anxiously. "They'll find out. The Elamites will flay the skins from our bodies. They'll throw us into the Insect Chamber—"

"Why?" said Semerket reassuringly. "Do they set spies to spy upon their spies?"

"I'd put nothing past them," the thin man said glumly. "You don't know them like we do." He grimaced, thinking perhaps of the punishments that would be his.

In the end, however, the two Dark Head spies agreed to Semerket's plan, though they warned him that if he did not emerge from the temple at sundown as he had promised, they would go immediately to the Elamite captain to report him missing. Semerket agreed to their single condition. A little more copper persuaded them to divulge the best route to the Egyptian Quarter. Under their guidance, he was able to reach it in a fraction of the time it had taken him on the previous day.

At the Egyptian temple, Semerket told Senmut and Wia that he must go over its rear wall so that he could explore Babylon without anyone's knowing he did. But Senmut showed him a long, underground passageway instead, damp from the waters of the Euphrates and smelling foully of waste, which connected the temple grounds to a distant alleyway. Wia gave him the ancient key that opened its bronze gate, and Semerket was at last alone in Babylon.

"WINE," he said. "Red."

As he frequently did when he first arrived in a strange city, Semerket went to a tavern. The owners of such establishments usually were the touchstones for all the gossip and intrigue of the neighborhood. As a rule, they were garrulous sorts, willing to share what they knew for a little cash, or even for a bowl of their own wine.

There was a surfeit of such places from which to choose in Babylon's Egyptian Quarter, and he sat in a shop that occupied the corner of a small square. The term "shop" was a misnomer, however, for only a single tattered awning barely kept the hot sun from Semerket's back. Everyone who passed could peek inside to see who drank there. Even at this relatively early hour there were more than a few patrons sitting on the pavement, huddled over their bowls of wine, like vultures over a corpse.

The owner himself brought the bowl to where Semerket sat, and Semerket gave him a copper snippet.

"Not enough," said the man shortly.

"Then you must import your wine directly from the Heavenly Fields, friend," Semerket said, smiling to show that he was joking.

The man regarded him with a blank expression. "Wonderful—a sense of humor. Now my day can begin. Three coppers, *friend.*"

"Three?" Semerket had never paid so much for wine before, even in Thebes' finest inns.

"There's been a war here, in case you hadn't noticed. When trade is down, the price goes up. Three copper pieces, or get out."

With a sourness that suddenly matched the innkeeper's, Semerket pulled out two more bits of copper from his sash and added them to the one already in the man's hand. The shop owner was about to depart when Semerket stopped him, attempting to arrange his features into something resembling cordiality.

"Wait," he said, "for that much copper I'd like some advice to go with it."

"Advice?"

"Help, then. I'm new to Babylon."

The shop owner's lip curled a fraction. "Go to one of the temples if you need charity. We're fresh out."

"It's information I want."

The man looked at him for a moment, eyes suddenly flat and ominous. "And you thought the wineseller could let you in on what's happening in our little world, eh? A few bowls of wine, a few coppers, and I'd tell you anything you want to know—is that it?"

"Something like it."

"Here's some 'advice,' then, and on the house: this is Babylon, friend, not Egypt."

"I'm aware of that."

"Then you should also be aware that any time some stranger from Egypt comes looking for information around here, it usually means someone ends up dead, or arrested, or hauled away for a turn in the Sinai mines. Stick your nose someplace else. We tend to get jittery when anybody starts asking questions—they're usually bounty hunters."

"I'm not a bounty hunter. I only want to find my friends," Semerket said, his voice becoming insistent. "Surely that's not—"

The wineseller bent down to where Semerket sat, bringing his heavy face close to Semerket's. "The only want of yours I'm interested in," said the man, enunciating, "is whether or not you want more wine." He paused. "Do you want more wine?"

"No."

"When you do, I'll be over there." The man pointed to the brick bench where his wine jars were stacked, and left him.

Semerket looked around the shop. Most of the people had overheard his conversation with the owner and now assiduously avoided his gaze. Only one person seemed friendly, an elderly man whose sagging jowls quivered excitedly when Semerket turned in his direction. The man lingered hopefully at the outer reaches of the canopy, in the white sunlight, and when the shop owner turned away, he gesticulated feverishly so that Semerket might call him into the shop.

Semerket inclined his head, indicating that the old man should join him. When he sat down, however, Semerket instantly regretted it. Stubble blossomed on his chin, and wine stained his grimy robes.

The old man brought his quivering hands together, saluting Semerket in the Egyptian fashion. "Thank you, young man, thank you," he burbled, taking a seat. "Most kind of you, indeed." A miasma of stale wine and garlic instantly stole over Semerket like a dank river fog.

The shop's owner appeared at their side. "Damn you, Kem-weset!" he said. "It gives my place a bad name when the likes of you comes begging."

"You have it all wrong, Hapi, dear fellow," the old man interrupted quickly, ducking his head as if he expected a blow. "This young man—" He nudged Semerket in the ribs.

"Semerket."

"My friend Semerket here invited me in. He wishes to consult with Babylon's greatest physician." He looked askance at Semerket, pleading with his cloudy eyes, smiling piteously. "Isn't that so, son? I can see you've had a touch of river fever recently, am I right?"

Semerket could have easily dismissed the old man, but after a moment's hesitation, he looked up at the wineseller with a trace of defiance. "Another bowl of red for Babylon's finest physician."

The old man's tongue darted to the crusted corners of his mouth.

"A jar would be better, I think," he said to Hapi. "It's devilish hot today."

Semerket nodded.

"Show me the copper, first," the wineseller demanded.

Semerket reached into his belt and tossed him the pieces.

Hapi the wine merchant delivered the jar with the usual bonhomie that distinguished his establishment. Semerket poured some for the old man, who eagerly raised the bowl to his lips after nodding a quick toast to Semerket. In his haste to drink, however, or because his hands were shaking, he spilled some wine onto the ground. Without hesitation he removed his sash and sopped it up, squeezing the few drops back into the bowl.

"Waste of good wine is a sin," the old man intoned firmly. "That's what the Babylonians say, and I believe them."

He seized the jar himself this time and poured another bowlful, drinking the second more slowly.

"Ah," he exhaled, "very soothing. Just the thing to counter this beastly heat."

He closed his eyes, sighing contentedly. Semerket noticed that the old man's trembling hands were calmer and that color was slowly returning to his blotched face.

"Are you truly a physician?" asked Semerket.

"None finer in all Babylonia, though that's not saying much." Kem-weset swallowed more wine. "They have no appreciation for the medical arts here. Whenever anyone falls ill, do they consult with a trained physician? No. Do they call in wizards for a proper exorcism? Certainly not. They just move them out of their homes, bed and all, into the Sick Square—"

"The what?"

"The Sick Square. That colossal joke where Babylon laughs at me, at Kem-Weset, physician of Egypt."

"But what is it?"

"What does it sound like, son? It's a square where they bring out the city's sick and ailing. The wretches are forced to call out—to total strangers, mind you—in the hope that someone might know a cure for their affliction."

"That sounds very backward."

"That's putting it mildly. But the Babylonians have a horror of the lancet and probe. And you can't really know medicine, true medicine, if you're squeamish. A body's about muscles and guts, sinews and organs, and all the liqueurs of life—phlegm, bile, blood, urine, sweat, semen, shit—"

Kem-weset's voice grew loud with his wine and indignation. Semerket noticed Hapi glancing sharply at them from his corner.

"Would you care for another jar?" Semerket asked hastily, hoping to divert the old man.

"A capital idea."

Semerket signaled the wineseller. Kem-weset became positively giddy. "I must say, my boy, you're being awfully generous. What can I do for you in return?"

"I'm here in Babylon to find some friends, to take them back to Egypt—"

"Back to *Egypt!*" the old man interrupted, his voice charged with ecstatic longing, as if the word Semerket had spoken were *heaven* or *paradise*. "How I long to lie in the shadows of the pyramids and drink from the waters of the Nile again. Alas…"

"What's keeping you here? Did you commit some crime that prevents you from returning?"

"Ah, no, nothing like that. I came here of my own accord, thinking they might need a real doctor in these parts." The old man sighed again. "It is my mistress who keeps me here."

Semerket blinked. Semerket tried to imagine the mistress of such a man, but found his powers unequal to the task. "A mistress?"

"Ah, dear me, yes. One whose heart is granite, yet whose embrace I've never left without wanting more. She is there in the bowl beside you."

"Oh," said Semerket, comprehending. "The wine."

Kem-weset nodded sadly. "I've no money to return to Egypt, Semerket. I've given all of it away to people like Hapi over there. I'm a physician with no patients, in a country with no doctors, who lives from bowl to bowl. Hope of ever returning to Egypt has withered in me."

Semerket remembered his own days as the town drunk, in the

weeks and months after Naia had divorced him. He might have become exactly like this pathetic old man, but the gods had been merciful, giving him honest work to do. Kem-weset, it seemed, had not even his profession to rescue him from despair.

"Surely the Egyptians here need your skills?"

"The occasional broken bone, some stitches—that's about all I'm good for. I'm still living on the remnants of a fee I got a few weeks ago for patching up some local lads. Last year I thought I'd latched onto something, but it came to nothing. As usual." Kem-weset wiped at his eyes with his wine-stained sash, burying his large nose in its folds and blowing.

Semerket poured him another bowl of wine.

Kem-weset raised his head. "Let's not talk anymore of sad things," he said. "This excellent wine won't permit us to be anything other than joyful. Now, you were telling me that you'd come here to find your friends?"

Semerket nodded. "But the city's so large. I don't know where to begin. Even the Egyptian Quarter here is so much bigger than I expected."

"Some twenty thousand of us in the city alone, last time anyone bothered to count, and that's not including the rest of Babylonia."

"Twenty thousand—!" Semerket choked. "How could the quarter hold them all?"

"We're all over the city, Semerket, not just in this little place." Kem-weset waved an extravagant hand to indicate a myriad of unseen vistas. "Egyptians are very desirable as servants, you know, because of our elegant manners."

Semerket considered what Kem-weset had told him. "Naia did write that she had become a maid in the Egyptian ambassador's residence—"

"Menef?" Kem-weset's voice was sharp.

Semerket nodded.

The old man's face lit up. "But I know him! I told you that I thought I was onto something last year—that's who it was. When Menef came to Babylon, I tried to interest him in making me his official physician. But he had brought his own doctor and luck deserted me once again."

"Do you know where he lives?"

"But of course."

"Can you take me there?"

"I can do more than that. I'll introduce him to you. I'm sure he'll remember me." Kem-weset preened importantly, and then sighed regretfully. "But before we go..."

"What?"

"I noticed you haven't touched that wine there at your side ...?"

Semerket passed his bowl to the physician.

DESPITE SEMERKET'S IMPATIENCE to get under way, Kem-weset insisted that they return to his nearby rooms, so that he could attire himself in his formal robes and don his physician's collar. A tedious hour passed before the old soak reappeared. The old man had dressed himself in a pleated linen tunic and shawl that even Semerket, who cared little for fashion's trends, ascertained was of no recent vintage.

For all his obvious decay, Kem-weset seemed jaunty enough. "Come, Semerket!" he cried, setting his walking stick firmly on the ground. Despite the copious amounts of wine he had imbibed that morning, he walked swiftly through the lanes and byways of Babylon without once stumbling—the sure sign of a true and committed drunkard, thought Semerket.

At the boundaries of the Egyptian Quarter, they paused at the canal so that Kem-weset could determine the best route to take to the ambassador's residence.

"It's been a while since I've been there," he fretted. "Now which street is it...? You'd think the Babylonians could lay down a straight road."

The ambassador, it turned out, lived in a walled-off enclave alongside the embassies and legations from other countries. It was not difficult to determine which estate belonged to the Egyptian ambassador, for twin spires flew the crimson and azure pennants that proclaimed it an official outpost of the kingdom of Egypt. It was a very imposing house, befitting the embassy of the greatest of nations, but the brightness of the mansion's recent whitewash and the glaring colors of its decorations made Semerket crawl with embarrassment. Its gaudiness was almost an assault amidst all the mud brick. Semerket abruptly recalled, too, how the temple in the Egyptian Quarter had gone untended, and how its two elderly acolytes starved within it.

He felt his heart harden against Menef, who would rather make his own home a palace than see the gods of Egypt well housed. Though he cautioned himself against leaping to conclusions, a tiny sneer began to pull irresistibly at his lips.

As he and Kem-weset drew nearer, Semerket heard the cacophony of many voices. Rounding the corner, he was appalled to see that perhaps two hundred litigants waited in the estate's shadow. They were Egyptian nationals, and each wore the same eager yet resigned expression of someone who knows his case to be hopeless, yet who hopes for a miracle. As they picked their way through the crowd, going to the guardhouse, Semerket heard their murmured conversations.

". . . a mistake, we shouldn't have been sent here . . ."

"A crooked judge was *my* downfall."

"If he will only review the facts of my case, they speak plain . . ."

"It was such a little crime . . . who did it harm?"

Semerket inhaled deeply. Would his own story sound so implausible and desperate? The difference was that he had in his possession two writs of freedom from the pharaoh of Egypt himself. Semerket reminded himself that he was only asking the ambassador for information concerning Naia and Rami's whereabouts, not for any official intercession on their behalf.

He anxiously turned to Kem-weset. "Can you get us in there ahead of these others? If Menef does indeed know who you are . . . ?"

A momentary glint of doubt clouded the physician's eye. Gone was Kem-weset's jaunty bravado, replaced by diffidence. "That is, yes . . . probably. I'll speak to the guard ahead. I'm sure he'll remember me— though it was some months ago, you must remember . . ."

Tentatively Kem-weset approached the small sentry house beside the gates. He raised his hand in a shaky greeting. The clerk continued to mark a clay tablet with his stylus, ignoring him. Kem-weset cleared his throat noisily.

"Good sir—a moment?"

The pimply clerk glanced at Kem-weset from beneath his lowered lids. When he saw who it was, the clerk grimaced slightly. He turned to murmur something to a nearby guard. The guard was a young man, anxious to make an impression, and immediately affixed a fierce glower to his features. He came from the shack to bark rudely into Kem-weset's face, "Back of the line, old sot!"

Yes, thought Semerket dismally, they did indeed know Kem-weset here.

When the old physician protested, saying that he wished an interview with Menef—that the ambassador would surely remember him, that he was a physician of some renown in Egypt—the young guard struck him savagely across his throat with the shaft of his spear. Kem-weset collapsed onto the ground like a sacrificed heifer, to lie gasping in the dust of the street, clutching his neck.

With a cry, Semerket ran to the old man's side. Kem-weset's eyes bulged from their sockets, tears oozing as he struggled for air. Quickly Semerket felt the physician's neck, and ascertained that his trachea had not collapsed. When Kem-weset could breathe again, Semerket raised his eyes to gaze into the young guard's face.

What the guard saw in those black eyes caused the young man to reconsider his own fierce glare for a moment. The youth blinked uncertainly, and swallowed. "You, too," he said, attempting again to be gruff and threatening, "go to the rear and wait like everyone else."

Semerket merely continued to stare at him. The lad suddenly remembered his courage and feinted at Semerket with his spear, obviously expecting him to cower. But Semerket abruptly wrenched the spear from his hands and broke it in two across his knee.

As Semerket threw the two ends into a nearby canal, cheers erupted from the crowd of supplicants. The young soldier, alarmed, sprinted to the sentry house to speak in earnest tones with the clerk. They both stared anxiously at Semerket, who was now advancing on them.

Before Semerket had a chance to confront them, however, the gates to the embassy unexpectedly opened from inside. The crowd surged forward, and Semerket had to struggle to keep them from trampling the still-prone Kem-weset.

A richly uniformed herald appeared and stood upon a stone. He loudly proclaimed that the ambassador would grant no more audiences to anyone that day, as he had been summoned to the royal palace. A great groan of disappointed anger rose in the throats of the crowd, sounding like a giant animal suddenly roused.

At the sound, an entire cohort of guards suddenly appeared from behind the gates and began to clear a pathway through the mob, herding the people away with the shafts of their spears. Semerket strained to see behind them and into the estate. He glimpsed a large carrying chair at the front door of the main house, ready for use.

A short, plump man emerged into the sunlight, sleek and spoiled as a temple cat, and stepped into the chair. From the richness of his robes and the glint of real gold in his elaborately braided wig, the man could only be Menef himself. With his hawk-tipped staff of office gripped firmly in his hands, he was raised high on the shoulders of his liveried bearers.

Semerket shook his head in derision, for no fewer than forty men carried Menef. He almost laughed aloud—no one, not even the great Ramses III himself, had been carried by so many bearers. This Menef's ostentation was unbelievable! Semerket suddenly wished he had brought his own badge of office that Pharaoh had bestowed on him, for he sensed that Menef might be intimidated by such a jewel.

The chair began to move forward. At that moment, a slimly built, sinewy man stepped forward through the gate. Seeing the crowd, the man's underslung jaw suddenly contorted into a wide grin that did not correspond with the flat menace of his ophidian eyes. The smile was a ghastly parody of good humor, a veritable rictus of disdain and spite. In a low voice, the man directed the guards to lash out at the crowd with their whips, to clear a pathway for the ambassador's approaching chair. Inexorably, the guards began to advance, flailing their short whips of hippopotamus hide at the people. Screams rang out, but still the stubborn mob would not disperse. Semerket felt the rush of air as one of the whips cracked too near his cheek. Rage began to build inside him.

The herald began to bawl instructions. "On your faces!" he said. "On your faces before Pharaoh's Beloved Friend!"

Semerket blinked in surprise. "Beloved Friend" was a rank usually held by only blood relations of Pharaoh.

Despite the royal epithet, the crowd continued to ignore the herald, and the grinning man realized that the whips were having no effect on the mob. He shouted orders to his men, and they brought the points of their spears forward. Only this quick action prevented the mob from overwhelming the ambassador.

As Menef's chair was carried past, Semerket shouted up, "Ambassador, where are your servants Naia and Rami?"

Menef jerked his face in Semerket's direction, his small eyes staring down in sudden alarm. Quickly, he directed his bearers to stop. "Who is that? What do you want?" cried Menef in a thin, petulant voice.

"Pharaoh wants them back, Menef, and expects your obedience."

"Who are you? Am I supposed to keep track of every whore and delinquent sent me, then? I'm not a wet-nurse, you know. Come back later, or tomorrow, if it's so important, and wait in line like everyone else." Menef turned to face forward again. With a nervous gesture, he bade his bearers move on.

Semerket would have kept walking beside the chair, pestering the ambassador, had not the commander of the guards suddenly appeared before him, grinning his macabre smile. Semerket noticed the man's tiny tattoo at the corner of his eye, a miniature asp, looking like a dirty tear.

Semerket attempted to lunge past him, but the Asp stood in his way, a block of unyielding stone. He shoved Semerket aside so that he half-fell into the dust. The Asp still grinned, silently daring Semerket to attempt another move toward Menef.

By this time, however, the ambassador was already far down the street, followed by his horde of desperate, importuning petitioners. Seeing the ambassador surrounded, the grinning man turned, almost reluctantly, and ran to catch up with his employer.

Only Semerket and Kem-weset remained in the now-quiet avenue. When Semerket bent to help the physician to his feet, he was distressed to see how the old man winced piteously, as if he expected Semerket to strike him.

"No," said Semerket, low, as to a child, "I'm only trying to help you stand. Why would you think otherwise? Here now, lean on me. Are you ready?"

The old man nodded slightly, unable to speak, and Semerket hoisted him upward. Kem-weset staggered slightly, but was able to stand on his own. Keeping a tight grip on the old man's bony shoulder, Semerket slowly walked him back to the Egyptian Quarter.

Semerket tried to think of something he could say that would comfort the physician, but his tongue was a useless sliver of wood in his head. They had reached the perimeters of the Egyptian Quarter. A sudden stab from his forehead's scar gave him inspiration.

"Kem-weset," he asked, rubbing his brow, "would you favor me with a look at an old injury of mine?"

The physician did not answer, or even acknowledge that he had heard. He continued to plod down the street, and his head seemed too heavy for his neck to bear.

"It's this old wound of mine—here, on my forehead." Semerket walked quickly to stand before the old man, forcing him to stop. He held his head close so that Kem-weset could see the jagged mark. "It stings like fire sometimes, and makes my head throb like a temple drum. Nothing but sleep will ease it. Can you help me?"

In the ensuing quiet, Semerket thought that perhaps the blow from Menef's young guard had driven the wits from the old man's mind. In the long shadows cast by the afternoon sun, standing beside the canal that girded the Egyptian Quarter, Kem-weset's wavery voice came to him at last. "You would consult with *me?*"

"Are you not the finest physician in Babylon?"

Kem-weset was silent for another moment. Then he brought his face close to Semerket's, looking at the scar with a professional eye. The old man's shoulders straightened imperceptibly as he turned to Semerket and spoke the ritual words.

"I will undertake your cure," Kem-weset said. "Come to me when you are next in pain."

IN THE SEARING RED LIGHT of the setting sun, the ziggurat Etemenanki was a beckoning flame. Always keeping its tumescent profile in front of him, Semerket was able to traverse Babylon's serpentine pathways rapidly. In a short time, he found himself crossing the great bridge that spanned the Euphrates, arriving on the other side of the river where the ziggurat towered. Kem-weset had said that the Square of the Sick was located somewhere nearby, and he wanted to reach the square before curfew was called.

He was curious to see the square, of course, in the way all foreign travelers seek the novel and esoteric, but he had another reason for going there as well. If Rami were indeed injured, as Pharaoh's cousin Elibar said he was, perhaps he would find him among the sick and ailing there. At worst, it might be that one of the ill could tell him if they had seen an Egyptian lad among their company.

Semerket smelled the square before he saw it—that curiously sweet scent of decay and human waste that accompanies all sickness. By simply following his nose to where the scent was strongest, he at last entered into the square from a side alleyway.

The Square of the Sick was enormous even by Egyptian standards, with thousands of Babylon's ill and injured lying side by side in the open air, a solid mass of writhing, living flesh stretching from one distant wall to another. Some lay on the bare ground, while others, the nobles, reclined in large beds of carved wood. Their moans and sighs filled his ears, crying out to passersby in various tones of desperation—wails, too, as families gathered to mourn their dying loved ones.

Semerket kept his head lowered, refusing to meet the imploring gazes of those who called out to him, scanning the square from side to side, careful not to catch anyone's glance. He jumped at the sudden appearance of a strangely attired priest, outfitted in copper-hued robes patterned like the scales of a fish.

Dimly, Semerket recalled that the Babylonians prayed to some water god—Ea, he believed the deity's name to be—who battled the demons that caused their maladies. He saw that those fellows he had once believed to be beekeepers, the undertakers of Babylon, also labored in the square. They culled the dead from the rows of sick, taking them on stretchers into a far tent where vats of honey awaited their remains. Still other attendants bore ewers of water, together with bandages and salves for the ill.

Gradually Semerket came to recognize that the city's sick had not been so wantonly abandoned as Kem-weset had intimated, but were well tended by the fish-robed priests and their acolytes. As he penetrated further into the square, Semerket noticed, too, that the priests had grouped the unwell according to the nature of their ailments. It was an ingenious system, he realized, making it easier for both Babylonians and tourists to go directly to where they could offer their help and counsel in the most efficient fashion.

Semerket screwed up his nerve to approach one of the priests. "Can you tell me——? Those with head injuries?" he asked.

The priest pointed, coppery fish scales gleaming in the sun's last rays, to the far corner of the square. Semerket went there without speaking to anyone. In truth, some of the square's inhabitants were of such horrifying appearance that he could not regard them without becoming ill himself. Ghastly wounds, hideous swellings, and deformities of every sort met his horrified gaze. By staring straight ahead, however, becoming deaf to their pleading words, he was able to reach his destination without incident.

When he reached the area the priest had indicated, he gazed around, looking for Rami's face. Most of the people sequestered in the area were recent victims of war, judging from their wounds. One man stared at him from beneath a bandage that revealed only a single fierce eye. The eye seemed intelligent enough, however, and Semerket approached him.

"I'm sorry to disturb you . . ." Semerket said.

The man did not move his head, but the one eye stared up angrily into Semerket's face.

"I'm looking for an Egyptian lad. His name is Rami. He was struck in the head. Have you seen him?"

Fierce Eye continued to stare, but made no answer.

"It happened about twelve weeks ago, by my reckoning," Semerket continued. But he ceased to speak when he saw the single tear that trickled down Fierce Eye's cheek and onto the pavement.

"Don't expect an answer from that one," came the words from behind.

Semerket whirled around. A boy carrying a water pail approached him. The boy knelt and dipped his ladle, bringing it to Fierce Eye's mouth. Most of the water ran down Fierce Eye's chin to pool in his lap, but some of the liquid made it into his mouth.

"He can't talk," the boy explained, bringing another ladle full of water to the man's lips. "The gods stunned his mind, and now he can't move a finger. What were you asking him?"

Semerket repeated his question.

"An Egyptian boy?" the boy mused. "There're no Egyptians here that I can recall—your people don't like our medicine much."

Semerket knelt beside the boy, to gaze into Fierce Eye's face. "In Egypt, we'd have a physician open his skull."

The boy suppressed a shudder. "I've heard they don't last very long when you do."

Semerket shrugged. "At least they don't linger, either. What a terrible life he has."

"Oh, I don't know," said the boy philosophically, wiping Fierce Eye's mouth with a rag. "At least here I feed him every day and wait on him like he's a noble. If you think about it, he's probably never had it so good."

"Still . . ." Semerket stood, shaking his head doubtfully. He hoped that when his own Day of Pain came, the gods would be merciful and kill him outright. He looked about the square, searching for Rami, but in the fading light of dusk, the faces of the sick were indistinguishable from one another.

The boy spoke to him. "Have you any other cure to suggest, other than to open his skull?" he asked.

"No," answered Semerket, still looking into the faces of the sick, "it's the only cure I know—"

He broke off, the words dying on his lips. Semerket quickly retraced the path his eye had taken; once again, he had seen someone he thought he knew.

"Marduk—?" he said aloud in wonder. Then Semerket yelled, "Marduk!"

Not fifty paces away, his one-time slave was speaking to one of the ailing. Marduk jerked his head up when he heard his name. Even in the twilight, Semerket thought he saw his eyes widen in surprise. Without hesitating, Marduk bolted for a nearby lane.

Semerket broke into pursuit. It was not easy to weave through the multitudes lying prone on the ground, but Semerket was like an eel among the reeds. He leapt over their heads, ignoring their yells and curses that followed him. Families visiting their relatives cowered as he flew by, staring after him as they would an escaped lunatic. The priests in their fish robes turned to frown at the commotion.

Semerket reached the lane seconds after Marduk had disappeared into it. There was no sign of him. Semerket stopped, panting, and hurried to where the lane divided into two streets. No one lingered there, nor were there any doors or gates through which Marduk could have gone.

"Marduk!" he called out again. He waited for an answer. "Marduk!"

When he was sure that he was completely alone, Semerket turned dispiritedly, beginning to doubt his own eyes—though if the man had not been Marduk, why would he have run away as he did? He sat on the lip of a nearby cistern, the only structure into which Marduk could have gone. But a bronze grille covered its top, and the grating was too narrow for any man to fit through. Nevertheless, just to make sure, he pulled on the grate; as he suspected, it was locked.

Semerket returned to the Square of the Sick. Ignoring the annoyed stares of those over whom he had so rudely leapt, he searched for the man to whom Marduk had been speaking. He located him in the area where the sufferers of skin afflictions were sequestered. Semerket grimaced when he realized that the man's face sported suppurating wounds, and tried to ignore the great patches of skin that peeled in sheets from his cheeks and chin.

"Do you know him?" Semerket asked the man abruptly.

"Pardon, lord?" the man said, startled.

"The man you were speaking with just now—who ran when I called out to him. Marduk is his name."

"No . . . no, my lord. I'm very sorry."

"What were you talking about?"

"I—I asked him if he knew a cure for my suffering," the man said unwillingly. "It's the custom here, you know."

Semerket did not believe the man, and brought his face closer to look into his eyes to ascertain if he were lying. When he drew near, the unmistakable scent of honey filled his nostrils. Semerket smiled, for the smell confirmed his suspicions.

Before he could say anything more, however, a sudden deep tolling of a bell came from the direction of the river. All around the square, people turned to listen to its sonorous, mournful notes. Families started to rise, gather their belongings together, and bid their farewells to their sick relations.

"What is that?" Semerket asked.

"The warning bell from the bridge. In a few minutes, its gangplank will be drawn back so that evildoers cannot cross it during the night."

Semerket knew he had to get back across the river. If he did not reappear through the Egyptian temple's gate, his Dark Head spies might panic and report him missing to the Elamite authorities. He cursed his luck, for he wanted to question this man more closely; Semerket was now absolutely convinced he was not telling the truth about Marduk.

"Tell him," Semerket said over his shoulder as he walked swiftly away, "tell him that I want to see him again."

"Believe me when I tell you, my lord—I don't know this man!"

"Tell him."

When he reached the street that would take him to the bridge, Semerket suddenly turned to call out. "I can help with that skin condition of yours, you know . . . !"

The man did not reply, but many heads turned in the dark to hear what Semerket had to say.

"Wash it with plain water!" Semerket yelled, his voice echoing through the dark square.

"WE WERE VERY WORRIED, SIR," the thin spy told him reproachfully as they walked down the alley, away from the Egyptian temple.

"I'm sorry."

"We almost went to our captain."

"I'll try to get here earlier tomorrow."

"We thought something had happened to you."

Semerket said nothing, and continued walking swiftly in the direction of his hostel.

As it was night, his spies no longer feared being seen with him. The fat spy puffed and wheezed without restraint. "Where did you go today, sir?" he asked Semerket companionably.

"But you know," said Semerket.

"How could I? We were waiting outside the temple all day, just as you paid us to do."

Semerket smiled. "I was praying."

"YOUR THUMB, my lord."

The priest pushed Semerket's thumb lightly onto a wedge of soft clay, using a rolling motion. He took the wedge into a shaft of light that streamed from an opening in the roof, comparing the print to the one Semerket had made on Pharaoh's tablet so many weeks before.

It was dawn, and Semerket was in the Temple of Marduk, which the Babylonians called the Esagila. Though the Great Temple of Amun in Thebes was far larger, it would be hard-pressed to compete in sheer opulence with the Marduk sanctuary. Alabaster pillars rose to coffered ceilings of hammered gold, while purple curtains hung from silver rings, cascading in rich folds to mosaic floors of malachite, turquoise, and mother-of-pearl. The Esagila existed in a perpetual and holy state of gloom, lit only by the small skylights in its roof. Everything in it, including the gold and silver threads woven into the vestments of its priests, seemed made for the shimmer of lamp and torchlight.

"All seems in order, my lord."

The priest indicated that Semerket was to follow him into the rear of the building. They soon came into the cool vaults where the priests secreted their treasure.

"If you will make your signature," the priest said in his low voice, "in cuneiform, please, here on this tablet where I have indicated . . . ?" He pushed a fresh wedge of clay toward Semerket. Several leather sacks already waited for him on a table of inlaid citron wood, each bulging with gold.

Semerket blinked in surprise. "But I can't take all this."

"I assure you, my lord, it's precisely the amount inscribed on the tablet you presented. If you'd care to count it . . . ?"

"I couldn't possible carry it all!"

"Perhaps your servants . . . ?"

"I have none."

A trace of suspicion lit the priest's eye. Who was this servantless man, Semerket could almost hear him thinking, who lays claim to Pharaoh's gold? In the end, the priest suggested that Semerket take only as much as he could conveniently carry. The rest would be returned to the vault until Semerket came for it. The priest smoothed out the figures he had previously inscribed onto the clay receipt, and quickly entered the new amount.

"Your gold will be safe with us, my lord."

Semerket once again affixed his thumbprint. When he left the room, his belt was stuffed with gold rings. Never before had he carried so much wealth on his person. And to think he had four more of Pharaoh's tablets waiting back in the hostel . . .

At the thought of Pharaoh, a sudden river of guilt surged through him. Since his arrival in Babylon, Naia's and Rami's rescue had so consumed him that he had given no thought to his other mission, that of obtaining Bel-Marduk's idol for his king. Since he was at the Esagila, Semerket reasoned, he might as well see the idol for himself, if only to gauge the effort it would take to transport it back to Egypt.

He stepped into the processional line, following it down a long sloping ramp into the underground chapel. It was perhaps an hour or more before the temple guardians allowed him into the presence of Babylon's most sacred idol.

The soft chanting of songstresses filled the halls, and the overpowering scent of smoky myrrh enveloped him. Semerket strained to see ahead to where the idol reposed, but the crowd of milling worshippers blocked his view. He did not know what to expect, but when he finally saw the thing standing beneath its cloth-of-gold canopy, his first feeling was of disappointment. The idol was no taller than he was, and not at all well crafted; glancing down, he saw the statue's wooden armature poking through a broken toe.

Fashioned in a crude, archaic style, the bearded god wore a high crown, and a girdle of starlike rosettes hung about his waist. A soft smile on his face gave the unfortunate impression of nothing so much as divine imbecility. In the god's left hand was a ring-and-rod scepter held close to his chest, while his right hand extended forward in greeting.

Pharaoh had told him that at the start of every reign, the new king of Babylon clasped the outstretched hand in his to receive the god's consent to rule. The hand was now almost featureless, its thumb and fingers smoothed almost entirely away. How many kings, how many millennia, Semerket wondered, had it taken to wear that hand to such slimness?

The god gradually became vibrant in his eyes, resplendent with the accumulated worship it had inspired over so many centuries. It was perhaps the oldest statue of any god in the whole world, and for that reason, the most revered. Semerket abruptly remembered the words Pharaoh had whispered to him. "I will take the god's hand in mine, and I shall be cured of all illness." Seeing the golden hand that had conferred power on so many kings, Semerket thought for the first time that perhaps the magic that resided in the idol might indeed help Pharaoh regain his health.

Semerket continued to stare at the statue until a temple guardian whispered that he must leave the chapel so that other worshippers might themselves approach the god. When he was again in the outer hall, he found a young priest waiting for him.

"Lord Semerket?" the man asked.

Semerket nodded, surprised.

"The Lord High Magus Adad requests a word."

"With me?" Semerket asked, wary.

The young priest inclined his head, pointing to a small, featureless door at the end of the hall, all but hidden from the public's view. It opened upon a narrow, private stairway leading to the temple's second floor.

The high magus's chambers were as dark and quiet as the god's sanctuary. The young priest put a finger to his lips, and nodded to the far end of the room. Semerket stared into the gloom and saw the back of a man, busy at a distant stone altar. The young priest closed the door softly behind him as he departed, and Semerket was alone with Adad. At that moment, the ferrous, salty smell of freshly spilled blood subtly infiltrated his nostrils, alarming him.

"I'll only be a moment, Lord Semerket," Adad called reassuringly from the table, though his next words were disturbing enough. "I've just finished reading your liver."

Semerket saw the discarded carcass of a sacrificed kid lying at the Magus's feet, its eyes half-lidded, its gray tongue protruding. Adad turned from the table, and Semerket noted that his hands were green with bile. Thrusting them into a basin of water, Adad cleansed himself before again addressing Semerket.

"I'm disappointed," said Adad casually, wiping his hands upon a cloth. "The kid's liver wasn't clear today, telling me first one thing and then another. I didn't learn as much about you as I wished."

"If the Lord High Magus wants to know anything about me, he has only to ask."

Adad looked at him, taking Semerket's measure. The magus was a large, powerfully built man, bearded like his god. "Words were invented to hide the truth, Semerket," he said. "Only a liver never lies. But for all its cloudiness, I did discover *some* interesting things about you."

Semerket arranged his features into polite curiosity.

"It told me you come here in search of someone. Two persons, in fact."

Semerket's expression did not change.

"It said that you and your pharaoh work to some secret purpose here in Babylon."

Semerket continued staring at the magus.

"It tells me that Egypt's wealth has been committed to the endeavor." Irritated by Semerket's continued stillness, Adad became suddenly impatient. "Well? Are you mute? What have you to say to all this?"

Semerket shrugged. "I would say the liver tells you nothing more than what you found by reading the contents of my pack the other night."

Semerket heard Adad's short intake of air. "Do you doubt my ability to read livers?"

"I'm beginning to."

Adad's tense jaws clenched several times before he answered. Few had ever spoken to him so impudently. The high magus began to pace, not looking at Semerket, and when he threw himself into his chair his fingers thrummed on its ivory armrest. "Since the Lord of All has given us the gift of prophecy and divination, Bel-Marduk's magi have no need for common snooping," he said firmly. "But if you would be so honest, then why don't you admit you come here to carry away our holy idol to Egypt?"

"Did you learn that from the liver?"

"I won't banter with you, Semerket. Ambassador Menef told me of Pharaoh's interest in it the moment Ramses' courier arrived in Babylon."

Semerket again did not respond. He was thinking instead of what possible motive Menef might have for telling Adad of Pharaoh's confidential words. Some might construe it a treasonous act. Was the ambassador seeking to thwart Semerket somehow, intending to send the idol to Egypt himself and thereby earn Pharaoh's favor and acclaim? As it was, Semerket cared little as to who successfully arranged the idol's state visit to Egypt. If Menef had already done so, all the better—Semerket would be thus free to continue his search for Naia and Rami, unhampered by other concerns.

Yet if that were true, what purpose had this high priest Adad for waylaying him like this? If the idol's visit to Egypt were already managed, what need for any of this discussion between them?

"And was Ambassador Menef successful?" Semerket asked. "Have you given your permission for the idol to visit Egypt?"

"It's not mine to give. The decision resides with King Kutir alone."

Semerket spoke his doubts aloud. "Then why did Menef go to you and not to him?"

Adad dropped his eyes. He looked at his hands, picking nervously at the golden tassels on his pectoral. "Because the magi must be consulted, of course." He raised his head to peer again at Semerket. "Because we alone can divine the god's disposition in these matters."

"I certainly hope you do a better job of it than with the liver,"

Semerket said lightly. Deciding that he could accomplish nothing more from the interview, he backed away, extending his hands to knee level, turning to leave. As he reached for the door, Adad's voice came to him, sharply.

"A moment, Semerket."

Semerket faced the high magus.

"Once, long ago, another king of Elam marched into Babylon. He laid unholy hands on the idol and carried it off to Susa in chains." Adad paused for effect. "Their crops failed. Plague struck. The Elamite armies went without victories. One after another their kings died. Finally, of their own accord, they returned the idol, paying us in gold to remove the god's curse from their land."

The high priest was warning him, Semerket knew. Nevertheless, he asked, "And the reason you tell me this, Lord High Magus?"

"Because it's what happens when the Lord of All is taken from Babylon against his will."

"You see me," replied Semerket. "What armies did I bring with me? What weapons? I don't even carry a knife."

Adad stood. "But there is about you an air of violence and mayhem. I've heard they call you a 'follower of Set' in Egypt—that you can wreck a nation simply by walking through it."

Semerket shrugged. "I am not your enemy, lord. It's true I seek the idol for my king, but you must decide whether it will go or stay. As I see it, my task is merely to convince you—and Kutir—of the advantages such a visit might bring to both our nations."

"And if the magi say that Bel-Marduk's idol must remain in Babylon—even though the king should give you his consent—?"

There it was, the reason why Semerket had been summoned to Adad's chamber. Semerket finally comprehended that the idol was at the center of some political contest being waged between the invader Kutir and the Babylonian clergy. It was clear the priests were afraid the Elamite conqueror might send the idol away against their will—and with it would go their power. Adad was warning Semerket that the real consent must come from the magi.

"I would never subject Egypt to the calamities you've described," Semerket answered.

Adad pursed his lips. Unwillingly, his eyes strayed again to the kid's liver glistening on the table beside him. Then, with an imperious wave of his hand, he dismissed Semerket.

IN THE NEIGHBORHOOD of the foreign legations, the only activity at the moment came from the energetic feints and parries of a young guard, practicing his fencing in the shadows of the Egyptian embassy's high walls. He was the same young man who had struck the physician Kem-weset with the shaft of his spear the previous day.

The young man lustily thrust and jabbed into the empty air, shouting and grunting. In his mind, he was slicing to pieces the man who had humiliated him by seizing his spear and breaking it in two. He could still hear the roars of laughter when his fellow guards learned how easily Semerket had disarmed him. Worse, they had told him that he must pay for a new spear out of his own wages—a whole month's worth!

Seething with shame, he vowed to never again be caught so unprepared. He would perfect his swordplay, so that the next time he met with the surly, black-eyed Egyptian, he would be ready. With every thrust he made into the empty air, with every slashing cut, he imagined Semerket skewered and bleeding before him. Soon the sweat ran from the young man in rivulets, soaking his tunic.

His hatred was hotter than the overhead sun bleaching the street to bone. Consumed by his need for revenge, the lad was completely unaware of the stranger who watched him from a nearby alleyway. As the youth whirled and feinted at his imaginary foe, his watcher moved from the shadows to stand at the lintel of Menef's gate. The clerk in the sentry house saw him, however, and frantically attempted to signal the young guard, to warn him of the stranger's approach.

"What—?" the young man said, puzzled by the clerk's grimaces. He leaned on his sword, and wiped the sweat from his forehead.

"Behind you!"

A tone in the clerk's voice made the young man spin around in panic, panting for breath. The man whom he had fought so furiously in his imagination now stood directly before him—and, worse, he carried a long, wicked spear in his hands. To his shame, the young man felt his bowels turning to water.

"Have you . . ." the young guard began, but his voice failed. "Have you come to kill me?"

"What?" Semerket said, surprised. "Of course not."

"W-why have you come here, then?" The lad's voice was still very faint. "With that?" He pointed to the spear.

"I mean to give it to you." The lad flinched when Semerket held out the spear for him to take. "I shouldn't have broken yours yesterday. I apologize."

Clearly dumbfounded, the young man reluctantly reached forward to take the spear into his hands. The instant he felt its weight and heft, he knew it to be of superb workmanship, better than any the legation had issued him.

"All the same," Semerket continued, "you shouldn't have struck my friend like you did. He's too old for such treatment. You could have killed him."

For some reason, perhaps because of the man's calm voice, the lad felt suddenly ashamed of himself. "They told me to make sure he didn't bother the ambassador," he muttered.

"Well, you'll find there are different ways of obeying orders. It's like hunting a hippo or a hare, isn't it?"

The lad looked at him, confused. "What?"

"Kem-weset is just an old hare. A little prod to his backside with the tip of your spear, and he'd have scooted away quick enough. But you went at him as if he were a hippo. Do you understand what I'm saying?"

"I suppose so," mumbled the lad. He lifted the spear, testing its weight and balance. "But—to bring me this spear... Why did you do it?"

"I was a guard once myself, and young. I remember how they'd make us pay if anything happened to our weapons."

"You were a guard?"

Semerket nodded. "On a caravan, yes."

The young man's mix of feelings played upon his face, one trumping the next in rapid succession. His hatred for Semerket had entirely dissipated, replaced finally by interest. "Well," the lad was nevertheless awkward, "thanks."

Semerket looked over to the clerk still staring wide-eyed in the sentry house. "You'd better tell your friend that I'm not here to kill you. In fact, I'm actually here to ask some questions."

The young guard's eyes filmed with suspicion. "Is that the reason you gave me the spear?"

"The spear is yours, in any case."

"Menef's not here. He stayed at the palace last night."

"I'd rather speak to you, if you don't mind—and your friend in the shack over there."

The young guard was silent for a moment, as if inwardly debating his answer. "Then it depends . . ."

"On what?"

"What it is you want to ask."

"Yes . . . yes," said the clerk in the sentry house, whose name was Nes-Amun. "She was as beautiful as you say—for a serving maid, I suppose. But that didn't mean she was very accommodating. Besides, she was a bit older than I like my women."

Semerket resisted the impulse to knock the clerk from his stool. He did not care for the hoarseness that crept into Nes-Amun's voice when, after much prodding, he at last remembered Naia. But the pimply-faced youth had worked at the legation for over two years and remembered many of the indentured servants who had come from Egypt with Menef. So Semerket was forced to endure his unpleasant words and character. "Yes, she was here—and the boy, too—and I can tell you this even though I'm charged with remembering only those who still work here."

"Can you remember what happened to them?"

Nes-Amun shook his head. "We get so many servants. They arrive with every caravan, hordes of them. Half of Egypt must be here by now—particularly after the conspiracy against old Ramses last year."

"Are they all sent to Menef?"

Nes-Amun nodded indifferently. "It's his right to dispense with them as he sees fit."

"Where does he send them?"

"Oh, some go to his friends, of course, if the servants are intelligent or good-looking. Most of the time he sends them on to Eshnunna."

"Who?"

Nes-Amun again emitted a high mirthless cackle. "It's not a 'who,' it's a 'where.' Eshnunna is the town where Babylon's slave market is, everybody knows that, about six leagues to the northeast of here."

"He sells their contracts to the slave traders?" Semerket felt the blood draining from his face.

"And a nice profit he makes, too." Nes-Amun was like so many of the clerks that Semerket had known back in Egypt, who took the first opportunity to snipe enviously at their masters behind their backs. "He gets at least thirty to forty deben of silver for each one. You'd better believe he'll go home to Egypt a richer man than when he came, the lucky sod."

If Naia and Rami had indeed been given over to the slave traders, they might have been sold anywhere in Babylonia—even beyond its borders. How was he to find them? The city in its immensity was bad enough; was he now required to search an entire nation, as well? Then he remembered Elibar's words to him, saying that Rami had been attacked somewhere in the northwest outskirts of Babylon, between the two rivers. His heart calmed a bit.

"Rami was at a plantation," he said, "somewhere to the northwest, outside Babylon's walls. Have you any idea if Menef knows anyone in that area?"

"Menef knows many people."

"Do you believe, then, that they were most likely sent to the slave market?"

Nes-Amun shrugged, scratching at the pustules on his face. "How should I know? You really must ask Menef these things."

"I will."

Nes-Amun unsuccessfully stifled a sardonic laugh. "*If* he'll receive you," he said. "Which I *doubt* very much; he doesn't see just *anybody*. I should know, shouldn't I, since *I* have the say of who comes and goes through these gates." He preened importantly.

Semerket did not tell Nes-Amun that he was Pharaoh's special envoy to King Kutir and therefore outranked the ambassador. Let these youths continue to think of him as an ordinary Egyptian citizen, attempting to find his unfortunate wife. He rose from his stool, feeling tired; Nes-Amun's answers had suddenly widened the scope of his investigation radically.

Semerket nodded to the young guard, who sat in the corner of the shed, carefully sharpening the blade of his new spear. "Enjoy the spear," he said to the lad in farewell. "But first learn the difference between a hippo and a hare, eh?"

The young guard smiled, and nodded.

BACK AT THE HOSTEL, Semerket approached one of his priestly hosts and asked if the inn could provide him with quick transport to Eshnunna. The moment his words were out of his mouth, the priest's eyes grew bright.

"Does the Egyptian lord wish a slave girl to warm his bed tonight?" he asked with a leer.

"Thank you, no."

"Well, then, perhaps a boy. What's a piece of mutton, then, without the bone, eh?"

Semerket held up his hand, interrupting the fellow. "I've no wish for a boy, either. Only a carry chair with running bearers. A chariot would be better, if you have one. I'll pay for its rental, of course."

It happened that the inn possessed its own chariot with a driver and that it would be the god Marduk's pleasure to bestow the equipage on him for the day.

"You vouch for its quickness?"

"Oh, yes, my lord. The horses are very fleet, and the chariot is practically weightless—constructed from river reeds!"

Semerket waited outside in the broiling sun for the chariot to appear. The grooms brought the vehicle around from the stables, its two cream-colored horses stepping high. The driver, though bowing his head to Semerket, never let go of the reins, and it was all he could do to keep the horses steady while Semerket climbed aboard.

With Semerket standing beside him, the driver eased the chariot into the Processional Way. As usual, the avenue overflowed with pedestrians, sedan chairs, and delivery wagons, making the going very slow indeed. Some long moments later, they came to the Damkina Gate, named for the goddess-mother of Bel-Marduk, located at the northeastern juncture of the city walls. Semerket informed the Elamite guards of his desire to go to the slave yards in Eshnunna. They checked his name from an official list of persons watched by the king, all the while making lubricious conjectures as to why he wanted to go there. In the end, the Elamites allowed them to pass, and the chariot and the team were at last on the road heading northeast. The flat river plain stretched before them, wavy with plumes of heat, and the sky was a colorless hue. Because it was full noon, there was little traffic to impede them, save for a few Elamite squadrons patrolling the river valley. Most people had sensibly gone indoors to avoid the worst of the sun's heat.

"Hold on, lord," muttered the driver.

Semerket clung to the chariot's reed frame and braced his sandaled feet on its woven floor. The driver spoke in a low voice to his steeds, though Semerket could not catch what he said. The horses touched their noses together, as if enjoying a conspiracy, and whinnied. Then Semerket felt the wheels leave the ground . . .

Semerket heard himself cry out in shrill terror, hardly knowing if his feet still touched the chariot. The horses cut directly across the plain, heedless of stones and boulders, so that at any moment Semerket thought the wheels might fly to pieces. No matter how hard he thumped on the driver's back with his fists—during those few times he dared to let loose a hand from the chariot frame—the man refused to acknowledge his shouts and blows. All Semerket could do, finally, was to hang on and pray to all the Egyptian gods to preserve his life.

Within a single measure of the water clock they saw the low walls of Eshnunna rising from the plain, and in another few minutes they were through its gates. When he was at last able to leap to the ground, cursing foully, Semerket reeled like a drunken sailor, unable to find his balance. As he collected himself, the driver calmly led the frothing horses to a nearby stable, telling Semerket that when he wished to return to Babylon, he could find him there.

When at last he could walk again, Semerket took a quick survey of the small town. It was essentially a village of low-slung barracks, used to house the ever-changing multitudes of newly arrived slaves. The Elamite invasion had swelled the inventory to bursting, and armed guards oversaw the vast yards where the slaves congregated. Semerket was surprised to see the complacent expressions on most of their faces; he had prepared himself for their miserable wails and cries of grief, but the slaves seemed content with their lot, not at all resentful of the guards. Nearby, he saw the raised stages on which the slave brokers exhibited their merchandise to prospective buyers. Painted signs posted on palm trunks advertised upcoming auctions. "Strong, healthy males from Subartu!" proclaimed one. "Fine girls of quality from Lullu, guaranteed none above fifteen!" said another.

Apparently, the brokers held their auctions on only two days of the week, and this was not one of them. The narrow streets were therefore empty save for the occasional businessman, and Semerket was able to traverse the town quickly to where the brokers made their homes.

The brokers, it happened, were a tight community of sharp professionals, each knowing his rivals' business intimately. Semerket had only to ask one of them to discover the identity of that broker who held the monopoly on Egyptian slaves. The man's name was Lugal, and he was in the midst of his midafternoon's rest when Semerket appeared at his door. Despite the interruption, he was glad to rise from his cushions, eager to do a little business. Like most Babylonians of a certain age, he was broad-shouldered and broad-bellied. He was not bearded, however, and, in fact, he had shaved the entirety of his body. The slaves who came there from barbaric countries were often crawling with lice, he explained. It was better to remain bald and hairless, since in the course of his business day he had to closely examine all the new arrivals. Semerket resisted an almost instant impulse to scratch himself.

Lugal called loudly for some beer. A servant brought a large bowl, with two flexible reeds, and he and Semerket sat companionably together in the room's center. The slave merchant's welcoming smile became a trifle fixed, however, when Semerket told him he had no wish to purchase a pretty girl—or a boy, thank you—but merely wanted to ask some questions regarding some of the merchant's old inventory.

"Of course, I'll be glad to pay you for your time," added Semerket, "for you're a man of business, and I would not expect something for nothing."

"Well, then," said Lugal expansively, patting his fat stomach as if it were a friendly dog, "you're a gentleman who commands my attention. How can I help you?"

Semerket explained how he sought his wife and friend, relating to Lugal how Naia had been married to one of those who conspired against Ramses III, while Rami was implicated in the looting of royal tombs. Lugal listened wide-eyed, as he would to a storyteller declaiming on the street corner, even applauding at the conclusion of Semerket's narrative.

"Stranger," he said, "put away your gold. Your tale is payment enough. Nothing in life is better than a good story, and a true one at that."

"Then you'll help me find them?"

"If I can, of course," said Lugal. "But our records are not always as accurate as we'd like. Sometimes the slaves come to us with the new names given them by their owners, and that's what we enter into our accounts. But take heart," he added, seeing Semerket's suddenly crestfallen expression, "if your Naia is as beautiful as you've described, I'm sure I'll remember her—if she came through here, that is."

"Is Menef in the habit of renaming his slaves?"

"Luckily he can't be bothered—another thing to be hopeful about. Come!"

Lugal led Semerket to a low building across the courtyard. Baskets full of clay tablets lined its myriad shelves. Lugal explained that he inventoried his sales by date, for taxation purposes, and that a detailed description existed for each slave that he sold.

Semerket gave him the approximate times that Naia might have left Menef's estate, and Lugal led him to those shelves where they might find the appropriate clay records. Together they went through each tablet, searching for a name or at least an indication of nationality among the hundreds of slaves that Lugal had bought and sold during that time.

As Semerket began to read, he saw that the trader entered each slave's name onto the clay, along with their age and nationality or tribe. If the sale were being made on behalf of another, with Lugal acting only as agent for the seller, that too was noted.

Semerket exclaimed at the detail of the documents.

"I have to do it, friend," Lugal said. "Slaves have the rights of law on their side, you know, and if they're clever they can easily win back their freedom. Some people actually indenture themselves to us, if they can't find work or have to flee their creditors. There's no shame in being a slave in Babylonia. Most of the time it's just a temporary condition—a bit of hard luck to endure."

Semerket was merely glad the reports were so detailed, for it made sifting through them a quick chore. Semerket discovered that, by far, the majority of Egyptians sent to Babylon were male—which made sense, when he thought about it, since males were more likely to become embroiled in the kinds of crimes that resulted in banishment. The few records of female Egyptian slaves he found did not correspond to Naia's age or general description—which both upset and relieved him. Quite a number of records were of Egyptian lads who might have been Rami, though none bore his name. Lugal was able to tell him, however, that none of the Egyptians he had sold had been sent to any plantation northwest of Babylon.

They continued searching through the tablets in silence, until Semerket heard Lugal give a victorious grunt. "Ah!" said the trader, staring at a clay tablet he had withdrawn from a basket. "This looks promising!"

Quickly Semerket went to his side. Lugal read from the tablet aloud. "'Egyptian female, twenty-three years of age. Slim, comely. Answers to the name of Aneku.' And it says here she came from Egypt in the company of Menef, aboard his own ship."

A sweat broke on Semerket's brow. Very few people knew that Naia's father had called her Aneku when she lived in his house. In

Egyptian it meant, "She belongs to me." He felt almost nauseous, torn between both exhilaration and fear. "It could be her," he breathed, "for Aneku was her infant name. Who was she sold to?"

Lugal eyed the tablet. His expression darkened. "Ah, well, it's not the best of news—particularly for a husband—but it could be worse, I suppose."

Semerket did not like the anxious look on Lugal's face. "Who bought her?" he asked again.

Lugal coughed, pretending great interest in the tablet, squinting at the marks inscribed on it. "The guardians of the Temple of Ishtar, I'm afraid."

Semerket let out a long breath. "You frightened me," he laughed. "From your look, I expected worse."

"Well, then," Lugal smiled in return, relieved. "If you're comfortable with it, so am I. Frankly, I thought that you'd despise me for selling her to the Ishtar eunuchs, and take your revenge somehow."

Semerket's sense of disquiet returned. "Why d'you say that?"

The grim, anxious look again appeared on Lugal's face. "Do you not know of the Temple of Ishtar?" he asked. "What it is . . . ?"

"I assume that Naia—if that's who she really is—helps to serve the goddess in some way."

"Aye," Lugal said, "but do you know in what way?"

Semerket shook his head, suddenly unable to speak for fear of what the answer would be.

"Ishtar is first and foremost a goddess of fertility . . ."

"Well?" Semerket asked.

"Aneku was bought to serve as a temple prostitute."

SEMERKET STOOD DAZEDLY outside Lugal's compound in the red afternoon sun. He wandered past a wagon train of slaves, recently arrived from the northern mountains. The strong scent of unwashed human flesh made him aware of where he was, reviving him better than even spirits of juniper. He pushed his way through the milling slaves, taking himself back to the stables where the chariot waited.

"I want to return to Babylon now," he announced to the driver.

"But, lord, it's getting dark. By the time we reach the city, the Elamite's curfew will have fallen." The man smiled encouragingly, hoping that Semerket might see reason. "Wouldn't it be better to stay here in Eshnunna tonight, and get a fresh start in the morning? The desert night is full of demons . . ."

"Now!" snarled Semerket, seizing a coiled whip from a peg and brandishing it dangerously.

The moon rose large and yellow over the desert, and the boulders and scrub cast weird, tangled shadows across the golden sands that stretched before them. Despite their eagerness to run as swiftly as before, the charioteer kept his horses to a brisk trot. For the first couple of leagues Semerket remained silent. He focused his troubled eyes forward, always on the red glow in the southwest that was Babylon.

The charioteer glanced covertly at him. The moon's rays picked out Semerket's bitter profile. The charioteer swallowed, musing on what the Egyptian must have discovered back in the slave yards that had turned him so sour. When Semerket spoke again, his words were not the ones the charioteer expected to hear. "What can you tell me of the Temple of Ishtar?" Semerket asked quietly.

So that was it, the charioteer nodded to himself. The man must be of an amorous nature that evening, and needed to relieve his tension in the time-honored way. The charioteer had noticed that eventually all foreigners wanted to go to the Lady's temple, to see for themselves if the stories were true. In fact, the charioteer received lavish gratuities from Ishtar's guardians to talk up the temple's allurements to the hostel's boarders.

The man launched into a full-throated description of the pleasures Semerket might find at the home of Ishtar. "Ah, my lord! It is a wonder of the world—"

"Is it a brothel?" Semerket curtly interrupted the charioteer's patter.

"It's a paradise come to earth, a city in itself, dedicated to love, with gardens of such exquisite—"

"What of the women there?"

"The Ishtaritu, my lord?" The charioteer blinked in confusion, trying to remember the order of his rehearsed speech. After a false start, he was once again able to pick up the thread of his words. "My lord, there are more than two thousand of them. Every new ship brings fresh beauties from around the world to serve there, each chosen to become a living manifestation of the goddess herself. Why, there are women from over sixty different races and countries, some with skin like polished ebony, others with eyes cut obliquely—"

"Are Egyptians among their company?"

"I—I suppose so, my lord." He hurried on to the next part of his speech. "And if you've tired of female companionship—as who among us has not?—there is no shortage of male Ishtaritu to whom an offering—"

"And the cost for all this beauty?"

"Ah, my lord, the act of love is the only offering the goddess requires." The charioteer coughed discreetly. "Of course, a present equal to the pleasure you receive is not turned away by the priests, if that should be your wish."

"Of course."

Stillness fell between them. The charioteer again looked sideways. The Egyptian certainly did not seem eager to sample the glories of Ishtar's temple. In fact, he seemed more morose than ever.

Just as they came to the outskirts of Babylon, however, Semerket cleared his throat to ask a final question of the charioteer. "Where is it? What part of the city?"

"The Ishtar Temple, my lord? Why, near the Ishtar Gate—where else?"

The moon had lost its skin of gold by the time they reached the city walls, and was now almost directly overhead, a flat pale disc of white. Contrary to the charioteer's predictions, the Elamite guards allowed them to enter Babylon, for Semerket demanded—and received—a pass permitting them to be on the streets after curfew.

The charioteer deposited him at the front door of Bel-Marduk's hostel. Semerket waited at the door in the light of the hostel's torches, watching as the charioteer drove the horses around to the stable. When he knew he was alone and unobserved, he slipped again into the street.

Since he had a pass allowing him to be abroad after curfew, he was certainly not going to be stupid enough to let it go to waste. He walked quickly down Processional Way, in the direction of the Ishtar Gate. It would be ironic if he found Naia no more than a furlong from where he had been staying all along . . .

Firmly, he forbade himself to sob.

DESPITE THE ELAMITES' CURFEW, Ishtar's temple was raucous with activity. Most of those who gathered in the street around its tall gates were Elamite soldiers on leave, drunk and loud, or foreigners with nighttime passes, also drunk and loud. As he came nearer the gate, he took out a silver piece to pay the temple guardians. Despite the chariot driver's reassurances, Semerket did not believe that Ishtar's priests demanded only an offering of love at her temple; if so, that in itself would have been reason enough to call the temple a wonder of the world.

A silver piece was coincidentally the exact price of admission required of him. Passing through a tunnel, he at last entered the gardens. A thousand torches gleamed, making the gardens blaze as brightly as if it had been noon. The temple grounds comprised a series of low-slung terraces planted in flowers and groves, rising to form an artificial hill. At their crest stood the temple itself, looking very much as the charioteer had described it to him, a paradise on earth. The scent of jasmine and honeysuckle wafted to him, borne in the arms of the night breezes.

A long line of men snaked through the gardens, climbing slowly through the terraces. Semerket crossed the courtyard to join it, for the line appeared to be the only way into the temple. There, he supposed, was where the sacred prostitutes were to be found.

When he had gone a few steps, however, he realized that the women concealed themselves in niches within the terraces. Watching the other men closely, he learned that one chose a woman by throwing yet another silver piece into her lap. The Ishtaritu then led her suitor into the temple, where Semerket presumed the cribs were located.

Semerket had no choice but to ogle every woman's face as he

passed, seeking Naia's. There were literally hundreds to choose from, each clad in the bizarre garb of her homeland. The charioteer had spoken true when he said that the women came from at least sixty nations from all around the world.

There were dark-skinned girls from the lands of the Ganges, who cultivated wispy mustaches on their upper lips; Africans with their crisp hair cut at an angle, their full breasts covered in heavy chains of bronze; yellow-skinned beauties from Cathay, with hair blacker than any Egyptian's. On and on he went, past yellow- and red-haired women with skins whiter than the sands of Libya; but Semerket saw no Egyptian woman.

He was close to the entrance of the temple now, and the only places left to explore outside were those parts of the gardens where the hot-eyed male Ishtaritu waited. Judging from what he saw, their ranks were as varied as the women's. Some were muscular, easily at home on any dockside, aggressively male, while others were indistinguishable from their sister Ishtaritu, dressed in women's robes, with faces painted as expertly as any courtesan's—only more so.

Semerket, who had not lain with a woman since Naia had divorced him, began to feel queasy. His pulse pounded in his limbs and his forehead became tight—a distant warning signal that his headaches would soon begin again.

It was not his simple unthinking prudery that disturbed him; it was that he had caught the unmistakable whiff of sex in the air and felt suddenly capable of rape. The women who had so brazenly displayed themselves to him in the gardens had aroused his long-dormant lust. Another few minutes at the temple and he would be lost. He stood at its doorway, breathing deeply, gathering up his courage to go inside.

At last, he stepped into the temple's dim and smoky interior. Hesitating in the entry hall, he thought that the eunuch priests might stop him, for no Ishtaritu accompanied him. But the eunuchs were indifferent to what he did or where he went. They conversed rapidly with one another in their alcoves, sibilants hissing like angry adders, and did not even condescend to look at him. His breath caught painfully in his chest, for the place was thick with incense. Semerket brought his mantle over his face and took another few steps into the dark.

The temple was a warren of reed partitions, erected so that hundreds of doorless cells existed in long rows. Within them, couples flagrantly copulated in every position that Semerket had ever imagined, and some he had not. Several single men, alone like him, strolled the hallways. They stopped occasionally to stare at or even cheer the more athletic or beautiful or imaginative pairs performing within the cubicles. Some even shamelessly stroked themselves as they watched, entranced by the carnal spectacle before them.

Semerket tasted bile in his throat. What if he found Naia in such a cubicle? How could he leave without killing the men who dared touched her—or even those who looked on? His breath came in shallow gulps, and his throat burned from inhaling the low-hanging incense.

He turned away in desperation—why did the eunuchs insist on burning so much of it? The answer occurred to him quickly: if there were no incense, then the scents of sex and bodily exudations would overwhelm everything within the temple. He looked down at the tiles on the floor, and was suddenly grateful that he wore his hard, hempen sandals; if he were barefoot, he would slide...

In desperation, he approached one of the priests. Seeing Semerket gasping before him like a hooked fish, he signaled a servant hurriedly. "Some wine over here, quickly!"

"No!" rasped Semerket. "No wine!"

But the eunuch was pouring a goblet full of mulled red, which the priests kept on hand for such occasions. Many men actually died from their exertions within the temple—one of Ishtar's more mordant jokes. The eunuchs privately believed that the goddess actually detested men—no doubt the reason why she required her priests to submit themselves to the knife.

"Water," insisted Semerket, "water is fine."

The eunuch looked at him doubtfully, but dipped a ladle into a nearby font. Semerket drank gratefully.

"Thank you." Semerket leaned against the wall, closing his eyes for a moment, and realized that his tunic had become sodden with sweat. The eunuch turned to leave, but Semerket called out, "Please. I need your help."

The eunuch began to wring his hands, grimacing. Eunuchs had a horror of physical distress, and Semerket did not look at all well. "It seems to me, sir, if you don't mind my saying so, that you've enjoyed altogether too much sport here tonight; you really need to go home."

"I want to find someone in the temple—one of the Ishtaritu. It's important."

"The goddess forbids you to see the same Ishtaritu more than once, sir. Come back another night—tomorrow, perhaps—and choose from the others."

"This is different—"

The eunuch rolled his eyes, and sighed. "It always is."

"She's my wife!"

Semerket said the words so loudly that several men turned to gaze at him.

"Your wife—?" the eunuch croaked.

Hastily, Semerket told the eunuch-priest that he had come to search for an Egyptian woman named Aneku. Her real name was Naia, he said. She was his wife, and she had been mistakenly sold to the temple. He had special papers from the pharaoh of Egypt, he insisted, guaranteeing her freedom. Semerket began pulling pieces of gold from his belt, not even bothering to count them, and shoved them into the eunuch's fat hands.

"Take them all, please! Just show me to Naia—to Aneku—take me to her. I beg you!"

Though it was against every stricture, the eunuch was a native Babylonian and knew the value of Egyptian gold. He was no fool, either, and foresaw a scandal of international proportions brewing. The fiction under which the temple existed was that all Ishtaritu were there by choice, each impersonating the goddess in his or her own way. How would it look if an Egyptian envoy's wife were found among the initiates, unfairly sold into prostitution?

"This way," the eunuch muttered, pulling Semerket by his now-sopping tunic over to the alcoves where his fellow eunuchs waited. On the wall behind them were squares outlined in chalk, and the eunuchs had affixed pegs to each square. From some of the pegs, clay markers hung on strings, each bearing the name of an Ishtaritu. This ingenious system allowed the eunuchs to know which cubicle was in use, and which Ishtaritu utilized it.

Quickly the eunuch-priest examined the markers, holding them in the light of a nearby torch. "Aneku, Aneku, Aneku," he muttered. Then he grunted, nodding. "Bin ninety-six." He seized Semerket by his sleeve and pulled him down a dark hall of reed cubicles. Semerket kept his eyes forward, refusing to look inside any of those he passed. Try as he would, however, he could not stop his ears against the groans and coughs and choking noises that assaulted him from all sides. His legs began to swim beneath him, as if his feet no longer touched the earth.

The eunuch stopped at the far end of the temple and peeked inside one of the reed enclosures. He held his hand up to prevent Semerket from advancing further. Even from a distance, Semerket heard the sounds of emphatic lovemaking that emanated from the cubicle. He grimaced, holding his hands over his ears.

Semerket waited in the dark for how long a time he did not know. At last, he saw a man emerge from the room, adjusting his garments. He was a tall, pale creature, with light eyes and long, dark hair. Semerket's glare burned into him as he passed. Momentarily discomfited, the man regarded Semerket with apprehension. He made a holy sign in the air to avert the evil eye and hurried away. As he sped down the corridor, he cast quick glances over his shoulder to see if Semerket followed him.

The eunuch beckoned Semerket to come forward. Semerket went into the cubicle with his head lowered, so that he saw only her long, shapely legs. He had forgotten the olive sheen of her complexion, and tried not to notice that she was wiping herself down with a cloth. Even these intimate gestures were imbued with her distinctive grace. He raised his eyes carefully and spied the beaded leather thong she wore around her loins; he glimpsed her small breasts with their hard brown nipples.

Still, he could not look at her face, and his shoulders began to shake. "Naia . . . Naia . . . my love," he moaned in Egyptian, "what have they made you do?"

Naia's voice in return sounded higher, more childish, than the one he remembered. "Who in hell are you?" she asked.

Semerket staggered forward, and felt the floor rising up to meet him . . .

WHEN HE AWOKE, he was lying on his back in the House of Ishtar, with his head in Aneku's lap. She was mopping his face with a moist rag, and before he opened his eyes he heard her high, thin voice rising loudly in the room, lashing out in Babylonian at the eunuchs who had gathered at the cubicle's entrance.

"Can't you let me alone with my husband?" she said in aggrieved tones. "Even you fat oafs must appreciate the shock he's just had."

When the eunuchs had scuttled from the room, Semerket muttered in Egyptian, "I'm not your husband."

"You and I know that," said Aneku, "but those fools don't."

"Why pretend?"

"Because you're my way out of this shit hole."

Semerket sat up wearily, his head throbbing. "Why should I get you out? I don't even know you."

"Because they told me you're looking for Naia. Well, it happens that she and I lived together at Menef's estate, before he sent me to the slave yards—may Set and all his devils blind and castrate him—and, if you're still interested, I happen to know where she is."

His black eyes grew clear. "Where?!" he asked eagerly. "Tell me!"

She shook her head. "Not so fast, my boy. First you're going to get me out of here."

As Semerket had learned, everything in Babylon had a price, and a sizeable donation of gold into the proper hands effected Aneku's release. The eunuchs gave him the woman's deed of indenturement, noting on the clay that Semerket was now her legal owner. They draped the near-naked girl in a blanket, and then both she and Semerket were spirited from the temple by means of an underground passage, to emerge into a neighborhood directly off the Processional Way. Within mere minutes, they were back in Semerket's rooms in Bel-Marduk's hostel.

Aneku exclaimed in delight over the spigots that gushed water into the large basin within the tiled privy. Immodestly, she cast off her blanket and stepped into the steaming water. Her shrill moans of ecstasy filled the rooms, so that Semerket's aching head throbbed even more fiercely. He plaintively begged her to quiet herself.

As she diffidently scrubbed herself with mounds of the perfumed lard and ash that the hostel priests provided, he sat watching her from a nearby stool.

"Tell me, now, as you promised," he said. "Where is Naia?"

She merely looked at him. "So you really are *the* Semerket?" she said by way of answer. "After all Naia told me of you, I feel we know one another."

"She spoke of me?"

Aneku scooped some soap from its bowl. "What a wonderful scent," she remarked, holding her frothy hands to her face and inhaling. "I'd forgotten what a real bath was like. The Babylonians are pigs, you know, despite all their fine plumbing."

"Did you really know her? You weren't just saying that so I'd rescue you?"

Aneku splashed irritatedly, and her little pointed chin grew petulant. "I said I knew her, didn't I? I'm not a liar, you know. We were sent here together on the same ship, with that swine Menef. Then we worked as maids at his estate for a while. But he sent us away, finally."

"Where is she, Aneku?"

She sat quietly in the water, still not looking at him.

"Answer me," he said softly. "Please."

She swallowed. "I'm sorry. It's just that Naia was my first woman friend. She was fair, you know? Just about the only woman who didn't say mean things about me behind my back…"

"Aneku—"

The girl looked at him then, and tears welled up in her slanted green eyes to mingle with the bathwater. "Oh, Semerket. Menef knew a prince and princess from Elam. They were the sister and brother-in-law of the new king, or something like that—I forget. Anyway, they needed servants when they arrived in Babylon. Menef sent her to their plantation outside of town, along with that boy who came with us—"

"Rami?"

Aneku nodded. "By then Menef was renting me out to anyone who had the right amount of silver. You can't believe what I was expected to do. When I refused to service his friends anymore, he sent me on to the slave yards with instructions to sell me as a trained whore. At first I cursed Naia and Rami for being the lucky ones."

Semerket found he was able only to nod dumbly.

"But it turns out that I was the fortunate one for once—can you believe it?"

"Why? What happened?"

She swallowed, and brought water to her face, bathing it before she answered. "Only a few days after she and Rami were sent to the plantation—it was during the last part of the war with Elam, you know?—the place was sacked by raiders." She fell silent, staring at Semerket as if she expected him to cuff her.

"Go on," he said.

"Oh, Semerket," she said softly. "They were all slaughtered. Every one of them. The plantation was burned to the ground. She's dead, Semerket—Naia's dead."

THE RIVER FEVER came upon him again that night. He lay on his bed and clutched the heavy skins around him, his body shaking with an onslaught of sudden fierce chills. Aneku crossed swiftly to the bed and crawled between its blankets, pressing close so that she might infuse her warmth into him. He would have shaken off her embrace, but she held him fast against her, shushing his protests as though he were a child. In truth, he was so starved for the closeness of another living body that he could not have moved away from her even if he had wanted.

As the lamp guttered fitfully in its niche, he turned over to regard the woman lying beside him. She stared back with slanted green eyes that were not Naia's. Aneku saw the lights that whirled and crashed in Semerket's black glance, and her hand slipped slowly down beneath the blankets.

"Don't," he said, wincing at her touch.

"Why not? Don't you think I recognize that look in a man's eyes?"

"That's not why I took you from the temple. No one will ever force you again."

"And if *I* choose . . . ?"

He sat up, brushing away her hand and turning his back on her. "Choose another."

She reached out to stroke his shoulders, dragging the tips of her nails down his slim, muscular back. "What's wrong, Semerket?" she asked. "Why do you turn away? Is it because of what I had to do at Ishtar's house?"

He said nothing, for his tongue clung inertly to his palate.

She pressed her lips to the small of his back. "Is it because of Naia?"

Semerket nodded.

Aneku reached around him. "She's no longer among the living, Semerket. You and I won't dishonor her with what we do."

"I said no."

Aneku fell back against a cushion, uncertain, making excuses for his indifference. "I—I can understand how you must take some time to accept it. After coming all that way from Egypt, it must be heartbreaking to discover that she's—"

He interrupted her curtly, turning to stare at her. "Did you see it happen?"

"What?"

"Did you *see* Naia killed?"

"How could I? I told you, I was in Eshnunna when I heard about the raid."

"Yes. You said how the bandits stormed the plantation, how everyone there was slaughtered, even the prince and princess from Elam." He turned to face her. "But how is it I received a message from Rami, asking for my help? Wasn't he supposed to have died there, too?"

Aneku sat up in the dark. "Rami's alive?"

He sighed. "Why do you think I came?"

Semerket rose from the bed then, clutching the woolen blanket to him, leaning against the wall so that he could look out through the door leading to the terrace. Silver light already suffused the eastern horizon. Semerket felt the faint half-flush of its heat rising in the breezes that stroked his body.

"Until I see her corpse for myself, I'll go on believing she's alive, that she escaped along with Rami. I must."

After a moment, he heard her thin, bitter chuckle.

"Why do you laugh?" he asked.

"How perverse it all is. After all those men I've slept with at the temple, the only one I'd freely give myself to won't have me." She sighed, laying her face upon her outstretched arm. "What's to become of me, then?"

"What do you mean?"

"I belong to you. You bought me from the Ishtar eunuchs. You have the deed that says I'm yours."

He shook his head. "You belong to yourself. I'll go to the authorities today and declare you a free woman. You can do what you want to after that."

Instead of showing gratitude, Aneku's eyes became stormy. "But where shall I go? What shall I do?" Her voice was edged with incipient panic. "You don't mean to abandon me here, do you? Better to have left me at the temple, then—at least there I was needed."

"Have you no friends you can go to, no relations?"

She looked at him with disbelief. "Of course I have relations," she said, as if speaking to a person of limited intelligence. "In Egypt!"

"I suppose you can't go back there . . . ?"

"No."

He did not press her to divulge the crime that had caused her banishment. Semerket rapidly considered his options. He could always give her a handful of Pharaoh's gold, he supposed, and be done with her. But that seemed a trifle callow, somehow—it had become his unthinking and rote solution to almost every problem he had encountered since his arrival in Babylonia. Reluctantly, he decided that the unfortunate girl deserved better from him. After considering her plight for a time, his face brightened.

"What?" Aneku said, suspicious.

"As your expertise lies in being a temple servant, how would you like to continue the profession?"

• • •

AS HE INTRODUCED Aneku to Senmut and Wia, he noticed how the old man perceptibly brightened when he looked upon the girl. Wia, however, narrowed her eyes in skeptical appraisal.

Aneku was dressed in an unassuming linen sheath that Semerket had purchased for her in a nearby souk, and a scarf of dark blue covered her hennaed hair. He had bought her three such outfits, along with the appropriate cosmetics and sandals, underwear, and some modest pieces of jewelry—everything that she would need to start her life as a free woman.

Semerket explained to the priestly couple that Aneku had been a friend of Naia's and had fallen on hard times. He had just that morning purchased her from a cruel owner, he said, and set her free. He showed them the clay tablet that manumitted her, witnessed by the Bel-Marduk priests at the hostel, which Wia read over very carefully.

Aneku had nowhere to go, Semerket went on, and as she had once served in a temple (he was careful not to say which one), would they consider taking Aneku in to work for them? He himself would guarantee her wages, Semerket promised.

"You can certainly use some help here," he urged, "and Aneku needs a place to stay."

Semerket glanced uneasily over at the girl. Aneku was staring aghast at the withered fig trees and broken tiles in the temple courtyard, all the while attempting to answer Wia's sharp questions.

"Do you cook, girl?" he heard Wia say.

"I never learned," said Aneku, shaking her head demurely.

"Do you know how to sing the litanies and chants we use?"

Again, a slight shake of the head.

"Well. Have you been instructed on how to make offerings to the gods in the proper fashion, then?"

"I don't think so . . ."

"Can you mend vestments, at least? Can you be trusted with the laundry?"

Aneku shrugged.

"By Set and all his devils," Wia shook her head in suspicious disbelief, "what duties *did* you perform in that temple of yours?"

Before she could answer, Semerket hastily assured them that Aneku was a fast learner. He pressed several gold pieces into Senmut's hands, saying that he was to use it in the girl's care and provisioning, and gave Aneku an equal amount.

Leaving the trio gawking at him, he departed quickly. Firmly, he crammed down his fast-rising sense of guilt. There was a reason to his lunacy in placing Aneku at the little temple, he told himself. Eventually, Naia's affection for the gods of her homeland would lead her to make an offering at the temple. And if—when—she came, Aneku would be the only person able to recognize her.

NOW THAT SEMERKET knew the raid on the plantation had also claimed members of the Elamite royal family, he could no longer put off consulting with the governing authorities. It was vital to find out what the Elamites knew. Semerket remembered that in Mari the Elamite commander had told him to seek out his friend, General Kidin, who commanded Babylon's garrison; General Kidin knew everything that transpired in the city, the commander had boasted, and could help him find his friends.

Semerket therefore took himself to the garrison's vast courtyard, in which the Elamites had pitched their long, even rows of tents. He crossed to the small, low, brick building that served as its headquarters, and asked if he could have a few minutes of General Kidin's time.

"Afraid not," the desk sergeant replied curtly.

"It really is a matter of some urgency."

The desk sergeant leaned forward, whispering confidentially. "He was executed," he said. "Last week. 'Failure in his duty to the king.'"

Semerket swore in vexation. Everywhere he turned in this benighted city, he seemed caught in some blind alley leading nowhere. "What did he fail to do?"

"Couldn't find them that killed the king's brother-in-law."

Semerket hesitated, surprised to hear the man mention only the prince. "But I'd heard his sister was also assassinated. Isn't that true?"

"No one knows. She's gone, vanished as if she were some spirit. No corpse, no traces. The king is wild with grief, as you can imagine, and we're the ones suffering for it. So when Kidin came up with nothing . . ." The man made a slicing gesture across his throat.

Despite the news of Kidin's death, Semerket felt his heart stir with hope. If the princess was missing, she had no doubt been kidnapped by raiders and was being held for ransom. And if that were true, perhaps Naia was a prisoner with her. It would then be a relatively simple task to ransom her freedom. "Was the princess captured, then?" he asked hopefully.

The desk sergeant shrugged. "No one's made any demands, though everyone thinks the Isins did it—and they're not exactly shy about asking for ransoms."

"Who's replaced the general?"

"Colonel Shepak has that honor."

"I will meet with him."

The sergeant's friendliness abruptly faded. "Shepak doesn't have time to meet with foreigners! Go to your own legation if you need help. We're stretched thin enough in Babylon as it is."

Semerket leaned in, murmuring to the man, "The name is Semerket. Why don't you check your official lists from the palace?"

The sergeant rose grumbling from his desk, and obediently went into the back rooms to consult with his commander. It was only a moment before he scuttled back, cringing and apologetic, to where Semerket waited. "This way," he said, bowing low. "This way to Colonel Shepak!"

Semerket followed the man to the courtyard behind the main building, located in the shadow of the royal palace. Looking up by chance to the high ramparts that surrounded the compound, Semerket was surprised to find they were thick with patrolling Elamite soldiers, each bristling with a formidable array of swords, spears, bows, and quivers of arrows. A chill feeling of foreboding ran up his spine. It seemed that the Elamites expected an attack, and soon. Before he could question the sergeant, however, Semerket was being shown into a nearby tent.

A sad-eyed man sat at a wooden table, his chin resting in his hand. The man was young, but his face sagged with a kind of world-weariness that was not all in keeping with his youth, and gray already streaked his beard.

"What now?" the man asked the sergeant in a low, resigned voice.

"An important person, sir," said the sergeant. "Lord Semerket, sent all the way from Egypt by Pharaoh Ramses. He wants to meet with you."

Shepak, unimpressed, gestured indifferently to Semerket that he should take the seat in front of him. Another tired gesture dismissed the sergeant.

"Felicitations on your recent promotion," Semerket said, by way of initiating their conversation.

Shepak stared at him, red-eyed. "I'm facing the Insect Chamber, while you make jokes."

Semerket opened his mouth to protest, but stopped. It was the second or third time he had heard reference to an "insect chamber." It had to be more than just a Babylonian idiom with which he was unfamiliar.

"I'm sorry——?" he asked. "What's this chamber you refer to? Someone mentioned it to me before."

"Merely the post I'll be assigned to next week this time," answered Shepak. He waved his hand, dismissing the subject. "How may I help my distinguished visitor from Egypt?"

Semerket came to the point. "I'm seeking information about the raid at the prince and princess's plantation—the one that happened about twelve weeks ago, to the northwest of here."

The colonel shot a penetrating glance at him. "Why, I ask myself, should an Egyptian be interested in what is only an internal affair of Elam?"

Semerket told him how the Egyptian ambassador had sent Naia and Rami to the plantation. He also mentioned that the pharaoh of Egypt was personally interested in their recovery, letting the tantalizing promise of a fat bribe remain discreetly unspoken.

But Shepak only shook his head. "You've come for nothing," Shepak said. "No one survived. The slaughter was painstaking, even by Isin standards." This from a man, Semerket noticed, who decorated his helmet with severed fingers and phalluses snipped from various Dark Head enemies.

"They left one person alive, however," Semerket said.

"Do you mean the princess?"

"Someone else."

"You're mistaken."

"I have proof."

Semerket reached into his leather pouch and fetched Rami's letter into the light. He laid the palm bark on the table before the colonel.

"This letter came to Pharaoh from the boy I told you about—Rami—wanting to be rescued." He pointed to the glyphs. "He was 'attacked by Isins,' it says there. We learned that he'd suffered a head wound, at a plantation to the northwest of Babylon—the same place, it turns out, where your prince and princess were also attacked. It may be that the lad's dead now—but he wasn't when he wrote it."

"By the Babylonians' sixty thousand gods," Shepak said, awestruck. "We'd very much like to meet this Rami of yours! If he could tell us what happened to the princess—"

"I was hoping you Elamites had found him."

Shepak rose, disgusted, to pace the tent. "*You* try to find anything in this demented country. Just when you think you've discovered something, you reach out only to find it wasn't there in the first place."

"So I've noticed."

"What more can you tell me?"

"Only this: I've talked to the Isins myself—"

Shepak interrupted him with a foul oath. "You've actually met with them?"

"When I came down the river, I went into Is and had a look. A couple of their men talked to me." Some instinct told him that it would be unwise to mention that Marduk had arranged the meeting. "They said they didn't do it."

"Egyptian," said Shepak, "you amaze me. I've offered rewards for anyone who can capture an Isin and bring him to me alive. They go unclaimed, even though the Isins are becoming quite plentiful here in Babylon—"

"What do you mean?"

"We've had reports that the Heir of Isin managed to slip into the city a few days ago—along with a great number of his men."

That explained the extra Elamite brigades on the ramparts.

"We expect an attack at any time," Shepak continued. "They'll want to stop Kutir from taking the hand of Bel-Marduk at the festival next week, for if he does, it means that heaven favors his claim to the throne. These Dark Heads are very backward, you know—very superstitious about such things." Shepak sat down across from him, leaning forward to stare into Semerket's face. "Did you believe the Isins, when they told you they had nothing to do with the raid?"

Semerket was cynical. "I'm not in a profession where I can afford to believe anyone."

"But if you were to wager . . . ?"

Semerket shrugged philosophically. "I don't know. If they'd done the deed, why wouldn't they boast of it? And if they have the princess, I think you'd have heard their demands by now."

Shepak looked through the tent flap to the garrison compound baking in the white sun, and bit his lip. "Why did you really come to see me, Egyptian? What is it you want?"

"I want to go to this plantation. I want to see for myself what happened."

Shepak shook his head doubtfully. "You won't find anything. We've scoured it clean."

"*I* haven't scoured it."

Shepak looked at him for a moment. Then he abruptly stood, seizing his grisly, trophy-bedecked helmet from its wooden perch. "All right. I'll take you there myself. Maybe you'll find something my own men have overlooked."

Semerket was surprised when Shepak also donned his bright crimson commander's mantle. "But surely . . ." Semerket began, and then stopped.

"What?" asked Shepak.

"If you expect an attack, won't you make a tempting target, wearing such a red cloak?"

"I certainly hope so," the colonel muttered dolefully.

SHEPAK LED SEMERKET to the stables and ordered two horses to be saddled. Semerket appreciated the aesthetics of a horse, certainly, its grace and power—but preferably from as far away from its mouth and hooves as possible. Overall, he said to Shepak, he preferred to ride a good little donkey whenever possible. In fact, there were those who said his rapport with donkeys was amazing . . .

Shepak gave him a disgusted look. "A donkey? It's almost twenty leagues to where we're going. We've no time to waste with a donkey."

Semerket suggested nervously that, if that were the case, perhaps it would be best if they rode together on a single horse. The Elamite colonel also dismissed this idea. "Too dangerous," Shepak said with finality. "If anyone comes after me, they'd be sure to kill you, too."

Semerket reluctantly allowed a groom to help him atop a dusty black nag, which the Elamite grooms assured him was as gentle as a pet rabbit. And though the beast plodded through the Babylonian streets in a complacent manner, Semerket grew uneasy at the way she kept rolling her eyes backward to see what kind of fool guided her. But the mare was a seasoned veteran of many wars and many riders, and did her best to keep Semerket from tumbling to the ground. Though he never quite lost his wariness of her, Semerket was soon able to unbend his spine a little and breathe regularly.

All the way to the Ishtar Gate, Shepak rode some fifty paces or so in front of Semerket, so that any lurking Isin assassin would not think they were together. It was not until they reached the lonely road leading to the northwest, far outside the city, that Shepak reined his horse and allowed Semerket to catch up to him.

"Let's pick up the pace a bit, shall we?" said Shepak.

With a click of his tongue, Shepak increased their speed to a slow gallop. Sometime after noon, they reached an area where rich fields had been plowed into long furrows. At the junction of a second road, they came upon a village of tenant farmers. Their curious round houses and barns, with pitched roofs made of dried reeds caulked with bitumen, made Semerket think of toadstools.

The children grew quiet as he and Shepak passed, running to their mothers to stare at the strangers from behind their skirts. He turned his head in time to see an old woman make the sign of evil at Shepak. Semerket made a mental note that if he came back to question these farmers later, he would do it without an Elamite colonel at his side.

As they neared the plantation, Semerket began to feel uneasy, his mouth growing dry. Everything seemed so weirdly familiar to him—the level brown land; the glimpse of the shimmering Euphrates in the distance; the upright, unbroken walls of the approaching estate. Then, with a start of horror, he realized that the place exactly conformed to the eerie landscape of his nightmares—the ones in which he had seen Naia repeatedly slain before the eyes of his wandering ka.

Then they turned down a path that Semerket knew, absolutely knew, he had seen before. In the afternoon's humid stillness, Semerket turned his head and finally saw the ruins.

The plantation's buildings were parodies of their original shapes, with an obscene smell to their ashes that Semerket doubted he would ever forget. Several structures had once stood in the compound—stables, worksheds, grain silos, servants' quarters. Now all of them were gone.

Semerket trod into what was left of the main house. Large and sumptuous at one time, it had been three stories or more when intact. Most of its floors had collapsed in on themselves, leaving its gaping husk open to the sky. Going from room to room, he glimpsed odd bits of pottery on the floors, fragments of furniture crushed beneath the charred rubble.

There was no logic to why something had survived the flames; a broom of palm leaves remained barely singed, while the stone statue beside it lay shattered in fragments. As he roamed, he vaguely wondered what Naia's duties had been within this house. Had she swept these rooms with the palm broom? Or carried the water jug to the pantry where it now lay in pieces? Perhaps she had polished the little statue of the Elamite household god, still standing in its niche, headless.

He went out the rear door. The thing hung on leather hinges, its paint charred and blistered. A few steps more and he was at the kitchen. Ironically, the structure had been built away from the main house so that its hearth would not set the larger building afire. Nearby was a well, and out of long habit Semerket stared down into its depths. The water's scent was fresh, smelling vaguely of citrus. The smell reminded Semerket of Naia, who habitually wore a perfume distilled from lemon blossoms.

He turned again and made another walk through the kitchen. Semerket found only copper pots, clay dishes, and broken cups. A sudden glint of gold caught his eye amid the rubble. He bent down to retrieve a flat serving tray, shaking off the ash and dust that covered it, and saw the design chased into its surface.

"The royal crest of Elam," whispered Shepak, who had silently followed him through the grounds. "The prince and princess must have brought it from Susa."

"It tells us one thing," Semerket grunted.

"What?"

"The raiders didn't come here for plunder." He threw the tray onto the ashes.

Semerket strode to a nearby grove of date palms. Wandering through the cool shadows, he examined the high brick walls that surrounded the estate. He saw the telltale marks at their top. "That's where they came over," he said to Shepak, pointing. "See how every few feet there are marks from grappling hooks? They would have been seen during daylight—but this far away, at night . . ."

Shepak looked up. "How many of them were there, do you suppose?"

Semerket shrugged. "I wouldn't imagine there were very many. Surprise and the dark were on their side. The raiders needed only a few of their men to scale the walls, to open the gates for the rest. If they were experienced, ten men could have handled the job from start to finish—"

Semerket stopped speaking when a cloud of flies darted past them. Alert to where they flew, he saw them disappear behind the wall and into the far courtyard. He followed for a few paces, and the flies' buzzing became louder and more frenetic as he approached.

When he came around the corner of the wall, he saw what attracted the flies—a massive stain of black blood stretching across the limestone tiles in a side courtyard.

"This is where they slaughtered them," he said to Shepak.

"You're right," Shepak confirmed curtly. "We found the bodies here, their hands bound together. There were thirty-three of them. All the water from the well couldn't wash the blood away."

"Then they had been at least two days dead before you found them."

Shepak looked at him oddly. "How did you know?"

"I know blood. You can wash it away if it hasn't been sitting for more than a day and half. After that, no matter how hard you scrub, some of it will remain."

Shepak swallowed uneasily. Despite being a hardened warrior, he possessed the same squeamishness about death and its detritus that all the peoples of Mesopotamia shared. "You Egyptians certainly possess a ghoulish streak, knowing such things," he said.

Semerket did not reply as he walked around the perimeter of the stain. Though the blood had long since dried, the flies were dense on the tiles, and the stain seemed to roil and heave iridescently in the sunlight.

"Where are they buried?" Semerket asked.

"Who?"

"The ones slaughtered here."

"Kutir brought their bodies back to the palace in Babylon, to bury them with the prince. He placed then into funeral jars, and embalmed them in honey."

"Everyone?"

Shepak nodded.

Semerket turned away, so the Elamite could not see the pleased look on his face. Honey would preserve the victim's features. "These jars—where are they?"

"In the royal crypts below the palace."

Semerket looked at Shepak with an enigmatic expression. He was remembering the vision he had had upon the river, searching the jars of honey. He knew he had to see those bodies for himself, to discover finally if Naia was among them. He did not intend to leave her behind in Babylon, alive or dead. Somehow, he must find a way to convince Shepak to get him inside the royal crypt.

"I must see their faces, before they've decomposed any further."

Shepak looked at him with revulsion. "They won't decompose. But it's against all our laws to interfere with the dead."

"How am I to learn the truth, then?"

"You'll have to figure it out another way, that's all."

"If you don't help me view those bodies," Semerket said shortly, "and find out what happened to your princess, how will I ever be able to save you from the Insect Chamber?"

The Elamite colonel raised his head abruptly, and stared at him.

They sat in the shade of the outer wall, near the broken gates. Shepak had brought a loaf of round bread and some cheese in his pack, but neither of them was hungry.

"I've only a week left to find Pinikir," Shepak said, drinking wine from a leather flask. "When the Day of the False King dawns, if I haven't produced the princess, I'll suffer the same fate as Kidin. Kutir's promised to go through the officers' ranks until either Princess Pinikir is recovered, or we're all dead."

"And execution will be in this Insect Chamber I've heard about?"

Shepak was quiet. Then he nodded. "Yes."

"But what is it? I mean, what is the method of . . . ?"

Shepak took a ragged breath before he spoke. "We found it in the palace dungeon and thought at first that it was just another prison cell—until we put one of our own men in there. He'd gotten drunk on duty, and needed a scare, we thought. We hadn't even closed the doors before the screaming began. Some mechanism is triggered when the door closes, we discovered, allowing other trapdoors inside the chamber to open."

He had to rinse his mouth with wine again.

"First come the shredders, those with their claws and pincers and beaks, the beetles and mantids, the scorpions and centipedes. Those that fly get there first. They flay the outer flesh open, crawling between the lips, competing for the tongue, burrowing into the ears and nose and eyes. When they've eaten their fill, then the next trapdoor opens. This time, it's the gray flesh eaters—the worms and grubs that go to work on the softer tissues, the organs and vessels. You can hear their jaws clacking together, thousands of them. Worms cluster in the victim's belly, feast in his skull. When they're finished, the third and final door opens—and the small parasites stream out, the most voracious of all, ants and mites and maggots. They clean the bones to a glistening white in a matter of minutes. It's said that the Kassites invented the chamber to secretly rid themselves of their most hated enemies, so that nothing would be left that could identify them."

Shepak fell silent. Semerket realized that he was staring at the Elamite with his mouth open. "I can't believe it," Semerket said.

"Believe it. Kutir forced the officers to watch Kidin when he was put in there." Shepak looked at him with the same haunted expression. "But I've not yet told you the most terrible part."

"What could be more terrible?" Semerket's voice was faint.

"You've seen the insects in this accursed country—how monstrous they are? How aggressive?"

Semerket nodded. He remembered that night outside the gates of Is, when he waited for Marduk to reappear from inside the city.

"Imagine them twice and three times that size," Shepak said. "It's what happens when they've a ready supply of meat." He drained his leather canteen. "And come next week, it'll be my turn."

Grim silence hung between them. Then Semerket moved decisively to his feet.

"Well," he said, with as much confidence as he could muster. "There's nothing for it, then, but to find the princess."

Shepak had to laugh, however morbidly. "And you think you can?"

"Why shouldn't I? She disappeared the very moment my own wife did, and in the same place." Semerket looked around, surveying the ruins of the vast estate. "If I can find one woman, I'll certainly be able to find the other."

BEFORE LEAVING, SEMERKET made one last search of the grounds. It was true that the Elamite forces had scrubbed the place clean of any evidence. When he mentioned this to Shepak, the colonel told him that there had not been much to discover in the first place; the raiders had themselves removed all traces of their attack, careful to leave nothing behind that might identify them. This in itself was curious.

A while later, however, Semerket glimpsed something embedded in the underside of a fallen cedar crossbeam. He had not seen the object when he first had come through the ruined chamber, for the beam had been in shadow. Now that the sun had moved across the sky, its rays revealed a single arrow, slightly charred but still intact. It pierced the beam deeply. When Semerket bent to pull it out, it did not move.

"Shepak—over here!" he called.

The Elamite hurried to where he stood. Semerket pointed to the arrow. Shepak used his sword to dig it out, and Semerket caught it in his hand as it fell.

"Odd-looking thing," Shepak said. "I don't remember seeing an arrow like it before."

"I have," said Semerket shortly. "See there—? The shaft isn't made of wood; it's a reed. Papyrus, in fact, dried and hardened with resin. Look at this arrow point—made from Sinai copper. And the feather here—gray, with white tips?—I'd wager anything that it's from a Theban goose."

He looked soberly at Shepak. "This arrow was made in Egypt."

IT WAS AFTERNOON when Semerket and Shepak began their journey back to Babylon. Since Semerket had divulged that the arrow was of Egyptian make, Shepak had grown distant, speaking to him only in grunts and monosyllables. It must seem more than coincidence that an Egyptian national should be investigating the murder of an Elamite prince and princess, only to turn up evidence of Egyptian complicity. It stank of conspiracy, in fact, and Shepak no doubt was reconsidering his alliance with Semerket.

They rode swiftly, if silently, back to the capital. Neither of them had any wish to be out on the open roads after dark. Even Shepak seemed relieved when they reached the Ishtar Gate.

Semerket gave the mare's reins to Shepak at the door of Bel-Marduk's hostel. Tersely, they agreed to meet the following morning, to determine their next course of action. Semerket gave the arrow to the colonel for safekeeping, telling him to hide it away and tell no one else of its existence; he did not want their only piece of tangible evidence to vanish mysteriously from his pack in the hostel.

Just as he was about to go inside, however, Semerket saw his two

Dark Head spies signaling him from the other side of the Processional Way. Though he wanted only to soak his tender, blistered backside in a cool bath, he picked his way through the traffic to where they stood.

When he approached them, the two men hung their heads, regarding him with fatalistic sadness. "Good evening, lord," said the fat one in a doleful voice, bowing slightly.

"Why so glum?" Semerket asked. "You look like your mother's just died."

"Our mother is well, thank you," said the thin Dark Head, and for the first time Semerket realized that the two men were brothers. "It's kind of you to inquire. We're disappointed because now that you've found your wife, you'll soon be leaving Babylon."

Semerket was momentarily without words. "What do you mean, I've 'found my wife'?"

"We know of the beautiful lady you hide at the Egyptian temple, my lord."

Semerket was amused. "She's not my wife."

The two Dark Head spies looked suspiciously at one another. "We have heard it from her own lips!"

"But she's not . . ." Semerket began, and then stopped. Aneku probably still believed that if her real identity were known, she would be forced back into the Ishtar Temple, having left it under false pretenses. Well, thought Semerket, if passing herself off as his wife would help her, what harm was there?

"I can assure you that I'm not yet done with Babylon."

"But if that's so, why would the Elamites no longer require us to follow you? You might as well know that we've been dismissed from their service."

So the Elamites had given up spying on him. Why? Most likely it was because he had gone to the Elamite garrison to consult with Colonel Shepak, something that would have been quickly reported to the palace.

"If it's all the same, lord," continued the fat spy, "since you plan on staying here, we would very much like to continue in your service."

Semerket snorted. "Now why should I pay you not to spy on me when I'm no longer being spied upon?"

"You need our help, lord."

"I don't."

"These are uncertain times in Babylon."

Semerket shrugged. "That may be, but you'll get no more gold from me."

Both of his Dark Head spies bowed their heads, saying nothing more.

Semerket was still laughing to himself as he entered the hostel's courtyard. He dimly noticed a contingent of Elamite guards over at the stables, arrayed in glittering livery. He was surprised when, at a signal from the Bel-Marduk priests, one of the Elamites accosted him as he began to climb the outer stairs to his rooms.

"Lord Semerket?" he asked.

Semerket, surprised, nodded.

"King Kutir requests your attendance at the palace."

"*Kutir?* Now?"

The guard crossed his arms and nodded.

"But I . . . I'm not dressed for the palace, as you can see. Nor am I bathed."

"Everything you need will be supplied upon your arrival, lord."

Semerket knew he was caught, and could no longer put off meeting with Babylon's latest ruler. Nevertheless, he insisted that he retrieve the badge of office that Pharaoh had given him. For the first time since receiving it, Semerket slipped the pectoral around his neck. Against his dusty leather traveling clothes, its richness gleamed improbably. The falcon badge, with its outstretched wings of hammered gold, swung heavily from carnelian and lapis beads in the shape of teardrops. Above the falcon's head, the eye of Horus stared out, the most potent of Egypt's charms.

A chair borne by twelve men awaited him on Processional Way. As he was carried aloft, the cynosure of all eyes on the avenue, Semerket felt thoroughly ridiculous. At least it was dusk, he thought, with shadows already concealing the long concourse.

"Lord Semerket!" The voice suddenly came to him from a darkened vendor's stall.

From the stall's depths, a man raised his hand tentatively to wave.

Squinting, Semerket was surprised to discover that the man was the same one who had been speaking to Marduk in the Sick Square.

"Halt!" Semerket cried to his Elamite guards. When they ignored him, he went through all the Babylonian words in his strained lexicon. "Stop! Cease! End! I will speak to this man!"

The Elamite guard protested. "My lord, I remind you that the king himself—"

"—must not be kept waiting, I agree," Semerket interjected. "Only a moment, Captain, to speak to my friend here." At the soldier's truculent expression, Semerket made his voice icy. "Or must I complain to the king of rudeness shown to Egypt?"

The Elamite guard quickly gestured to the bearers to set the chair upon the ground. Semerket leapt from the chair, trotting to where the man waited.

"I see your complexion is much improved," Semerket said as he approached. Indeed, the man's smooth face seemed as if he had never suffered from a skin ailment.

"I used plain water, as my lord suggested. Its effects were truly miraculous."

"How did you know I'd be coming this way?"

"I was told to meet you here and give you a message."

"From whom?"

"I cannot say, my lord."

Semerket looked into the fellow's face, trying to ascertain if the man concealed anything behind his servile manner. But the man's expression remained bland and innocent.

"What is the message, then?"

The man took a breath, and recited. "'It is noticed that you go to the garrison of the Elamites, my lord. It is devoutly wished that you avoid the area in the future.'"

"Why?"

"There is no more to the message, my lord." The man shifted uncomfortably. "But, if you please, there is something that *I* would like to know . . ."

Semerket nodded.

"H-how is it that you knew water alone would cure my affliction?"

Semerket laughed. "Do you think I can't recognize an old beggar's trick when I see one? If you want to appear worse than a leper, you have only to paste moldy bread to your face with honey."

A slow smile broke on the Babylonian's face. "You're the first to ever find out, lord."

When Semerket blinked, the man disappeared into the shadows of the market stall. Semerket went back to the chair and his bearers raised him high once again. All the short way to the palace, he thought of what the fellow had told him. Why must he avoid the Elamite garrison? Was he being warned—or threatened? And who had sent the message? Also, why would an apparently healthy man be stationed in the Sick Square . . . ?

If it had been Marduk who had sent the message (a logical thought, as Semerket had seen him in the company of the man, or at least believed he had), he of all people would know that Semerket would feel duty-bound to act contrary to the message's instructions. But Marduk was a mere Dark Head renegade. No, the warning had to have come from someone else. But who? He was deep in thought when he noticed that he and his escort had crossed into the royal citadel.

Shining tiles depicting stylized trees of blue, green, and gold sheathed the royal palace, raising their mosaic limbs to the sky. Ahead, an immense door opened as Semerket's chair approached. The temperature dropped pleasantly once he was inside, for the palace's brick walls were at least four cubits thick.

In the dim interior, courtiers bowed low as he was borne through the winding hallways. The high chamberlain appeared almost instantly from a side hall, a thin, nervous eunuch of indeterminate age. His nostrils twitched to catch the reek of sweat and horse that emanated so richly from Semerket. The eunuch firmly pulled him from the chair and hustled him down a long hall into a side room, where a tub of steaming water waited. Serving maids suddenly appeared to strip Semerket's clothes away, and he was embarrassed when they pointed at him, laughing, for they declaimed loudly that they had never before seen a circumcised man. Several of the women threw him suggestive looks, but he pretended indifference.

After they had soaped and rinsed him, the eunuch ushered him to a room where a valet offered up a choice of garments to wear. Picking the simplest robe, he allowed them to place thin sandals of gilded kid on his feet. The valet would have draped ropes of gold about his neck, but Semerket insisted that his only jewel be his badge of office. Satisfied with Semerket's appearance at last, but still lamenting his lack of ornamentation, the high chamberlain then led him up a narrow winding staircase, trudging the many steps to emerge finally into the indigo twilight.

Many Babylonian buildings sported rooftop gardens, but the one he now beheld caused him to gape. It was terraced, rising in irregular heights as a real hillside might, and its pink marble planters were verdant with greenery. Perfectly framed by boughs of flowering trees, King Kutir stood with his back to Semerket, seeming to admire the moonrise. A woman was at his side, her hand resting delicately on the young king's arm. The tableau was so perfectly composed that Semerket knew the king must have staged it just for him.

The herald announced him in ringing tones, and the king turned, as if surprised. Semerket bowed low, in the Egyptian manner, arms outstretched, and Pharaoh's pendant swung from his chest.

"Semerket, you have come to us at last," said the king. "I am saddened to have torn you away from your prayers, for I've heard how devout you are." Kutir's mouth twitched when he said this.

Semerket's tongue, for once, was usable. "But my prayers have been answered, Majesty—to meet with you at last, amid all this splendor."

The king snickered. The lady on his arm, however, turned her back—a deliberate snub that effectively silenced the king's laughter. Kutir, embarrassed, forcibly turned her around again to face Semerket. The king's fingers made white impressions in the flesh of her arm.

"May I present the queen, my wife, Narunte, who is as eager to meet you as I."

This was so patently a lie that all Semerket could do was bow again, concealing his smile. The queen wrenched her arm from her husband's grip and sank into a chair of carved ivory. She signaled for a slave to fetch her a bowl of beer, and sat glaring at Semerket as she sucked on the reed.

At first glance, Queen Narunte seemed far older than her young husband, for her face was gaunt, her neck creased. She looked at Semerket with eyes of a demonic silver color, and in them her tiny pupils were pinpoints of hate. Had she not been introduced to him as the queen, her rudeness should have branded her a common trull.

Kutir on the other hand was a prince out of legend—virile, with his beard curled and his long hair gathered into a knot at the back of his neck. His only flaw was that his eyes were small, set close together, while the tiny lines at their corners betrayed his anxiety.

Semerket was suddenly aware that he was studying the royal pair as he would suspects in a crime, and hastily looked away. It was then he saw that Ambassador Menef was also in the gardens, standing behind the queen's chair. Menef's bodyguard, the man whose macabre smile was so remarkable, also waited there, stationing himself discreetly apart from the ambassador. The moment Semerket saw them, the pair genuflected extravagantly.

At that point, Kutir came forward and draped his arm around Semerket's shoulders. "Come and let us talk now that you're here," he urged, "as men would, away from these others."

Kutir guided Semerket up a flight of stairs to a copse of fragrant pines growing at the top level of the gardens. Kutir would have taken a seat on a marble bench had not a very large peacock already roosted there. He kicked it away, and the bird flew with great flapping wings to a pine bough above them, shrieking. The king then indicated that Semerket should join him on the bench. Attentive to the fresh droppings that covered it, Semerket sat carefully.

"So," Kutir said eagerly, "what is the offer?"

"Sire?"

"For the Marduk statue—what will Ramses give me?"

Semerket, surprised, guessed that Menef had told Kutir of Pharaoh's request, just as he had informed High Priest Adad. Once again, he grew alarmed at the ambassador's intentions; any sensible emissary would have kept secret the fact of Pharaoh's ill health. If other nations knew that Ramses was sick or dying, diplomatic communities throughout Asia would defer making any long-term treaties with Egypt, preferring instead to deal with his successor.

Semerket breathed deeply, and began to list carefully the concessions Ramses had indicated he was to make. "Pharaoh is prepared to acknowledge you the true king of Babylon."

"And?"

"And to offer assistance in subduing the various native factions."

Kutir snorted. "Hmmph. That's at least a change in policy from his father's."

"Sire?"

"The Isin heir was raised in Egypt—from where he was set loose last year to pester and bedevil us. But of course you knew that."

Semerket knew nothing of the sort. Though it was customary to invite foreign princes to be educated in Egypt, and thereby civilized, Semerket had never heard any mention of the Isin heir from either the present pharaoh or his father. But Kutir was not interested in pursuing the subject.

"And?" he prodded. "What else?"

Semerket cast about for more. "And gold."

"And?"

"Weapons. Grain. Armor. Supplies."

"And?"

"I'm sorry, but I've not been authorized to offer more."

Kutir sighed in exaggerated disappointment. "And yet it's not enough."

Kutir rose from the marble bench then, and stared over the edge of the gardens into the city below. Babylon stretched before them in purple shadow. Cooking fires began to flare in the darkened urban expanse. Kutir turned again to face Semerket.

"Ramses is Pharaoh today because of you. If you hadn't discovered the plot hatched in his father's own harem, a traitor would sit on the Falcon Throne today. Everyone knows it."

Semerket began to voice his protests. "Majesty, I stumbled on the plot without knowing I did—"

"Modesty, too, they told me, was a hallmark of your character."

Semerket's voice rose in agitation. "Pharaoh's father *died* because of me. If I hadn't been so blind, so stupid . . ." He stopped, not wishing to remember those times. "Anyway, I'm not what you think I am. And what does it have to do with your demands, Sire?"

Kutir took a breath. "I have only one demand. And that is for you to join my service. I want *you* to find my sister—or find what happened to her."

The king began to explain himself quickly, a thread of nervousness running through his voice. "Of all his children, Pinikir was Father's favorite. If I cannot recover her—even if it's just her body—my father will take some steps of his own." The thread pulled, his fear unraveled, and the king's voice collapsed in a strangulated gasp.

Semerket tried to offer him some comfort. "If that's so, perhaps he'll send you the troops you need to quell the rebels—"

Kutir turned haunted eyes upon him. "No, you don't understand. He'll take steps against *me*. I'm no more than a vassal king to him, now—one not performing his duties too well at the moment."

Semerket stared at Kutir. He knew of Kutir's father, King Shutruk, the ruler of Elam. Like the rest of the world he had heard, fascinated, as conquest by conquest, Shutruk transformed Elam into a world power. Babylonia was merely the first of his son's western victories, and beyond that were the new and tempting nations of the Levant—Assyria, Israel, Canaan. Even Egypt, Semerket supposed, would some-day lie within the ambitions of so voracious a dynast.

"But you are his eldest son," Semerket reminded him. "What is there to fear?"

Kutir looked at him with a strange glint in his eye. "We have a say-ing in Elam about an unlucky man. 'If he were to pick up gold, it would turn to dirt.' Well, Babylon has turned to dirt in *my* hands, Semerket. My sister's disappearance was the start of it all—the bad luck, the turn in the war, the ongoing defeat of my armies—and now you must help me to find her, to bring her back. Perhaps then my luck will change, when my touch will once more be golden."

"Majesty—" Semerket began patiently.

But Kutir cut short his objections before he had a chance to voice them. "If you will not do this, Semerket, then the idol will remain here, forever. Never will it visit Egypt. Never will it restore your pharaoh's health." Kutir's voice became supplicating. "But where is the risk, eh? If you can find your wife in this godforsaken city, I know you'll be able to find my sister."

Again, Aneku's lie rose up before him. Everyone in Babylon, it seemed, believed that he had already rescued Naia.

"Are not our objectives well-matched, after all?" the king continued in a pleading voice: "My sister for the idol."

"Why do you think I can succeed when your own secret police have failed?"

Kutir blinked. "Because you're Semerket."

Semerket was appalled at the king's misplaced trust. Still, by accepting the task—and one, after all, that he was already pursuing—he would be free to continue his search for Naia and Rami unimpeded, with all the resources of Babylon's king at his disposal. At the end of it, too, the idol would be allowed to visit Egypt.

Semerket made his decision quickly. "Will you allow me to come and go freely in the city and countryside?"

"Have I not already?"

"Will you call off your spies?"

"Are they not gone?"

"I'll need a pass against the curfew."

"You'll have it."

"I've been told the victim's bodies are entombed here beneath the palace," Semerket said.

"Everyone except my sister, yes."

"I will need to examine their bodies."

Kutir started, a furtive look of disgust crossing his face, quickly banished. "That's impossible."

"Majesty, it's extremely important for me to examine their wounds, to see how they were killed. Just as every nation has its own way of living, its way of murder is unique as well. Seeing the bodies might help me to determine who killed them."

"But we know the Isins did it!"

"No, Majesty, we don't." He was thinking of the arrow he had found that afternoon, and how the Isins themselves had vehemently denied the crime.

"Semerket, you're an Egyptian and don't know our ways. Once the dead are placed in the crypt, we believe they're in the underworld. The doors to the crypt are literally the portals to our next life. No one may

open them until another burial, and then only after the priests have driven away the demons who guard the entrance. You can't just go in there—it simply isn't done. Nor should it be done."

When Semerket began to protest, Kutir turned away with a grimace, holding up his hand. "I've said no. It's impossible."

With little grace, Semerket inclined his head. "I will need one of your men to help me, then—someone who knows the city."

"Name him."

"Colonel Shepak."

Kutir hesitated. "Shepak? Certainly another man more capable—?"

"He is a good man, and loyal to your majesty."

Kutir nodded, though doubtfully. "I'll relieve him of his current duties immediately, if that's what you truly want."

Semerket exhaled. Though he had not yet saved Shepak entirely, at least he had extended his life past the Day of the False King. Now that they had reached an understanding, Kutir's face no longer seemed so pinched and frightened. But at a sudden sharp shriek from the peacock above them, Kutir leapt to his feet.

"I'll have that bird's neck wrung," the king grumbled, breathing hard. He gazed up resentfully into the branches.

There was only one thing more Semerket needed to say. "Sire, you must know I am doing this only for Pharaoh. At the end of it, if I'm successful, I expect not only your own consent for the idol to leave Babylon, but the priests' as well."

Kutir nodded confidently. "They will give it."

"But willingly? I cannot chance the use of black magic against Egypt."

Kutir remained confident. "I guarantee it. For if they don't agree, another priceless relic of Babylon's past will never be returned to the city."

"What relic?"

"King Hammurabi's stone, inscribed with all the laws of Babylonia. Five hundred years old, and almost as venerated as Bel-Marduk's idol. It's in Susa now—a gift to my father after I took the city. I will offer the priests an exchange—let the idol visit Egypt for a year and the stone will be returned to Babylon."

Semerket thought that he would have liked to see such a stone, to understand how laws were composed. In Egypt, laws were traditions handed down over many generations and had no need to be written.

"And the magi will agree?" he asked.

"As it says on the stone, Semerket, 'An eye for an eye, a tooth for a tooth.'"

"And a statue for a stone . . . ?"

"Precisely."

AS SEMERKET LEFT the palace, intending to tell Shepak of his reversal of fortune, a waiting woman intercepted him. "My lord... ?" she asked, laying a hand upon his arm. The woman was clad in the same high-necked raiment that Queen Narunte wore, livid with fringes and garish embroidery. "The queen desires a word with you, my lord."

Semerket regarded her without enthusiasm. After the hostile reception the queen had shown him in the gardens above, he could see no purpose for such a conference. But he could hardly decline, and said that he would be pleased to meet with the lady.

The woman led him outside through a series of courtyards. They entered a low building, which Semerket ascertained was Kutir's harem, for he saw that eunuchs guarded every door. But there were no women about, and Semerket ruefully surmised that they were locked away into their rooms, fearful that his lustful male gaze might somehow befoul them.

In a far hall of thin alabaster columns, Narunte reclined on a divan, the inevitable cup of beer clutched in her hand. Semerket was surprised to see that Ambassador Menef sat at her side, and that the Asp, his bodyguard, leaned against a pillar at the chamber's rear. Menef instantly stood when he approached, and offered his chair to Semerket.

"Well," said the queen in a voice that was as harsh as two millstones scraping together. "Did my husband ask you to find his sister?" She raised the cup to her lips, drinking the beer straight and unfiltered, not bothering to sip it through a reed. Semerket realized she was drunk.

"I promised his majesty that I would, yes."

The queen let out a whoop of shrill laughter, and nodded her head to Menef. "Didn't I tell you?" After a moment, her silver demon's eyes found Semerket's again.

"Ever since my husband heard you were coming, it's been 'Semerket will find her, Semerket will save us.' I had to see for myself if you were an actual man of flesh and blood, and not some god." She looked on him as if assessing the flesh of a slave. "Now that I see you close to, you don't look either to me."

Semerket heard Menef's bodyguard making choking sounds in the back of the room, and Semerket looked over to see that his shoulders were shaking. An amused smile also played on the ambassador's lips.

When Semerket continued silent, Narunte made a peremptory gesture to her waiting handmaidens to bring some silver ewers forward. "Beer," she said, "wine?"

"No, ma'am."

"You don't drink either, I suppose."

"On the contrary, I drink too much. Wine has become a poison to me."

The queen screwed up her sharp features, as if trying to retrieve some fading piece of information in her blurred memory. "Yes . . . yes . . . I remember. You drank because your wife divorced you. Yet you rescued her, all the same; loyal to the end. It's almost like a folk song, isn't it?"

The image of the woman Aneku entered the room to hover between them, and still Semerket did not correct the queen. "Your majesty is well informed," he said obliquely.

Lost to the fumes of her potent brew, Narunte turned her silver eyes to the distant shadows. "How Pinikir hated me," Narunte said, "with her narrow head and her pale, delicate skin. I was never good enough for her brother, she said—because I was crude, and couldn't read, and preferred beer to her fine vintages."

The queen's lip curled and Semerket saw her sharp white teeth beneath her twisted smile. "How she hated me. Pinikir did all she could to push me aside—throwing her maids into my husband's path, trying to tempt him from my bed."

The harshness of her wild laughter scarred the room, reminding Semerket of the shrieks of the peacocks in the rooftop gardens.

"But he spurned his other wives, those highborn ones who looked just like her, because I told him the truth about his family—about her. And she hated *me* because he listened." Her face contorted itself into a mask of utter loathing. "I know the real reason his father sent them here from Susa—don't think I don't!—her and that weak husband of hers!"

"Your Majesty!" Menef sharply interrupted her.

Narunte, startled, looked up fuzzily into his face. The ambassador had successfully torn her from her reveries, damming her spate of ugly words. It took her a moment to recognize him, and when she did, she smiled—a stiff, automatic smile taught her by some expert in court protocol.

Gently, the ambassador took her by the arm. "Come, ma'am. You'll make yourself ill with such memories. I'm sure that after the tragedy at the plantation, everyone desires only the safe return of Princess Pinikir. Our Lord Semerket here will do his best to bring her back—you'll see."

Menef took her hand in his, urging her from the couch, and handed her over to her waiting women. She tripped suddenly, lurching forward, and her maids leapt to catch her. The queen's alabaster cup smashed on the floor. She turned her pale eyes on Semerket a final time.

"I didn't weep overmuch when the plantation was sacked, you know. I only weep to think she might still be alive—like that wife of yours."

After her maids escorted the queen to her bedchamber, Semerket, Menef, and the Asp stood awkwardly regarding one another. Menef put a finger to his lips, and gestured that they should withdraw into the outer courtyard, where the three conferred in whispers beneath a flickering torch.

"I'm sorry you had to hear that," Menef said in his high-pitched, oleaginous voice.

"On the contrary, I only wish I could have heard more," Semerket said. "But you saw to it that I couldn't. And I find this strange in someone who's usually so eager to spread knowledge throughout the world."

Menef was uncertain what Semerket meant. "My lord . . . ?"

Semerket fixed him with a level gaze. "Everywhere I go in Babylon, from Bel-Marduk's temple to the palace itself, I find that Pharaoh's private wishes are known by everyone—told to them by you."

The chubby little ambassador was unprepared for this direct assault. Nevertheless, he inclined his head, instantly comprehending the crux of the matter. "My Lord Semerket is new to Babylon, and unfamiliar with the political realities here. Much has changed since the Elamites invaded," he said. "If I erred by informing certain high personages of Pharaoh's request for the idol, it was merely to facilitate your enterprise. If I may instruct you on the situation . . . ?"

The black fires in Semerket's eyes instantly ignited. "You may not. But *I* will instruct *you*, Lord Ambassador."

Menef raised his head abruptly, unused to being addressed as an underling.

"Your first and only care is the protection of Egypt's interest and Pharaoh's good name—"

"As it ever has been, great lord," Menef murmured. "I'm surprised you'd think I'd do otherwise."

"Yet because of you, the subject of Pharaoh's health is probably being discussed at this very moment in courts from Keftiu to India."

Droplets of sweat began to appear on Menef's upper lip. "Surely, my lord, it's naive to think such knowledge can be kept a secret for long."

"Yes. Particularly when indiscreet ministers such as you serve Pharaoh."

Semerket thought he saw a flash of alarm in Menef's slippery expression, while the Asp's hand moved to clutch the hilt of his sword.

Ignoring the glowering bodyguard, Semerket continued his harangue. "I'll say it frankly, Menef: whether or not I report this treachery of yours to Pharaoh will depend on the level of cooperation I get from you from now on."

Menef hunched his shoulders, reminding Semerket of a tortoise seeking protection from a lion's fangs. "What will it take to convince you of my loyalty, Great Lord?" he asked meekly.

"Decide first whom you serve, Pharaoh or the Elamites."

Menef came close to groveling. "My lord, I do indeed apologize if I offended, but what was I to do? The king himself asked me to look after

Queen Narunte. You can see how she is when she's . . ." He gestured, not wanting to say the obvious word.

Semerket supplied it for him. "When she's drunk?"

Menef winced delicately, and looked around into the shadows of the courtyard before he nodded. "My lord," he said. "There are many things to say, and this is perhaps not the best place in which to say them."

"I have only one thing more that I *will* say, Menef." Semerket's voice was colder than the breezes in any winter night. "And that's to tell you that I'll never forgive you for sending my wife to that plantation. Never."

Semerket noted the quick glance Menef and the Asp exchanged. "Again, my lord, what was I to do? The prince and princess were newly arrived. They needed servants. The queen asked me to send a few of mine to them—"

"The queen?" Semerket was doubtful. "She didn't sound as if she'd lift a finger to help her sister-in-law."

"It was the king, then, who asked me. Who can say? It was many weeks ago, and hard to recall." A crafty look crept across the ambassador's face upon those words. "But surely, now that your wife has been recovered, aren't we really arguing over nothing?"

Damn Aneku and her lies! Still wishing to protect the former Ishtaritu, however, Semerket held his tongue.

Sensing Semerket's indecision, Menef became all unctuousness. "I feel we've started badly here, my lord, first outside the embassy— where you really should have made yourself known to me—and now tonight at the palace. If you will permit me, I'll make it up to you. Would you please be my guest tonight at an entertainment?"

"I'm hardly inclined—"

"But it's a most extraordinary entertainment, the singer Nidaba. Perhaps you've heard of her?"

"Nidaba?" Semerket pricked up his ears.

"Yes, my lord, an extraordinary woman, a most accomplished singer. They say hers is the greatest voice in the world. Will you come? Will you allow me to demonstrate my hospitality to my most honored guest?"

Semerket hesitated. He had wanted to explore this singer's house since Senmut and Wia had mentioned it to him earlier. "Yes," he said abruptly. "I'll come."

"And, of course, you must share my chair." Menef smiled toothily.

Semerket instantly remembered the ostentatious equipage in which the ambassador traveled, with its forty liveried bearers. He shuddered.

"If I must," he said.

NIDABA'S HOUSE WAS NEAR the old quarter, at the ancient center of Babylon. Her concierge, a Syrian clad in the florid garments of his race, flung open the gates and hurried over to the grotesque carry chair and its forty bearers. He and Menef fell into each other's arms. When they had unclasped, the Syrian's gaze shifted almost imperceptibly to Semerket. "My. Isn't the map of the Nile all over *your* face."

Menef made the introductions.

"'Special envoy from the Pharaoh'?" murmured the man, reaching out to finger Semerket's falcon badge. "Wait until she feasts her eyes on this." He scanned the courtyard for available seats. "Well, we'd better hide you far away, hadn't we? Otherwise this little trinket will surely be in her treasure box before morning."

The concierge, generously tipped by Menef, led them to a grouping of couches at the edge of the courtyard. The Asp melted discreetly away, to watch over them from the shadows. Just as Semerket and Menef became comfortable, a thin, cringing fellow wrapped in an enormous robe crept furtively to their divan.

"Pardon me, good lords," he said, opening his robe slightly. Stuffed into its interior pockets were a variety of clay tablets and rolled papyri. "Would the gentlemen be interested in a letter of transit to Nineveh, perhaps, signed by the vizier himself?"

"Do I look like a fugitive to you?" asked Menef irritably.

"Joppa, then? Ilium?"

"Go away, you rogue."

"Perhaps you have one to sell? I pay good gold for them." He jingled his leather purse significantly.

The sudden appearance of the Asp cut short the man's wheedling. One glance at the Asp's bared yellow teeth was all it took to send the man fleeing across the courtyard. Semerket noticed that many such peddlers filled the rooms. He remembered old Wia's saying to him that at Nidaba's house one could buy the kinds of things not sold in the regular marketplace.

Semerket turned abruptly to Menef. "I wonder how Nidaba can flourish like this. Is she perhaps a member of this gagu I've heard so much about?"

Menef turned an incredulous eye on him. "Let's just say she's not the sort of woman the gagu would admit and leave it at that."

But Semerket could never leave anything "at that" and opened his mouth to demand the reason. Just then, however, a voice pealed richly from the upstairs gallery. "Hello, my darlings!"

Nidaba stood behind the balustrade, her arms flung wide in greeting. The men abandoned their gambling games in the back rooms to come running into the courtyard. Those who sat in divans rose to their feet, cheering loudly, intoning her name as though she were a goddess.

Nidaba descended the stairway one step at a time, spying her favorites among the crowd, calling out warmly to them. "How are you, sweetheart? Oh, marvelous! . . . There you are, my spirit, safe home at last! I was fantastically worried!" Her speaking voice was indeed lovely, Semerket admitted, a low, simmering tenor. As Nidaba paused on the final step, one of her waiting women gave her the leash fastened to a pet cheetah. Nidaba was now ready to circulate.

Semerket sat back down on the divan, allowing a serving maid to refill his bowl of beer. He amused himself by looking about the villa, staring into the distant rooms. He watched as documents were produced and examined, as gold and silver exchanged hands, as kisses were traded to seal pacts.

Semerket turned to gaze again into the courtyard, only to realize that he now stared directly into the face of the cheetah. With a strangled cry, Semerket leapt back against the cushions. The big cat took a few uncertain steps backward, straining to hide behind the skirts of her mistress.

Collecting himself, Semerket raised his head to stare into the eyes of Nidaba.

"Don't be afraid of Inanna," she said in her low, sultry voice. "She's really quite docile."

"I . . . I was taken by surprise," Semerket stammered, rising to his feet.

He noted that Nidaba was far from the voluptuous odalisque she appeared from afar, being in fact rather reedy. She was very tall for a woman, and her robes of rare silk picked out her angular form. Semerket noticed that she had painted her face to create a countenance that might not even have existed in real life, a masterpiece of subtle shadings of ocher and cochineal, highlighted by powdered fish scales.

"Such black eyes," Nidaba crooned, staring at him. "I've never seen blacker. Do they match your heart?"

It was the kind of question deserving the kind of witty riposte he had always been incapable of producing quickly. "I—I don't know," Semerket stammered out.

As her concierge had done, she reached out to fondle the falcon badge that hung from his neck. Nidaba's eyes became full of acquisitive greed. "You've no idea what I would do to possess that," she said, her voice full of sordid insinuation. "You'll give it to me as a gift, no? To seal our friendship?"

"No."

Nidaba laughed regretfully. She let the badge go, and it fell heavily to his chest. To his intense relief, she began to turn away. She paused, however, and spoke to him from over a bare shoulder. "You are still welcome in my house, Semerket, though you have been very cruel to me. But I have heard others speak well of you, and I am of a forgiving nature."

Raised voices suddenly intruded from the gardens, preventing Semerket from asking who had spoken well of him. The concierge broke through the horde of men surrounding Nidaba to whisper urgently into her ear. The word "Elamites!" was murmured and Nidaba threw a warning glance around the courtyard.

The Dark Heads in the back rooms and courtyard instantly faded away, some even slipping over the walls into the streets behind the villa. Such behavior confirmed what Semerket had suspected, that Nidaba's house was a hub of Dark Head resistance.

A group of drunken Elamite officers suddenly burst into the courtyard, laughing loudly. Nidaba strode leisurely toward them, smiling seductively, the cheetah's leash in hand. Semerket noticed with satisfaction how a couple of the Elamite officers hung back as the cat approached.

"Captain Khutran!" Nidaba trilled to their leader, dressed in glittering armor of overlapping metal discs. "This is a surprise."

"Not an unpleasant one, I hope!" he brayed. Khutran clung to the shoulders of his companions, so drunk he could barely stand.

"You seem very pleased with yourselves tonight," Nidaba purred to the officers. "Have you something to celebrate, then?"

One of the captains spoke up, "Khutran here has been promoted— and by the king himself, no less! He's now colonel of the garrison forces!"

Semerket grunted to himself, satisfied. Already Kutir had replaced Shepak. He wondered if his friend had been told the reason for his reassignment, and hoped that Shepak realized that it brought with it the promise of survival.

"So we thought," Khutran shouted, "screw any Isin attack! Screw the Babylonians! Let's go over to Nidaba's and hear some love songs tonight, for we're all in a lusty mood!" He reached to pull Nidaba toward him, but she sidestepped his drunken lunge. A warning rattle issued from deep inside the cheetah's throat.

"I've another song in mind," answered Nidaba, "to mark the occasion of my lord Khutran's promotion."

The concierge appeared to escort the Elamites to their seats. With their armor rattling loudly, the soldiers finally sat. A hush fell over the crowd, and servants went about the villa extinguishing the lamps, giving many who hid in the back rooms another chance to escape. Only the dais at the center of the courtyard remained lit by lanterns, shining down on a hassock upholstered in rich purple.

A palpable excitement charged the crowd when a serving woman brought Nidaba a lyre. As the crowd quieted, Nidaba tuned the strings of her instrument, taking her seat. Then Nidaba plucked a fierce, loud note, and her voice rang out in the night air—a thing of such vitality and power that Semerket was hard-pressed to believe it came from a human.

> *Mistress of Holy Ur am I—*
> *This is my House!*
> *Where good food is not eaten anymore*
> *Where good drink is not drunk anymore . . .*

Semerket heard Menef gasp. "What audacity—she sings 'The Lament'!"

Semerket had no idea what the ambassador meant, but as he listened it became clear how daring Nidaba's choice of song was, particularly because she sang her defiance of Elam's rule directly to Elamite officers.

> *My house,*
> > *Where good chairs are not sat in*
> *My house,*
> > *Where good beds are not lain in*
> *My house,*
> > *In which I, its mistress, dwell no more . . .*

Nidaba's voice throbbed with grief.

> *Let me go into my house, let me go in,*
> > *Let me lie down!*
> *Its sleep was sweet,*
> *Its beds were soft,*
> *Its walls were strong,*
> *Let me go into my house!*

Beside him, in other chairs and divans, Semerket heard the muffled sobs of the listeners, and glanced in the direction of the Elamites to gauge their reaction. They, too, began to screw up their faces and dab at their eyes. Soon they were bawling as loudly as the other guests. The impact of Nidaba's incredible voice was such that even Semerket felt his eyes begin to overfill.

After the recitation of many stanzas Nidaba finished, her voice rising in even more full-throated misery, scarring the night with its melancholy:

> *Alas my city! Alas my house!*
> *Bitter are the wails of Ur*
> *She has been ravaged*
> *Her people scattered.*

Nidaba stilled the strings with her hand, and her voice died away with them. She dropped her head as if she had no more strength to lift it. Then she rose quietly and left the dais, to disappear into a back room.

No one moved for a few moments. Servants again relit the lamps, and wine was brought. The guests stood gazing embarrassedly at one another, overcome by emotion. Then, gradually, they broke apart into groups. He could hear Menef's gurgling voice: "Can you believe it? 'The Lament!' Do you think they suspected?"

Semerket took the opportunity to slip away from the courtyard and into the gardens. Sounds of the night floated to him; crickets chirped, an owl hooted in a tall palm, while a vole ducked for cover in the ivy at his feet. Then a different sound altogether came to him from the rear of the villa. A far gate opened, and with it came the low murmur of feminine voices. One of them was Nidaba's; after tonight's performance, he was sure of it.

Picking his way through the dark, careful not to stumble on the vines crossing his path, he followed the voices to a rear courtyard. As he came nearer, he smelled the ammoniac reek of pack animals. A small donkey train had just arrived, stripped of their bells. Their hooves, he noticed, were wrapped in thick woolen cloths, preventing them from being heard on the streets.

Women were removing the donkey's packs under Nidaba's direction—members of the gagu, he thought. In a hushed voice, Nidaba told them to take their loads into the kitchen cellar. One of them, smaller than the others, staggered under a pack's weight, and cried out softly when it dropped to the ground. Instantly, shiny chunks of black bitumen spilled out, clanging heavily across the tiles of the courtyard. The woman apologized in desperate whispers, looking nervously at Nidaba and then at a tall elderly woman who emerged from the shadows. Semerket had not seen her lurking there, and her instant appearance was almost shocking, as if she had conjured herself into being. Her dark robes were embroidered in mystic symbols, and atop her head was a tall crown of intricate workmanship that exaggerated her already impressive height.

Nidaba bent down to gather up the spilled bitumen herself, hoisting the sack almost effortlessly to her shoulders and disappearing down the cellar stairs. Emerging once more into the feeble torchlight, she led the older woman to the well, speaking with her in low tones. Semerket strained to hear. They spoke so quickly that he could comprehend only a fraction of what they said. But a single word caught his ear—his own name.

Their voices rose to a climax of fierce whispers, and then subsided. He leaned forward, hoping to hear more, but the women of the gagu took that moment to depart. In a moment, Semerket emerged from his hiding place. If she was startled to see him, Nidaba did not show it.

"You wouldn't have been spying on me, would you?" she said.

He made no answer at first. His deliberate hush seemed at last to penetrate her indifferent facade and, for a moment, Nidaba's face betrayed frenzied panic.

"Will you tell the Elamites?" she asked breathlessly.

"Tell them what? That you receive supplies of bitumen from the gagu? I'm sure they have more pressing concerns."

Nidaba's face visibly relaxed, but tensed again at his next words.

"I need to speak with the Heir of Isin," he said bluntly.

She stopped. "What makes you think I know him?"

He looked at her with irony. "Do you really think I can't guess what's going on here? That this place—and you—are part of the resistance?"

She shook her head, dropping her eyes. "You're mistaken. I cannot help you."

"I'm not mistaken. Why can't you help me? Did that woman forbid it just now?"

Her eyes flashed in the dark. "So you *were* spying on me."

"I heard her say my name, and not in a friendly way."

Nidaba made a vague gesture. "You should leave my house, Semerket. I'm sorry."

He was silent. The set of her jaw told him he would get nothing more from her. He inclined his head to her, and kissed his fingertips. "Thank you for your hospitality this evening," he said. "For all my life, I will be able to boast that I heard the great Nidaba sing in person."

Semerket found Menef in the courtyard, and informed him that he was leaving. The ambassador made a great show of regret, but, strangely, did not offer his chair, nor did he suggest that one of his men accompany Semerket back to the hostel for his protection. His bodyguard, the Asp, was nowhere to be seen. Semerket was forced to set out into the dark streets alone, and hoped that he could remember the way back to his hostel.

Using the flames atop Etemenanki's ramparts as his touchstone, he went west to the river where he expected to meet the Processional Way. From there it was a straight route back to his hostel. But again, Babylon's twisting streets and the near total darkness served to confuse him utterly. Despite the suddenly chill air, he began to perspire. Soon he had to admit the truth to himself: he was lost. Semerket forced his thumping heart to calm itself. What was the worst thing that could happen? He would have to wait in some town square until first light, and then find his way back, that was all.

Ahead of him, barely visible in the starlight, he spied a well. His thirst suddenly powerful, he groped for its bucket and tossed it down into the water. The bucket's splash was loud in the deserted square, and Semerket winced when he heard it. He pulled it up by its rope and cupped his hands to drink. As he bent over the bucket, he felt his falcon badge lightly strike its edge.

He raised his head at a distant footfall, so slight he might have imagined it. Semerket turned in the direction from which the sound came.

His heart was beating so fiercely he could hear nothing but its own frantic pulse. He probed the dark with his eyes, trying to see something, anything.

Then, black upon black, he saw them framed in the narrow street—two shapes moving stealthily toward him.

"Who is it?" he said loudly. "What do you want?"

The shapes stopped. If they had continued walking, or if they had hailed him, he would have stayed by the well. But when they froze, silent and guilty, their sinister intentions were betrayed.

Semerket threw the bucket in their path and ran. From behind, he heard one of his pursuers trip over it, coming up cursing. Semerket darted down an alley, trying not to dash himself senseless against any lurking walls or steps.

The men who followed him did not even try to hide their footsteps now. He heard them split up, one following him down the alley, the other taking off in another direction. Semerket ran full out, heedless of the dark and the snares it contained. He heard his pursuer's breath coming fast upon him. How was it that they could follow him in all this gloom? Then he realized his new linen robes must gleam like a beacon. He could not even hide in some doorway, hoping they would pass him by. His only chance was to keep running.

Twice he struck his shoulder painfully on a jutting wall, and another time sent a clay pot flying with his foot. Pain radiated up his leg from the blow, for he wore only the light kidskin sandals the high chamberlain had given him—good for an audience in the royal gardens, perhaps, but scarcely adequate for the evasion of assassins.

Semerket had no idea where he went, for his terror had by now claimed all his tenuous sense of direction. He splashed through gutters filled with stinking waste, following the streets' curves and twists with outstretched hands. He no longer heard his assassin running behind him. He canted his head to listen, to make sure that he had lost him.

Semerket turned, staggering backward, staring into the dark. With an "oomph!" he crashed into something hard and unyielding directly behind him. It was the second assassin, waiting for him. Semerket felt powerful arms encircling him, holding him fast. He tried to struggle, but the arms were like manacles.

"I've got him!" his captor shouted in strangely accented Babylonian.

"Cut his throat and be done with it! Hurry!" came the distant cry.

Semerket pulled at the iron arm that clamped him, and he felt his captor's other hand fumble for the knife in his belt. Then he saw a flash in the dark as a blade of shiny bronze came toward his neck.

He screamed silently to himself. In the moment before the blade tore out his throat, he uttered a wordless prayer to all the gods of Egypt. Too soon he felt the sting of its cold bronze edge bite into his neck. Hot blood spilled from the wound down his chest. But then he heard the knife scrape across the outspread wings of his falcon badge. In the struggle, the pectoral had been pushed up by the man's arm, wedged like a protective shield across his throat.

Semerket sensed the moment when the man's grip loosened, and he suddenly went limp, slipping out and under his attacker's arms. He rolled into the street, trying to get as far away from his assailant as possible. He tried to regain his footing, but his limbs were like lead. At any moment, he knew, the other assassin would be upon him to finish the work.

Sudden footsteps were indeed echoing in the dark, rushing upon him. This was the end, he thought. The other assailant reached him, and now there were two against him. Semerket braced himself to feel the terrible kiss of that freezing blade once again on his throat. He closed his eyes.

But the footsteps went past on either side of him, going in the direction of his attacker. Semerket heard the sounds of a man's labored breathing, like the wheezing of a punctured bellows. A tremendous invisible scuffle occurred. From the black came a single, aborted scream, and then a ghastly, gurgling moan.

Semerket, still lying in the street, felt the shock of impact as a body fell beside him in the dark. A rush of air enveloped him, and warm drops of something splashed upon his face. He was too dazed to register what it was, too confused. Then none-too-gentle hands were pulling him to his feet, and he was being reassured in strangely familiar voices—

"Do you see now, my lord, why you need us to watch over you? Didn't we tell you these were uncertain times in Babylon?"

．　．　．

"DOES HE BREATHE?" Semerket rasped to his Dark Head spies, pressing his hand against his neck to stop the flow from his wound.

One of the spies moved to the prone form of the assassin, laying his head on the man's chest to listen. "He lives," said the stout brother, his familiar wheeze rumbling through the desolate alley. "But barely."

"I stabbed him, lord," the thin one's voice came to him from his left. "It was a good thrust—in his back, I think."

Vaguely, Semerket saw the outline of the thinner spy as he leaned forward over the body. Semerket heard the high-pitched sigh of metal sliding through flesh followed by the gurgle of escaping air as the man removed the knife.

"What should we do with him, lord?" the thin spy asked. "Throw him in the canal?"

Semerket tried to piece together some kind of plan, but the attack had numbed his mind. "Where are we?" he asked. "What part of the city?"

"Just up the road from the Egyptian Quarter, my lord. Near its main square."

That was a bit of luck. They could go to Kem-weset's house, where the physician would be able to tend them both. Semerket directed the Dark Heads to get the man to his feet.

"He's going fast, lord," wheezed the fat spy doubtfully. "I don't think he'll make it."

"Kem-weset will know what to do."

It was some time later when they found the house where Kem-weset lived. It took all of Semerket's strength to climb the three stories to the physician's apartment. To his surprise, a young woman opened the door. Wrapped in a thin blanket, she carried an oil lamp in her hand. Her dark eyes widened in fear when she saw him, and her shrill scream filled the stairwell.

"Kemi!" she cried in Egyptian. "Kemi, come quickly!"

In the flickering lamplight, Semerket looked down and comprehended the reason for her fright: blood saturated his robe's pleated bosom. The sight made Semerket feel suddenly faint, and he had to push his way past her to grasp the back of a rickety chair, weaving uncertainly.

The physician was in the sleeping room, fastening a robe about himself. He did not seem in the least abashed about the young woman. Though Semerket had feared the old man might be bleary from drink, the moment Kem-weset saw the wound on his neck his physician's eye hardened in professional appraisal.

"I thought you meant to come to me only for headaches," he said with a slight smile. Then he spoke softly to the young woman. "Dearest, my medicine chest, please."

Casting a stricken glance at Semerket, the young woman slipped from the room. Kem-weset sat Semerket in the chair, and looked at his throat.

"My attacker," Semerket said, "he's downstairs. Punctured lung, I think."

"So you're diagnosing now?" Kem-weset took Semerket's chin in his hand and pushed his head slowly from side to side. Semerket winced, expecting pain, but there was none.

The young woman emerged from the other room, lugging a cedar box. Kem-weset unlatched the casket's top and eyed the jumble of vials and bottles. He removed a small clay jug and unplugged its stopper. The sharp scent of juniper spirits jabbed Semerket's nostrils.

"A cloth, please, my child."

The woman bent to retrieve a piece of folded linen from the chest.

"A few drops of this on it, I think," he told her, handing her the tiny jug.

The physician began to clean the wound quickly. As he worked, he made the introductions. "Sitamun," he said, "meet Semerket, a special envoy from our own dear pharaoh. And a man with enemies, I think."

Sitamun bobbed her head shyly.

"Your nurse?" Semerket murmured.

Kem-weset coughed, and explained, "I removed a few disfiguring moles from her bottom a few weeks ago. Sitamun repays me in her own way."

"Kem-weset is the finest physician in all Babylonia," the woman said reverently, gazing at the old physician.

"A bowl of wine, please, Sitamun," Kem-weset directed. As the girl poured, Kem-weset quickly wrote out a prayer on a strip of papyrus in red ink. He placed the bowl of wine on the floor in front of him, and dipped the papyrus into the bowl. As the glyphs gradually dissolved into the liquid, Kem-weset added to it a few tinctures of some foul-smelling elixir. He handed the bowl to Semerket.

"You know I don't drink wine—"

"You'll drink this."

Semerket gulped it rapidly, hoping the wine's taste would not linger on his tongue to torment him. As it reached his belly, he felt its warm, familiar glow radiating into all his limbs. It felt very pleasant... too pleasant.

"Your wound," pronounced Kem-weset, "is only a superficial puncture, nothing more."

"Superficial?" Semerket said, incensed. "The man tried to cut my throat!"

"Sorry to disappoint you, but it wasn't even made with a knife."

Semerket was incredulous. "What cut me, then?"

"This is the culprit." Kem-weset pointed to the falcon badge on Semerket's chest. "The tip of this wing, here—it somehow got wedged into your neck and probably nicked a vessel. See there, how it's bent? How the blood has caked on it?"

Semerket lifted the pectoral from around his head. He held the badge up to the oil lamp. There, scoring the gold, was the jagged gouge where the assassin's blade had scraped across the wing, futilely seeking the flesh beneath.

Semerket swallowed, inhaling raggedly. "The gods were protecting me tonight," he said.

Kem-weset fashioned a poultice of honey and herbs, and pressed it to the wound, then tied it around Semerket's neck with light gauze. The physician leaned back on his heels, satisfied. "Now to your attacker," he announced. "Outside, you said?"

"In the stairwell with—" Semerket hesitated. He had never bothered to learn the names of his two Dark Head spies. "With my friends."

During the time Kem-weset was gone, Semerket asked Sitamun for some water and a sponge. As she fetched it, Semerket removed his once-fine palace robe, peeling away its sticky, reddened layers. Sitamun brought him a jug, and he began to wash himself.

He was presentable by the time Kem-weset opened the door. The two Dark Heads staggered into the dim light half-carrying, half-dragging his attacker. At Kem-weset's command, they laid the man on the floor next to the medicine chest. The assassin's eyes were closed and the old physician felt for a pulse. Not finding one, he deliberately gouged the man's right eye with his thumb. There was no response.

"I'm afraid he's gone, Semerket," Kem-weset said simply.

Semerket muttered a foul word.

Kem-weset brought the oil lamp close to the man's face. The assassin was bearded, precluding any possibility that he might be Egyptian. In fact, he did not even seem to be Babylonian, for he was of a slender build and his long hair was braided, tied off at the ends with amber beads.

"Is he an Elamite?" asked Semerket.

"No, he's from the mountains to the northeast of Elam," said the wheezing Dark Head. "That's how they dress their hair."

On a sudden impulse, Semerket reached forward to open the assassin's eye. Its color was pale silver—like Queen Narunte's eyes. A shiver ran down his spine. Had she sent this man against him that evening to prevent the rescue of her despised sister-in-law? He immediately dismissed the thought as being too farfetched. In her drunken state, the queen would have been incapable of arranging anything, much less the assassination of a foreign dignitary so recently employed by her husband.

"But I know this man!" Kem-weset said suddenly. "I'm almost sure of it!" He handed the lamp to Sitamun, and then withdrew a lancet from his medicine chest. He cut at the man's sleeve, tearing the cloth up to the elbow. A long and vivid scar, crosshatched with stitch marks, ran down the man's forearm.

Kem-weset nodded. "That's my work there. He and six others came to me one night, all bruised and bloodied. They'd been in a tavern brawl, they said. I remember thinking at the time that their story wasn't true."

"Why?" Semerket asked.

"Because they were all stinking of soot and fire. There'd been no fire in Babylon that night and no brawl, either."

Semerket blinked. "When did this happen?" he asked the physician.

"Some weeks ago. Early winter. Just about the time you say your wife disappeared . . ." Kem-weset's voice trailed off. He shot a stricken glance at Semerket.

"Were the other men you treated from the mountains as well?" Semerket breathed.

"No, they were Dark Heads. At least, they were dressed like Dark Heads." Kem-weset's voice was uncertain.

"You doubt it?"

Kem-weset reluctantly nodded.

"Why?"

"Because they spoke an excellent Egyptian."

SOMETIME BEFORE DAWN, Semerket and his Dark Head spies took the assassin's body to a nearby canal. Semerket, clad in an old tunic borrowed from Kem-weset, watched as the two noiselessly rolled the corpse into the water.

Semerket was almost certain the man had been at the Elamite plantation the night of the raid, and he deeply regretted being unable to force a confession from him. If the man had indeed been one of the raiders, it would go a long way to bolster the Isins' claims that they had nothing to do with the crime. Then, too, this man's companions had spoken "an excellent Egyptian," as Kem-weset purported. Had they been armed with Egyptian arrows, as well? Semerket wondered.

Semerket forced down a sudden surge of rage. This man, now sinking beneath the canal's surface, might be the same one he had seen so often in his nightmares, who had stood exultant over Naia's fallen body.

"If only you could die twice . . ." he muttered to the corpse.

In the dark, he felt a slight gust of warm air from the east, the harbinger of dawn. He looked at his two companions in the silvering light, whose names he had finally learned—they were the brothers Galzu and Kuri.

"Tell me," he whispered to them, "how did you know I was in trouble tonight? Why did you show up just when I needed you?"

"That's very simple, lord," Kuri, the thin one, said almost blithely. "We knew you'd need us sooner or later, at the rate you were going, so we kept you always in sight. We hoped to prove our worthiness to you."

The explanation, glib as it was, made sense. The two Dark Heads had indeed saved his life—and one does not question too closely a gift from the gods.

"All right," Semerket said at last, though halfheartedly. "I'll continue paying you."

"A wise decision, lord," Galzu said, rubbing his fat hands together gleefully. "You will have no regrets."

Semerket eyes were flinty. "You don't know what I want you to do, yet."

Galzu spoke with supreme confidence, "Of course we do, my lord. You want us to continue what we've been doing all along. We will watch over you."

"But this, too, you must know—they've attempted to kill me once and when they find out they've failed, they'll do it again. In a way it's good news; it means I'm onto something they don't want me to know. All I have to do is figure out what it is. Next time, though, I want them alive. Understand?"

Solemnly, the two Dark Heads promised him that they would do as he wished. To ensure it, he filled their fists with pieces of Pharaoh's gold. Murmuring their joyous thanks, they left him at the canal to take up their positions in the shadows.

The scent of dung fires lightly stung Semerket's nostrils. Another day had begun in Babylon, and the indigo sky was turning crimson. Resolutely, Semerket brought his tunic up around his neck, hiding his bandage, and went down the nearby alley.

"YOU MUST STOP telling people you're my wife," he said.

Semerket was in the little courtyard of the Egyptian temple, seated beside Aneku. Hearing him, she hugged her arms around her knees and her sigh was a hollow sound of longing and wistfulness.

"Am I so hideous to you that you could not be married to me, even in pretense?"

Semerket knew if he answered that question, he would end up having to meticulously list Aneku's charms, if only to reassure her that she was not ugly or repellent—something she knew well enough on her own. Why must women always be told such things, he asked himself with rising irritation. Seeking to divert her, he gestured to the forecourt.

"I've never seen this place so clean. Wia must be grateful to have you here."

"She hates me."

"I'm sure she doesn't," Semerket said without conviction.

Aneku's mouth twisted into a wry smile, and a spark of mischief lighted her eye. "It doesn't matter. I like the way she scolds me; it reminds me of my mother. 'Just a wild girl who'll come to no good!' she used to say." Aneku's fleeting cheer deserted her, and her slanted green eyes grew bleak. "She was right about that."

"Was she?" Semerket replied carefully. "Is it your wildness that brought you here, then?"

"Are you finally asking me why I was banished from Egypt?" Aneku asked archly.

"Only if you want to tell me."

"I was banished because I dared to love someone above me."

It was not the answer that Semerket expected, and he looked at her with frank curiosity.

"He was a noble," she explained. "And I was only a serving maid in a tavern. Every night he came to see me. We fell in love. As soon as he could divorce his wife, he promised, we were going to break the jar together. I didn't know at the time that his brother-in-law was Menef."

Semerket blinked. "Menef? The ambassador?"

"Yes, Menef—who had me hauled into court on charges of adultery so that his sister's reputation remained unsullied. A few bribes later I was named an adulteress and banished from Egypt."

"But if your lover was so high up, surely he could have forbidden the trial?"

"Menef threatened him with exposure and he didn't dare."

Semerket shook his head in confusion. "Exposure of what? Adultery's not exactly an unknown sin in lordly circles."

"It was something else. I don't know what. But Menef knew about it and once my trial began, I never saw him again." She looked away, pulling a withered leaf from the fig tree beside her. "Naia knew the man, you know. He'd been a friend of her husband."

Semerket's black eyes grew wide. "Nakht was your lover's friend? *Nakht?* Well, then, I can tell you exactly what your lover was involved in, what he didn't want exposed—the conspiracy to kill Pharaoh Ramses, that's what! No wonder he feared Menef."

"No," Aneku said firmly. "You're mistaken. He wouldn't have been involved in anything like that. He was a good man."

Semerket made a dismissive gesture, heartless. "You're lucky you escaped him. Your marriage would have been cursed. Egypt was brought near to ruin because of 'good men' just like him."

Her slanted green eyes hardened into emeralds. *"Egypt?* Don't talk to me of Egypt—Egypt can sink! What did it ever do for me except destroy everything I ever wanted, and then throw me out in the bargain? I'm fed up with Egyptian hypocrisy—and you're the worst, Semerket! So fine, so upstanding, Pharaoh's 'special envoy' chasing after a dead woman—"

Her mouth was an ugly twist and her words reverberated in his head: "Dead woman, dead woman!" Semerket turned on her, hot words rising to his lips. Before he could say them, however, Wia's voice rose sharply in the courtyard.

"Aneku! Semerket!"

Both of them whirled guiltily, like a pair of squabbling adolescents. The old priestess stood in the doorway of the temple, glaring at them. She nodded to Aneku, "Senmut needs your help with the morning sacrifices, girl."

As Aneku defiantly stalked through the little courtyard to the distant altar, she shot a final hate-filled glance at Semerket. Semerket stared after her, breathing hard.

"Did you hear us?" he asked Wia, finally.

"I heard enough."

Semerket looked away sullenly. "I'm not sorry I said it."

Wia exhaled a long, sad gust of air. "Oh, Semerket, you should be. What's it to you if her lover was a scoundrel? He's long gone from her life, and the memory is all she has left of him."

He thrust out his stubborn bottom lip. "She can't live her life in a dream."

But Wia's words made him feel ashamed. The only thing that had seen him through these last couple years of his life was the memory of Naia's love. Despite all that had happened between them—his inability to father a child, her marriage to another man—he had always known that she never had stopped loving him. Poor Aneku did not even have that to comfort her.

He looked into the temple doorway where Aneku had fled. "I should go in to her, apologize."

"Let her alone, Semerket," Wia said. "You're only bound to anger one another now. Come back tomorrow, and you can patch things up." She patted him on the shoulder encouragingly. "I'll speak to her in the meantime."

Semerket nodded. Mumbling a farewell, he slipped out the temple gate. At the street corner, he turned to look back and saw Wia still standing beneath the miniature pylon. She waved when she saw him turn.

As he trudged through the streets, his guilt gave way to sudden anxious reflection. If Aneku's words were true and Menef had threatened her lover with exposure of some crime—and if the crime were indeed what Semerket suspected it was—then Menef must have known about the plot to murder the Great Ramses before it happened. This meant that he had been at least a peripheral member of the conspiracy or, at best, that he had done nothing to prevent it.

Even in the scorching air, Semerket felt his skin suddenly prickle. Were the remnants of that same conspiracy to be found here within Babylon itself? Is that why the gods had sent him to the city on the plain—to once again battle the very demons he thought he had vanquished?

And why, wherever he went, was Ambassador Menef seemingly at the source of every ill? The unbidden thought came to him—could the fey, plump ambassador actually have been responsible for the attack on Naia and Rami?

He shook his head to clear it of cobwebs, for he knew that he was at the point in his investigation where he became so burdened by disparate facts and suspicions that all and everyone seemed guilty of almost everything. It would do no good to bedevil himself with imagining more than what there was; all would be revealed within the province of time.

Picking up his pace, he did not realize that he had forgotten to warn Aneku that she should take extra care around strangers.

WHILE ON HIS WAY to his morning appointment with Shepak, Semerket caught the faint, alarming scent of fire. Far in the distance ahead, a flat wall of smoke advanced slowly down Processional Way, concealing the Royal Quarter behind it. He began to run.

At the garrison's gate, the gray shroud of smoke thinned a bit, allowing him to glimpse a flurry of activity behind it. Scores of Elamite soldiers lay dead, or moaned in agony. Others shouted hoarsely to one another, attempting to organize the survivors into fire brigades, to throw buckets of water onto the flames, now quickly consuming the once-orderly rows of tents. Most of them were already smoldering tatters, but a quick glance told him that Shepak's larger tent was among those still blazing.

In the confusion, no one challenged him as he hurried across the compound. At Shepak's tent, the smoke was so thick that he had to hold his mantle over his face to breathe. Squinting into the wreckage, he saw a bright heap of glittering armor. A bare arm stretched toward him, lying in a pool of blackening blood. A tangle of blood-soaked hair hid the man's face.

"Shepak?" he said.

He might have thoughtlessly plunged inside had he not suddenly remembered where he had seen that golden armor—at Nidaba's only the night before. It belonged to the newly appointed garrison commander, Khutran, the man who had drunkenly demanded that Nidaba sing him love songs.

Though the heat was fierce, Semerket took a few tentative steps closer and saw that a stone-tipped mace had smashed in the man's head. By now, the roof of the tent was afire, and Semerket retreated into the courtyard. Choking, eyes watering, he did not see the man who had come up behind him. With a crash, Semerket lurched into him. Semerket looked up.

"Shepak!" he coughed in surprise. "Bless the gods, you're alive. I thought it was you in there."

"Didn't you hear me shouting at you?"

Semerket could only shake his head, choking. Shepak bundled him away to a distant part of the courtyard, where Semerket could soothe his smoke-singed throat with well water. "What happened here?" Semerket managed to ask between coughs.

"The Isins struck us a short while ago," Shepak related grimly, "just after first light. Over two hundred garrison dead, and twenty horses."

"How many Isin dead?"

Shepak was unwilling to meet Semerket's eyes. "Not a one," he admitted. "They appeared out of nowhere, like desert djins. Before anyone knew it, they'd picked off the guards on the upper walls and taken their places. There wasn't even time to sound the alarm. They sent flaming arrows into the hay bales at the stables and then into the tents. Their archers picked us off like sheep in a pen. Then they broke down the gates and went straight for the officers still alive."

"You weren't here?" Semerket asked.

"No," Shepak shuddered. "I was at the palace getting my new orders. By the time I got here, it was all over. It didn't take the Isins more than a few minutes to do their worst, and then they disappeared as quickly as they'd come."

Semerket scratched his brow. "How many of them?"

"Sixty or seventy, I'm told."

"But I was on the street this morning," Semerket said, surprised.

"There wasn't any force like that to be seen—and one that size can't just disappear. They must have broken ranks, blended into the neighborhoods somehow—"

"Perhaps. But the Dark Heads are saying that the Isins are using magic to make themselves invisible—that our arrows are useless against them."

"Is that what *you* believe?"

Shepak shook his head. "I don't know."

Semerket looked over the ruined compound. He was thinking, I was warned not to come here today . . .

He gazed at Shepak's morose face. Should he tell the Elamite of the message he'd received from the man at the Sick Square? No—the admonition had been meant for him alone. In a city where assassins had tried to kill him once, where he owed allegiance to only those who furthered his quest, it would be unwise to displease any who might be watching out for him.

Semerket took another drink and turned to Shepak. "Let's leave all this death and stink. You're free of this place now. Come, we've a princess and my wife to find."

"But I can't just leave! What about my men? I'm needed here." Shepak looked around at the garrison yard, where bodies lay amid the smoke and ruin.

"They're not your men any longer; you've been assigned to me. And look at it this way: the best thing you can do for them is to find the princess, before Kutir in his wrath hurls these survivors into the Insect Chamber."

Shepak saw the sense in Semerket's words, and nodded, though reluctantly. "Where are we going, then?"

"To find out what those living near the plantation have to say about that night."

Shepak's lip curled into a sneer. "Those peasants? But we've already questioned them. It was like speaking to cattle."

Semerket fixed him with a skeptical eye. "When you investigated them, did you by any chance wear your uniform and that helmet?"

"I was on official business, wasn't I?"

Semerket was silent.

"What?" demanded Shepak.

"Nothing. It's just I'm reminded of a Nubian saying my friend Qar is fond of quoting. 'When the Great Lord passes, a wise peasant bows and farts silently.'"

Semerket pretended not to see the color rising in Shepak's neck. Instead, he told him to shed his armor and change into civilian clothes. The last thing he needed was the intimidating presence of an Elamite soldier at his side when he questioned the villagers.

"But you might want to keep that sword of yours handy," Semerket added, bringing his hand to the bandage at his throat.

THEY WENT TO three villages before they learned anything. At the first two, when Semerket mentioned that they sought an Elamite princess, the villagers feigned a sudden inability to comprehend him, shrinking back into their smoky mushroom-shaped huts. Their behavior confirmed Shepak's previous observation that the peasants' sensibilities were bovine at best.

But when they reached the third village, Semerket tried a different tack. He made no mention of the Elamite princess, saying only that he was an Egyptian in search of his wife and young friend, whom he believed to have been victims of the plantation massacre. These villagers, moved that he had come so far to seek his loved ones, allowed Semerket and Shepak to pass into their town.

They brought the two men to a low doorway in a round brick building. Semerket and Shepak had to crawl into its gloomy interior. As his eyes adjusted to the dark, Semerket saw that many of the villagers already awaited them. A woman took an ember from a brazier and lighted a lantern, throwing the interior of the building into sudden relief.

Surprised by the room's large size, Semerket saw that its walls were thick with the oily grime from generations of bitumen lamps. Looking up into the high conical reed roof above him, he heard the soft rustlings of rats and birds.

With gestures, a woman indicated that he and Shepak were to recline on the flyblown cushions she brought them. When they were comfortable, an old, toothless man came forward into the center of the room, taking up his position under the lantern's soft light.

"Is this the mayor, then?" Semerket asked eagerly.

Before anyone spoke, however, the old man began to chant. "She came to us that night," he sang loudly. "Rings of lapis were on her fingers, and precious beads hung from her neck. A band of gold encircled . . ."

As the old man droned on, Semerket grew uneasy. He feared that the villagers' hospitality might include long-winded poetry recitations before the matter at hand could be discussed. Loudly, he cleared his throat, interrupting the old man.

"I'm sorry," he said as earnestly as possible, "but we've no time for entertainment, superb as it is. We've come to ask you about the raid."

The old man glanced at Semerket with something like irritation, and his tongue darted around his rubbery lips. "Yes! Yes!" he snapped. "I know that!"

Once again, he started to sing, and he made his voice a trifle louder. "She came to us that night! Rings of lapis were on her fingers, and precious beads hung from her neck. A band of gold encircled her brow. She came to this very house, with the scent of death clinging to her, an immortal spirit who dwelt in the river. She came to us that night, to this very house, and sought our help. Desert demons had risen to beset her, she said; out of the night they had risen—"

"What is this?" This time it was Shepak who spoke. "D'you mean that some woman survived the raid and came *here?*"

This time the villagers groaned audibly at the interruption. Semerket could hear them whispering their disapproval to one another.

"Quiet," Semerket murmured to Shepak. "When you stop him, he has to start all over again from the beginning."

"But what's it *mean?*"

"She came to us that night!" The old man glared at Shepak, defying him to speak again. Shepak fell abruptly silent.

As Semerket listened, he soon realized that not only had these villagers known about the raid, they had also begun to commemorate it in the florid and repetitious imagery of song. But disturbing, nonsensical elements were also couched within their recitation. Semerket closely observed the rapt faces of the villagers as they listened to the old man; not one of them scoffed or looked askance as the song became even more fanciful. They appeared, truly, to believe a super-natural being had touched them that night, one who had come to them from the river.

"And though she spoke only the language of spirits and not the tongue of human folk," the old man at last came to the end of his song, "we understood her and gave her shelter."

The old man fell silent. There was a great exhalation of the villagers' collective breath, and then much hooting and applause for the old man's recitation. Semerket waited until the room quieted before he spoke.

"What you've told us—all this truly happened that night? Just as the old gentleman sang it?"

A chorus of voices rang out, each swearing on their children that the story was true and verifiable.

"And the woman who came to you," he asked, "—how do you know she was a river spirit?"

The villagers broke into loud exclamations. "Why, she was soaking wet, as if she'd just leapt from the river itself!" "Beautiful, too, like a goddess!" "Clad in silks, in jewels!" "What else could she have been, but a river nymph?"

Semerket looked over at Shepak, perplexed.

In response, Shepak shot Semerket an impatient, disgusted glance, clearly implying that they were wasting their time by interviewing such backward people. But Semerket stubbornly continued to believe that from their poetry real information could be gleaned.

"How long after the raid did she come to you?"

Several of them loudly counted out the hours it had taken for this strange woman to appear. They finally agreed that she had appeared some six or seven measures of the water clock from the time the desert demons had attacked the plantation, or just before dawn.

"Was there a boy named Rami with her? He would have had a head wound—"

Vigorously, they denied that a boy traveled with the goddess.

Shepak, who had been silent until now, leaned forward to ask sud-denly, "These desert demons who attacked her—did any of you actu-ally see them?"

The villagers shook their heads. They had been warned not to venture outdoors that night, they said.

"Warned?" Semerket raised his head sharply. *"Who* warned you?"

The rustics stared at one another, as if gauging how much they should tell him. The mayor's wife at last broke the strained silence. "Mother Mylitta came to our village that evening. She told us that she was going to the plantation to warn the Elamites, that we must hide—"

"She said that blood was in the sky!" The mayor excitedly interrupted his wife. "She told us that it'd be too dangerous to come out. Stay inside, she said. Blood in the sky, she said!"

"Who is this Mother Mylitta?" mused Semerket, looking around the room. "Another goddess from the river?"

Surprisingly, it was Shepak who answered him. "Mylitta's as human as you or I, Semerket; she's the head woman of Babylon's gagu."

Semerket's eyes widened in surprise. "The gagu?"

Once again, the mysterious women of that strange convent had surfaced in the deepening mystery surrounding Naia's disappearance. From the first day he had come to the city, these women had hovered at the fringes of his investigation. He had seen them at the river's edge, when he and Marduk had first arrived at the city, then again at Nidaba's house only the night before. Now they appeared to have some connection to the raid itself—though perhaps a benign one, if this Mother Mylitta woman had been truly bent on warning the Elamites. But the inevitable question had to be asked: how did Mother Mylitta know that such a raid was coming?

Semerket turned again to address the room full of villagers. "How long did this woman—this 'river spirit'—stay with you?"

"A single day. At the end of it, she indicated that we must take her to Mother Mylitta. So we hid her in a cart full of straw and drove her into Babylon, past the Elamite guards."

Semerket's heart began rapidly beating with excitement; the woman, whoever she was, mortal or goddess, was at the gagu! Without appearing eager to leave, Semerket nodded his thanks and edged toward the low doorway. Shepak followed, and together they walked to the canal where their horses were tethered.

"What do you make of it all?" asked Shepak.

"They told us the truth," Semerket said simply.

Shepak was disdainful. "So you believe that a nymph appeared to them from out of the river that night? That desert demons attacked her?" When Semerket nodded, he snorted contemptuously. "You Egyptians are so credulous!"

Semerket looked at him sideways. "If you can believe that entire armies of Isins vanish into thin air, why can't I believe in river nymphs?" Semerket came around to stand in front of him. "Don't you see? In their own way, they told us how the princess survived—and that she can be found at the gagu."

"Has the river fever seized you again?"

"What was the first thing the peasants sang about? It was how richly the woman dressed—the rings on her fingers, her necklaces. And what did she wear on her head?"

"A golden band," Shepak sneered. "So?"

"Doesn't that suggest a royal diadem to you?"

Self-doubt began to soften Shepak's features.

Semerket pressed on. "To these people, a royal woman stumbling out of the dark, alone—mightn't she seem like a goddess or spirit to them?"

"But this woman was dripping wet, they said. How do you explain that?"

Semerket shrugged. "Perhaps she hid in a canal or the river." He smiled suddenly. "But that's it! That's how she got away from them!"

"You truly believe it was Pinikir? Perhaps it was your own wife."

Semerket sighed, momentarily dispirited, staring at the ground. "No. Naia was only a servant. She wouldn't have been clothed in jewels and silks." He looked up again. "It *has* to be the princess. Look at what their song told us. The demons are obviously the raiders. The woman who came to them spoke only the language of spirits. I'll wager that Pinikir couldn't speak Babylonian, and babbled away in Elamite to them. And if I'm right, she's hiding at the gagu right now."

"But—" Shepak almost shouted his frustration. "Why would she be in hiding? It makes no sense."

Semerket continued blithely. "Perhaps there was a conspiracy and Pinikir caught wind of it. It's obvious this Mother Mylitta knew something, else why would she have rushed to the plantation that night?"

"But surely Pinikir would tell Kutir that she was at the gagu—he's her brother!"

Semerket looked soberly at his friend. "Not if she suspects her brother was behind the attack," he said quietly. "After all, I know that Queen Narunte hated her."

Shepak gave a great start. Before he could speak, however, a woman's voice hissed at them from behind.

"Egyptian!"

They turned, looking back into the village. The wife of the mayor beckoned to him, the red sun of evening flickering in eyes as black as his own.

"The boy you seek . . . ?" she began.

"What about him?" Semerket's voice was suddenly very forceful, and the woman shrank from him, intimidated. When she did not speak, he said again insistently, *"What* about him?"

She swallowed her fear. "That night of the attack, a caravan was at the oasis—"

"What oasis? Where?"

Shepak answered. "One a few leagues north of here, along the river; I know of it."

They both turned again to the woman. She pulled nervously at the strands of hair that escaped her headscarf. "Some of the caravan merchants went to the plantation, after the demons had fled. They saw what had been done."

"How do you know this?"

"The merchants trade with us sometimes, when they come through here. Women talk, you know?"

Semerket nodded.

"All the people were dead, they said. Tied together, slaughtered all at once."

Semerket remembered the bloodstained courtyard in the rear of the plantation. He nodded, urging her to continue with her story, for that detail confirmed to him that she spoke the truth.

"But as they looked around, one of the dead moaned. He was alive—this one you seek, the Egyptian boy! He called to them from beneath the bodies."

"Go on."

"The merchants bound his wounds and took him to their camp."

"What happened to him? Where is he now?"

The woman shrugged elaborately, palms outward.

Semerket took out a gold ring from his belt and gave it to the woman. She gasped in delight, taking his hands and kissing them. Then, looking slyly about to see if any of the villagers had seen the exchange, she quickly slipped the gold into the folds of her headscarf, running back to her own little round hut and slipping inside.

Semerket and Shepak decided to separate. "You go to the oasis," Semerket told his friend, "since you know where it is. Question anyone there. Find out what happened to Rami, if he's still alive, where he might be. But remember, you're not an Elamite commander any longer. If you frighten them, they won't tell you anything."

At the junction of the north–south road, the two men parted with the promise that they would meet later at the Bel-Marduk hostel. Semerket turned his mount to the south, riding quickly back to Babylon. He was in time to see the movement of many Elamite troops converging on the city. They were the last of the armies withdrawing from the northern part of the country. Though they stopped him, suspicious of any galloping horseman, they recognized his pass from Kutir and let him ride on.

WHEN HE RETURNED his horse, the stableman told him where the gagu was located—in the Etemenanki complex.

"But you won't be able to go there tonight, if that's what you're planning," he said.

Semerket raised his eyebrows. "But I've a pass."

The man looked at him as if he'd gone mad. "You don't know what's been going on in Babylon today, do you?"

Semerket admitted that he did not.

The stableman told him that the Elamites—might they all be flung into the Eternal Pit!—had swiftly revenged themselves on the city in retaliation for the Isins' dawn raid. Suspecting that the Babylonian citizenry hid the raiders in their homes, the Elamites initiated a door-to-door search. But no Isin had turned up, clad in mufti or otherwise. Many Babylonian citizens had been slaughtered in the process.

"But this hasn't been enough for those damned murderers," lamented the stableman. "They've even shut down the city's granaries. Go out into city, anywhere, and you'll hear the wails of our hungry children. The gods alone know how my wife is coping, or even if she's alive!"

Semerket wondered if he should even attempt going out onto the streets that night. But his need to know if Princess Pinikir was at the gagu was too compelling to ignore, and he set out alone on the avenues. Only by sheer luck did he manage to avoid every Elamite patrol.

The gagu, he discovered, was a large structure to the rear of the Etemenanki complex, hidden behind its own wall and moat. A tall cylindrical tower of mud bricks rose from its confines, around which a winding staircase snaked. He had often seen the structure from afar during his peregrinations throughout the city, but never knew what it was. Idly, he wondered what purpose the tower served.

The gagu's gate was closed tightly, and its bridge was winched up over the moat so that no one could enter. Behind the walls, however, Semerket saw the flare of torches and heard the murmurs of many feminine voices. As he drew near, the sulfurous scent of burning bitumen grew suddenly strong. Above the gagu's walls he saw thick roiling clouds of smoke spewing into the night sky from some hidden smelter. Semerket, who had seen no such clouds billowing forth during the day, was immediately suspicious. What were these women doing with the bitumen that could not bear examination by daylight?

Semerket walked to the edge of the moat. "Hello!" he yelled out loudly into the dark. When there was no answer, he yelled again. "My name is Semerket, from Egypt. I want to speak to Mother Mylitta! Tell her!"

A harsh though distinctly feminine voice answered. "Go away, Egyptian! Mother Mylitta decides to whom she speaks, not the other way round!"

He stood defiantly, hands on hips. "Tell her that it concerns the Princess Pinikir. Tell her I know she was at the plantation that night— and that if she won't see me, I'll go to Kutir."

The women's helmeted heads disappeared from the watchtower. Semerket assumed that they went to inform Mother Mylitta that he was at their gate. Placidly, he sat down before the moat, cross-legged, to wait her reply.

Mother Mylitta's response was not long in coming. With a great scraping of chains, the women lowered their bridge and Semerket crossed into the gagu's courtyard. As he blinked in the bright torch-light, the gate was quickly shut behind him and the bridge rose again over the moat, locking him inside. He scrutinized the shadows for any available exits, but there were none; he saw only that several donkeys were hitched together, bearing their usual loads of black bitumen. As he waited for an escort, he went over to one of the asses to take a closer look at the bitumen.

As if idly, he pulled out a gleaming black chunk from a donkey's sack, tossing it into the air. It was surprisingly weighty for its small size, and oddly shaped—so rectangular it seemed almost fabricated. As the torchlight hit it, he saw a sudden telltale glint of metal. Semerket caught the piece in his hand again, paling, and turned to face the guards.

Two spears were at his chest, their points almost touching his flesh.

"Put it back," one of the female guards said evenly.

Carefully, Semerket returned the bitumen into the sack.

"Step away from the donkey," she ordered.

"I'm sorry if I offended," he said, affecting an expression of mortifi-cation. But he was not in the least sorry he had done it, for as the bitu-men had flown into the torchlight he had discovered—finally—what the gagu was doing with the mineral.

The two guards led him to the cylindrical tower of mud bricks he had seen from afar, and halted. The tower was very wide at its base—almost thirty cubits, he gauged—and as he looked up, he saw that it tapered inward as it reached toward the heavens.

"Up there," his escort instructed, nodding to the tower. She pointed her spear to the outer staircase. "Mother Mylitta's in her observatory."

"Up?" he gasped.

"You said you wanted to meet her, didn't you?"

Sweet Isis! How would he ever scale the thing? He looked at the staircase; it extended out from the tower no more than a cubit at most, and possessed no railing or balustrade. Semerket felt his legs starting to swim beneath him.

"Can she not meet me down here?" he asked faintly, trying not to sound like he was pleading.

"She cannot. It's coming on the New Year and she reads the heavens for its portents."

There was nothing for him to do but put his sandaled foot tentatively on the first step. As he did, he realized that he was not breathing. Firmly, he bade himself to show a little fortitude. He inhaled and took another step, going up a single riser, and even felt brave enough to try the third.

The curving stairs were steeply inclined, and his rise upward was precipitous. Semerket was careful to face inward, concentrating on the next stair in front of him. Though the women muttered under their breath at the slowness of their ascent, he was deaf to anything but his own terror.

At last, many eons later, Semerket edged his way onto the uppermost level of the tower. Only about half the diameter of the base, it was crammed with bronze and copper instruments made for the calculation of the heavens. Semerket rejoiced to see that a waist-high wall surrounded the platform.

A tall woman across from him peered through a long bronze tube affixed to a tripod. As he stepped onto the platform, she turned to stare at him. Semerket was dumbfounded to see who it was. "You!" he said.

Mother Mylitta regarded him suspiciously. "We've met?"

Semerket shook his head. "No. But I saw you at the singer Nidaba's house, only last night."

Mother Mylitta was the older woman who had accompanied the donkey train to Nidaba's back courtyard—the one he had heard speak his name so vengefully in the dark. If she was surprised that he knew her, her cold, dark eyes indicated only contempt. She bent to make another notation on a clay tablet. While she did this, Semerket finally screwed up his courage to look finally out and over the tower. From above the lingering smoke of cooking fires, the desert plains beyond the city were silver, especially brilliant in the dry, clear, starlit air.

Semerket took a single step forward, looking down upon the wide walls surrounding the city. He was almost disappointed to see no chariots galloping atop them, four abreast.

Without looking up from her notations, the woman spoke. "I'm told you stand in our courtyard and fling accusations at me from the dark."

He decided to come straight to the point. "I'm Semerket, envoy of Pharaoh—"

"I know who you are."

He stopped, irritation plucking at him. He took another breath and began again. "Because of the friendship between our nations, I've been asked by King Kutir—"

"To find his sister, yes," Mother Mylitta interrupted him again. "Go on."

Semerket gritted his teeth. All right, he thought, I can do it your way. "I know that Princess Pinikir survived the massacre. I know she came here."

Mother Mylitta looked up from her note-taking. She pursed her thin, wrinkled lips. Laying down her stylus, she placed her hands into the sleeves of her robes and stared at him. "It was not the princess who sought sanctuary that night."

"Who was it, then?"

"A woman needing our help."

"Who was she? What was her name?"

Mother Mylitta's expression did not change and she said nothing.

He sighed. "You're not going to tell me?"

Mylitta gave a haughty shake of her head. "I cannot. Our bylaws prohibit us from divulging the names of our members. Not even a woman's husband may claim her once she enters the gagu."

"And if I should tell the king that I suspect his sister is behind these walls . . . ?"

An amused smile of indulgence creased the old woman's face. "Do it, Semerket, and see what happens. There's not a prince in Mesopotamia who doesn't owe his throne to the gold we lend them, including Kutir."

"Then if you'll answer none of my questions, why did you let me in here? You could have chased me away, or simply ignored me."

She did not answer him at once, but continued to gaze at him with the same hard, unforgiving expression. Then, as if she had come to some sort of inner decision, she turned suddenly, squinting into the tube of bronze. Mother Mylitta aimed the tube almost to the level of the horizon line, scanning the skies intently. Then she stopped and beckoned him to approach.

"I brought you up here for one reason, to show you this. Look into the scope," she commanded.

Careful not to get too near the edge of the tower, he edged forward to put his eye to the tube, not knowing what he would see. The tube, it turned out, was simply that—a hollow piece of cast metal that allowed the user to follow a single star exclusively among all the others.

"Well?" he said.

"It's the star of Egypt—the Seshat star, you Egyptians call it."

Semerket looked through the tube again. The Seshat star seemed very much like all the rest of the anonymous lights in the sky, though perhaps a trifle redder. Then he remembered what the villagers had told him.

"Blood in the sky," he murmured.

"Yes," Mother Mylitta said, not surprised by his words. "The reason I cannot help you."

Mother Mylitta pointed a knobby finger at the Seshat star. "Never before has Egypt's star been seen in our part of the sky, nor blazing with such ominous color. Worse, we've discovered it reverses its orbit. The omen cannot be clearer. A great evil has come out of Egypt to threaten us. It is the gods themselves who have decreed that we can give no Egyptian our help."

"But I am not this evil."

"Until a clearer message is sent us, all Egyptians are suspect. Even you, Semerket. Or perhaps I should say—*especially* you."

He would have attempted to reason with the woman, but before he had a chance to say anything more, Mother Mylitta made a gesture to the two female guards. They came forward and seized him by the arms, removing him from the observatory. The one beneficial outcome of that evening was that Mother Mylitta had so confused him with her talk of malevolent stars that he made his descent in a kind of daze and was not quite so aware of the tower's giddy height. It was small consolation for losing Pinikir's trail again, however.

Semerket retraced his steps to the hostel. There was no one on the streets, and the profound quiet disturbed him; it reminded him too much of the previous night, when the assassins had leapt upon him from the dark. He wondered vaguely if his two Dark Head spies, Galzu and Kuri, were watching over him as they had promised. Semerket doubted it, for the Elamite patrols were too diligent to allow many Dark Heads on the streets. He was somewhat heartened to realize that if the Elamites made it difficult for his bodyguards to be abroad, they did as much for any assassins. With that thought, he stopped to risk a drink from a nearby well.

"Lord Semerket!" a strangely familiar voice whispered to him.

He jumped, dropping the drinking gourd in the well, his heart racing. But it was only the man from the Sick Square.

"I apologize for frightening you," said the man. "But there is a message—"

"Another one?"

"You are warned to avoid the harbor this evening, my lord. Particularly that area where the Elamite fleet is moored."

So now the Isins were planning an assault on Kutir's navy. Even Semerket, who was no military strategist, could recognize it for the bold move it was; simply put, the Isins would cut off the Elamites' only means of escape. The war for the hand of Babylon would be played to the death.

"Who sends me this warning?" Semerket asked the man, knowing what his answer would be.

"Alas, my lord, I don't know myself."

SEMERKET REACHED THE HOSTEL at the same time as Shepak. Upstairs in Semerket's rooms they whispered together. Semerket confessed his inability to extract any information from Mother Mylitta, other than her insistence that the princess was not at the gagu.

"Do you believe her?" Shepak asked.

Semerket nodded glumly. "Yes, I do—though I don't think she'd hesitate to lie to me, if she felt she needed to."

He did not tell Shepak what Mother Mylitta had told him of the great evil supposedly arising from Egypt. Nor did he tell Shepak about the impending Isin attack in the harbor. The civil strife in Babylon was none of his affair, he kept telling himself, and the warning was for him alone. Of course, he would do all he could to prevent Shepak from going in the direction of the harbors that night.

Shepak, on the other hand, had been more successful in his quest. "The boy is still alive," he said resolutely.

"Thank the gods!" Semerket exclaimed. "Tell me!"

"I went to the oasis and found that the boy was left with a local farmer who lived a few leagues up the road. I got to the place just before dark. Apparently this Rami was so seriously hurt that the caravan merchants didn't want to take him on their journey, fearing a death would curse their enterprise. That's when Rami wrote his message to you, giving it to the caravan masters."

Semerket immediately threw his cape over his shoulders. "Take me to him! We'll have trouble getting out of the city, but maybe Kutir's pass will be enough—"

"Hold on," interrupted Shepak, a warning glint in his eye. "Rami's no longer there. Not a week ago, a band of Isins swooped down on the place and took him hostage. The last the farmer saw of the boy, he'd been flung across a saddle and taken north."

It was all too much for Semerket. He let out a torrent of profanity that impressed even Shepak.

Semerket at last collected himself. For a while, all he could do was pant, leaning his head against the wall in dejection. "What in hell do we do now?" he asked, turning to Shepak.

Shepak pulled a cushion from the bed, throwing it on the floor. "We sleep on it," he answered shortly.

THAT NIGHT THE ISINS attacked the Elamite fleet, burning the ships on the river. As the Elamite troops converged on the harbor, the Isins again evaporated as if by magic, only to reappear at the city granaries. While the Elamites fought to save their ships, the Isins emptied their silos. As a result, now the Elamites were starving, too.

The last place the marauders attacked that night was a small, out-of-the-way building not far from where Semerket and Shepak slumbered. The raiders forced open the gates of the Egyptian temple, going into its shrines with brands and torches, where the greasy soot of candles and incense instantly caught fire. The temple's three inhabitants—an elderly couple and a young, beautiful woman with slanted green eyes—were hacked to pieces as they called upon their gods to save them.

BOOK THREE

DESCENT
INTO THE
UNDERWORLD

 SEMERKET WANDERED, BEWILDERED AND speechless, through the ruined Egyptian temple. The roof had collapsed from the heat of the flames, and he had to crawl over heaps of brick and plaster. The colored mural pieces littering the floor caught his eye—the smile of a goddess, the green hand of Osiris clutching his scourge, wavy blue lines that had depicted the Nile . . .

The Babylonian civil police and their servants—all whose duty it was to make the ashes and blood go away—spoke to him as he passed. Their words sounded like the singsong clacking of alien birds. Semerket simply could not comprehend another Babylonian word at that moment. At the officials' questions, he merely averted his eyes and kept walking through the ruins, deaf to everything but the scream in his head.

Fortunately, Shepak was there. The workers deferred to him, for they knew Shepak was a highly ranked Elamite officer. He barked questions at the witnesses, asking all the things that Semerket was too tired and heartsore to ask.

Leaving Shepak to deal with them, Semerket at last came to the little temple's granite altar. Wildflowers were still standing upright in its vases, and its surface was slick with the black blood of sacrifice. But it was not a heifer or ewe that had been slaughtered on it. Three unmoving figures lay at the altar's granite base, draped in shrouds: Senmut, Wia, and Aneku.

Who had been the first to die? Semerket wondered.

The wind suddenly gusted, lifting the shroud a little. A shaft of light happened to fall upon a frail, withered hand—Senmut's hand, the old priest who had been too proud to beg for alms on the street. Semerket saw the deep cuts that ran across its palm, telling him that the priest had tried to fend off his assassin's blade.

He pulled the thin cloth over the hand again, accidentally brushing his fingers against the priest's flesh. Its coldness was a shock; even the fierce Babylonian sun could do nothing to kindle warmth in it.

When the wind once again lifted the shroud, Semerket turned away. He did not wish to see their bodies, did not want to remember his friends so torn and bloodied. He cursed himself for having forgotten to warn Aneku that such an attack might occur. Though such a warning would have done his friends little good, still he blamed himself.

Semerket was standing beside the bodies when Shepak found him. "I've questioned everyone who saw or heard the attack," he announced. "It was a force of Isins who did it, about ten strong."

Semerket raised his brows in surprise. "Isins again?" he remarked coldly. "And did they suddenly appear from nowhere to attack this little Egyptian temple, and did they vanish again just as quickly?"

Shepak ignored his bitter jest. "They came on foot, around midnight, yelling and cursing. They woke up the whole quarter, it seems. Plenty of witnesses saw them—not just the Egyptians from around the neighborhood, but Dark Heads, too."

"Or thought they saw them," Semerket murmured. He stood up, turning soberly to Shepak. "A favor . . . ?"

"Of course. Anything."

Semerket took some gold and silver rings from his belt and gave them to Shepak. "See that my friends' bodies are taken to the House of Purification. The locals will know where one is. Give the priests this cash, and say that you want them to receive the best possible embalming."

Shepak looked squeamish but he nodded, knowing how important such things were to Egyptians.

"While you're there I want you to do something else." Semerket swallowed, dropping his eyes.

Shepak's expression now became apprehensive. "What?"

"Ask them to check their records for last winter. Find out if they embalmed a woman named Naia."

Shepak, appalled, protested. "Don't you think *you're* the one to do that?" he said. "You can describe her for them. I can't."

"She was beautiful, tell them, just twenty-three years old. Her skin was the color of ash, and her eyes like the Nile at flood season."

Because he could no longer speak, Semerket turned abruptly, heading down the stairs that led to the secret tunnel beneath the temple.

"Where are you going?" Shepak called after him.

There was no answer, for Semerket was already gone.

"I MUST SEE HER," Semerket said, pushing against the gate.

The Syrian pushed back. "My lord, be reasonable. I told you Nidaba isn't awake—"

Semerket suddenly threw all his strength against the gate. It flew back, striking the wall loudly. He stalked through the portal, into the gardens. The concierge ran up the outer stairs to the villa's second floor, flinging terrified glances over his shoulder, as though Semerket were some barbarian intent on ravishing his mistress.

From the gardens, Semerket went into the courtyard and waited in the veranda. In the harsh sunlight, the flowering vines were scraggly. The silken cushions on the divans seemed faded and wine-stained. Without the dark and the soft glow of oil lamps, the villa resembled a dead wizard's palace in some ancient folk tale, its magic withered away.

A short while later, Semerket heard a noise above him. A young man stood on the balustrade grimacing into the bright light and rubbing his eyes. The concierge held a fluttering tunic for the young man, which he donned while descending the stairs.

"Semerket?" he asked. "What are you doing here?"

Semerket went to meet him in the courtyard. The youth was very pale and his chin was dusted blue-black with morning beard.

"I came to see Nidaba," Semerket said firmly. "It's important. Take me to her."

The young man was momentarily shocked. With a stricken glance at the concierge, he brought his hands up to his face to hide his smirk. "Oh, dear," he said, "I'd forgotten how Egyptians can be so naive about such things."

Then Semerket saw the young man's nails, lacquered in gold dust, while tiny lines at the corner of his eyes still held smudges of antimony. The dawn broke at last in Semerket's frail mind.

"*You're* Nidaba?" Semerket asked faintly.

The young man nodded, laughing softly. His low and sultry tenor convinced Semerket of the truth. No wonder Nidaba's voice was so forceful, Semerket thought—a man's lungs powered it.

"Surely you know," Nidaba explained with a touch of defiance, "that Ishtar is male and female both—the god of war and the goddess of love together. I've dedicated my life to serving both their holy guises."

Semerket nodded, a man of the world, though he was thinking, Sweet Osiris, is anything in Babylon truly what it seems to be?

"So," Nidaba said, "since I've told you my secret, you must tell me the reason you've come to see me."

"Some friends of mine were murdered last night."

"Were they at the harbor?"

Semerket looked at Nidaba squarely. "How do you know about the harbor?"

Nidaba picked at an imaginary thread. "I heard something about it this morning. My concierge told me."

"My friends were killed in the Egyptian temple," Semerket said. "They're saying that Isins were behind it."

Nidaba eyes glittered. "I'm very sorry, but what can I do?"

"The same thing I asked you to do before: take me to the Heir of Isin. I want to question him myself about the attack."

"Impossible. I told you before. I don't even know him."

"I think you do." Semerket said nothing more, letting his black eyes bore into Nidaba's.

"Haven't you forgotten, Semerket? I'm forbidden to help any Egyptian."

"No, I haven't forgotten. And I know that it was Mother Mylitta who forbade it. I also know that she was here the other night—just as I know what was in those donkey sacks."

Nidaba gave a start. Gone were the graceful movements and languid smiles.

"Now," said Semerket evenly, leaning forward to speak in a low tone, "what would happen, do you think, if Kutir knew that the women of the gagu were sending the Isin rebels their gold, coated in melted bitumen?"

Nidaba gasped. "How did you find out they were sending it to them?"

"I saw the gold for myself. As for who it was being sent to, that was a guess—one you just confirmed."

Nidaba had succumbed to the oldest trick in an investigator's arsenal, and glared at Semerket. "The stars were right," Nidaba said. "You really are a bastard."

"HOW ARE WE GOING to get past the Elamite blockades?" Nidaba whispered to him.

"Just bat your lashes at them; that should do it."

"I'm serious."

Semerket explained that he possessed a pass from the king that should see them easily through any checkpoint.

"Well, aren't we the fortunate ones," sniffed Nidaba scathingly, no longer bothering to hide her loathing of the Elamites from him.

They walked down a narrow, crooked side street in the old part of the city. Nidaba, clad in all her finery, strolled with her usual grace— due, perhaps, to the jeweled clogs she had insisted on wearing. Freshly barbered and painted, she explained to him when he complained at how long her toilette took, that if she were going to be murdered, she certainly did not intend to die a frump.

The little street they traveled on ended abruptly at the grated entrance to a large cistern. When Semerket looked questioningly at her, Nidaba merely walked over to lean casually against the grate, idly scanning the rooftops and doorways. Semerket realized she looked to see if anyone watched them. Satisfied that no eyes were turned in their direction, Nidaba abruptly reached her hand through the grate's bars. He heard a latch open.

"Hurry!" Nidaba hissed at him. She had lifted up the grate, something no ordinary woman could have done so effortlessly. "Get in!"

Semerket did not ask questions, just crawled under the opening. He braced his back against the grille so that Nidaba could join him. When they were both inside, she led him forward into the dark. They went about twenty paces before they found a curving stairway leading to a lower level.

Nidaba seized a torch from the wall, knowing just where to find it. She took a flint from her gilded leather sash and quickly lighted it. The torch threw the staircase into bright relief, allowing them to descend in safety. When they reached the lower level, a long tunnel loomed before them, beside which an underground canal gabbled softly.

"What *is* this place?" Semerket asked in wonder. "A sewer?" It certainly did not smell like one, for though the air was dank, it was not foul.

Nidaba began to lead him forward. "It's a sort of underground highway," she whispered. "Babylon's laced with them. A queen built these tunnels hundreds of years ago. She wanted to be able to rush her troops to any place in the city in case of riot."

"Amazing," Semerket said, awestruck by the engineering effort it must have taken to build them. Expensive glazed brick sheathed the tunnel's surface. Over the centuries, however, a mare's nest of spidery roots had grown down from the street above, snaking into the canal. It made their going very tricky, for the roots clutched at their feet as they passed.

"Why don't the Elamites use these tunnels?"

"As I said, they're very old. Not many people even know they exist."

"But the Isins do," he said, realizing just how their troops were able to come and go so quickly. It was magic, yes, but not the kind the Elamites believed in.

He and Nidaba reached a well of light that fell from a vertical shaft leading up to the street. They heard an Elamite captain distantly shouting orders to his men. Nidaba flashed a warning look at Semerket, putting her finger to her lips, and they continued forward in silence.

Semerket reflected how much easier it would have been for the Elamites to control Babylon had they known about these cisterns. But they had marched into the city with all the arrogance and conceit with which conquerors possessing superior forces are usually imbued, no doubt believing they could easily subdue such a corrupt and vitiated people as the Babylonians. If only the Elamites had taken a little time to do some reconnaissance, Semerket thought—or at least some cursory investigation into the city's history—they might not now be fighting for their lives.

Such an odd people, these Babylonians, he thought. And the woman—man—walking beside him had turned out to be the oddest of them all. At that moment, Nidaba happened to glance over at him. "Why do you look at me like that?"

"I'd never have taken you for a freedom fighter."

"Well, why should you? An Ishtaritu is only ever expected to be amusing, never brave or daring—or even patriotic." There was bitterness in her lovely voice.

They had reached another cistern opening, and Nidaba cautioned Semerket again to be quiet. As the minutes passed and the dark grew even more stygian, he began to feel almost buried alive. He suddenly remembered the time when he had been locked inside a pharaoh's tomb in the Great Place. A trickle of sweat snaked down his spine as the long-repressed panic came flooding back. Before it completely engulfed him, however, Nidaba stopped abruptly.

"We're here," she said.

They stood in front of another metal grille, chained and locked. They could go no further.

"Where are we?" he whispered.

"Beneath the Royal Quarter."

He almost smiled. "You mean the Heir of Isin can be found only a few cubits below Kutir himself?" He marveled at both the irony and the daring.

"That's right."

Nidaba bent to run her fingertips near the base of the wall. She stood a moment later, holding a short copper spike in her hand. Nidaba tapped out a code on the grille. From deep inside the dark tunnel, Semerket heard the answering tones. Then a torchlight appeared from far away, carried in the hand of a tall, bearded man.

Semerket resisted the urge to flee, for in the gloom the man resembled nothing so much as one of hell's demons coming to claim him. Dimly, he heard Nidaba introducing him as Pharaoh Ramses' friend.

"No need to tell me who it is," the man chortled. "We've already met!"

Shocked, Semerket recognized the man as one of those Isins he had met in Mari—the man who had first told him that Isins had never attacked the Elamite plantation. At that time, the man had not been particularly amiable. Now he smiled broadly in the torchlight and clamped his arm around Semerket's shoulders as though he were an old friend.

"So you want to see the Heir? Well, it's been a few days since you've had chance to talk together, eh? I imagine there's a lot to catch up on."

"Pardon?" Semerket asked. Had they confused him with someone else?

But the man was already heading down the tunnel with Nidaba at his side, and Semerket had to hurry after them. They came to the place where four of the cisterns, along with their attendant canals, emptied into one enormous arched cavern. Several levels deep, the place echoed from the roaring of water. He became gradually aware that hundreds of Isin soldiers camped there. As he looked down on them from above, they shot him suspicious glances.

Another abrupt twist in the tunnel, and he was shown into a small chamber lit by a number of oil lamps. After all the darkness, the lamplight temporarily dazzled him. All he could see were the silhouettes of several persons milling in the room.

Then he heard his guide's gruff voice saying, "Here's your Egyptian friend, lord."

A silhouette advanced toward him, arms outstretched. Semerket felt himself embraced.

"So you found me at last, Semerket!" the figure said in perfect Egyptian, albeit in a flat, northern accent.

Semerket realized that, of course, he had indeed met this Heir of Isin before, the princeling raised in the court of Ramses III. His eyes adjusted to the glittering light at last.

Standing before him was his one-time slave, Marduk.

HIS FIRST REACTION WAS RAGE—more at himself for having been the stooge once again of duplicity perpetrated by his former servant.

"You abandoned me," he snarled coldly at Marduk.

Marduk's smile vanished.

"What did you expect?" he snarled back. "That I would lead you by the hand through the city, point out the sights? I had to meet up with my men, you fool!"

"How was I supposed to know that? You never told me who you were, what you were doing here—"

"I *couldn't* tell you! If you had known I was the Heir, your own life would have been in danger."

"A little help in finding my wife and friend, that's all I wanted. And I had saved your life!"

"Haven't I looked out for you? Didn't I send those messages to you, warning you away from the garrison and the harbor?"

"How was I supposed to know who they came from?"

"I thought if anyone could figure it out, it'd be the great investigator from Egypt. Apparently, it was beyond your limited capabilities."

"What hurts most is that you never trusted me enough to tell me who you really were."

"I *did* trust you."

"Oh, yes," scoffed Semerket, "when you needed to sneak into the city, acting like some moron, drooling—"

"I had to get past the Elamites, Semerket. Surely, even you must realize that. They'd been alerted I might attempt to enter Babylon. And you have to admit, no one ever willingly looks at the simple-minded."

Semerket regarded Marduk with exasperation. "I suppose that kind old master of yours back in Egypt was Ramses III?"

Marduk nodded. "He took me into his court to raise me out of harm's way, as a favor to my father. When the Kassite kings were set to fall, he sent me back to claim my throne. Unfortunately, that's also when the Elamites chose to invade."

They stared at one another for a moment. Now that he had voiced all his resentments, Semerket had nothing else to say. "Well, anyway," Semerket admitted grudgingly, "it's good to see you again, Marduk. The truth is, I missed you."

The tension in the small underground chamber evaporated. Marduk's soldiers, who had retreated to watch the fracas from the outer tunnel, suddenly crowded back inside the room, relieved and laughing.

"Ah, Semerket, Semerket," said Marduk, sitting down on a brick bench. "Tell me how you are, and how your investigation proceeds."

Semerket winced to hear Marduk's question, for there were painful things he had to ask his friend. He sat beside Marduk to tell his story. It never occurred to him that Marduk could become the next king of Babylon and that it might be better to stand in his presence; to Semerket, Marduk would always be the prisoner he had saved from the Elamites, his one-time slave. Marduk himself did not take offense, and listened intently while Semerket related the events of the previous week.

Semerket told Marduk how he had learned that Naia and Rami had been at the plantation where the Elamite prince and princess were attacked. Marduk was not unfamiliar with this; he only nodded, asking how it was that Kutir had seen fit to retain Semerket in locating his missing sister.

At this, Semerket spoke in Egyptian, informing his friend of Ramses' urgent need for Bel-Marduk's idol. Marduk had not known of Pharaoh's sickness, and was shocked. He looked upon the fourth Ramses as his elder brother, Marduk insisted.

Semerket also told him of Queen Narunte's hatred for her sister-in-law, Princess Pinikir, and how he himself had been attacked by someone he believed might have had some connection to her. This, also, was not a surprise to Marduk; it seemed that the Heir of Isin had a host of informants throughout the city who kept him aware of all that transpired, particularly if it concerned his Egyptian "master."

Semerket fell silent now and bit his lip. His growing uneasiness was plain to see. Marduk laid his hand on Semerket's arm, forcing him to look into his face. "What do you need to ask me, Semerket?"

Semerket had always been incapable of dissimulation, and decided to ask the dreaded question. "Marduk, did you order the massacre at the Egyptian temple? If you did, then you're responsible for the deaths of three people I considered friends."

Marduk gave a start. There was an angry stirring in the room. "Isins don't attack civilian targets, Semerket," he said in a cold voice, "particularly the houses of gods."

"A rogue band, perhaps drunk—?"

"Impossible."

Semerket reasoned that Marduk had nothing to gain by lying to him, and nodded. "I do believe you. But since your Isins didn't do it, you must know that someone—some group—wants everyone to think you did. Just as they want everyone to believe that you attacked the plantation, as well."

Before Marduk could react, the tall Isin from Mari stepped forward, bringing his face close to Semerket's.

"I told you back in Mari we didn't attack that damned farm! What is it with Egyptians, anyway? The other one tried to accuse us of the same thing!"

Perhaps it was the omnipresent sound of rushing water from the nearby canal that prevented Semerket from hearing clearly, for it was a moment before he comprehended what the man had said.

"What other one?"

Marduk turned to nod to a soldier waiting in the doorway. The man walked swiftly down the outer hallway, the echoes of his boots receding with him.

"Now," said Marduk, when they heard footsteps again approaching the chamber, "you'll see how I take care of you, Semerket. When you told me the story of how the plantation was attacked by Isins, I put some men on it back in Mari. We were able to discover a few things, one of which should interest you exceedingly—"

A small commotion at the door interrupted Marduk. The soldier had returned, and the milling Isin warriors moved clumsily aside to allow him into the room. Semerket noticed that a second person followed the soldier.

Semerket blinked. He rose to his feet slowly, staring.

He's no longer a boy, Semerket thought. He's lost his adolescent reediness, and his shoulders are broader.

"Rami?" he said at last, so quietly that he might have mouthed the name.

The boy stared at him, his expression unreadable. Semerket had been largely responsible for Rami's banishment from Egypt, having uncovered his parents' complicity in rifling the tombs within the Great Place. Though he had managed to save Rami from the executioner, getting him exiled instead, the lad had blamed him for having destroyed the life he had known. Semerket was therefore unsure what kind of welcome he would receive from the young man.

Perhaps Rami had not altogether grown up, for his face suddenly crumpled like any child's when he recognized Semerket, and he flung himself into Semerket's arms. "I knew you'd come," he said in Egyptian. "Naia told me you would."

At the sound of his wife's name, Semerket's chest thudded. Rami alone knew the truth of what had happened that night. But the boy was clearly in too vulnerable a state to answer any questions about it; and perhaps, too, for the first time in his life, Semerket did not want to know the answers.

"Of course I came," Semerket said. "I'm the one who got you into this, didn't I?" He extracted himself from Rami's grasp, gazing at him at arm's length. The lad was emaciated, pale, with dark circles ringing his eyes. Semerket saw the boy stagger slightly; clearly, Rami had not recovered and would need the services of a good physician quickly.

"Rami, I know an Egyptian doctor here in Babylon," Semerket said. "I'm going to have him brought here."

Before he could finish, Rami grew even paler, and put his hand up to his ear. "I'm sorry . . . sometimes when I stand for too long—"

Rami's eyes began to quiver, then rolled upward into their sockets. Without another sound, he fell to the floor.

"I MUST OPEN YOUR SKULL," Kem-weset said to Rami.

At Semerket's request, Marduk had sent a man through the tunnels to fetch the physician. When he arrived, Kem-weset evinced no surprise to find Semerket surrounded by Isin rebels, as well as a male Ishtaritu, for he had long before accepted that Semerket was a Follower of Set, allied to danger, chaos, and trouble. Rami, meanwhile, had regained consciousness in the interval between his collapse and the physician's appearance, and resisted Kem-weset's first attempts to examine him. He was well, the boy insisted. All he needed was sleep. Rami tried to shake off the physician's hands that continued to press gently on his skull, but then he cried out sharply.

Kem-weset withdrew a razor from his medicine chest and carefully shaved away the hair over the boy's left ear. Even Semerket could see that though the skin had healed, the skull was no longer rounded at the area, but indented. Kem-weset said that he must perform the surgery immediately.

"No!" was Rami's instant response.

Kem-weset spoke calmly. "Then you won't get well. Your attacks will become more frequent, until finally you will die from them."

"I'll die from the operation!"

"Quite possibly," Kem-weset agreed. "But you also have one chance in three of surviving. If I do nothing, you have no chance at all."

"It'll hurt!"

"I have drugs to calm the pain. You'll feel very little."

In the end, Rami had to agree to the treatment. Kem-weset then shaved his head entirely and applied a numbing salve to the area where he would cut. The physician called for wine.

"Is that wise?" asked Semerket, alarmed. "Surely your hands will be steadier without it?"

"It's for Rami, you idiot," answered Kem-weset shortly. "I'll mix the poppy paste into it."

The wine was brought, and Kem-weset spooned a thick, viscous brown substance into it, stirring until it was completely dissolved. Following the custom of centuries, just as he had done for Semerket, Kem-weset wrote out a prayer of supplication on a strip of papyrus and ran it through the liquid. The glyphs melted, the inks bled away, and Kem-weset brought the bowl to Rami's lips.

"Drink it all down," he commanded.

Kem-weset beckoned Semerket to join him at the corner of the room, and spoke to him in a low tone. "If you have anything to ask him, Semerket, you'd best ask now."

Semerket shook his head. "If these are to be his last moments, I'd rather not torment him with useless questions. There are more important things." But he was saying to himself, Coward!

Kem-weset gruffly patted his arm. He returned to his box of instruments and asked one of the Isins to bring a flame in which to purify them. He also asked Semerket for a silver piece, though he did not say what it was for. Semerket did not ask. Marduk offered up his own mattress, helping Semerket carry Rami into another small room, where they laid the boy upon it. Every oil lamp in the cistern was collected from the soldiers and brought there, until the area was bright as day.

Rami attempted to lie quietly while the drug worked its magic, but it was apparent that the sedative was having the opposite effect on him than the one intended. "Semerket," he said anxiously, "Semerket, my Day of Pain has come, hasn't it?"

"Of course it hasn't," came his automatic reply.

"I heard what the old man told you, that you'd better ask me about Naia, now, while I'm still alive."

"There's no need. It can wait," replied Semerket, too quickly. "Tomorrow, perhaps, when you're well enough." When I can bear it, he was thinking.

But the boy was not listening. Once he began to speak, his words poured out in a torrent of confession and self-reproach. "I know I'll die today," he said in a quivery voice. "I think I only lived long enough so I could ask for your forgiveness . . . because you loved her so much."

Fear began blowing coldly into Semerket's soul. He knew that he could not let Rami die in such torment, and tried to keep the fright from his voice when he answered. "What is it, then, Rami? What do you need to tell me?"

Rami's eyes grew wide. "Semerket, it was because of me that Naia died! It was my fault!"

Semerket stared. So there it was, he thought; the confirmation that Naia was well and truly dead. Strange to feel nothing. In fact, he felt only a relief to hear the words at last spoken aloud. No more hope. Everything gone; finished at last. Oddly, it was an unexpectedly pleasant feeling, an almost buoyant sensation of complete and utter emptiness.

"I'm sure it wasn't," Semerket said tonelessly.

The boy began to ramble. "No! I should have saved her! I *could* have, if I'd only known what they were saying. But it's such a difficult language—even Naia had trouble with it. When we were at the ambassador's, it didn't matter. Everybody spoke Egyptian there. But Naia said we must learn the language—Babylon was our home now—but I was too stupid—"

If anything, the drug was making the boy more fretful. Semerket canted his head to see if Kem-weset was nearby, but the old physician was pounding at something in the corridor. Semerket swabbed Rami's sweaty forehead with a damp cloth. "It doesn't matter," he said.

"We were happy at the embassy." Rami ignored him, and his rush of words came even more quickly. "But when Prince Mayatum came, everything changed. Why? We hadn't done anything! Why did Menef send us away?"

Semerket's raised his head slowly. *"Who* came to the embassy?"

The boy writhed in sudden pain, and he gasped the name. "Prince Mayatum!"

Semerket sat back on his heels, stunned. He put his hand to the wall to steady himself. Prince Mayatum had been in Babylon? But why should he travel all the way to Babylon just to see Menef? For what purpose? The alliance between Egypt and Babylon had existed for hundreds of years; there was no need to send any royal personage here. Then he remembered Mayatum's own words that day so long before in Djamet Temple. The prince had told Semerket that he had only then returned from a trip to meet with Egypt's Asian allies. It would have been a simple thing for the prince to make a secret journey into Babylon at that time. Semerket shook his head, forcing down the terrible suspicion that was fast rising in him.

"Do you know *why* he came here, Rami?"

As his spasm of pain subsided, Rami shook his head slightly. "No . . . no. I only know that Naia and I were chosen to serve him at the feast that night. Out of all the servants, Menef chose us."

Menef again! Always Menef at the root of every nasty little evil in this wretched city!

"All during the banquet, the prince kept looking at Naia, making comments about you, about what a hero you were to Egypt. But it sounded like an insult, the way he said it. She got so nervous she spilled her tray all over him." The boy spoke with increasing difficulty, for the medicine was drying his mouth. Semerket soaked the rag in a jar of water and squeezed a few drops between Rami's lips.

"Then what happened?"

"Next day, we were sent away to the Elamite plantation. But Naia went to Menef, before we left. She told him that we didn't want to go. Menef hit her across the face. Said we had no choice, that he could do what he wanted with us."

Semerket's voice went flat. "He struck her?"

But Rami ignored the question. "I didn't like it at the plantation," he said, "couldn't understand anyone. But Naia and the princess got along. Naia found out the reason why she'd come to Babylon . . . a secret reason . . ."

"What was the secret, Rami? Did she tell you?"

Rami shook his head. His eyelids were drooping.

"Rami!" Semerket's voice cracked like whip. "Tell me what happened that night!"

Rami grimaced as if he had been struck. He screwed up his face, trying to remember. "An old woman came there after sundown, telling us that . . . that something was in the sky . . . blood . . . a warning, she said."

Mother Mylitta. Semerket could see her tall figure in his mind, banging on the plantation gates, demanding entry. He closed his eyes, deliberately forcing his ka up and out of his body. As Rami continued to speak, it left the underground world, rising to the streets above, plunging through the avenues and out the Ishtar Gate. Soon it was soaring over the hilltops and wheat fields, heading to the north, gliding effortlessly past the river levees.

Semerket was at the plantation now, its walls rising abruptly before him. The guards were closing the gates against the night and Naia was there—she was carrying a basket of laundry into the house. As always in his nightmares, he tried to call out to her, but his voice was wedged in his throat.

He gripped Rami's shoulder.

"And Mother Mylitta has just arrived," he said softly into Rami's ear, prompting him, "she's come through the gate. Where are you, Rami?"

"Outside, in the kitchens, with the cook . . ."

Semerket's eyelids flickered. He tried to open them, but his ka was gone and would not return. Semerket was once again on his plain of nightmares.

"Where were you when the old woman came, Rami?"

"In the kitchens, helping the cook prepare the meal. Then he sent me upstairs to the garden, to help serve it with Naia. The old woman was already there. She was waving her arms about and pointing to a star in the sky. I thought she was crazy, but Naia told me she was a kind of sorceress, that she'd seen a great evil coming from Egypt to attack us."

So far, Rami's story was consistent with the one that Mylitta had told him. "Go on, Rami. What happened next?"

"Everyone turned to look at Naia and me, since we were the only Egyptians. But the woman asked us questions—"

"What kind of questions?"

"When we were born—the date, what time it was, where . . ."

"Go on."

"She said that we weren't the evil ones, and that we were all to go with her to Babylon. She said she could protect us there."

According to Rami, however, the prince did not trust Mylitta, believing instead that she intended to lure him and his wife into a Dark Head trap. He had guards enough at the plantation to protect them, he told her, and would allow neither his wife nor his servants to come with her. Knowing that her trip to the plantation had been in vain, Mother Mylitta departed.

"We kept all the bonfires burning that night," said Rami. "But everything was quiet as usual. The prince told us that the old woman was insane, and that we should be laughing at her. But we were frightened, all the servants were."

"Where was Naia during this, Rami?"

"She was upstairs with Princess Pinikir. The princess was scared, too, so Naia came to the kitchens to make her a sleeping brew. I remember she told me that the princess was distressed."

As the hours wore on and nothing happened, Rami said, jangling nerves became calmer at the plantation. The cook heated some wine for the guards and the boy delivered it to the watchtower. He climbed the ladder to distribute the clay cups among the men, taking a moment to look out into the blackness beyond the walls. Across the plain, Rami believed he saw the movement of the swift-flowing Euphrates in the starlight. But he suddenly realized that the river was in fact behind the estate, to the west. Thinking that he had only imagined the movement in the dark, Rami climbed down to the courtyard.

When he was on the ground, he turned to look back at the watchtower.

"But something was wrong! The guards were suddenly falling over—arrows had struck them!"

Everything happened then in extreme, exaggerated slowness, he told Semerket. Not until one of the soldiers in the tower fell upon the tocsin bell, not until he heard the man's dying gasps, did Rami's tongue loosen enough so he could yell an alarm—

"Help! Assassins!" he called. "Help!"

Prince Nugash was in the courtyard and heard Rami screaming. By then the raiders were throwing grappling hooks over the wall. Nugash turned in time to see the shadowy figures of men appearing over the ramparts. The raiders' heads were swathed in black cloths, Rami said, so everyone knew it was the Isins who attacked them.

"Prince Nugash rushed up to one of them, with a battle-ax in his hand, but their archers got him first. Then they drove a lance through him, to make sure he was dead. All that time, I just stood there. I couldn't move!"

The Isins rounded up all the servants and tied them together in the courtyard. Rami stood rooted to the ground, hidden in the shadows, still holding his tray. No one noticed him. When everyone had left the houses, the marauders pitched torches into the buildings. They caught fire quickly, for their reed roofs became instant tinder.

"That's when I thought about Naia. I remember saying her name aloud," Rami said, looking up at Semerket. "I should have been searching for her. I could have saved her if I hadn't been so stupid!"

"That's when you saw her coming out of the house," Semerket said, his eyes closed, remembering the image from his own nightmares. "That's when she came into the courtyard."

Rami nodded. "I saw her in the doorway, with fire raging behind her. I knew it was Naia, because she was wearing the scarf you gave her—the blue one with the stars."

"What happened? She was in the doorway, and—"

"They surrounded her, kept her apart from the others." The boy was weeping now, unabashedly, and he thrashed about on the mattress, so that Semerket had to grip his arm to quiet him.

"They were on horseback," Rami said. "One of them, the leader I think, rode over to her. The fire was so loud, like a furnace roaring, but I heard him to say to her, 'You're the Egyptian woman? You're Naia?'"

"Those were his words, Rami? His *exact* words?"

"I heard him say it! Naia didn't answer. I couldn't see her face, but I could tell that she was looking up at him. Then I saw her nod her head. And that's when he took his lance and drove it through her! I saw it happen! He killed her!"

In the underground chamber, Rami brought his hands up to his face, covering his tear-stained cheeks. "I remember running at him, then. I dropped the tray and I ran toward the man on horseback. I screamed at him, yelling curses at him. The horse reared up and the man fell to the ground. Then I was on top of him—strangling him, hitting his face. I kept trying to get his black hood off him so I could see what he looked like. Even if they killed me, I wanted to come back to haunt him. Then the hood came off, just like that. Right into my hands. And I saw—I'll never forget—"

"What, Rami? What won't you forget?"

"His face, like a skeleton's, with awful yellow teeth and that mark at his eye."

Semerket exhaled. "Was it an asp . . . so small it could have been a tear?"

Rami nodded, looking at him wide-eyed.

"That's when they struck you."

"I don't remember when it happened, except that my head exploded. I know that I fell on top of the man. 'Get him off me!' he kept screaming. 'Get him off me!' And the funny thing is . . ."

Rami's voice was barely audible now, and his words were slurring together. Semerket laid his ear against Rami's lips.

"What was it, Rami? What was so funny?"

". . . I could understand everything they said . . . all of a sudden, I could speak Babylonian . . ."

"No, Rami," said Semerket. "You understood them because they were speaking Egyptian."

RAMI WAS SUFFICIENTLY DRUGGED that Kem-weset felt it safe to begin the surgery. But the old physician was adamant that Rami was not to move by so much as a fraction. "You two will need to hold his arms," Kem-weset said to Semerket and Marduk.

Though Semerket was averse to the task, at least he had been schooled in the House of Purification and was fairly inured to the cutting and stitching of flesh. Marduk, on the other hand, instantly paled and instead ordered one of his men to Rami's side. But the man fell to his knees, weeping in fear. It was sacrilegious to open a body with a knife, he said, contrary to the will of the gods—this from a warrior who had probably disemboweled hundreds on the battlefield.

Marduk was about to order that lots be drawn, when a low voice came from outside the room. "I'll do it," said Nidaba, pushing her way past the warriors and approaching the mattress. Semerket made sure to take the side where the incision would be made, sparing her the sight of the wound. She sank to the floor and took Rami's head onto her lap. Her gold-tipped fingers gripped his skull tightly.

Kem-weset then demanded that the Isins bring forth a blood-stauncher. The Isins looked at one another in bewilderment, for they had never heard of such a person. Muttering to himself about the backwardness of such people, Kem-weset took his scalpel and made a cut across his thigh. The blood ran freely down his leg.

"Let your men be brought here in single file," Kem-weset said to Marduk. "Quickly now, before it clots."

At least twenty soldiers passed into the chamber before Kem-weset found his blood-stauncher, a young Isin man who had once been a farmer. When he approached the old physician, the wound on Kem-weset's thigh instantly stopped its flow.

"This is the man!" Kem-weset declared. "Bring him into the room."

The Isin warriors became alarmed and stared at the farmer as if he were suddenly revealed to be a demon. Kem-weset patiently explained that the Egyptians, being more advanced, had long known of the existence of staunchers—and that approximately one in every ten persons possessed the power to stop the flow of blood by their mere presence.

"Of course, these persons rarely know they possess the talent," he explained, as he beckoned the farmer into the chamber, placing him near Rami's head.

Kem-weset was ready to begin. Quickly, he made the incision, a half circle around the indentation above Rami's ear. The boy groaned, but did not wake. Carefully, Kem-weset peeled the flesh up to expose the bone. Blood oozed from the cut, spilling across Nidaba's lap. She made no sound, and her expression remained stoic.

"Where is that stauncher?" Kem-weset asked crossly.

The man had backed unseen into the corner of the room. Marduk dragged him into position, and the blood stopped its flow.

"Stay there!" Marduk growled.

Kem-weset took up a chisel and mallet, and began hammering at

Rami's skull. Finally, the physician inserted a bore into the wound. A few taps of the mallet, a twist, and he pulled away a neat plug of bone, exposing the pinkish-gray brain inside. It pulsed in the lamplight, and even Semerket noticed the black blood and fragment of bone that pressed against it.

"Now," said Kem-weset, "all I must do is remove this chip—like so—and tweeze away the bits of old blood. Yes . . . there!" Deftly, Kem-weset inserted the flattened disc of polished silver he had fashioned from the piece that Semerket had given him, then sealed it with mastic.

"They say the brain's a worthless organ," said Kem-weset as he threaded a needle with lamb's sinew. "But see what this minuscule piece of bone was able to do to the poor lad?" He held the fragment in the lamplight, where it glistened bloodily for all to see. With gasps and curses, the Isin warriors sharply averted their eyes. But Kem-weset continued his discourse, fascinated. "What it tells me is that the brain must be good for something," he said. "Don't you agree?"

When no one answered him, Kem-weset shrugged and began stitching up the flap of skin. Then he made a paste of honey and herbs, lathering it onto a bandage, and pressed it against the wound. Finally, he wrapped a cloth tightly around Rami's head.

It was not until Kem-weset rose to his feet, saying, "I'll have that wine now," that everyone realized the surgery was over. A collective sigh of relief sounded through the room.

Semerket found that he was drenched in sweat, that his forehead blazed with pain. The headache that had threatened to overtake him all day had at last arrived. He did not mention it to Kem-weset, however, lest the physician in his enthusiasm suggest a second surgery.

"When will you know if the boy will live?" Semerket asked him.

"The next ten measures of the water clock are critical," replied the physician. "If he develops a fever, he will die."

Ten hours. He could not wait ten hours. He would go mad in this tomblike place. He needed to walk, to wander, to breathe fresh air. And then he knew what he needed more than anything else in the world at that particular moment; a demon had taken possession of him, thirsting with a demon's ferociousness—he needed wine.

"I must leave," Semerket said abruptly. "I'll come back later. I have business in the city."

Kem-weset reassured him that he would stay with the boy until they knew his fate, one way or another.

Without a word to even Marduk or Nidaba, Semerket had already turned on heel and started to sprint down the tunnels. Marduk called out, saying that if he waited he would send a man with Semerket to lead him out. But Semerket would not wait. Even when Nidaba called after him, offering to take him back through the cisterns herself—even then he ran.

Possessing no torch, he had no idea where he went. He simply kept running forward, tripping over the roots and broken tiles, sometimes falling. A faint light appeared in the distance, seeping down from a cistern grate, and he ran to it. He found a curving stairway and climbed, coming upon the grate at its far end. It took him a moment to figure out its latch, but he was finally able to lunge into the Babylonian twilight after a few moments, gasping.

Semerket leaned against a wall. The street was unfamiliar to him. As always, he attempted to orient himself to Etemenanki, but the angle of the buildings in the area prevented a clear view of the tower. At the end of the street, however, he saw the pediment of the Ishtar Temple. He knew he was near the Egyptian Quarter. From deep within the cistern he heard Nidaba faintly calling to him. But he was unable to face her—anyone—and began to run.

"WINE," he said. "Red."

"Going to drink it this time?" the wineseller asked, his disdain for Semerket as marked as ever.

"What's it to you whether I drink or not?" The black jets in Semerket's eyes flashed dangerously.

The wineseller swallowed his impertinent retort; there was something about Semerket that night that reminded him of a coiled serpent. Best not to tease it into striking.

Semerket sat at the rear of the tavern, away from the lantern light. Though the Elamites patrolled the city, enforcing the curfew where they could, they ignored the Egyptian Quarter. Semerket had known instinctively that this tavern, where he had first met Kem-weset, would continue to serve wine regardless of riot, upheaval, or war.

"Planning on staying long?" the wineseller asked.

"What's it to you?"

"No reason, no reason—just making conversation."

"Bring me the wine."

The wineseller shrugged and went back to where his wine jars were stacked. Semerket watched him as he poured out a bowl. The seller caught the eye of his servant, a sheep-faced youth who collected the empty bowls strewn about the disordered place. The wineseller whispered into the boy's ear, then nodded in the direction of Semerket.

"He's telling him to charge me double," Semerket thought morosely. He dropped his eyes, past caring, for his body throbbed with fatigue and grief. The bowl was set before him. It was not the servant who put it there, but the wineseller himself. Semerket looked around in dim surprise, and noticed that the serving boy was gone. Pulling out a gold piece from his belt, he flipped it into the air. "Keep the wine coming," he said shortly.

The wineseller caught the ring in his fist. He saluted Semerket smartly, and returned to his jars.

Semerket brought the bowl to his lips and the red flowed into his throat. For a whole year he had not tasted wine, save for the cup that Kem-weset had forced into him, mixed with medicines. On the Theban docks, when Naia had sailed away from Egypt forever, he had solemnly promised her that he would never again drink it. She had placed her son in his arms, saying that if Semerket ever tasted wine again, then her child could not thrive and she would grieve for them both.

For an entire year, he had kept his promise.

But Naia was dead. Gone from him forever. Surely that invalidated his pledge.

A paroxysm of grief shook him, starting from his stomach where the wine lay cold and sour, refusing to do its work. He called for another bowl. It was delivered. Then another. It was doing nothing for him, this wine. What kind of piss did they serve here? Rage suddenly blazed through him, and he hurled the bowl across the room.

"I still feel!" he shouted. "Bring me another bowl!"

"Why don't I just bring you a jar of my very finest?" the wineseller suggested from across the room.

The establishment's very finest tasted suspiciously like the wine he had been drinking all along. By the end of the jar, however, he didn't care, for it had finally succeeded in calming his roiling mind. Now he could take out the terrible revelations that Rami's confession had stirred; he had the courage to examine them at last.

He stared into the distance, allowing the spectre of Prince Mayatum to appear before him. Semerket finally acknowledged to himself the thought he had been trying to keep at bay, that the prince had come to Babylon not for any diplomatic discussions, nor for pleasure.

The prince had come simply to arrange the murder of Naia and Rami.

It seemed almost a ridiculous thing to admit. Semerket could not comprehend why the prince had gone to such lengths to strike at him. Semerket was a nobody, beneath his notice. Mayatum and his brothers were princes of the blood, tracing their lineage to the great god Amun himself, while Semerket was only a generation from the peasantry.

Self-effacing, willfully naive, Semerket had always considered himself scarcely worth the attention of even ordinary people. That was why, when Naia had approached him, seeking him out above all the other youths who trailed in her wake, he had lost his heart to her.

Then he remembered something else and his tears dried.

Menef had struck her!

Icy wrath surged through his body, and the thought came upon him succinctly—I will kill him. Tonight. Before the dawn arrives, I will drive the life out of him.

His rage was not directed at the ambassador's bodyguard, the Asp, the one who had impaled Naia on his lance. No, the Asp was an animal, scarcely human, who gloried in pain and suffering. Semerket had known it the moment he had seen him, with his ghoul's smile and yellow teeth. Why expect an animal to be something other than what its nature compelled it to be? No, it was Menef who said, "Fetch!" and it was Menef who said, "Kill!" and the animal went just as willingly to either task.

He was convinced now that Menef had been a member of Queen Tiya's foul conspiracy. Prince Mayatum's secret visit to Babylon proved it. The remnants of the terrible cabal were alive, Semerket realized, and their sinister hand had reached all the way into Mesopotamia to take their revenge upon him. He had been the one who foiled their ambitions, who had also been the author of their subsequent humiliations, testifying at the trials against them. How stupid he had been to consider their conspiracy dead and forgotten! Though the queen had mysteriously disappeared, rumored to be the victim of her husband's secret revenge, as long as her remaining sons were still alive, how could it ever be over? By killing Naia they had sought the most vicious and painful way possible to kill him as well.

Well, he was not dead yet.

He would go that very night to Kutir, to make his accusations against them. They had caused the massacre at the plantation, to make Rami's and Naia's murder look like the work of Isin terrorists. But he shook his head, uncomfortable with the logic. Was it not strange that so many had to die because of some distant Egyptian quarrel—that a massacre of more than thirty Mesopotamians was perpetrated just to kill two ordinary Egyptians?

He looked at the empty wine jar in front of him. Perhaps another would help him reason out why so many had to die at the same time. Semerket raised his head to call again to the wineseller, but discovered that a group of men had quietly stolen around him.

Rough hands suddenly pulled him to his feet. "Whoa there, my lord!" a harsh voice came to him, loud enough for all to hear. "It seems you've drunk a wee bit too much tonight—as usual. Don't want you to go making a spectacle of yourself again, eh? You might fall into the wrong hands!"

The Asp leered at him. Semerket whirled around to see the other man who gripped his shoulder; the young man's face was very familiar and he strained to remember who it was. Then he knew—it was the guard from the embassy, the one to whom he had given the new spear.

"What're you doing here?" Semerket mumbled to him. "I thought we were friends . . ."

The young man glanced fearfully at the Asp, and his grip on Semerket's arm became tighter. "Come along quietly now, sir," he urged.

But that was precisely what Semerket would not do. He struggled, cursing, shrieking for help, but none in the shop made a move to aid him. He was just another obstreperous drunk to them, fortunate to have people who cared enough to rescue him before he passed out. As they dragged him from the wineshop into the dark street, Semerket saw the Asp toss a couple of gold pieces to the wineseller and his serving boy. He suddenly knew where the boy had disappeared to that evening: he had been sent to fetch the Asp.

In the empty streets, Semerket's screams caromed off the brick walls of the shuttered buildings. He saw heads peeping at him from over the balustrades, and he shrieked up to them for help. But they quickly withdrew into the shadows; in times of war, no one willingly went into the dark to aid a stranger.

In his hysteria, Semerket noticed that he and his captors were skirting the Processional Way, heading in the direction of the royal quarter. Surely there must be Elamite soldiers on the avenues, he thought, and craned his neck to see. But the dark was by now so pervasive that he could not even see the faces of his captors.

"I know it was you who attacked the plantation," he hissed in the direction of the Asp.

"We suspected as much," came the indifferent answer.

"Kutir knows," Semerket lied. "I told him."

"No, he doesn't."

"Even now his men are searching for you."

"No, they aren't."

"How do you know? Where do you think I've been all day? I've been at the palace! I told Kutir everything—how it was you who dressed up as Isins and killed his brother-in-law. I showed him the Egyptian arrow I found!"

"Did you, now? I'm curious to learn, then, what Ambassador Menef had to say. He's been at the court all day, too, you see. Did you have an opportunity to chat?"

Semerket cursed inwardly at his slip, but continued to hurl his accusations into the dark "I told him that it was you who attacked the Egyptian temple, that you thought my wife was there—"

"No. We knew your wife wasn't there."

The Asp and his men came to a halt. The man's ghastly yellow smile lit up the dark as he drew close to Semerket. "We knew your wife was dead, you see. Because I'm the one who killed her. My only regret is I hadn't the time to rape her first, for she seemed a tasty little morsel." His jeering laughter filled the street.

Semerket hung between the two men that held him, dead-eyed. He suddenly hawked up deeply and spat in the Asp's face. Though the man's frozen rictus of a smile remained unchanged, Semerket saw his eyes become lethal.

"Hand me that spear, will you?" the Asp said calmly to the young embassy guard. "Nice," he said when he held it in his hands. "Good weight. Expensive."

The guard merely swallowed, saying nothing.

Semerket knew he was going to be impaled, just as Naia had been, and closed his eyes. He braced himself for the terrible thrust. Instead of freezing metal in his guts, it was his head that erupted in a blaze of golden sparks. The Asp had struck him with the butt-end of the spear. A metallic taste filled Semerket's mouth, and a pitiless black overtook him. The last sense to go was his hearing.

"There," the Asp said. "That ought to shut him up for a while."

THEY WERE STILL carrying him when he wakened. Hearing the loud echo of his captors' footsteps, he thought that he was once again in the cisterns beneath the city. But there was no accompanying sound of running water, and through the slits of his eyes he saw no roots snaking along the footpaths and up the walls. Torches lit the long hallway at regular intervals, telling him that the place was inhabited.

His head ached and his mouth tasted of blood, but he was no longer drunk; either the Asp's blow or sheer terror had driven the wine fumes from him. Semerket decided that if he continued to lie motionless in

their grip, a dead weight, the men would have to lay him down eventually. The moment they did, he would spring away.

The men stopped at a doorway. Semerket tensed. This was where he
would have to make his move. But he heard a bolt drawn and then a
heavy door pulled open.

They had brought him to some sort of cell, he realized. Semerket
was simultaneously relieved and fearful; it meant that they were not
going to execute him immediately, yet it precluded any attempt at
flight. The men carried him inside, dropping him roughly onto the
brick floor. From the movement of light through his closed eyelids, he
sensed that they had brought a torch into the room with them.

When he felt rough hands begin to remove his clothes, he surrendered all pretense at unconsciousness. Semerket yelled loudly, striking
out at them, and rolled away from their grasp.

"He's awake!" one of the guards shouted.

"Ah, good," said the Asp from outside the cell. "That should make
it all the more interesting for him."

Without much difficulty, the Asp's men caught him again and continued to strip off his garments. All the while, he noticed, they glanced
nervously over their shoulders to the rear of the cell. At last he was
quite naked, for they had removed even his sandals. They shoved him
roughly against the wall and backed out of the room, holding their
swords in front of them to foil any attempt to rush past them.

The last to leave was the young guard to whom he had given the
spear. The lad said nothing, but his glance was peculiarly intense. He
looked from Semerket to the wall, indicating with his eyes that Semerket should look up as well. Semerket moved his head to see that the
guard had left the torch in its socket.

What was the lad getting at? Semerket thought. So what if he could
see the cell where he was imprisoned? Of what value was that?

As the guards closed the door, he threw himself upon it, pushing at
it, pounding, but he heard only its bolt slide into place. Then a small
grilled window set high in the door opened, and a pair of dark brown
eyes stared at him—the Asp's.

"Let me out of here," Semerket pleaded. "I have gold. I'll make you
rich."

"I've gold enough," the Asp said. His indifference was chilling; how many people had offered him gold to spare their lives? It was hopeless, anyway, Semerket thought, suffering, not gold, was what the Asp relished.

Semerket heard the sound of approaching footsteps from down the hallway. The high whinny of Menef's voice reached him. "Is he in there?"

"He's there," replied the Asp.

"Let me see!"

The ambassador was so short that he had to struggle to put his eyes to the grille.

"You'll answer to Pharaoh for this, Menef! You'll be lucky if you're not burned to death for it! I know you were part of Tiya's conspiracy—"

Menef turned unconcernedly to the unseen Asp. "I told you that Aneku would burble everything to him."

"Does it matter?" murmured the Asp. "She can't talk anymore."

Semerket pounded on the door in rage. "When I get out of here, Menef, I'll tell Kutir you ordered the attack on the plantation, that your own men did it—"

The ambassador interrupted nonchalantly. "But I didn't order it, Semerket."

Semerket fell silent. Even at that moment of extremity, his mind sought to solve the puzzle. Another person suddenly pushed Menef away from the grille. A pair of familiar silver eyes took the place of the ambassador's.

"I ordered it," said the heavily accented voice. This time, however, the queen's voice was not slurry from beer. "Surely you had guessed by now."

Semerket shook his head slowly.

Narunte's laugh was a vulgar cackle. "And my husband thought you were such a brilliant investigator!" Behind her, Menef tittered immoderately.

"But why?" Semerket asked faintly.

Narunte sighed, rolling her demon's eyes, and spoke in an indulgent tone. "Because Nugash and Pinikir had been sent to undermine my husband. Shutruk, his own father, had sent them—he could not have a son who outshone him. Not even his own blood could compete with that monster. Well, I couldn't have that. I wouldn't."

Was that what Rami meant when he said that Naia had known Pinikir's secret reason for coming to Babylon?

"Menef and I put our heads together," the queen continued, "and came up with a perfect solution to both our problems. We could eliminate all our enemies at once, and make everyone think that the Isins had done it." Her voice grew petulant. "It was a perfect plan—perfect! Until you came here. You even foiled the assassin we sent against you. Did you kill him, Semerket?"

"Yes."

He saw her silver eyes darken. "He was my kinsman. The Asp said he had seen your followers do it."

"I was there that night, Semerket," said the Asp.

So he had been the second man!

Menef's voice behind the door was solicitous. "Don't fret, Majesty. In a few moments, Semerket will die and the king will never know about any of this. Your kinsman will be avenged. You've nothing more to worry about."

Semerket pounded on the door. "Pharaoh will scour this country looking for me, Menef!"

"Alas, Semerket, you'll have disappeared. As completely and utterly as anyone *can* disappear. There won't even be a fingernail left to identify you."

In the hallway, a bronze stirrup hung from a chain. The last thing Semerket saw before they closed the grated window was the Asp reaching for it, his death's-head smile etched on his face.

"Goodbye, Semerket," he heard Menef's faint voice from behind the thick door. "We'd stay and watch, but the king will be wondering where we are. Mustn't keep royalty waiting, you know." There was a pause. "Pull the lever," Menef said. Semerket heard the fading echoes of their footsteps as they walked swiftly away.

With a great rasping of chain, the sound of moving machinery came to him from the floor above. Wheels were turning, latches falling into place, hidden doors springing open. From behind him, in the cell itself, he heard another noise, and turned swiftly to look. A small portal in the far wall opened. He had not noticed it before, for it was located close to the floor, in the shadows. Two other doors were beside it, but they remained closed.

A slight movement in the portal's black recess caught his eye. Something was crawling forward into the light. A rat, Semerket thought. Yet the thing was not gray, as a rat would be, but gleamed iridescently as if it were made of metal. He looked closer. It skittered forward. Its flat, shiny eyes shone in the flickering torchlight, and mandibles moved in its head. Then its long back broke apart. As two wings sprouted, the thing lifted from the ground, and the giant black beetle flew straight at him.

With a shout of terror, Semerket realized where he was . . .

SEMERKET POUNDED ON the chamber's door, scratching at the wood with his nails, screaming for help. He felt the thing hit his back. Searing pain radiated from the nape of his neck. The beetle had sunk its mandibles into his flesh and clung there, already feasting. Its legs wrapped obscenely around the contours of his shoulders, so that it pressed against him in an almost intimate way. Semerket's mouth filled with bile.

He reached behind to pry it away. The beetle made a hissing noise, and he felt it move across his back to avoid his hands. He could not reach it. Swiftly, he turned and rammed himself against the brick wall. There was a satisfying crunch, and the beetle fell to the floor, writhing, legs and mandibles still working spasmodically.

Other beetles were beginning to emerge from the portal, equal in size to the monster he had just killed. He saw them begin to twitch and quiver as they sought to break open their carapaces and stretch their wings. Though he could barely stand to touch it, he kicked the dying insect over to where the others teemed. They fell on their cousin, swarming over it, devouring it. Even at the opposite end of the chamber, he heard the awful sounds of their jaws working in unison.

He pounded on the doors again, screaming, "Help! Somebody! Please! Open the door!"

Semerket pressed his ear to the wood to ascertain if anyone in the corridor moved, but the only thing he heard was another clanging movement from the hidden mechanism above. He turned, gasping, and saw the second portal open across the chamber.

The scorpion emerged slowly, creeping warily into the light, keeping near the door while it studied the chamber. Semerket saw it raise its forearm, and heard the clack of its pincer, as big as an infant's fist. Even in his primal state of horror, he stopped to gape at the thing.

Semerket remembered those scorpions he had seen by the river at Mari, and almost laughed aloud to think that he had once thought them large. The creature he now faced was easily the size of his foot, and its lethal sting curled up over its back like a miniature scimitar.

Semerket remembered the desert nomads telling him that the larger scorpions possessed the least-toxic venom; it was the sting of the smaller ones that caused the greatest numbers of deaths, and the most agony. But Shepak had told him that these insects in the chamber had reached their grotesque size from a steady diet of human flesh; for all he knew this could be one of the smaller specimens grown large.

He heard the dry skittering of countless others of its kin trying to wedge themselves out from the portal. But the giant scorpion did not move, and the others behind it could not enter the chamber; the first scorpion seemed to be taking Semerket's measure before attacking him. Fortunately, it sensed that easier prey was nearby, and it turned, rushing with a blur of legs to the beetle's carcass. The beetles that feasted on it fled backward, giving the scorpion ample room to dine alone. It was clear which was the dominant insect in the chamber—so far. Semerket watched, sickened, as its claws delicately sheared off pieces of the dead beetle, bringing them to its mouth where its jaws worked busily.

Other scorpions and beetles boiled out from their hidden lairs. Semerket again pounded on the door, screaming. The insects began to venture near him, and he lunged threateningly at them. He was gratified to see them retreat, but only for a moment.

Sweet Isis, what was he to do?

Then, as though Isis herself had sent the thought, he suddenly remembered the young guard.

The torch!

Now he knew why the boy had looked so intently at it before he left—and Semerket called down all the gods' blessings on the lad, who had left it there for his defense. Kind lad, intelligent lad—sweet and wonderful lad—!

In one leap, Semerket had the torch in his hand.

He brought it low in a wide circle in front of him. To his relief, the insects clambered away, hysterically piling atop one another, some even attempting to crawl back into their portals. Savagely, he held the torch to them, gleefully watching as they shriveled and died. Even the stench of their bursting carcasses was like perfume to him.

Semerket heard the overhead mechanism stir itself again, and this time maggots and grubs poured out from the third and final portal—fat squirming things the color of mucus and the size of a man's thumb. These were the things that were supposed to cleanse his carcass of all the shreds the others had left behind. He burned them as they spilled from the portal, glorying in the sounds their shriveling bodies made, like tiny shrieks as they withered into nothing.

He actually might survive this, he thought.

But the hope was dashed as soon as it was born, when he saw the torch begin to sputter, going dim for a moment.

Oh, Sweet Isis, no! He could not run short of fuel—not now! Please, please, he begged the torch soundlessly, trying to shake more melted wax from its cone into the flame. But its light was irretrievably dying, and the chamber was becoming dim.

Once again he banged on the door, screaming. The torch in his hand gutted and flared, plunging the chamber into total darkness, then lighting it up again. To his horror, he saw the insects begin to peek from their portals once more. Their flat, unblinking eyes reflected the momentary bursts of light. Antennae moved, tasting the air, seeking his smell.

Semerket sank to the floor, his back against the door, and he wept in despair. He had faced death many times, but always at the hands of humans—not like this, engulfed by thousands of tearing jaws and ripping pincers. Worse, at the end of it there would be nothing left of his body. His ka would be doomed to wander the earth forever, looking for it, never able to rest in the eons ahead. Menef had even stolen his eternal life from him . . .

The chamber echoed with his sobs. The torch sputtered for a final time and died. Not long now, he thought. He began to mouth the ritual prayer for the dead. "Osiris, who made me," he began, "raise my arms up again, fill my lungs with your breath. Let me stand at your side . . ."

From across the chamber he heard scratching movements coming nearer.

He inhaled raggedly, rushing to complete his prayer. "In the fields of Iaru . . ." But terror had burgled the prayer from his memory. "In the fields of Iaru . . ." he kept whimpering, "of Iaru . . ."

Semerket closed his eyes. He held his hands over his ears to shut out the sounds of the skittering, advancing insects. He braced himself for their onslaught . . .

Then the world fell out from behind him.

With his hands to his ears, he had not heard the door's latch unbolted. Before he even realized what was happening, arms were reaching in to drag him swiftly from the cell. He was dimly aware that the chamber door was being slammed shut, and a moment later, he heard the noise of a thousand chitinous bodies hitting the back of it at full force. Then he was looking up from the floor at the inverted face of Shepak hovering over him.

"Semerket!" Shepak whispered. "Thank the gods! You're not hurt?"

He could not speak. He could not move. He was thinking, I've died, I've passed through the gates of darkness—and this is what heaven looks like.

SEMERKET COULD NOT rise from the floor. He was only able to lie on the bricks, staring upward.

"How did you know I was here?"

"Your servants found me," Shepak said.

Servants? Semerket craned his neck. The brothers Kuri and Galzu, his two Dark Head spies, bent their heads in greeting. He was shocked to see Nidaba as well, standing apart from the rest.

"Don't look at me like that," she said languidly. "I'm not your servant."

"But how did you find me here? How did you know?"

"We had you in sight most of the day, my lord," said Galzu, wheezing. "Didn't we promise you that we would? I confess, though, we lost you after you left this lady's house. You both seemed to disappear suddenly at the end of a street. Luckily, around sunset, we checked the wineshop—merely as a last resort, you know—and saw you there."

"I had followed you from . . ." Nidaba turned away, eyeing Shepak, her Elamite enemy, and bit her lip; she could hardly mention the cisterns to him. "I followed you to the Egyptian Quarter. It took me a while to find where you had gone, but then I heard your shouts. I saw those men surrounding you."

"We knew you were in trouble," said Kuri. "The lady here joined us, then, when she saw that we were also following you. She was most concerned, and wanted us all to attack the men. We convinced her that such a job was hardly fit for a woman. The lady hid here in the corridors while we went to fetch Colonel Shepak from the garrison."

Semerket blinked, interrupting them dazedly. "But where is 'here'? Where am I?" he asked.

"The palace dungeon, Semerket," Nidaba told him.

The dungeon. Of course; that's why Queen Narunte had been there. And if they were in the dungeon, then—

Shepak interrupted his fevered thoughts. "When I got here, this lady was trying to rip the door from its hinges. I daresay she would have done it, too." He looked at Nidaba admiringly. "I've never seen a woman so brave—or so strong."

Despite the fact that Shepak was the hated invader, Nidaba dimpled prettily.

Under the full force of Nidaba's gaze, Shepak had to swallow before he spoke again. "I must tell you, Semerket," he said, "we didn't know what we'd find in there."

"A few seconds more and you wouldn't have found anything," Semerket answered. Shakily, he sat up. It was then that he noticed he was still naked. Hastily, he covered himself with his hands, looking askance at Nidaba; but Nidaba was staring only at Shepak. And Shepak, he noticed, was staring back.

"Did they happen to leave my clothes behind?" Semerket asked plaintively.

Shepak and Nidaba joined Kuri and Galzu to search the dim hallway. They found his garments on top of a nearby midden. So sure were his captors of his imminent demise, they hadn't even bothered to hide them. Shepak and Nidaba helped him dress, for his limbs were still so rubbery that he could barely manage the task. As he donned his clothes, he told his four friends of what he had learned—that Menef and the Asp had been responsible for the raid on the plantation, as well as the Egyptian temple, and that the queen had assisted them in their crimes.

When he had clothed himself at last, they huddled together, conferring in whispers. "We'll go to the garrison and put a guard around you," said Shepak. "Then we'll ask for an audience with the king. You'll have to tell him what you know."

"No," said Semerket after a moment. "Not yet. There's something else I must do here first, one final task."

"But what?" asked a puzzled Shepak. "You've solved the riddle—at least enough to tell Kutir who the culprits were. What else is there?"

"If we're truly in the palace dungeon, then we must be near the burial vaults . . . ?"

Nidaba and the Dark Heads looked at him quizzically, but it took only a fraction of time for Shepak to comprehend what he meant. Semerket saw the Elamite's face slam shut. "No," Shepak said.

"I must."

"I told you before—it's sacrilege!"

"Shepak, listen to me. Naia's body is in one of those jars. I know it now. The last possible thing I can do for her is to take her back with me to Egypt. My one comfort is to know that we'll be able to lie together in our tomb."

Shepak remained obstinate. "How would you like it if we were to come to Egypt and sift through your dead? You need a priest to recite the proper prayers and spells before you can go inside a crypt. It isn't just a tomb to us—it's the underworld itself. Ghosts and demons lurk there!"

Before Semerket could reply, Nidaba delicately coughed, interjecting in a small voice, "I'm a priest." She shot an alarmed glance at Shepak. "Er, priestess. I serve Ishtar."

Semerket looked at Shepak, silently pleading for his consent.

With a resigned curse, Shepak seized a nearby torch from its sconce.

THERE WERE ACTUALLY several floors to the palace cellar. Over the generations the Babylonian kings had been forced to dig ever deeper into the fine river soil, creating chambers in which to store the detritus of their reigns—unwanted gifts of tribute, old furniture, tattered hangings. Statues from faraway lands, outlandishly formed and bizarrely colored, emerged from the darkness, caught in the passing light of Shepak's torch. They seemed, indeed, to lunge forward when the light caught them, like the underworld demons Shepak feared.

They came to a pair of immense copper-plated doors, set into a blood-red wall. Nidaba began to chant a prayer in her loveliest voice, while Galzu came forward with his knife to dig out the lead that had been poured, molten, into the crack between the doors. Only when Nidaba stopped her chanting and indicated that he could, did Shepak pull them open.

The first thing Semerket noticed was the overwhelming smell of honey, overlaid by the sweeter smell of rot. Semerket placed a tentative foot inside the crypt. Nidaba's prayers must have been effective, for no demons or ghosts rose to do battle with him. With a nod to the others, Semerket reached for the torch that Shepak held.

"I'm coming with you," Shepak said.

"You don't have to."

"You'll need someone to hold the torch for you."

Semerket nodded, grateful for the company.

"I'm coming, too," Nidaba said. "I must say the Prayer for the Dead over the jars you unseal."

Shepak shook his head in wonder to see such courage in so delicate a creature. Leaving Kuri and Galzu to guard the crypt's entrance, the three walked silently forward. To Semerket's eyes, the place looked like one of the huge river warehouses in Thebes, with thousands of clay jars filled with grain or olives. But these jars held a different treasure—the preserved corpses of Babylonian kings, their wives and nobles, families and servants.

Semerket had no idea how he was ever to find Naia in them. But Shepak said they would locate Kutir's brother-in-law in the far end of the crypt, where the most recent chambers had been dug. As they walked further into the crypt, Semerket noted that each jar was inscribed with the name of the entombed, together with the clay seal of the king or queen they had served. Semerket was surprised by the fact that king and servant alike were buried in exactly the same kind of jar. In Babylonia, kings were not gods as they were in Egypt; in death, all were equal before an unforgiving and indifferent heaven.

As they penetrated into the most distant reaches of the crypt, the jars were newer-looking, not covered with the dust of centuries. The honey smelled fresher, too. Soon the jars became pristine in their new-ness, shiny with brown glaze, and the honey was still sticky on their sides.

"Here they are," whispered Shepak.

Shepak pointed to the seal on the jar in front of him. It was Kutir's seal, and the name below it said that the body within belonged to Nugash, the husband of Princess Pinikir. To Semerket's dismay, many of the jars bore only the words "servant of Nugash" or "servant of Pinikir." As there had been no one left alive to identify the servants, Shepak explained, there had been no record of their names. Semerket groaned aloud. It meant that he must search every jar reading "Servant of Pinikir." He counted them—there were at least six such jars in the row before him, perhaps more behind.

He went to the first jar that bore the inscription. Nidaba, white-lipped, came forward to say a prayer to the jar's inhabitant, begging their forgiveness. At its conclusion, she nodded to Semerket. His hands were trembling as he smashed the jar's seal of dried clay. The moment he did, the foul stench of putrefaction flooded the room.

Shepak brought the torch nearer so Semerket could look inside. It was worse than he thought—a foamy scum of rot was on top of the honey. The Babylonians did not remove the soft inner organs as the Egyptians did; all the gases and liquids of corruption had therefore been released, to rise and pool at the top of the jar.

Semerket felt his stomach twisting, and a sour taste rose again in the back of his throat. Firmly, he willed his nausea away; he simply could not give in to it now. Holding his breath, he fiercely plunged his hand into the viscous mess. He closed his eyes, reaching further, until he felt his hand brush against a nose, and then an ear.

He gasped, took another quick breath, and held it. Moving his hand slowly through the thick honey, he reached for the woman's floating hair and pulled. The weight of the body was much heavier than he had imagined, for the honey did not want to release it so easily. Suddenly the scalp tore loose from the skull, and he stumbled backward.

Semerket stood in the middle of the crypt, clutching a wad of dripping hair in his hand. Shepak's face was a mask of horror, and Nidaba made a strange noise, turning away. Semerket looked down at the gooey mess. The hair was white; the woman had been elderly.

Naia was not in that jar.

He and Nidaba went to the next jar. Again, a prayer was intoned, and again he broke the jar's seal. Once more, the fetid, sour odor rose in his nostrils. He plunged his hand once more into the mess; this time, however, he reached down further than the corpse's head, hoping to snag an arm. Semerket was surprised when he felt a piece of cloth, wrapped around the body's shoulders; for some reason, he had assumed the dead would be buried in the nude. His job became a bit simpler by this discovery, for a robe or mantle would be far easier to grasp than a slippery piece of flesh.

Bracing himself against the side of the jar, he pulled on the cloth. Slowly the body rose; finally, the top of the head emerged. This time the color of its streaming hair was black, and he strained to lift the rest of the body into the light.

"Bring the torch closer," he panted.

Shepak moved the torch, angling it toward the face. Both of them winced to see it. Even with the natural slackening the features had undergone, Semerket could not remember ever having seen a picture of such affecting and hideous agony. The woman had suffered massive burns, and one side of her face was gone. The features that remained were horribly distorted; her torn mouth a hideous grimace.

But the woman was not Naia.

Semerket let the body slip back again into the dark, golden ooze, where it settled slowly. Honey drizzled across the tiles from his arm as he went to the next jar. He did not know how much more of this horrific gruesomeness he could endure. But when he broke the seal, he knew his search was over.

There, floating at the top of the jar, fouled by putrefaction, was Naia's mantle. It was the one he had given her on the Theban docks, as she was about to set sail for Babylonia. It had been the color of the Egyptian sky, embroidered in five-pointed stars of gold thread.

Tears ran down his face as he reached his arm into the jar. Sobs began to wrench from him. Shepak had to look away, seeing his friend so grief-stricken. Nidaba dropped her head to stare at the tiles. Within the thick honey, Semerket felt his fingers move across his beloved's features, reaching to the lips that he used to kiss so fondly, to the nose, over the closed eyes fringed in black lashes. Summoning all of his resolve, he reached for the yoke of her rough servant's dress and gently lifted her into the light.

Her head emerged, the honey streaming over her domed forehead, black hair glued to her narrow skull. The honey had altered her lovely dark features, however, for her skin seemed bleached of all color...

Then Semerket looked again.

"That isn't Naia," he whispered.

Both Nidaba and Shepak jerked their heads to see.

"Why, no," Shepak said, after a moment, and his voice was faint with shock. "That's Princess Pinikir."

BOOK FOUR

DAY OF THE
FALSE KING

THE FIRST WHEAT HAD BEGUN TO SPROUT across Babylonia's fields. Overnight, the bearded spears covered the tamped, rutted earth left behind by the retreating Elamite armies. The priests of Bel-Marduk, after consulting many sheep livers, went into the cities of Babylonia to declare that the New Year had begun. After the proper rites and observances were made, after sacrifice and prayer had propitiated the sixty thousand gods of Babylonia, the priests proclaimed that the Day of the False King had at last arrived.

The drab, mud-brick cities of the river plain transformed themselves overnight into riotous fairgrounds, decked in floating streamers that flew from every building. Babylon, of course, was the loudest and most riotous of all. On the Euphrates, the gilded barges of the gods assembled in a magnificent river procession, parading in splendor around its walls. The flotilla's progress signaled to the thousands who lined the banks that the gods had returned from their annual retreat into the high mountains to extend once again their blessings to humankind for another year.

The Day of the False King was above all a topsy-turvy day, when every role and law in the land were reversed. In private homes, masters waited on their servants, while in the thoroughfares, vendors good-naturedly opened their shops to looters. But the most important part of the festival was the coronation of the False King. Every year the priests of Marduk launched a citywide search for the most foolish man in the kingdom, to name him Babylon's king for a day.

That very morning the priests had gone through the city, breaking into the homes of rich and poor alike, shouting the ancient words, "Where is the king? Bring him forth! He must be arrayed in his royal robes and given the rod and ring so that he can dispense justice to his people! Show us where he is, for we have lost him!" And the people ran about, pretending to be frightened, shouting with alarm, "Where is our king? He is lost! Let him be found at once!"

Of course, everyone knew that the real king was safe in his palace, and that he had already chosen the most foolish man in the kingdom to rule in his place. This year's festival promised to be among the most memorable in all of Babylon's long history, for there were not one, but two False Kings, and they sat enthroned together in the vast courtyard of Etemenanki. One of them was a short, plump man, who wept piteously and bewailed his fate, even though his elite guards jabbed him with their spears, urging him to put on a better face for the crowds. The other, a scary-looking fellow with a macabre smile and a mark at the corner of his eye, thrilled the Babylonians with his glowering stare and defiant posture. Though the pair's lack of humor was disappointing, the crowds had every faith that their new king had chosen wisely.

The new king of Babylonia was in fact such a beloved figure that nothing he did could ever be amiss in the eyes of his subjects. He was so handsome and so clever, his subjects boasted, that people vied to see how extravagantly they could praise him, and even predicted that Babylon was poised to embark on a new golden age.

The proof of all this?

Why, hadn't the new king delivered the country from the detested invader without a blow being struck? Such a hero had not walked the streets of Babylon since Gilgamesh himself was a lad!

As the crowds laughed and caroused drunkenly in the corridors of the city, they did not know or even notice the true author of their good fortune—the black-eyed Egyptian man, slim and long-limbed, who skirted the crowd's edge. Some of the more spirited Dark Heads tried to pull him into the streets to join their shameless dances, but he slipped from their hands, smiling but firm, intent on his own business. His prudery did not offend them, for they soon found other amusements to divert themselves.

As he entered the forecourt of Etemenanki, Semerket slowly forced his way through the crowds to where the two False Kings were enthroned together on their raised dais. Menef was weeping copious tears, which only seemed to induce more cruel behavior on the part of his "subjects," who expected their False Kings to be foolish and ridiculous, not sad. The crowds pelted him with waste and spat on him as they came near, enjoining him to laugh and prattle as a proper False King should. Menef did his best to placate the Babylonians with half-hearted antics, but the crowds still covered him with offal.

The Asp's aggression was more satisfying to them, for it somehow seemed more kingly in their eyes that he should roar and stamp his feet when they ventured near him. Chains bound the False Kings to their thrones, but the Asp's cruel expression was enough to deter the people from taunting him as they did Menef. But when Semerket emerged from the horde to stand at the base of their thrones, to stare at them and nothing more, the behavior of the two False Kings changed abruptly.

Menef's eyes bugged out of his head, and he began to scream in fright. He struggled to turn away, dementedly gibbering. Even the Asp cowered, calling on the gods of Egypt to protect him from vengeful ghosts. The crowd roared in delight to see the two False Kings behave in so cowardly a fashion.

This was more like it!

Semerket merely watched the two kings, a scornful smile tugging at his lips. Menef and the Asp had not been told that he had survived the Insect Chamber, and they no doubt believed that he had come back from behind the Gates of Darkness to snatch them both into hell. Semerket made a sudden lunging gesture at them, and the crowd screamed with laughter to see the two False Kings fall backward, tugging at their chains, shrieking in terror.

Bored with his game, Semerket moved away. When Menef and the Asp dared to look up again, he was gone, confirming their supposition that they had indeed seen his vengeful spirit.

Semerket did not pause to look at the wrestlers or jugglers who entertained the mobs. He was too intent on his final task to clutter his mind with nonessentials. Semerket usually detested festivals, discomfited by the crowds and the noise, but Mother Mylitta had told him to wait by the gagu's drawbridge. Nothing that morning—neither riot nor war nor even a festival—could have kept him away.

Semerket did not call out his arrival to the female guards, for Mother Mylitta had warned him that the gagu had its own rituals to perform and he was not to disturb them. So Semerket joined the others who took their ease near the gagu's moat and did as he had been told; he waited quietly.

The Babylonian sun was its usual savage self, and Semerket wished that he had bought one of the wide-brimmed straw hats that the mat-weavers sold in the streets. Removing his sandals, he plunged his feet into the moat's cool water. With the sounds of a mirthful people all around him and the pleasant feeling of tiny fish nibbling at his toes, he was soon lulled into an agreeable torpor.

Though he was not exactly dozing, he was able to reflect at last on all that had happened to him since his discovery of Princess Pinikir's body. Whether he could make sense of it all was an entirely different matter . . .

DOWN IN THE CRYPT, he and Shepak had decided that it was too dangerous for Semerket to appear immediately at the palace. They reasoned that if Queen Narunte or Menef saw him, the two might even then engineer some desperate attempt upon his life. Shepak therefore went alone to fetch King Kutir to the crypt in secret. Shepak later told Semerket that he had found the solitary king in a council chamber, pale and anxious, reading some recent dispatches from his father's capital city of Susa.

"Sire," Shepak said, "we've found your sister."

Kutir gave a start, rising to his feet slowly. "Alive?"

Shepak dropped his eyes, staring at the floor, and the king had his answer.

"So the Isins killed her, then . . ."

"No, Sire."

Kutir looked up sharply.

"Semerket is in the crypt below the palace, where we found the princess's body. He will be able to explain——"

"The crypt?" Kutir was appalled.

"Will you come, Sire?"

Kutir glared, unused to interruption. "Yes—and my bodyguards will arrest him for heresy. I told him specifically he was not to violate our dead."

"I think it best, Sire, that you hear his tale first, without your bodyguards as witnesses. Afterward, you can decide for yourself who can know the truth."

Kutir immediately comprehended Shepak's meaning. "Is it conspiracy, then?"

Again, Shepak said nothing. Kutir strapped his sword to his side and thrust a dagger into his belt. Though he had every confidence in both Semerket and Shepak, he did not intend to walk blithely into a trap, for in the past Elamite kings had been slain by trusted underlings.

In the palace cellars, they came to the red wall that separated this world from the next. Nidaba and the two Dark Heads were gone, dismissed by Semerket. Their presence would have only served to alarm the Elamite king.

Shepak and Kutir found Semerket, stained and sticky, in the far end of the crypt. Kutir saw the shards of the shattered seals littering the floor, and his eyes flashed indignation.

"Sire," Semerket said before the king could vilify him, "rest assured that a priestess said every proper prayer over the dead before I searched here."

Kutir fell silent, and Semerket continued warily. "We believe that your sister's body was mistakenly identified as a servant and placed into this jar. Will you look?"

Kutir exhaled, then nodded shortly.

Semerket reached again into the jar and gently pulled the princess's head into the torchlight. The honey streamed in oozing rivulets from her nose and forehead, and the torch picked out her features in wavering outline.

"Is this your sister, lord?" Semerket asked.

The king looked away quickly. He nodded. "Who did this?" muttered Kutir darkly.

"I'm ashamed to say, Sire, that Egyptians committed the crime. It was Menef who sent the raiders to your sister's home. And it was the Asp, his bodyguard, who carried out the murders."

Semerket related how he had discovered that Menef had been part of the conspiracy that had taken the life of the Great Ramses III, and that Menef kept his ties to the remaining conspirators in Egypt, principally Prince Mayatum, who himself had instructed Menef to execute Naia and Rami.

"Are you saying that my sister and her husband were killed because this Egyptian prince wanted to revenge himself—on *you?*"

"No, Sire. It was not Menef, but your wife who ordered your sister's death. All the killings occurred at the plantation to make it seem as if Isins had carried them out. The queen admitted this to me herself."

Kutir, who must have known of his wife's hatred for his sister, put a hand to his forehead and looked as if he might have fallen had not Shepak assisted him to a bench. Leaning heavily against the wall, the king listened in wonder as Semerket told of being locked in the Insect Chamber by Narunte and the scheming Menef.

Kutir was incredulous, and he shook his head. "The Insect Chamber? But that's impossible. No one survives it—"

"Shepak rescued me at the last possible moment. If you don't believe me, I'll show you the marks." Without waiting for Kutir's consent, Semerket turned and pulled down the yoke of his tunic. The wound where the beetle's jaws had dug into him was swollen and discolored.

The sight of the still-bleeding lesion at last convinced Kutir that Semerket's tale was true. "But why?" he asked dully. "Why would she do it?"

"Queen Narunte discovered that your sister and her husband came here with secret orders from your father. Your victories in Babylonia threatened him. They had been charged to undermine your successes where they could."

"Successes!" Kutir echoed bitterly. He abruptly brought his hands to his face, and his shoulders shook silently. He regained control of himself quickly, however, looking off into the dark. "Narunte's only a mountain chieftain's daughter, unused to more enlightened ways, fierce in her love for me. She's rough, sometimes, I acknowledge it . . ."

At that moment, Semerket knew that Kutir would never bring the queen to justice for what she had done to him. He shrugged philosophically and said, "Then let the blame fall on Menef and his henchmen alone, Sire. They come from a civilized nation and should have known better."

Kutir regarded him gratefully. "You've lived up to your reputation, Semerket. You found my sister, as I knew you would, and were honorable enough to tell me of your compatriots' part in her murder. Many other men would not have had the courage to tell me the truth. I will order the arrest of Egypt's ambassador and his men. Their punishment will be left to you." Then his eyes filled with shame. "As to my part of the bargain, I regret that my current strategic position prevents me from allowing Bel-Marduk's idol to leave Babylon. The god's magi, I'm afraid, would laugh in my face if I ordered it. They're counting on another king to give the orders in Babylon soon; I wish you luck with him."

"I understand, Sire." He felt it would only cloud the issue to tell Kutir that he was already on extremely friendly terms with his likely successor. Why trouble the poor man with inconsequentials?

It was dawn when they emerged from the palace cellars. To Semerket, who had spent most of the previous day in the tunnels beneath Babylon and the long night hours searching through the palace crypt, it seemed as if he had lived for a time in perpetual darkness. It was almost startling to see the rays of the sun again.

Kutir told them both to wait at the garrison. He would send for them after he arrested the pair, he promised, when it was safe for Semerket to appear. But the hours passed and no message came. Concerned, Semerket and Shepak took themselves to a side entrance of the palace used by tradesmen and servants. They hoped to waylay some butler or serving woman, to ask if they might know why the king tarried. But the servants were just as ignorant as they.

Semerket began to feel uneasy. He sensed that something strange, even profound, was taking place within the palace. His sense of discomfort increased with the arrival of several couriers from the south. They rode their foaming mounts at full gallop into the palace courtyard, dismounting before their horses had even stopped. They ran swiftly into the palace, clutching their important-looking leather pouches, not even pausing to wipe the dirt from their faces.

"They're from King Shutruk," said Shepak, recognizing their livery. He attempted to hail the next courier in Elamite, but the man simply barreled passed him and into the palace without even looking at him.

Semerket, who had his own vital reasons for not wanting to stay, was on the verge of suggesting that Shepak should meet alone with Kutir. He did not need to be present when they locked Menef and the Asp away; Shepak, as former commander of the garrison, was no doubt admirably versed in the detention of prisoners. At that moment, however, a steward approached, saying that Kutir would see them.

He and Shepak entered the throne room, where huge carved bulls' heads topped thick square pillars. The Gryphon Throne itself sat on a dais of intricately carved ivory panels. But Kutir, Semerket noticed, did not sit on it. Instead, he was at the corner of the room, in close conversation with Queen Narunte. They both raised their heads to stare at him as he approached.

Fear shot through Semerket, particularly when Shepak was detained by the chamberlain at the edge of the hall. Semerket squinted into the dim light, trying to read the expression on Narunte's face. He expected rage, guilt, even shock that he had survived the Insect Chamber, but her reaction to his presence was of the most casual indifference, as if he were some stranger she had not met before.

Courtiers moved aside as Semerket came forward alone, his footsteps echoing loudly on the malachite tiles. Was this an ambush? Was he once again to be cast into the Insect Chamber for what he had discovered?

He genuflected before the royal pair.

"Semerket," Kutir said quietly. "I must tell you, as representative of

Egypt's Falcon Throne, that King Shutruk of Elam, my father, has mounted his golden chariot."

Semerket looked up, staring blankly. "What?"

"He's dead, Semerket," elucidated Kutir tersely. "Couriers brought the news today. After a meal of pigeon pie and figs, his bowels turned to a bloody flux and he was struck dumb. He succumbed a few hours ago without speaking another word." Kutir's voice broke, and he began to weep, though Semerket believed his tears were only for show. "He may have been poisoned, my spies tell me. Can you believe it? Who could ever commit such a terrible deed against Elam's greatest king?"

Without thinking, Semerket glanced at Queen Narunte. She was not afraid to meet his glance. Her silver eyes did not glitter; Semerket could read nothing in their pale depths, not even satisfaction. Nevertheless, he knew the answer to Kutir's question stood at his side. What a career lay ahead of Narunte, he thought in wonder—provided she avoided the strong brew that loosened her tongue.

"I am grief-stricken, Sire," Semerket mumbled. "As I'm sure Pharaoh will be when he receives this dreadful news." Semerket hoped that his words were adequate to the situation. He could not help but think that the entire world—and especially his son—would breathe easier now that the old tyrant was dead.

"What will you do now, Sire?"

"I must return to Susa. I must go there before my brother can raise an army and stake his own claim to the throne. But . . ."

The king fell silent, looking at Semerket helplessly.

Yes, indeed—but! Semerket knew that with the Isins hidden in the city, with the food stocks gone and the Elamite fleet destroyed, there was little chance of Kutir's reaching the border with his armies intact. The king could, of course, easily escape the city in disguise, but what good would it do him to enter Elam without his armies? If he pursued so rash a course, he would be able to count his life in moments.

Well, Semerket thought, these were the occupational hazards of being an invader in a hostile country. It was none of his affair, or Egypt's. Though Semerket had not found Kutir to be the savage despot he had been led to expect, neither was he particularly fond of him. In addition, if he were being truthful with himself, he much preferred it if his friend Marduk ruled in Babylonia.

So much for Egyptian neutrality, Semerket thought grimly.

It was then that the idea occurred to him. He coughed politely, and spoke.

"YOU MEAN HE'LL LEAVE—just like that?" Marduk was incredulous.

"I mean exactly that."

Semerket was once again in the tunnels beneath the city. He sat in the small dark room off the cistern that Marduk and his generals called their headquarters.

The tall Isin from Mari made an angry gesture. "Don't believe him, my lord. The Elamite king sent this Egyptian to tempt you into some kind of trap."

Semerket rolled his eyes. "How can it be a trap, you moron, when it was my own idea?"

The Isin struggled to dispute him, finally muttering, "Because everyone knows that Egyptians can't be trusted."

"Semerket can," said Marduk flatly. "But I must admit that I'm finding it difficult to believe Kutir's telling the truth. I mean, after all the men he's lost, all the supplies and treasure—to believe that he'd simply abandon this misbegotten war of his . . ."

"He knows he's trapped in the Royal Quarter, Marduk. The only way he can leave is for you to agree to this truce. If you don't, you'll face a siege that might last for months, even years. Kutir's brother will seize Elam's throne and Kutir will have no kingdom except what he can manage to hold on to here. Wouldn't you rather let him go now, when he has another kingdom to go to, rather than create an enemy who knows that he has nothing to lose?"

The Isins erupted into loud, angry debate, saying that they must punish Kutir for his invasion of Babylonia. "We have a chance to kill him," said the tall Isin, pounding his fist into his palm. "And then we will be the ones to march into Elam! With Kutir and his armies slaughtered, Elam can only drop into our hands like a ripe fig!"

"And so it begins all over again . . ." Semerket muttered darkly.

"Semerket is right," Marduk said. "For the first time in almost three centuries, a native-born Dark Head will sit on the Gryphon Throne. We've achieved everything we set out to do; let's not risk the gods' anger by asking for more. We will let the Elamite invader and his armies leave peaceably. Besides," he continued, smiling craftily, "these Elamites will soon be engaged in a long and bloody civil war. At the end of it, they will be weak and spiritless. What better time to sweep in and seize that ripe fig? Time is on our side, gentlemen—we can afford to be generous for once."

Mesopotamia never changes, Semerket thought in disgust. Thus it had been, and thus it ever would be—a succession of "strong men" seizing power from one another. He took that moment to slip away into the little room where Kem-weset waited with Rami. The boy's eyes were open and they brightened to see him.

"No fever?" Semerket asked Kem-weset.

"Not under my care!" said the physician forcefully. But he added in a humbler tone, "The gods were kind."

"To us all," Semerket agreed with unusual enthusiasm. He turned his black eyes on Rami. "How do you feel, boy?"

"I have a headache."

"Headache or no, it seems that you won't be standing in front of Osiris anytime soon. So you didn't have to ask for my forgiveness, after all. It simply wasn't needed."

Patting Rami's hand in farewell, Semerket then took himself into the outer hallway. Marduk soon joined him.

"You look very morose," said Semerket. "I'd have thought you'd be ecstatic." Semerket even laughed aloud. "You'd best be careful, Marduk. People might start mistaking you for me."

Marduk sighed before he answered. "All my life, I've been trained for one thing—to struggle for my heritage. I had prepared myself to die for it, just as my own father did. But thanks to you, Semerket, my struggle is over."

"And that makes you sad?"

"The truth is, life prepared me only to struggle, never for the victory." He shook his head impatiently. "I'm talking nonsense. You can't possibly understand what I mean."

Semerket smiled. "Maybe I'm the only person in the world who can."

Later that day, after many trips on Semerket's part between the various levels of the city, a truce between the two rivals for the hand of Babylon was announced. Heralds went into the cities of the plain, proclaiming in an edict from King Marduk-kabit-ahhešu, the first king of the second Isin dynasty, that he would allow the Elamites to leave Babylonia unmolested. Marduk dispatched the Isin troops themselves to escort the retreating armies to the border, not only to protect them from any unwarranted violence on the part of a people who had suffered so much at their hands, but also to make sure they well and truly left the nation.

AS THE ELAMITES were making ready to depart, Semerket found Shepak in the garrison compound.

"You saved my life," said Shepak simply.

"You saved mine."

The two men stared awkwardly at the ground for a moment, and then spoke simultaneously:

"If ever you're in Elam . . ."

"If you're ever in Egypt . . ."

They laughed. Embraced.

"Say goodbye to that goddess friend of yours," said Shepak. "Tell her that had it been another day, another time, she might have been the woman I took back with me to Elam."

Semerket, biting his tongue, promised that he would convey the message to Nidaba. Then Shepak mounted his horse and put on his helmet (which had been stripped of its grisly body parts, lest such mementos incite the Dark Heads into final acts of revenge). The last Semerket saw of him, Shepak was riding at Kutir's side through the Ishtar Gate.

Only then, at last, was Semerket able to attend to the penultimate task that awaited him. There were no more international disputes to settle, no more crypts to search, no foul insect chambers to escape. Semerket's step was light and confident as he made his way for the second time to the gagu.

• • •

As determined as he was, difficulties beset his short journey. Upon learning the news that the Elamites would vacate the country, a spontaneous festival erupted on the streets of Babylon that night; people left their homes for the first time in two days to converge on the temples and palaces, eager to make their devotions to the gods and perhaps catch a glimpse of their handsome, dashing new king Marduk.

By the time Semerket at last arrived at the gagu, it was well after dark. Its drawbridge was down, and Semerket walked across it and into the courtyard without asking permission to enter. For once, none of its women were loading donkey trains, nor did he see the smoke of melting bitumen rising into the night skies.

Yet, just as before, the women guards once again surrounded him, spears leveled. Even in times of celebration, it seemed, the gagu women never lost their wariness of men.

"What do you want, Semerket?" the guard asked.

He raised his brow in surprise; at least they knew his name. "I would see Mother Mylitta."

This time they did not run to Mylitta to ask if she would condescend to receive him. Instead, they took him directly into the gagu, once again delivering him to the base of Mylitta's soaring observatory tower.

"Doesn't she ever come down from up there?" Semerket asked forlornly as he set his unwilling foot upon the steps.

Slowly, hugging the tower, turning his face inward, he crept up its long height. At the top, Mother Mylitta was, as ever, peering through her tubes of bronze and making her notes on tablets of clay. She did not even look up as Semerket stepped into the enclosure.

"Good news," she said in her deep, masculine voice. "The Seshat star has turned forward in its arc again, and will soon be back in its proper place above Egypt. It seems you weren't the evil it predicted, Semerket. In fact, I'm beginning to think that you've brought great fortune to Babylon instead."

"Had you bothered to read my horoscope, perhaps you might have known that."

"You fool," she said, not unkindly. "Do you think I hadn't?"

He looked at her, his black eyes suddenly flaming like melted bitumen. "Then why didn't you tell me who the woman truly was?" he whispered fiercely, unable to keep his emotions in hand.

"I take it you mean the one who came here after the raid?"

"You know I do. The one dressed as a princess."

"You have to realize, Semerket, that the gagu exists not for the sake of trade, as most people think, but for the protection of all women who suffer at the hands of men. Why do you think I went out to the plantation that night? After what I learned from the stars, it didn't matter if the princess was an Elamite, a Dark head—or even an Egyptian. A woman in peril will always find a home with us as long as we exist."

"But it was cruel to let me go without telling me that night I came here; savage. If you'd read my chart, couldn't you see my love for her in it?"

"Yes, I saw it there. I don't think I've ever seen anything like it in the heavens before. It's almost as strong as your love of truth, your desire to see all things clearly. Both traits impel you equally through your life."

"Then why did you let me leave? I almost died afterward! I might never have seen her again!"

Her voice was harsh, without emotion. "It's precisely because of what I saw in your chart that I couldn't tell you who she was."

Semerket felt his scalp prickle; he had not considered this possibility. "What else have you seen in your heavens, Mother Mylitta?" he asked quietly.

"This I have seen. I've seen how you destroy those who love you. I've seen how death dogs your every step. You're a catastrophe to those who attach themselves to you, for you bring such pain to them that you can in a trice annihilate all their joy of living."

Semerket dropped his eyes, unable to withstand her forthright gaze. Everything she said was true.

"Now you know why I could not let her go to you, or even tell you she was here—not until I showed her myself what the stars predicted for you."

"And have you told her?"

"Tonight. Then she will decide for herself what her future will be. Know that she has been offered a place here. It's the right we grant to all the women who ask our help. No man may claim her from these premises without her own consent."

He swallowed. "When will I know her decision?"

"Wait outside the gate at midmorning, tomorrow. You will have your answer then. But mind you, do not yell at our gate, for it is the Day of the False King and we have our own rituals to perform."

So HE SAT in the hot sun on the Day of the False King, his feet dangling in the gagu's moat. Hope seared Semerket's soul, yet despair also chilled him. What would she decide, knowing that life with him meant having death for their constant companion? But Mother Mylitta had done nothing other than confirm what everyone in Egypt already instinctively knew—that Semerket was a Follower of Set, a man of chaos and danger.

Screams erupted in the nearby courtyard, and he quickly turned his head, his heart in his throat. But the crowd was only watching the antics of gymnasts walking a tight rope; one of them had pretended to fall, catching herself at the last moment.

Semerket breathed deeply to calm himself.

There were a myriad of smells in the air that day—fish from the river sizzled on the food vendors' griddles; fresh-baked bread dipped in honey was given free to children (his gorge rose, for after the crypts he doubted that he would ever willingly taste honey again); waterfowl turned on spits, their skins crackling in the flames' heat, fat dripping down to sputter on the orange coals.

Yet he knew at once when her familiar scent of citrus oil came over him, obliterating every other smell.

He turned.

"My love," she said.

Then she was in his arms.

•   •   •

IN LATER YEARS, Semerket would remember those short weeks that followed the Day of the False King as the happiest of his life. He and Naia were honored guests in the sanctuary of Bel-Marduk, where his one-time slave was crowned king of Babylonia. They winced when High Magus Adad slapped Marduk smartly across the face before setting the mitered crown on his head. Tersely, Adad reminded both Marduk and the crowded room that kings in Babylonia are mortal, and that kingship is a painful duty. Despite that moment of shock, the ceremony proved so long and intricate that he and Naia fidgeted with boredom. They leaned forward, rapt, however, when Marduk stepped forward to grasp the outstretched golden hand of Bel-Marduk's idol. Semerket half-expected that lightning would strike, or that the fonts of holy water would begin to boil, but nothing of the sort happened. Yet, when he thought about it later, he realized that something holy and mystical had indeed occurred, the quiet miracle of a people taking back their nation after three hundred years of servitude to foreigners. And, perhaps most miraculous of all, he had played a part in it.

At the festivities that night, Nidaba sang a special song of praise to Semerket. Sitting with Naia at the royal dais, he was more embarrassed than flattered. Naia snickered behind her hand as he flushed red, struggling to assume a dignified air as Nidaba intoned the thanks of a grateful nation. Though her voice was thrilling as ever, the ancient text Nidaba sang alluded to tales with which he and Naia had little familiarity. The two of them slipped away from the festivities as early as decency would allow.

More than the honors and gifts that Marduk showered on them, it was their time alone in their hostel's bed, whispering the night away, that Semerket would remember always as their happiest moments. And it was there, as she nestled in his arms, that Naia revealed the remaining pieces of the mystery to him.

"When did you know I was alive?" she asked, stroking the scar on his forehead.

"The moment I saw Princess Pinikir in that terrible jar, wearing the scarf I gave you. I knew exactly what you'd done, you stupid woman—"

"*What* did you call me?"

"You changed clothes with her, didn't you? To save her life."

"What if I did?" she admitted, unwilling but still defiant.

"Stupid."

"But, Semerket! I didn't think they'd come after a servant. She had a child at home waiting for her—"

"And you didn't?"

"But I had no hope of ever returning to him." Naia's eyes became moist. "Poor woman. I thought she might have a chance of seeing him again if she was dressed like a servant. How could I know that my poor robes actually made her a target?"

"As hers made you one."

"Ah, but by then the mansion was in flames and there was no one to see me go out the back door."

He held her close. "And then you hid in the river."

"I?" she said, surprised. "No."

"But you were dripping wet when you went into the village, jabbering madly in Egyptian. Did you know that the villagers thought you were a river nymph, speaking the language of immortals?"

"Did they really?" she said, momentarily charmed by the notion. "No, when the raiders set fire to the plantation, I ran out the back way through the flames. The princess's mantle had caught fire, so I jumped into the well. The river was much too far away, and they would surely have seen me in the light of the flames. It took me all night to climb back up that rope."

"Clever girl."

"So now I'm clever!"

"I admit it. And beautiful, too."

They kissed, for how long a time Semerket did not know.

"So after you hid in the village, you went to the gagu."

"It was the only place I knew to go. Mother Mylitta had offered us sanctuary earlier that night. Rami was dead—at least I thought he was—and you certainly weren't there to rescue me. I didn't know what else to do, other than go to her."

A sudden horrid thought struck him. "When you were at the gagu," he asked, "what were your duties there?"

"They sent me out with the donkey trains sometimes, to help deliver the gold they covered in bitumen. Why?"

He thought back to that moment when he had arrived in Babylon, when he had seen the gagu's women for the first time. Semerket had almost called out to one of them because she had reminded him of Naia.

Sweet Isis, he wondered—what if that woman truly had been his wife all along?

Naia saw his brow furrow in self-reproach. "Ketty, what's wrong?"

"Nothing," he said quickly. Firmly he put the thought aside. Everything had turned out well in the end and there was no use in rebuking himself for things that might have been.

"Were you happy in the gagu?" he asked.

"I suppose."

"What changed your mind about staying there?"

"What do you mean, 'changed my mind'? I never intended to stay there in the first place. I am not the type to spend my life among women. You should know me well enough by now to realize that." She pressed herself close to him.

"Even after Mother Mylitta told you about my future? How dangerous it would be?"

"Even then."

"What convinced you I was worth the risk?"

"Oh, really, as if she were telling me anything I didn't already know! These astrologers always predict the obvious and then expect everybody to gasp in awe. Ketty, I've always known you work in a dangerous profession. And I've always known you're worth the risk. As for the rest of it, the dangers ahead—if they really exist—we'll face them together, won't we?"

"Kiss me," he said.

"I just did."

"Again."

AT THE END of the festival, guards escorted the two False Kings into a nearby temple. There, magi and shamans read from prayer books, rattling their sistra and blowing into shrill pipes.

"What are these fools doing now?" muttered the Asp.

"I don't know!" hissed Menef in misery. He was bruised and stinking from the many pieces of offal and shards of broken pottery hurled at him during the festival.

The two were unaware that their most important function as False Kings would soon commence. The priests began to cast spells, ensuring that all the sins committed by King Marduk during the previous year were magically transferred to them. They also did not know that at the end of every festival, the False King was slain so that he could take the true king's sins with him into the underworld. In ancient days, when the country had been poor, a goat was used for the ceremony. But as Babylon grew more prosperous and sophisticated, men were given the honor instead.

It was the prerogative of the reigning king to decide whether to be merciful when slaying a False King. Since Menef had been a dignitary and the Asp a soldier, Marduk (after consulting with Semerket) decided to administer a drug-laced wine to them. Shortly thereafter, they fell into a coma.

It was not a deep sleep, however, for the drug was not a powerful one. When they awoke, almost simultaneously, they found themselves in a brick cell, stripped of all their royal raiment. They had no idea where they were, and looked about in hazy wonder.

A small window in a nearby door suddenly snapped shut.

They heard a muffled order given from outside the cell. Only when Menef heard the grinding sound of gears moving into place above him did he know, finally, where he was. Then he began to scream, just as Semerket had.

The Asp, however, did not waste his breath with screaming. He reached out and seized the former Egyptian ambassador by his shoulders, and threw him to where the insects were streaming from their lairs. They immediately engulfed Menef, his body becoming a roiling mass of double-jointed legs and jaws and fluttering wings. Soon the ambassador was dead, yet still his body moved and writhed.

If the Asp thought the insects would be content with only Menef, he was mistaken. When the insects had reduced the ambassador to a glistening pile of milky bones, they turned with clicks and hisses toward the second False King, staring at him with their flat, shiny eyes.

Then it was the Asp's turn to scream. Briefly.

. . .

SOME WEEKS LATER, on a day that the magi declared the most auspicious, the priests moved Bel-Marduk's idol into his shrine of carved and gilded wood, to be strapped atop a wagon drawn by a hundred oxen. The wagon itself had twelve wooden wheels, inlaid with ivory, surmounted by two carved, winged dragons. The wagon gleamed with a fresh coat of paint, and its traceries of gold and inset gems gleamed in the hot sun. Silver bells strung around the wagon rang riotously in the morning air, frightening away any ill-intentioned demons that might be lurking. The ox-drivers eased the huge wagon onto the road that led to the northwest; as it moved slowly forward, it seemed indeed a coach fit for heaven's corridors.

Behind it was a secondary wagon, where Semerket rode beside High Magus Adad. Semerket was clad in a plain white linen tunic, wearing the scarred and bent badge of office that Pharaoh had bestowed on him. Never again would he be without it; the falcon jewel had saved his life, and he now regarded it with superstitious awe.

As the secondary coach was pulled into position behind the god's equipage, the high magus leaned over to Semerket, whispering into his ear, "I knew all along we'd be going to Egypt together, you know. A sheep's liver told me."

Semerket merely smiled, saying nothing, and turned to look at the god's entourage that followed behind.

An array of carts, chariots, and drays composed the rest of the god's train. In them were Bel-Marduk's lesser magi and his singers, as well as a bevy of beautiful virgins to warm his nights. A long line of Isin soldiers marched beside them, protection for their journey into Egypt.

Also in the entourage, at its rear, was a small cart bearing three coffins carved in the Egyptian manner. They contained the newly mummified bodies of Senmut, Wia, and Aneku. Semerket himself would ensure that a fine tomb would be fashioned for them in Thebes' City of the Dead. It was the least he could do for them, he reasoned.

Behind that cart was the litter that carried Rami. Though the boy declared himself well enough to sit beside Semerket at the front of the queue, both Naia and his attending physician, Kem-weset, forbade him to do so. Despite his sternness, the old physician was all smiles that morning, for he had eagerly accepted Semerket's invitation to care for them along their tedious, dangerous passage. Babylon was thus losing its greatest physician, and its wineshops their most devout patron. Naia and Kem-weset rode close to Rami's litter on little white donkeys, fiercely guarding the lad like a pair of eagles watching over their chick.

Cheering crowds of Dark Heads lined the road, come to bid their god a safe journey. Prominent in the crowd were the brothers Galzu and Kuri, Semerket's former spies. The night before, Semerket had given them a sack full of Pharaoh's gold (for had they not twice saved the life of Pharaoh's envoy?), and they were now counted among the richest men in Babylon. Arrayed in splendid robes and feathered turbans, the brothers bowed elaborately as Semerket passed. He nodded his head gravely to them, saluting them in the Egyptian fashion.

At the crossroads, King Marduk waited on his stallion. "Semerket!" he called out in his flat, northern Egyptian accent. "I find that I cannot do without your dour face and sad eyes. When will you come back to us?"

Semerket could not say to Babylon's new king that he hoped never to lay foot in his cursed kingdom again. So he merely shook his head. "You must speak to my wife, Sire," he answered, "for she has the say of my coming and going now."

Marduk rode to where Semerket sat in the coach. He leaned forward in his saddle to clasp Semerket's arm. Suddenly unable to speak, the king thrust a leather packet into Semerket's hands, and turned his horse away. Without looking back, he rode swiftly through the Ishtar Gate and into his capital city. It was not until some hours had passed that Semerket even thought to look inside the packet. Five pieces of gold glinted out at him from its folds. Semerket laughed aloud—for the king of Babylon had at last redeemed the purchase price that Semerket had paid the Elamites for him all those days back in Mari.

Semerket raised his head. By every measure, he was returning to Egypt in triumph. He had found the woman who was his life and the boy who had called across nations for his help. He was bringing the sacred idol back to his king, just as he had vowed he would. Yet even then, a part of Semerket remained sorely troubled. He knew now that there were those in Egypt who still sought his death, and that the terrible queen Tiya had reached even through the Gates of Darkness to try to gather those he loved into her vengeful embrace. And he knew as surely as he lived that her restless spirit would try to do it again. But with Naia at his side, he would never fear the future. Though Mother Mylitta's stars had predicted terrible times ahead, he would face them boldly.

What other choice had he, really?

Toward afternoon, winds from the west began blowing over the river plains. Semerket lifted his head and inhaled deeply, and in them was the scent of Egypt—of home.

EPILOGUE

 PRINCE MAYATUM'S MAJOR-DOMO COUGHED discreetly at the door to his bedchamber, holding a terracotta lantern in his hand. When the sounds of slumber continued unabated, the man hissed to the servant girl lying beside the prince. "Wake him," he said. "For pity's sake—his brother's guards are all over the front hall!"

The girl's eyes shot open. Whenever the prince demanded her for the night, she was careful never to disturb him when he slept, not even to leave the room to make water. She had discovered over the few weeks she had been in his house that if she inadvertently roused him from sleep, it often engendered a hard slap—or worse, another bout of rough lovemaking. Already bruises around her throat were beginning to darken, inflicted by the prince's hands where he had held her as he climaxed.

The girl's eyes grew wide and pleading. She shook her head so slightly that it might have been a tremor. "No!" she mouthed silently. "You do it!"

Cursing his luck, the man tentatively approached the prince's side.

"Highness," he whispered, leaning down to the royal ear. "Highness, wake . . ."

There was a stirring on the bed. It was a moment before Mayatum recognized who had called to him. Mayatum reached out to pinch the major-domo's fleshy upper arm. "I told you I wasn't to be wakened until noon."

Stifling his yelp of pain, the man spoke in a soothing voice. "I would never dare to disturb your slumber, Great Prince, were it not for that fact that Pharaoh has sent his heralds for you."

Prince Mayatum sat up, swinging his legs to the floor. It was the middle of the night. "What are they doing here at this hour?" he whined petulantly.

"They gave no reason, Highness—only that you must go to Djamet at once."

While the prince and his butler spoke, the servant girl crept noiselessly from the bed, passing the other servants who waited, cringing, outside the door to dress and barber their master. The major-domo himself quickly laid out the vestments that Mayatum would wear.

Naked, Mayatum wandered into his privy and sat on the bench in his tiled bath, yawning. He was not much concerned with the summons; convinced that he had so far successfully enacted the part of loyal brother and patriot. As his valet poured scented water over his shoulders, he ruminated on the reasons why Ramses had called for him at such an odd time of day.

Irresistibly, a smile stole over his lips. Perhaps his half-brother was dying at last. Ramses had not been well during the few times that Mayatum had seen him during the previous months. Now that Semerket was dead, killed by the loyal Menef in far-off Mesopotamia, there would be no foreign idol to cure the rottenness in his brother's lungs. Mayatum frowned, remembering that for six months he had heard nothing from Menef, no confirmation that Semerket's assassination had indeed occurred. But he remembered that Babylon was yet again in the throes of establishing a new dynasty, and this undoubtedly explained the slowness of the post.

Then a happy thought occurred to the prince. Perhaps Mayatum had been summoned so that he could be named official regent to

Ramses' young son, his nephew. His smile grew wider still as he tenderly contemplated his young charge, so sadly soon to lie within the Great Place in a tomb next to his father's, another of those forgotten boy-kings Egypt produced with such frequency.

A shadow crossed Mayatum's handsome face. Alert to his fickle moods, his barber stepped hastily backward, avoiding the prince's pinching fingers. But Mayatum was not thinking of the barber, but of his mother Tiya.

She should be here, he thought bitterly. Tiya should be the one going to Djamet Temple. How she would have relished it, this triumph over her husband's Canaanite whore, mother of Ramses IV. Upon this thought, Mayatum's smile grew even more malignant. He positively chuckled as the valet fastened the leopard skin around his shoulders, denoting him the high priest of On, then placed Mayatum's most formal wig upon his head.

Preceded by his attendants, Mayatum made his way to the temple barge that awaited him at his private wharf. Mayatum lived a few leagues north of the city, on his own vast estate, situated far away from the stink and sprawl of Thebes. Not for him the cramped, private apartments at Djamet, so coveted by other nobles because of their proximity to Pharaoh. Living in so teeming a place would not allow him to practice his secret pastimes—ones that he preferred to keep far from the prying eyes of his family. His thoughts turned reminiscently to the little serving girl who had shared his bed that night. He must remember to ask whether she had any relatives still among the living who might miss her and start to ask questions after she had disappeared.

His midsection was beginning to pulse pleasantly as the gilded ship rounded the bend in the river, bringing Djamet Temple into view. When he saw it, however, the pleasant feeling in his groin died away, replaced by a dull knot of disquiet. Instead of the mournful chants and dirges he expected to hear, signifying the end of his brother's life, Djamet Temple was alive with lights and celebration, and the music of drums, panpipes, and lutes wafted over the water to him. The docks were crowded with the barques of other nobles and gentry, summoned in the dead of night just as he had been.

As the sailors rushed to tie his ship to the pilings, Mayatum stared in dismay at the avenue in front of the temple, lit by bonfires and smoky with thick clouds of incense cascading from great stone censers. Then he saw the reason for all the commotion: a bizarre and splendid wagon had halted before the gates of the Great Pylons. There must have been a hundred oxen tethered to its reins, and the thing was painted in bright, barbaric colors, its sides inset with gems and gilded traceries that twinkled in the firelight. In its bed, the wagon bore some kind of shrine, the doors of which had been thrown open to the night. But whatever had been inside it was gone.

As Mayatum stepped forward onto the dock, he saw that an entire train of accompanying carts and drays extended down almost the entire concourse to the Nile. The noise and congestion around the temple were intolerable, and he had to wait as his attendants lashed at the people, shouting at them to step aside so that Prince Mayatum might pass inside the gates.

The moment he was through the Pylons, the pounding of drums insinuated itself into the ground beneath his feet. He made his way with the rest of the puzzled, excited courtiers to the rear of the temple grounds, where a great pavilion awaited them. Purple curtains hanging from silver rings kept its interior hidden. But lanterns and torches illuminated it from within, making it blaze like a comet in the night sky.

Pharaoh's elite Shardana guards met him at the pavilion's entrance, and they indicated that Mayatum was to go into a small ancillary hall around the corner—a private reception, they told him. There, he found his brother surrounded by his favored courtiers. Mayatum noticed that Ramses was arrayed in his most formal robes of pleated linen. His head bent under the red and white crowns, and his thin neck sagged under the weight of jeweled collars, heavy pectorals, and chains of gold. But Mayatum also saw that Pharaoh's eyes shone brightly (though this may have been from fever) and that his normally pallid complexion was livid with color (though this may have been from the rouge). When Ramses glanced in his direction, Mayatum made quick obeisance before him.

"Brother!" exclaimed Ramses. "You are here at last. Now the ritual can begin." He nodded to an attendant, who hurried into the pavilion. Ramses bent to lift Mayatum to his feet. "I wanted you particularly to come tonight, to see it for yourself."

"But . . . what am I to see, Majesty?"

"Something about which you must be sure to tell my other half-brothers in Pi-Ramesse. I wanted them both here, of course, but I could not tarry another moment. So you must describe to them exactly what you see here tonight."

"I will of course do whatever Pharaoh desires."

The drums from the pavilion increased their fierce tempo, and the attendant returned, whispering into Pharaoh's ear. Pharaoh took off at a quick pace, going through the tent's flap and into the pavilion. Mayatum stared after him with foreboding. Pharaoh's odd, smiling manner troubled him deeply.

The remaining courtiers deserted the small tent and Mayatum was alone, save for two loiterers. Being royal, Mayatum scarcely noted them. But as he looked about for his own attendants, he chanced to notice that the two people—a lad and a beautiful woman—were now looking directly at him with piercing glances. Such an act was in flagrant defiance of royal protocol.

Mayatum's eyes began to snap fire—a prince of the royal blood must never be gawked at—and hot words of condemnation bubbled to his lips. But he choked them back when he looked fully at the woman. There was something reminiscent in her glance, now as scornful as his own. He tried to think where he had seen her, she with her skin the color of smoke, with her eyes like the Nile at flood . . .

"Do you not recognize me, Great Prince?" murmured the woman, as if reading his thoughts.

"Should I?" Mayatum said tightly, annoyed that she should address him so boldly. By rights, she should have waited until he had spoken to her. He disliked how informal his brother's court had become, when any courtier felt free to burble anything to a member of the royal family without invitation. When it was his turn on the throne, he thought—

"I thought you would remember the occasion," the woman continued blithely, determined to interrupt his sanguine thoughts. She turned to the youth beside her. "My friend here met you at the same time. Perhaps you recall *him* . . . ?" The youth's expression was strangely malevolent, and he did not even bow his head to the prince.

"Am I expected to remember everyone I meet?" asked Mayatum coldly. "My life in Egypt is full—"

"But it wasn't in Egypt that we met, Great Prince," the woman interrupted him. "It was during your recent visit to Babylon."

Mayatum paled. No one was supposed to know of his secret visit to Mesopotamia, where he had commanded Menef to kill the wife and friend of the hated Semerket. "But I've never been to Babylon . . ." he began to sputter.

Once again the woman defiantly interrupted him. "I spilled a tray of sweetmeats upon your lap. Do you remember now?"

Mayatum felt a film of sweat break upon his upper lip. Now he knew who they were. By the gods—by the gods—were they ghosts, then? Spirits come to bedevil him? He began to back slowly from the tent, his shaking hands clutching the linen drapes behind him. *They were supposed to be dead!*

The woman laughed charmingly to see him so undone. "I can admit it now," she said, "spilling the food was no accident. I do hope you'll forgive me, but you'd said such distressing things about my husband that night, you see."

Mayatum was at the tent flap, and he turned quickly, only to careen into a slim, long-limbed man with eyes of blackest jet.

"Semerket!" he gasped.

"Highness."

Mayatum marveled how in that single word, uttered in such a flat and toneless way, there could be found such malevolence. Semerket, not even inclining his head, shot a glance over the prince's shoulder to the woman and lad.

"It's time," he said.

Mayatum was alone in the tent, now. He was soaked with sweat and his hands were shaking uncontrollably. He was feverishly thinking that if Semerket had returned—if Semerket's wife and friend were truly alive—then Pharaoh must know of his own secret journey to Babylon, and how he had plotted with Menef to kill one of Pharaoh's most trusted envoys. Sudden images of his dead brother Pentwere danced in his mind. Mayatum suddenly felt the slick, braided white cord of silk slipping over his head, just as it had Pentwere's—how it tightened beneath his chin as it was thrown over the cedar beam and made secure. Then he imagined himself stepping forward from the stool into space—and heard the sudden crack of his own neck breaking—

Mayatum screamed aloud. He would have run from Djamet then had not Pharaoh's Shardana guards been waiting for him outside the tent. When he emerged, shaking and sweating, they urged him firmly into the purple-curtained pavilion.

What he saw there confirmed all his darkest fears. The magi of Bel-Marduk whirled in frenzied circles before their golden idol, spinning faster and faster to the shrill piping of priestesses and the primordial pounding of their drums. The magi held sharp knives in their frenzied hands, and they slashed at themselves in ecstasy, so that blood ran from their limbs and spattered the faces and robes of the courtiers who stood nearest them. Mayatum could already see that Pharaoh, standing in their center, was sodden with red. The furor of the music increased so that Mayatum felt that even his heart's own beating had been seized by it. Then, at a final roar of the drums, the magi ceased their frantic twirling and the musicians fell silent.

The high magus stepped forward, his hands dripping green bile from the liver he had ripped from a she-goat, intoning a short prayer in Babylonian as he genuflected before the idol. With a gesture, he beckoned Pharaoh to approach the god with him. Before Pharaoh's family, before his court, before all the important personages who were the witnesses for the rest of Egypt, Ramses turned and seized the idol's outstretched hand in his.

Mayatum saw for himself how Pharaoh's limbs became infused with sudden strength, how his shoulders appeared no longer so rounded, how his neck straightened beneath the heavy crowns, saw that his stance became more solidly planted upon the earth. And then Mayatum saw the look of triumph in Pharaoh's suddenly unclouded eye.

Mayatum fled the pavilion. This time no Shardana guards rose to stop him. He ran through the temple grounds, panting, out between the Pylons and to the docks. His attendants had been so entranced by the spectacle in the pavilion that they had not seen him leave. Mayatum was forced to look himself for a ferryman to take him across the river. As they traversed the Nile, he looked back to see if he was being followed. But he was not.

Alone in Eastern Thebes, he stumbled into the street that led to the foreign quarter. Only a tiny, silver scrap of moon lit the twisting alleys. Though he was a prince and wore enough gold to make him a tempting target, not one of the denizens who lingered in the lightless doorways dared to make a move against him. Mayatum was known and protected in these parts.

Soon he stood before the rotting gates of the Hyksos temple, the one-time abode of the King of the Beggars. The place was ruled by another now, a female this time, but it was just as foul a place as it ever had been. Mayatum pounded hysterically on the gates, crying, "The queen! I must see her! Open up!"

The black door slowly opened. An old woman appeared, giggling in delight to see him. Once, long ago, she had been his wet nurse at the palace. Quickly she bolted the gates behind him. Still chuckling fondly, she pulled him by the sleeve past the overgrown oasis of reeds and grasses that had once been the temple's sacred lake.

Inside the temple proper, only a few oil lamps lighted its twisting hallways, and he had to be careful where he trod. Hundreds of beggars slept on the floor—like bees in a hive, he thought, guarding their queen—and he was loath to touch them even with his gilded sandal.

His one-time nurse led him to a suite of rooms, high in the back of the temple, overlooking the Nile. "Majesty," the old woman whispered into the gloom, "our Mayatum has come to visit you!"

There was a rustling from the darkened recess. A black, bent shape crept into the dim circle of candlelight. Even now, after so many months, he was shocked by her appearance. All his tension broke then, and tears of despair stung his eyes, for she was hideous to see, almost immobile from the injuries she had suffered. Her flesh seemed fused together, as if she had been caught in some terrible conflagration, barely escaping with her life. Flaps of melted skin covered her eyes, so that she had to crane her neck up from her crooked back to see him.

Her voice was an ugly rasp, barely intelligible as language. "You've come to tell me that the rumors are true," she said, slowly hauling her bulk toward him. "That Semerket is back in Thebes."

"Yes, it's true—and he's brought the idol with him!"

"Has Ramses taken its hand in his?"

"I saw it with my own eyes! Ramses forced me to watch while he did it!"

The woman emitted a demented shriek, her damaged scream a thing of broken stones and gravel. Mayatum winced to hear it. He saw the furious tears running down her wrinkled cheeks, tinted with red. Even now, almost two years since she had come there, the Beggar Queen had not yet healed from the Cripple Maker's artful attentions.

"He should never have done it!" she railed, tearing at herself with talonlike fingers. "It's heresy for a king of Egypt to seek the protection of a foreign idol!"

Mayatum was too numb to say anything.

"Well," the woman said finally, "what can you expect from a northerner whose mother is a Canaanite whore?"

Mayatum began to shake again, and he blurted out shrilly, "That's hardly important! Semerket has brought his wife and friend back to Egypt with him. They survived. Menef failed us. Now Pharaoh will know of my secret trip to Babylonia, and how the conspiracy still lives. I will be judged and condemned a traitor, given the white cord to strangle myself with—just as my brother Pentwere was!"

His tension broke at last and he fell into choking sobs, hiding his face in his hands. The crippled woman crawled painfully toward him. She took him into her arms then, and laid his head upon her bosom.

"Don't be afraid," she croaked to him. "Remember that you are a royal prince, and that the blood of Amun-Ra himself flows within you. Semerket is less than the dust beneath your feet. And remember, too, that I—and all the beggars who serve me—will protect you."

"But how . . . ?"

"You will stay here, with me, for the time being. No one will think to look for you here, not even Semerket. It's been half a year since he left Thebes. He doesn't know of the changes that have occurred in the city."

"What of his brother? Won't he tell?"

"Do you mean the mayor? That twitching halfwit?"

"He must know that you're the Beggar Queen now."

"Doubtless he's heard that a woman rules the beggar kingdom. But that's all he knows, and ever will."

"But what can we do against them?"

"We wait. Semerket will be afraid of losing his wife again. This will make him either ferocious or timid. We must see how he plays out the game. In the meantime, I shall make new spells against him." She grasped the prince's head in her hands, peering at him from beneath the folds of melted skin. "Do you trust me? Do you know I love you best of all?"

Mayatum swallowed. He nodded his head. As always, her presence served to reassure him. Even as a little boy, she had possessed this same power to make everything seem possible. It all would turn out all right; he knew it now.

"Yes, mother," he sighed contentedly, laying his cheek once more on Tiya's slowly heaving breast.

THANK YOU

THERE ARE MANY PERSONS TO THANK in the creation of this book, and most of them know who they are. But there are six people in particular who deserve to be singled out...

Michael Korda, my editor, whose wisdom and taste permeate every page of this book.

Gypsy da Silva, Queen of copyediting, Mother Courage, and a dear friend.

Ellen Sasahara, whose design skills lift my books into the realm of the sublime. (If they just read as good as they look, I'm home free.)

Katie de Koster, whose fact- and grammar-checking are nothing short of phenomenal; I am humbled each time she returns a manuscript to me, being permanently dissuaded that I know anything about either history *or* writing.

And finally, to **Elizabeth Hayes** and **Deirdre Mueller**, my publicists at Simon & Schuster; their excellent stewardship ensures my tomes don't slip into the mire of obscurity. They are my angels.

Thank you, one and all.

Brad Geagley

ABOUT THE AUTHOR

Brad Geagley worked for many years as a producer of virtual reality environments in the entertainment industry. History and writing were Geagley's real loves, however. His first book, *Year of the Hyenas*, which featured the debut of his detective Semerket, clerk of Investigations and Secrets, appeared in 2005. Geagley currently lives in Palm Springs, California, where he is completing his third novel.